"I SAY—IT AIN'T A HER, IS IT?"
—*Uncle Jim and Uncle Billy*

"ARGONAUT EDITION" OF
THE WORKS OF BRET HARTE

# STORIES
# IN LIGHT AND SHADOW

## THE ARGONAUTS OF NORTH LIBERTY

BY

BRET HARTE

ILLUSTRATED

VIGILANS ET AUDAX

P. F. COLLIER & SON
NEW YORK

*Published under special arrangement with
the Houghton Mifflin Company*

# CONTENTS

# STORIES IN LIGHT AND SHADOW

## "UNSER KARL"

THE American consul for Schlachtstadt
had just turned out of the broad König's
Allée into the little square that held his consulate. Its residences always seemed to him
to wear that singularly uninhabited air peculiar to a street scene in a theatre. The
façades, with their stiff, striped wooden awn-
ings over the windows, were of the regularity, color, and pattern only seen on the stage,
and conversation carried on in the street below always seemed to be invested with that
perfect confidence and security which sur-
rounds the actor in his painted desert of
urban perspective. Yet it was a peaceful
change to the other byways and highways
of Schlachtstadt which were always filled
with an equally unreal and mechanical sol-
diery, who appeared to be daily taken out
of their boxes of "caserne" or "depôt" and

loosely scattered all over the pretty linden-haunted German town. There were soldiers standing on street corners; soldiers staring woodenly into shop windows; soldiers halted suddenly into stone, like lizards, at the approach of Offiziere; Offiziere lounging stiffly four abreast, sweeping the pavement with their trailing sabres all at one angle. There were cavalcades of red hussars, cavalcades of blue hussars, cavalcades of Uhlans, with glittering lances and pennons — with or without a band — formally parading; there were straggling "fatigues" or "details" coming round the corners; there were dusty, businesslike columns of infantry, going nowhere and to no purpose. And they one and all seemed to be *wound up* — for that service — and apparently always in the same place. In the band of their caps — invariably of one pattern — was a button, in the centre of which was a square opening or key-hole. The consul was always convinced that through this keyhole opening, by means of a key, the humblest caporal wound up his file, the Hauptmann controlled his lieutenants and non-commissioned officers, and even the general himself, wearing the same cap, was subject through his cap to a higher moving power. In the suburbs, when the supply of soldiers gave out, there were sentry-boxes; when these dropped off, there were "caissons," or commissary wagons. And, lest the military idea should ever fail from out the Schlachtstadt's burgher's mind, there were police in uniform, street-sweepers in uniform; the ticket-takers, guards, and sweepers at the Bahnhof were in uniform, — but all wearing the same kind of cap, with the probability of having been wound up freshly each morning for their daily work. Even the postman delivered peaceful invoices to the consul with his side-arms and the air of bringing dispatches from the field of battle; and the consul saluted, and felt for a few moments the whole weight of his consular responsibility.

Yet, in spite of this military precedence, it did not seem in the least inconsistent with the decidedly peaceful character of the town, and this again suggested its utter unreality; wandering cows sometimes got mixed up with squadrons of cavalry, and did not seem to mind it; sheep passed singly between files of infantry, or preceded them in a flock when on the march; indeed, nothing could be more delightful and innocent than to see a regiment of infantry in heavy marching order, laden with every conceivable thing they could want for a week, returning after a cheerful search for an invisible enemy in the suburbs, to bivouac peacefully among the cabbages in the market-place. Nobody was ever imposed upon for a moment by their tremendous energy and severe display; drums might beat, trumpets blow, dragoons charge furiously all over the Exercier Platz, or suddenly flash their naked swords in the streets to the guttural command of an offi-cer — nobody seemed to mind it. People glanced up to recognize Rudolf or Max "do-ing their service," nodded, and went about their business. And although the officers always wore their side-arms, and at the most peaceful of social dinners only relinquished their swords in the hall, apparently that they might be ready to buckle them on again and rush out to do battle for the Fatherland be-tween the courses, the other guests only looked upon these weapons in the light of sticks and umbrellas, and possessed their souls in peace. And when, added to this singular incongruity, many of these warriors were spectacled, studious men, and, despite their lethal weapons, wore a slightly profes-

sional air, and were — to a man — deeply
sentimental and singularly simple, their attitude in this eternal Kriegspiel seemed to
the consul more puzzling than ever.

As he entered his consulate he was confronted with another aspect of Schlachtstadt
quite as wonderful, yet already familiar to
him. For, in spite of these "alarums without," which, however, never seem to penetrate beyond the town itself, Schlachtstadt
and its suburbs were known all over the
world for the manufactures of certain beautiful textile fabrics, and many of the rank
and file of those warriors had built up the
fame and prosperity of the district over their
peaceful looms in wayside cottages. There
were great depôts and counting-houses, larger
than even the cavalry barracks, where no
other uniform but that of the postman was
known. Hence it was that the consul's
chief duty was to uphold the flag of his own
country by the examination and certification
of divers invoices sent to his office by the
manufacturers. But, oddly enough, these
business messengers were chiefly women, —
not clerks, but ordinary household servants,
and, on busy days, the consulate might have
been mistaken for a female registry office,

so filled and possessed it was by waiting
Mädchen. Here it was that Gretchen, Lieschen, and Clärchen, in the cleanest of blue
gowns, and stoutly but smartly shod, brought
their invoices in a piece of clean paper, or
folded in a blue handkerchief, and laid them,
with fingers more or less worn and stubby
from hard service, before the consul for his
signature. Once, in the case of a very young
Mädchen, that signature was blotted by the
sweep of a flaxen braid upon it as the child
turned to go; but generally there was a
grave, serious business instinct and sense of
responsibility in these girls of ordinary peasant origin which, equally with their sisters
of France, were unknown to the English or
American woman of any class.

That morning, however, there was a slight
stir among those who, with their knitting,
were waiting their turn in the outer office
as the vice-consul ushered the police inspector
into the consul's private office. He was in
uniform, of course, and it took him a moment to recover from his habitual stiff, military salute, — a little stiffer than that of the
actual soldier.

It was a matter of importance! A stranger
had that morning been arrested in the town

and identified as a military deserter. He claimed to be an American citizen; he was now in the outer office, waiting the consul's interrogation.

The consul knew, however, that the ominous accusation had only a mild significance here. The term "military deserter" included any one who had in youth emigrated to a foreign country without first fulfilling his military duty to his fatherland. His first experiences of these cases had been tedious and difficult, — involving a reference to his Minister at Berlin, a correspondence with the American State Department, a condition of unpleasant tension, and finally the prolonged detention of some innocent German — naturalized — American citizen, who had forgotten to bring his papers with him in revisiting his own native country. It so chanced, however, that the consul enjoyed the friendship and confidence of the General Adlerkreutz, who commanded the 20th Division, and it further chanced that the same Adlerkreutz was as gallant a soldier as ever cried Vorwärts! at the head of his men, as profound a military strategist and organizer as ever carried his own and his enemy's plans in his iron head and spiked helmet, and yet with as simple and unaffected a soul breathing under his gray mustache as ever issued from the lips of a child. So this grim but gentle veteran had arranged with the consul that in cases where the presumption of nationality was strong, although the evidence was not present, he would take the consul's parole for the appearance of the "deserter" or his papers, without the aid of prolonged diplomacy. In this way the consul had saved to Milwaukee a worthy but imprudent brewer, and to New York an excellent sausage butcher and possible alderman; but had returned to martial duty one or two tramps or journeymen who had never seen America except from the decks of the ships in which they were "stowaways," and on which they were returned, — and thus the temper and peace of two great nations were preserved.

"He says," said the inspector severely, "that he is an American citizen, but has lost his naturalization papers. Yet he has made the damaging admission to others that he lived several years in Rome! And," continued the inspector, looking over his shoulder at the closed door as he placed his finger beside his nose, "he says he has relations living at Palmyra, whom he frequently visited. Ach! Observe this unheard-of-and-not-to-be-trusted statement!"

The consul, however, smiled with a slight flash of intelligence. "Let me see him," he said.

They passed into the outer office; another policeman and a corporal of infantry saluted and rose. In the centre of an admiring and sympathetic crowd of Dienstmädchen sat the culprit, the least concerned of the party; a stripling — a boy — scarcely out of his teens! Indeed, it was impossible to conceive of a more innocent, bucolic, and almost angelic looking derelict. With a skin that had the peculiar white and rosiness of fresh pork, he had blue eyes, celestially wide open and staring, and the thick flocculent yellow curls of the sun god! He might have been an overgrown and badly dressed Cupid who had innocently wandered from Paphian shores. He smiled as the consul entered, and wiped from his full red lips with the back of his hand the traces of a sausage he was eating. The consul recognized the flavor at once, — he had smelled it before in Lieschen's little hand-basket.

"You say you lived at Rome?" began

the consul pleasantly. "Did you take out your first declaration of your intention of becoming an American citizen there?"

The inspector cast an approving glance at the consul, fixed a stern eye on the cherubic prisoner, and leaned back in his chair to hear the reply to this terrible question.

"I don't remember," said the culprit, knitting his brows in infantine thought. "It was either there, or at Madrid or Syracuse."

The inspector was about to rise; this was really trifling with the dignity of the municipality. But the consul laid his hand on the official's sleeve, and, opening an American atlas to a map of the State of New York, said to the prisoner, as he placed the inspector's hand on the sheet, "I see you know the names of the *towns* on the Erie and New York Central Railroad. But " —

"I can tell you the number of people in each town and what are the manufactures," interrupted the young fellow, with youthful vanity. "Madrid has six thousand, and there are over sixty thousand in " —

"That will do," said the consul, as a murmur of Wunderschön! went round the group of listening servant girls, while glances of admiration were shot at the beaming accused.

"But you ought to remember the name of the town where your naturalization papers were afterwards sent."

"But I was a citizen from the moment I made my declaration," said the stranger smiling, and looking triumphantly at his admirers, "and I could vote!"

The inspector, since he had come to grief over American geographical nomenclature, was grimly taciturn. The consul, however, was by no means certain of his victory. His alleged fellow citizen was too encyclopædic in his knowledge: a clever youth might have crammed for this with a textbook, but then he did not *look* at all clever; indeed, he had rather the stupidity of the mythological subject he represented. "Leave him with me," said the consul. The inspector handed him a *précis* of the case. The cherub's name was Karl Schwartz, an orphan, missing from Schlachtstadt since the age of twelve. Relations not living, or in emigration. Identity established by prisoner's admission and record.

"Now, Karl," said the consul cheerfully, as the door of his private office closed upon them, "what is your little game? Have you *ever* had any papers? And if you were

clever enough to study the map of New York
State, why were n't you clever enough to see
that it would n't stand you in place of your
papers?"

"Dot 's joost it," said Karl in English;
"but you see dot if I haf declairet mine intention of begomming a citizen, it 's all the
same, don't it?"

"By no means, for you seem to have no
evidence of the *declaration;* no papers at
all."

"Zo!" said Karl. Nevertheless, he
pushed his small, rosy, pickled-pig's-feet of
fingers through his fleecy curls and beamed
pleasantly at the consul. "Dot 's vot 's der
matter," he said, as if taking a kindly interest in some private trouble of the consul's.
"Dot 's vere you vos, eh?"

The consul looked steadily at him for a
moment. Such stupidity was by no means
phenomenal, nor at all inconsistent with his
appearance. "And," continued the consul
gravely, "I must tell you that, unless you
have other proofs than you have shown, it
will be my duty to give you up to the authorities."

"Dot means I shall serve my time, eh?"
said Karl, with an unchanged smile.

"Exactly so," returned the consul.

"Zo!" said Karl. "Dese town — dese Schlachtstadt — is fine town, eh? Fine vomens. Goot men. Und beer und sausage. Blenty to eat and drink, eh? Und," looking around the room, "you and te poys haf a gay times."

"Yes," said the consul shortly, turning away. But he presently faced round again on the unfettered Karl, who was evidently indulging in a gormandizing reverie.

"What on earth brought you here, anyway?"

"Was it das?"

"What brought you here from America, or wherever you ran away from?"

"To see der volks."

"But you are an *orphan*, you know, and you have no folks living here."

"But all Shermany is mine volks, — de whole gountry, don't it? Pet your poots! How's dot, eh?"

The consul turned back to his desk and wrote a short note to General Adlerkreutz in his own American German. He did not think it his duty in the present case to interfere with the authorities or to offer his parole for Karl Schwartz. But he would claim

that, as the offender was evidently an innocent emigrant and still young, any punish-
ment or military degradation be omitted,
and he be allowed to take his place like any
other recruit in the ranks. If he might
have the temerity to the undoubted, far-see-
ing military authority of suggestion making here, he would suggest that Karl was
for the commissariat fitted! Of course, he
still retained the right, on production of satisfactory proof, his discharge to claim.

The consul read this aloud to Karl. The
cherubic youth smiled and said, "Zo!"
Then, extending his hand, he added the
word "Zshake!"

The consul shook his hand a little remorse-
fully, and, preceding him to the outer room,
resigned him with the note into the inspector's hands. A universal sigh went up from
the girls, and glances of appeal sought the
consul; but he wisely concluded that it
would be well, for a while, that Karl — a
helpless orphan — should be under some
sort of discipline! And the securer business
of certifying invoices recommenced.

Late that afternoon he received a folded
bit of blue paper from the waistbelt of an
orderly, which contained in English charac-

ters and as a single word "Alright," followed by certain jagged pen-marks, which
he recognized as Adlerkreutz's signature.
But it was not until a week later that he
learned anything definite. He was returning one night to his lodgings in the residen-
tial part of the city, and, in opening the door
with his pass-key, perceived in the rear of
the hall his handmaiden Trudschen, attended
by the usual blue or yellow or red shadow.
He was passing by them with the local
*'n' Abend!* on his lips when the soldier
turned his face and saluted. The consul
stopped. It was the cherub Karl in uniform!

But it had not subdued a single one of
his characteristics. His hair had been
cropped a little more closely under his cap,
but there was its color and woolliness still
intact; his plump figure was girt by belt and
buttons, but he only looked the more unreal,
and more like a combination of pen-wiper
and pincushion, until his puffy breast and
shoulders seemed to offer a positive invitation to any one who had picked up a pin.
But, wonderful! — according to his brief
story — he had been so proficient in the
goose step that he had been put in uniform

already, and allowed certain small privileges,
— among them, evidently, the present one.
The consul smiled and passed on. But it
seemed strange to him that Trudschen, who
was a tall strapping girl, exceedingly popular with the military, and who had never
looked lower than a corporal at least, should
accept the attentions of an Einjähriger like
that. Later he interrogated her.

Ach! it was only Unser Karl! And the
consul knew he was Amerikanisch!

"Indeed!"

"Yes! It was such a tearful story!"

"Tell me what it is," said the consul, with
a faint hope that Karl had volunteered some
communication of his past.

"Ach Gott! There in America he was
a man, and could ' vote,' make laws, and,
God willing, become a town councilor, —
or Ober Intendant, — and here he was nothing but a soldier for years. And this
America was a fine country. Wunderschön!
There were such big cities, and one —
' Booflo ' — could hold all Schlachtstadt,
and had of people five hundred thousand!"

The consul sighed. Karl had evidently
not yet got off the line of the New York
Central and Erie roads. "But does he re-

member yet what he did with his papers?"
said the consul persuasively.

"Ach! What does he want with *papers*
when he could make the laws? They were
dumb, stupid things — these papers — to
him."

"But his appetite remains good, I hope?"
suggested the consul.

This closed the conversation, although
Karl came on many other nights, and his
toy figure quite supplanted the tall corporal
of hussars in the remote shadows of the hall.
One night, however, the consul returned
home from a visit to a neighboring town a
day earlier than he was expected. As he
neared his house he was a little surprised
to find the windows of his sitting-room lit
up, and that there were no signs of Trudschen in the lower hall or passages. He
made his way upstairs in the dark and pushed
open the door of his apartment. To his astonishment, Karl was sitting comfortably in
his own chair, his cap off before a student-
lamp on the table, deeply engaged in apparent study. So profound was his abstraction
that it was a moment before he looked up,
and the consul had a good look at his usually
beaming and responsive face, which, how-

ever, now struck him as wearing a singular
air of thought and concentration. When
their eyes at last met, he rose instantly and
saluted, and his beaming smile returned.
But, either from his natural phlegm or extraordinary self-control, he betrayed neither
embarrassment nor alarm.

The explanation he gave was direct and
simple. Trudschen had gone out with the
Corporal Fritz for a short walk, and had
asked him to "keep house" during their absence. He had no books, no papers, nothing
to read in the barracks, and no chance to
improve his mind. He thought the Herr
Consul would not object to his looking at
his books. The consul was touched; it was
really a trivial indiscretion, and as much
Trudschen's fault as Karl's! And if the
poor fellow had any mind to improve, — his
recent attitude certainly suggested thought
and reflection, — the consul were a brute to
reprove him. He smiled pleasantly as Karl
returned a stubby bit of pencil and some
greasy memoranda to his breast pocket, and
glanced at the table. But to his surprise it
was a large map that Karl had been study-
ing, and, to his still greater surprise, a map
of the consul's own district.

"You seem to be fond of map-studying," said the consul pleasantly. "You are not thinking of emigrating again?"

"Ach, no!" said Karl simply; "it is my cousine vot haf lif near here. I find her."

But he left on Trudschen's return, and the consul was surprised to see that, while Karl's attitude towards her had not changed, the girl exhibited less effusiveness than before. Believing it to be partly the effect of the return of the corporal, the consul taxed her with faithlessness. But Trudschen looked grave.

"Ah! He has new friends, this Karl of ours. He cares no more for poor girls like us. When fine ladies like the old Frau von Wimpfel make much of him, what will you?"

It appeared, indeed, from Trudschen's account, that the widow of a wealthy shopkeeper had made a kind of protégé of the young soldier, and given him presents. Furthermore, that the wife of his colonel had employed him to act as page or attendant at an afternoon Gesellschaft, and that since then the wives of other officers had sought him. Did not the Herr Consul think it was dreadful that this American, who could vote

and make laws, should be subjected to such
things?

The consul did not know what to think.
It seemed to him, however, that Karl was
"getting on," and that he was not in need
of his assistance. It was in the expectation
of hearing more about him, however, that
he cheerfully accepted an invitation from
Adlerkreutz to dine at the Caserne one evening with the staff. Here he found, somewhat to his embarrassment, that the dinner
was partly in his own honor, and at the close
of five courses, and the emptying of many
bottles, his health was proposed by the gallant veteran Adlerkreutz in a neat address
of many syllables containing all the parts of
speech and a single verb. It was to the effect
that in his soul-friend the Herr Consul and
himself was the never-to-be-severed union
of Germania and Columbia, and in their
perfect understanding was the war-defying
alliance of two great nations, and that in the
consul's noble restoration of Unser Karl to
the German army there was the astute diplomacy of a great mind. He was satisfied
that himself and the Herr Consul still united
in the great future, looking down upon a
common brotherhood, — the great Germanic-

American Confederation, — would feel satisfied with themselves and each other and
their never - to - be - forgotten earth - labors.
Cries of "Hoch! Hoch!" resounded through
the apartment with the grinding roll of
heavy-bottomed beer-glasses, and the consul, tremulous with emotion and a reserve
verb in his pocket, rose to reply. Fully
embarked upon this perilous voyage, and
steering wide and clear of any treacherous
shore of intelligence or fancied harbor of
understanding and rest, he kept boldly out
at sea. He said that, while his loving adversary in this battle of compliment had dis-
armed him and left him no words to reply
to his generous panegyric, he could not but
join with that gallant soldier in his heartfelt
aspirations for the peaceful alliance of both
countries. But while he fully reciprocated
all his host's broader and higher sentiments,
he must point out to this gallant assembly,
this glorious brotherhood, that even a greater
tie of sympathy knitted him to the general,
— the tie of kinship! For while it was well
known to the present company that their
gallant commander had married an Englishwoman, he, the consul, although always an
American, would now for the first time con-

fess to them that he *himself* was of Dutch
descent on his mother's side! He would
say no more, but confidently leave them in
possession of the tremendous significance of
this until-then-unknown fact! He sat down,
with the forgotten verb still in his pocket,
but the applause that followed this perfectly
conclusive, satisfying, and logical climax
convinced him of his success. His hand
was grasped eagerly by successive warriors;
the general turned and embraced him before
the breathless assembly; there were tears in
the consul's eyes.

As the festivities progressed, however, he
found to his surprise that Karl had not only
become the fashion as a military page, but
that his naïve stupidity and sublime simplicity was the wondering theme and inexhaus-
tible delight of the whole barracks. Stories
were told of his genius for blundering which
rivaled Handy Andy's; old stories of fatuous ignorance were rearranged and fitted to
"our Karl." It was "our Karl" who, on
receiving a tip of two marks from the hands
of a young lady to whom he had brought
the bouquet of a gallant lieutenant, exhibited some hesitation, and finally said, "Yes,
but, gnädiges Fräulein, that *cost* us nine

marks!" It was "our Karl" who, inter-
rupting the regrets of another lady that she
was unable to accept his master's invitation,
said politely, "Ah! what matter, Gnädigste?
I have still a letter for Fräulein Kopp [her
rival], and I was told that I must not invite
you both." It was "our Karl" who astonished the hostess to whom he was sent at
the last moment with apologies from an officer, unexpectedly detained at barrack duty,
by suggesting that he should bring that unfortunate officer his dinner from the just
served table. Nor were these charming in-
felicities confined to his social and domestic
service. Although ready, mechanical, and
invariably docile in the manual and physical
duties of a soldier, — which endeared him to
the German drill-master, — he was still in-
vincibly ignorant as to its purport, or even
the meaning and structure of the military
instruments he handled or vacantly looked
upon. It was "our Karl" who suggested
to his instructors that in field-firing it was
quicker and easier to load his musket to the
muzzle at once, and get rid of its death-deal-
ing contents at a single discharge, than to
load and fire consecutively. It was "our
Karl" who nearly killed the instructor at

sentry drill by adhering to the letter of his
instructions when that instructor had forgotten the password. It was the same Karl
who, severely admonished for his recklessness, the next time added to his challenge
the precaution, "Unless you instantly say
'Fatherland' I'll fire!" Yet his perfect
good humor and childlike curiosity were
unmistakable throughout, and incited his
comrades and his superiors to show him
everything in the hope of getting some characteristic comment from him. Everything
and everybody were open to Karl and his
good-humored simplicity.

That evening, as the general accompanied
the consul down to the gateway and the
waiting carriage, a figure in uniform ran
spontaneously before them and shouted
"Heraus!" to the sentries. But the general promptly checked "the turning out" of
the guard with a paternal shake of his finger
to the over-zealous soldier, in whom the consul recognized Karl. "He is my Bursche
now," said the general explanatorily. "My
wife has taken a fancy to him. Ach! he is
very popular with these women." The consul was still more surprised. The Frau
Generalin Adlerkreutz he knew to be a pro-

nounced Englishwoman, — carrying out her English ways, proprieties, and prejudices in the very heart of Schlachtstadt, uncompromisingly, without fear and without reproach. That she should follow a merely foreign society craze, or alter her English household so as to admit the impossible Karl, struck him oddly.

A month or two elapsed without further news of Karl, when one afternoon he suddenly turned up at the consulate. He had again sought the consular quiet to write a few letters home; he had no chance in the confinement of the barracks.

"But by this time you must be in the family of a field-marshal, at least," suggested the consul pleasantly.

"Not to-day, but next week," said Karl, with sublime simplicity; "*then* I am going to serve with the governor commandant of Rheinfestung."

The consul smiled, motioned him to a seat at a table in the outer office, and left him undisturbed to his correspondence.

Returning later, he found Karl, his letters finished, gazing with childish curiosity and admiration at some thick official envelopes, bearing the stamp of the consulate, which were lying on the table. He was evidently struck with the contrast between them and the thin, flimsy affairs he was holding in his hand. He appeared still more impressed when the consul told him what they were.

"Are you writing to your friends?" continued the consul, touched by his simplicity.

"Ach ja!" said Karl eagerly.

"Would you like to put your letter in one of these envelopes?" continued the official.

The beaming face and eyes of Karl were a sufficient answer. After all, it was a small favor granted to this odd waif, who seemed to still cling to the consular protection. He handed him the envelope and left him addressing it in boyish pride.

It was Karl's last visit to the consulate. He appeared to have spoken truly, and the consul presently learned that he had indeed been transferred, through some high official manipulation, to the personal service of the governor of Rheinfestung. There was weeping among the Dienstmädchen of Schlachtstadt, and a distinct loss of originality and lightness in the gatherings of the gentler Hausfrauen. His memory still survived in the barracks through the later editions of

his former delightful stupidities, — many of
them, it is to be feared, were inventions, —
and stories that were supposed to have come
from Rheinfestung were described in the
slang of the Offiziere as being "colossal."
But the consul remembered Rheinfestung,
and could not imagine it as a home for Karl,
or in any way fostering his peculiar qualities. For it was eminently a fortress of for-
tresses, a magazine of magazines, a depôt of
depôts. It was the key of the Rhine, the
citadel of Westphalia, the "Clapham Junc-
tion" of German railways, but defended,
fortified, encompassed, and controlled by the
newest as well as the oldest devices of military strategy and science. Even in the pip-
ingest time of peace, whole railway trains
went into it like a rat in a trap, and might
have never come out of it; it stretched out
an inviting hand and arm across the river
that might in the twinkling of an eye be
changed into a closed fist of menace. You
"defiled" into it, commanded at every step
by enfilading walls; you "debouched" out
of it, as you thought, and found yourself
only before the walls; you "reëntered" it
at every possible angle; you did everything
apparently but pass through it. You thought

'yourself well out of it, and were stopped by a bastion. Its circumvallations haunted you until you came to the next station. It had pressed even the current of the river into its defensive service. There were secrets of its foundations and mines that only the highest military despots knew and kept to themselves. In a word — it was impregnable.

That such a place could not be triflea with or misunderstood in its right-and-acute-angled severities seemed plain to every one. But set on by his companions, who were showing him its defensive foundations, or in his own idle curiosity, Karl managed to fall into the Rhine and was fished out with difficulty. The immersion may have chilled his military ardor or soured his good humor, for later the consul heard that he had visited the American consular agent at an adjacent town with the old story of his American citizenship. "He seemed," said the consul's colleague, "to be well posted about American railways and American towns, but he had no papers. He lounged around the office for a while and " —

"Wrote letters home?" suggested the consul, with a flash of reminiscence.

"Yes, the poor chap had no privacy at the barracks, and I reckon was overlooked or bedeviled."

This was the last the consul heard of Karl Schwartz directly; for a week or two later he again fell into the Rhine, this time so fatally and effectually that in spite of the efforts of his companions he was swept away by the rapid current, and thus ended his service to his country. His body was never recovered.

A few months before the consul was transferred from Schlachtstadt to another post his memory of the departed Karl was revived by a visit from Adlerkreutz. The general looked grave.

"You remember Unser Karl?" he said.

"Yes."

"Do you think he was an impostor?"

"As regards his American citizenship, yes! But I could not say more."

"So!" said the general. "A very singular thing has happened," he added, twirling his mustache. "The inspector of police has notified us of the arrival of a Karl Schwartz in this town. It appears he is the *real* Karl Schwartz, identified by his sister as the only one. The other, who was drowned, was an impostor. Hein?"

"Then you have secured another recruit?" said the consul smilingly.

"No. For this one has already served his time in Elsass, where he went when he left here as a boy. But, Donnerwetter, why should that dumb fool take his name?"

"By chance, I fancy. Then he stupidly stuck to it, and had to take the responsibilities with it. Don't you see?" said the consul, pleased with his own cleverness.

"Zo-o!" said the general slowly, in his deepest voice. But the German exclamation has a variety of significance, according to the inflection, and Adlerkreutz's ejaculation seemed to contain them all.

. . . . . . . .

It was in Paris, where the consul had lingered on his way to his new post. He was sitting in a well-known café, among whose habitués were several military officers of high rank. A group of them were gathered round a table near him. He was idly watching them with an odd recollection of Schlachtstadt in his mind, and as idly glancing from them to the more attractive Boulevard without. The consul was getting a little tired of soldiers.

Suddenly there was a slight stir in the

gesticulating group and a cry of greeting. The consul looked up mechanically, and then his eyes remained fixed and staring at the newcomer. For it was the dead Karl; Karl, surely! Karl! — his plump figure belted in a French officer's tunic; his flaxen hair clipped a little closer, but still its fleece showing under his kepi. Karl, his cheeks more cherubic than ever — unchanged but for a tiny yellow toy mustache curling up over the corners of his full lips. Karl, beaming at his companions in his old way, but rattling off French vivacities without the faintest trace of accent. Could he be mistaken? Was it some phenomenal resemblance, or had the soul of the German private been transmigrated to the French officer.

The consul hurriedly called the *garçon*. "Who is that officer who has just arrived?"

"It is the Captain Christian, of the Intelligence Bureau," said the waiter, with proud alacrity. "A famous officer, brave as a rabbit, — un fier lapin, — and one of our best clients. So *drôle*, too, such a *farceur* and mimic. M'sieur would be ravished to hear his imitations."

"But he looks like a German; and his name!"

"Ah, he is from Alsace. But not a German!" said the waiter, absolutely whitening with indignation. "He was at Belfort. So was I. Mon Dieu! No, a thousand times no!"

"But has he been living here long?" said the consul.

"In Paris, a few months. But his Department, M'sieur understands, takes him *everywhere!* Everywhere where he can gain information."

The consul's eyes were still on the Captain Christian. Presently the officer, perhaps instinctively conscious of the scrutiny, looked towards him. Their eyes met. To the consul's surprise, the *ci-devant* Karl beamed upon him, and advanced with outstretched hand.

But the consul stiffened slightly, and remained so with his glass in his hand. At which Captain Christian brought his own easily to a military salute, and said politely: —

"Monsieur le Consul has been promoted from his post. Permit me to congratulate him."

"You have heard, then?" said the consul dryly.

"Otherwise I should not presume. For our Department makes it a business — in Monsieur le Consul's case it becomes a pleasure — to know everything."

"Did your Department know that the real Karl Schwartz has returned?" said the consul dryly.

Captain Christian shrugged his shoulders. "Then it appears that the sham Karl died none too soon," he said lightly. "And yet" — he bent his eyes with mischievous reproach upon the consul.

"Yet what?" demanded the consul sternly.

"Monsieur le Consul might have saved the unfortunate man by accepting him as an American citizen and not helping to force him into the German service."

The consul saw in a flash the full military significance of this logic, and could not repress a smile. At which Captain Christian dropped easily into a chair beside him, and as easily into broken German English: —

"Und," he went on, "dees town — dees Schlachtstadt is fine town, eh? Fine womens? Goot men? Und peer and sausage? Blenty to eat and trink, eh? Und you und te poys haf a gay times?"

The consul tried to recover his dignity.

The waiter behind him, recognizing only the delightful mimicry of this adorable officer, was in fits of laughter. Nevertheless, the consul managed to say dryly: —

"And the barracks, the magazines, the commissariat, the details, the reserves of Schlachtstadt were very interesting?"

"Assuredly."

"And Rheinfestung — its plans — its details, even its dangerous foundations by the river — they were to a soldier singularly instructive?"

"You have reason to say so," said Captain Christian, curling his little mustache.

"And the fortress — you think?"

"Imprenable! Mais" —

The consul remembered General Adlerkreutz's "Zo-o," and wondered.

# UNCLE JIM AND UNCLE BILLY

THEY were partners. The avuncular title
was bestowed on them by Cedar Camp, possibly in recognition of a certain matured
good humor, quite distinct from the spasmodic exuberant spirits of its other members, and possibly from what, to its youthful sense, seemed their advanced ages —
which must have been at least forty! They
had also set habits even in their improvi-
dence, lost incalculable and unpayable sums
to each other over euchre regularly every
evening, and inspected their sluice-boxes
punctually every Saturday for repairs —
which they never made. They even got to
resemble each other, after the fashion of old
married couples, or, rather, as in matrimonial partnerships, were subject to the dom-
ination of the stronger character; although
in their case it is to be feared that it was
the feminine Uncle Billy — enthusiastic, im-
aginative, and loquacious — who swayed the
masculine, steady-going, and practical Un-

cle Jim.   They had lived in the camp since
its foundation in 1849; there seemed to be
no reason why they should not remain there
until its inevitable evolution into a mining-
town.   The younger members might leave
through restless ambition or a desire for
change or novelty; they were subject to no
such trifling mutation.   Yet Cedar Camp
was surprised one day to hear that Uncle
Billy was going away.

The rain was softly falling on the bark
thatch of the cabin with a muffled murmur,
like a sound heard through sleep.   The
southwest trades were warm even at that
altitude, as the open door testified, although
a fire of pine bark was flickering on the
adobe hearth and striking out answering
fires from the freshly scoured culinary uten-
sils on the rude sideboard, which Uncle Jim
had cleaned that morning with his usual serious persistency.   Their best clothes, which
were interchangeable and worn alternately
by each other on festal occasions, hung on
the walls, which were covered with a coarse
sailcloth canvas instead of lath-and-plaster,
and were diversified by pictures from illustrated papers and stains from the exterior
weather.   Two "bunks," like ships' berths,

— an upper and lower one, — occupied the gable-end of this single apartment, and on beds of coarse sacking, filled with dry moss, were carefully rolled their respective blankets and pillows. They were the only articles not used in common, and whose individuality was respected.

Uncle Jim, who had been sitting before the fire, rose as the square bulk of his partner appeared at the doorway with an armful of wood for the evening stove. By that sign he knew it was nine o'clock: for the last six years Uncle Billy had regularly brought in the wood at that hour, and Uncle Jim had as regularly closed the door after him, and set out their single table, containing a greasy pack of cards taken from its drawer, a bottle of whiskey, and two tin drinking-cups. To this was added a ragged memorandum-book and a stick of pencil. The two men drew their stools to the table.

"Hol' on a minit," said Uncle Billy.

His partner laid down the cards as Uncle Billy extracted from his pocket a pill-box, and, opening it, gravely took a pill. This was clearly an innovation on their regular proceedings, for Uncle Billy was always in perfect health.

"What's this for?" asked Uncle Jim half scornfully.

"Agin ager."

"You ain't got no ager," said Uncle Jim, with the assurance of intimate cognizance of his partner's physical condition.

"But it's a pow'ful preventive! Quinine! Saw this box at Riley's store, and laid out a quarter on it. We kin keep it here, comfortable, for evenings. It's mighty soothin' arter a man's done a hard day's work on the river-bar. Take one."

Uncle Jim gravely took a pill and swallowed it, and handed the box back to his partner.

"We'll leave it on the table, sociable like, in case any of the boys come in," said Uncle Billy, taking up the cards. "Well. How do we stand?"

Uncle Jim consulted the memorandum-book. "You were owin' me sixty-two thousand dollars on the last game, and the limit's seventy-five thousand!"

"Je whillikins!" ejaculated Uncle Billy. "Let me see."

He examined the book, feebly attempted to challenge the additions, but with no effect on the total. "We oughter hev made the limit a hundred thousand," he said seriously; "seventy-five thousand is only triflin' in a game like ours. And you 've set down my claim at Angel's?" he continued.

"I allowed you ten thousand dollars for that," said Uncle Jim, with equal gravity, "and it 's a fancy price too."

The claim in question being an unprospected hillside ten miles distant, which Uncle Jim had never seen, and Uncle Billy had not visited for years, the statement was probably true; nevertheless, Uncle Billy retorted: —

"Ye kin never tell how these things will pan out. Why, only this mornin' I was taking a turn round Shot Up Hill, that ye know is just rotten with quartz and gold, and I could n't help thinkin' how much it was like my ole claim at Angel's. I must take a day off to go on there and strike a pick in it, if only for luck."

Suddenly he paused and said, "Strange, ain't it, you should speak of it to-night? Now I call that queer!"

He laid down his cards and gazed mysteriously at his companion. Uncle Jim knew perfectly that Uncle Billy had regularly once a week for many years declared his final

determination to go over to Angel's and
prospect his claim, yet nevertheless he half
responded to his partner's suggestion of
mystery, and a look of fatuous wonder crept
into his eyes.   But he contented himself by
saying cautiously, "You spoke of it first."

"That's the more sing'lar," said Uncle
Billy confidently.   "And I've been thinking about it, and kinder seeing myself thar
all day.   It's mighty queer!"   He got up
and began to rummage among some torn
and coverless books in the corner.

"Where's that 'Dream Book' gone to?"

"The Carson boys borrowed it," replied
Uncle Jim.   "Anyhow, yours wasn't no
dream — only a kind o' vision, and the book
don't take no stock in visions."   Nevertheless, he watched his partner with some sympathy, and added, "That reminds me that I
had a dream the other night of being in
'Frisco at a small hotel, with heaps o'
money, and all the time being sort o' scared
and bewildered over it."

"No?" queried his partner eagerly yet
reproachfully.   "You never let on anything
about it to *me!*   It's mighty queer you havin' these strange feelin's, for I've had
'em myself.   And only to-night, comin' up

from the spring, I saw two crows hopping
in the trail, and I says, ' If I see another,
it 's luck, sure! ' And you 'll think I 'm
lyin', but when I went to the wood-pile just
now there was the *third* one sittin' up on a
log as plain as I see you. Tell 'e what folks
ken laugh — but that 's just what Jim Filgee
saw the night before he made the big strike! ' "

They were both smiling, yet with an un-
derlying credulity and seriousness as singularly pathetic as it seemed incongruous to
their years and intelligence. Small wonder,
however, that in their occupation and environment — living daily in an atmosphere of
hope, expectation, and chance, looking forward each morning to the blind stroke of a
pick that might bring fortune — they should
see signs in nature and hear mystic voices
in the trackless woods that surrounded them.
Still less strange that they were peculiarly
susceptible to the more recognized diversions
of chance, and were gamblers on the turning
of a card who trusted to the revelation of a
shovelful of upturned earth.

It was quite natural, therefore, that they
should return from their abstract form of
divination to the table and their cards. But
they were scarcely seated before they heard

a crackling step in the brush outside, and
the free latch of their door was lifted. A
younger member of the camp entered. He
uttered a peevish "Halloo!" which might
have passed for a greeting, or might have
been a slight protest at finding the door
closed, drew the stool from which Uncle Jim
had just risen before the fire, shook his wet
clothes like a Newfoundland dog, and sat
down. Yet he was by no means churlish
nor coarse-looking, and this act was rather
one of easy-going, selfish, youthful familiarity than of rudeness. The cabin of Uncles
Billy and Jim was considered a public right
or "common" of the camp. Conferences
between individual miners were appointed
there. "I'll meet you at Uncle Billy's"
was a common tryst. Added to this was a
tacit claim upon the partners' arbitrative
powers, or the equal right to request them
to step outside if the interviews were of a
private nature. Yet there was never any
objection on the part of the partners, and
to-night there was not a shadow of resentment of this intrusion in the patient, good-
humored, tolerant eyes of Uncles Jim and
Billy as they gazed at their guest. Perhaps
there was a slight gleam of relief in Uncle

Jim's when he found that the guest was un-
accompanied by any one, and that it was
not a tryst. It would have been unpleasant
for the two partners to have stayed out in
the rain while their guests were exchanging
private confidences in their cabin. While
there might have been no limit to their good
will, there might have been some to their
capacity for exposure.

Uncle Jim drew a huge log from beside
the hearth and sat on the driest end of it,
while their guest occupied the stool. The
young man, without turning away from his
discontented, peevish brooding over the fire,
vaguely reached backward for the whiskey-
bottle and Uncle Billy's tin cup, to which
he was assisted by the latter's hospitable
hand. But on setting down the cup his eye
caught sight of the pill-box.

"Wot's that?" he said, with gloomy
scorn. "Rat poison?"

"Quinine pills — agin ager," said Uncle
Jim. "The newest thing out. Keeps out
damp like Injin-rubber! Take one to follow
yer whiskey. Me and Uncle Billy would n't
think o' settin' down, quiet like, in the evening arter work, without 'em. Take one —
ye 'r' welcome! We keep 'em out here for
the boys."

Accustomed as the partners were to adopt and wear each other's opinions before folks, as they did each other's clothing, Uncle Billy was, nevertheless, astonished and delighted at Uncle Jim's enthusiasm over *his* pills. The guest took one and swallowed it.

"Mighty bitter!" he said, glancing at his hosts with the quick Californian suspicion of some practical joke. But the honest faces of the partners reassured him.

"That bitterness ye taste," said Uncle Jim quickly, "is whar the thing's gittin' in its work. Sorter sickenin' the malaria — and kinder water-proofin' the insides all to onct and at the same lick! Don't yer see? Put another in yer vest pocket; you'll be cryin' for 'em like a child afore ye get home. Thar! Well, how's things agoin' on your claim, Dick? Boomin', eh?"

The guest raised his head and turned it sufficiently to fling his answer back over his shoulder at his hosts. "I don't know what *you*'d call ' boomin','" he said gloomily; "I suppose you two men sitting here comfortably by the fire, without caring whether school keeps or not, would call two feet of backwater over one's claim ' boomin'; ' I reckon *you*'d consider a hundred and fifty

feet of sluicing carried away, and drifting
to thunder down the South Fork, something
in the way of advertising to your old camp!
I suppose *you* 'd think it was an inducement
to investors! I should n't wonder," he
added still more gloomily, as a sudden dash
of rain down the wide-throated chimney
dropped in his tin cup — "and it would be
just like you two chaps, sittin' there gormandizing over your quinine — if yer said
this rain that's lasted three weeks was something to be proud of!"

It was the cheerful and the satisfying custom of the rest of the camp, for no reason
whatever, to hold Uncle Jim and Uncle
Billy responsible for its present location, its
vicissitudes, the weather, or any convulsion
of nature; and it was equally the partners'
habit, for no reason whatever, to accept
these animadversions and apologize.

"It's a rain that's soft and mellowin',"
said Uncle Billy gently, "and supplin' to
the sinews and muscles. Did ye ever notice, Jim" — ostentatiously to his partner —
"did ye ever notice that you get inter a
kind o' sweaty lather workin' in it? Sorter
openin' to the pores!"

"Fetches 'em every time," said Uncle
Billy. "Better nor fancy soap."

Their guest laughed bitterly. "Well, I'm going to leave it to you. I reckon to cut the whole concern to-morrow, and 'lite' out for something new. It can't be worse than this."

The two partners looked grieved, albeit they were accustomed to these outbursts. Everybody who thought of going away from Cedar Camp used it first as a threat to these patient men, after the fashion of runaway nephews, or made an exemplary scene of their going.

"Better think twice afore ye go," said Uncle Billy.

"I've seen worse weather afore ye came," said Uncle Jim slowly. "Water all over the Bar; the mud so deep ye couldn't get to Angel's for a sack o' flour, and we had to grub on pine nuts and jackass-rabbits. And yet — we stuck by the camp, and here we are!"

The mild answer apparently goaded their guest to fury. He rose from his seat, threw back his long dripping hair from his handsome but querulous face, and scattered a few drops on the partners. "Yes, that's just it. That's what gets me! Here you stick, and here you are! And here you'll

stick and rust until you starve or drown! Here you are, — two men who ought to be out in the world, playing your part as grown men, — stuck here like children ' playing house' in the woods; playing work in your wretched mud - pie ditches, and content. Two men not so old that you might n't be taking your part in the fun of the world, going to balls or theatres, or paying attention to girls, and yet old enough to have married and have your families around you, content to stay in this God-forsaken place; old bachelors, pigging together like poor-house paupers. That's what gets me! Say you *like* it? Say you expect by hanging on to make a strike — and what does that amount to? What are *your* chances? How many of us have made, or are making, more than grub wages? Say you're willing to share and share alike as you do — have you got enough for two? Are n't you actually living off each other? Are n't you grinding each other down, choking each other's struggles, as you sink together deeper and deeper in the mud of this cussed camp? And while you're doing this, are n't you, by your age and position here, holding out hopes to others that you know cannot be fulfilled?''

Accustomed as they were to the half-queru-
lous, half-humorous, but always extravagant,
criticism of the others, there was something
so new in this arraignment of themselves
that the partners for a moment sat silent.
There was a slight flush on Uncle Billy's
cheek, there was a slight paleness on Uncle
Jim's.  He was the first to reply.  But he
did so with a certain dignity which neither
his partner nor their guest had ever seen on
his face before.

"As it's *our* fire that's warmed ye up
like this, Dick Bullen," he said, slowly rising, with his hand resting on Uncle Billy's
shoulder, "and as it's *our* whiskey that's
loosened your tongue, I reckon we must put
up with what ye 'r' saying, just as we 've
managed to put up with our own way o' living, and not quo'll with ye under our own
roof."

The young fellow saw the change in Uncle
Jim's face and quickly extended his hand,
with an apologetic backward shake of his
long hair.  "Hang it all, old man," he said,
with a laugh of mingled contrition and amusement, "you must n't mind what I said just
now.  I 've been so worried thinking of
things about *myself*, and, maybe, a little

about you, that I quite forgot I had n't a call
to preach to anybody — least of all to you.
So we part friends, Uncle Jim, and you too,
Uncle Billy, and you 'll forget what I said.
In fact, I don't know why I spoke at all —
only I was passing your claim just now, and
wondering how much longer your old sluice-
boxes would hold out, and where in thunder you 'd get others when they caved in!
I reckon that sent me off. That 's all, old
chap!"

Uncle Billy's face broke into a beaming
smile of relief, and it was *his* hand that first
grasped his guest's; Uncle Jim quickly followed with as honest a pressure, but with
eyes that did not seem to be looking at Bullen, though all trace of resentment had died
out of them. He walked to the door with
him, again shook hands, but remained looking out in the darkness some time after Dick
Bullen's tangled hair and broad shoulders
had disappeared.

Meantime, Uncle Billy had resumed his
seat and was chuckling and reminiscent as
he cleaned out his pipe.

"Kinder reminds me of Jo Sharp, when
he was cleaned out at poker by his own
partners in his own cabin, comin' up here

and bedevilin' *us* about it! What was it
you lint him?"

But Uncle Jim did not reply; and Uncle
Billy, taking up the cards, began to shuffle
them, smiling vaguely, yet at the same time
somewhat painfully. "Arter all, Dick was
mighty cut up about what he said, and I
felt kinder sorry for him. And, you know,
I rather cotton to a man that speaks his
mind. Sorter clears him out, you know, of
all the slumgullion that's in him. It's just
like washin' out a pan o' prospecting: you
pour in the water, and keep slushing it
round and round, and out comes first the
mud and dirt, and then the gravel, and then
the black sand, and then — it's all out, and
there's a speck o' gold glistenin' at the bot-
tom!"

"Then you think there *was* suthin' in
what he said?" said Uncle Jim, facing
about slowly.

An odd tone in his voice made Uncle Billy
look up. "No," he said quickly, shying
with the instinct of an easy pleasure-loving
nature from a possible grave situation. "No,
I don't think he ever got the color! But
wot are ye moonin' about for? Ain't ye
goin' to play? It's mor' 'n half past nine
now."

Thus adjured, Uncle Jim moved up to
the table and sat down, while Uncle Billy
dealt the cards, turning up the Jack or right
bower — but *without* that exclamation of
delight which always accompanied his good
fortune, nor did Uncle Jim respond with
the usual corresponding simulation of deep
disgust. Such a circumstance had not occurred before in the history of their partnership. They both played in silence — a
silence only interrupted by a larger splash
of raindrops down the chimney.

"We orter put a couple of stones on the
chimney-top, edgewise, like Jack Curtis
does. It keeps out the rain without inter-
ferin' with the draft," said Uncle Billy
musingly.

"What's the use if" —

"If what?" said Uncle Billy quietly.

"If we don't make it broader," said Uncle
Jim half wearily.

They both stared at the chimney, but
Uncle Jim's eye followed the wall around to
the bunks. There were many discolorations
on the canvas, and a picture of the Goddess
of Liberty from an illustrated paper had
broken out in a kind of damp, measly erup-
tion. "I'll stick that funny handbill of the

' Washin' Soda ' I got at the grocery store
the other day right over the Liberty gal.
It's a mighty perty woman washin' with
short sleeves," said Uncle Billy.   "That's
the comfort of them picters, you kin always
get somethin' new, and it adds thickness to
the wall."

Uncle Jim went back to the cards in silence.   After a moment he rose again, and
hung his overcoat against the door.

"Wind 's comin' in," he said briefly.

"Yes," said Uncle Billy cheerfully, "but
it would n't seem nat'ral if there was n't
that crack in the door to let the sunlight in
o' mornin's.   Makes a kind o' sundial, you
know.   When the streak o' light 's in that
corner, I says ' six o'clock! ' when it 's across
the chimney I say ' seven! ' and so 't is!' "

It certainly had grown chilly, and the
wind was rising.   The candle guttered and
flickered; the embers on the hearth bright-
ened occasionally, as if trying to dispel the
gathering shadows, but always ineffectually.
The game was frequently interrupted by the
necessity of stirring the fire.   After an interval of gloom, in which each partner suc-
cessively drew the candle to his side to examine his cards, Uncle Jim said: —

"Say?"

"Well!" responded Uncle Billy.

"Are you sure you saw that third crow on the wood-pile?"

"Sure as I see you now — and a darned sight plainer. Why?"

"Nothin', I was just thinkin'. Look here! How do we stand now?"

Uncle Billy was still losing. "Nevertheless," he said cheerfully, "I'm owin' you a matter of sixty thousand dollars."

Uncle Jim examined the book abstractedly. "Suppose," he said slowly, but without looking at his partner, "suppose, as it's gettin' late now, we play for my half share of the claim agin the limit — seventy thousand — to square up."

"Your half share!" repeated Uncle Billy, with amused incredulity.

"My half share of the claim, — of this yer house, you know, — one half of all that Dick Bullen calls our rotten starvation property," reiterated Uncle Jim, with a half smile.

Uncle Billy laughed. It was a novel idea; it was, of course, "all in the air," like the rest of their game, yet even then he had an odd feeling that he would have liked Dick Bullen to have known it. "Wade in, old pard," he said. "I'm on it."

Uncle Jim lit another candle to reinforce
the fading light, and the deal fell to Uncle
Billy. He turned up Jack of clubs. He
also turned a little redder as he took up his
cards, looked at them, and glanced hastily
at his partner. "It's no use playing," he
said. "Look here!" He laid down his
cards on the table. They were the ace,
king and queen of clubs, and Jack of spades,
— or left bower, — which, with the turned-
up Jack of clubs, — or right bower, — com-
prised *all* the winning cards!

"By jingo! If we'd been playin' four-
handed, say you an' me agin some other
ducks, we'd have made ' four ' in that deal,
and h'isted some money — eh?" and his
eyes sparkled. Uncle Jim, also, had a slight
tremulous light in his own.

"Oh no! I didn't see no three crows
this afternoon," added Uncle Billy glee-
fully, as his partner, in turn, began to shuffle
the cards with laborious and conscientious
exactitude. Then dealing, he turned up a
heart for trumps. Uncle Billy took up his
cards one by one, but when he had finished
his face had become as pale as it had been
red before. "What's the matter?" said
Uncle Jim quickly, his own face growing
white.

Uncle Billy slowly and with breathless awe laid down his cards, face up on the table. It was exactly the same sequence *in hearts*, with the knave of diamonds added. He could again take every trick.

They stared at each other with vacant faces and a half-drawn smile of fear. They could hear the wind moaning in the trees beyond; there was a sudden rattling at the door. Uncle Billy started to his feet, but Uncle Jim caught his arm. "*Don't leave the cards!* It's only the wind; sit down," he said in a low awe-hushed voice, "it's your deal; you were two before, and two now, that makes your four; you've only one point to make to win the game. Go on."

They both poured out a cup of whiskey, smiling vaguely, yet with a certain terror in their eyes. Their hands were cold; the cards slipped from Uncle Billy's benumbed fingers; when he had shuffled them he passed them to his partner to shuffle them also, but did not speak. When Uncle Jim had shuffled them methodically he handed them back fatefully to his partner. Uncle Billy dealt them with a trembling hand. He turned up a club. "If you are sure of these tricks you know you 've won," said Uncle Jim in a voice that was scarcely audible. Uncle Billy did not reply, but tremulously laid down the ace and right and left bowers.

He had won!

A feeling of relief came over each, and they laughed hysterically and discordantly. Ridiculous and childish as their contest might have seemed to a looker-on, to each the tension had been as great as that of the greatest gambler, without the gambler's trained restraint, coolness, and composure. Uncle Billy nervously took up the cards again.

"Don't," said Uncle Jim gravely; "it 's no use — the luck 's gone now."

"Just one more deal," pleaded his partner.

Uncle Jim looked at the fire, Uncle Billy hastily dealt, and threw the two hands face up on the table. They were the ordinary average cards. He dealt again, with the same result. "I told you so," said Uncle Jim, without looking up.

It certainly seemed a tame performance after their wonderful hands, and after another trial Uncle Billy threw the cards aside and drew his stool before the fire. "Mighty queer, warn't it?" he said, with reminiscent awe. "Three times running. Do you know, I felt a kind o' creepy feelin' down my back all the time. Criky! what luck! None of the boys would believe it if we told 'em — least of all that Dick Bullen, who don't believe in luck, anyway. Wonder what he'd have said! and, Lord! how he'd have looked! Wall! what are you starin' so for?"

Uncle Jim had faced around, and was gazing at Uncle Billy's good-humored, simple face. "Nothin'!" he said briefly, and his eyes again sought the fire.

"Then don't look as if you was seein' suthin' — you give me the creeps," returned Uncle Billy a little petulantly. "Let's turn in, afore the fire goes out!"

The fateful cards were put back into the drawer, the table shoved against the wall. The operation of undressing was quickly got over, the clothes they wore being put on top of their blankets. Uncle Billy yawned, "I wonder what kind of a dream I'll have to-night — it oughter be suthin' to explain that luck." This was his "good-night" to his partner. In a few moments he was sound asleep.

Not so Uncle Jim. He heard the wind gradually go down, and in the oppressive silence that followed could detect the deep breathing of his companion and the far-off yelp of a coyote. His eyesight becoming accustomed to the semi-darkness, broken only by the scintillation of the dying embers of their fire, he could take in every detail of their sordid cabin and the rude environment in which they had lived so long. The dismal patches on the bark roof, the wretched makeshifts of each day, the dreary prolongation of discomfort, were all plain to him now, without the sanguine hope that had made them bearable. And when he shut his eyes upon them, it was only to travel in fancy down the steep mountain side that he had trodden so often to the dreary claim on the overflowed river, to the heaps of "tailings" that encumbered it, like empty shells of the hollow, profitless days spent there, which they were always waiting for the stroke of good fortune to clear away. He saw again the rotten "sluicing," through whose hopeless rifts and holes even their scant daily earnings had become scantier. At last he arose, and with infinite gentleness let himself down from his berth without disturbing his sleeping partner, and wrapping himself in his blanket, went to the door, which he noiselessly opened. From the position of a few stars that were glittering in the northern sky he knew that it was yet scarcely midnight; there were still long, restless hours before the day! In the feverish state into which he had gradually worked himself it seemed to him impossible to wait the coming of the dawn.

But he was mistaken. For even as he stood there all nature seemed to invade his humble cabin with its free and fragrant breath, and invest him with its great companionship. He felt again, in that breath, that strange sense of freedom, that mystic touch of partnership with the birds and beasts, the shrubs and trees, in this greater home before him. It was this vague communion that had kept him there, that still held these world-sick, weary workers in their rude cabins on the slopes around him; and he felt upon his brow that balm that had nightly lulled him and them to sleep and forgetfulness. He closed the door, turned away, crept as noiselessly as before into his bunk again, and presently fell into a profound slumber.

But when Uncle Billy awoke the next morning he saw it was late; for the sun, piercing the crack of the closed door, was sending a pencil of light across the cold hearth, like a match to rekindle its dead embers. His first thought was of his strange luck the night before, and of disappointment that he had not had the dream of divination that he had looked for. He sprang to the floor, but as he stood upright his glance fell on Uncle Jim's bunk. It was empty. Not only that, but his *blankets* — Uncle Jim's own particular blankets — *were gone!*

A sudden revelation of his partner's manner the night before struck him now with the cruelty of a blow; a sudden intelligence, perhaps the very divination he had sought, flashed upon him like lightning! He glanced wildly around the cabin. The table was drawn out from the wall a little ostentatiously, as if to catch his eye. On it was lying the stained chamois-skin purse in which they had kept the few grains of gold remaining from their last week's "clean up." The grains had been carefully divided, and half had been taken! But near it lay the little memorandum-book, open, with the stick of pencil lying across it. A

deep line was drawn across the page on which
was recorded their imaginary extravagant
gains and losses, even to the entry of Uncle
Jim's half share of the claim which he had
risked and lost! Underneath were hurriedly
scrawled the words: —

"Settled by *your* luck, last night, old
pard. — JAMES FOSTER."

It was nearly a month before Cedar Camp
was convinced that Uncle Billy and Uncle
Jim had dissolved partnership. Pride had
prevented Uncle Billy from revealing his
suspicions of the truth, or of relating the
events that preceded Uncle Jim's clandestine
flight, and Dick Bullen had gone to Sacramento by stage-coach the same morning.
He briefly gave out that his partner had
been called to San Francisco on important
business of their own, that indeed might ne-
cessitate his own removal there later. In
this he was singularly assisted by a letter
from the absent Jim, dated at San Francisco, begging him not to be anxious about
his success, as he had hopes of presently
entering into a profitable business, but with
no further allusions to his precipitate departure, nor any suggestion of a reason for it.

For two or three days Uncle Billy was staggered and bewildered; in his profound simplicity he wondered if his extraordinary good fortune that night had made him deaf to some explanation of his partner's, or, more terrible, if he had shown some "low" and incredible intimation of taking his partner's extravagant bet as *real* and binding. In this distress he wrote to Uncle Jim an appealing and apologetic letter, albeit somewhat incoherent and inaccurate, and bristling with misspelling, camp slang, and old partnership jibes. But to this elaborate epistle he received only Uncle Jim's repeated assurances of his own bright prospects, and his hopes that his old partner would be more fortunate, single-handed, on the old claim. For a whole week or two Uncle Billy sulked, but his invincible optimism and good humor got the better of him, and he thought only of his old partner's good fortune. He wrote him regularly, but always to one address — a box at the San Francisco post-office, which to the simple-minded Uncle Billy suggested a certain official importance. To these letters Uncle Jim responded regularly but briefly.

From a certain intuitive pride in his part-

ner and his affection, Uncle Billy did not
show these letters openly to the camp, although he spoke freely of his former partner's promising future, and even read them
short extracts. It is needless to say that
the camp did not accept Uncle Billy's story
with unsuspecting confidence. On the contrary, a hundred surmises, humorous or serious, but always extravagant, were afloat
in Cedar Camp. The partners had quarreled over their clothes — Uncle Jim, who
was taller than Uncle Billy, had refused to
wear his partner's trousers. They had quarreled over cards — Uncle Jim had discovered that Uncle Billy was in possession of
a "cold deck," or marked pack. They had
quarreled over Uncle Billy's carelessness in
grinding up half a box of "bilious pills" in
the morning's coffee. A gloomily imagina-
tive mule-driver had darkly suggested that,
as no one had really seen Uncle Jim leave
the camp, he was still there, and his bones
would yet be found in one of the ditches;
while a still more credulous miner averred
that what he had thought was the cry of a
screech-owl the night previous to Uncle
Jim's disappearance, might have been the
agonized utterance of that murdered man.

It was highly characteristic of that camp —
and, indeed, of others in California — that
nobody, not even the ingenious theorists
themselves, believed their story, and that
no one took the slightest pains to verify or
disprove it.  Happily, Uncle Billy never
knew it, and moved all unconsciously in this
atmosphere of burlesque suspicion.  And
then a singular change took place in the attitude of the camp towards him and the dis-
rupted partnership.  Hitherto, for no reason whatever, all had agreed to put the blame
upon Billy — possibly because he was present to receive it.  As days passed that
slight reticence and dejection in his manner,
which they had at first attributed to remorse
and a guilty conscience, now began to tell
as absurdly in his favor.  Here was poor
Uncle Billy toiling through the ditches,
while his selfish partner was lolling in the
lap of luxury in San Francisco!  Uncle
Billy's glowing accounts of Uncle Jim's success only contributed to the sympathy now
fully given in his behalf and their execration
of the absconding partner.  It was proposed
at Biggs's store that a letter expressing the
indignation of the camp over his heartless
conduct to his late partner, William Fall,

should be forwarded to him. Condolences were offered to Uncle Billy, and uncouth attempts were made to cheer his loneliness. A procession of half a dozen men twice a week to his cabin, carrying their own whiskey and winding up with a "stag dance" before the premises, was sufficient to lighten his eclipsed gayety and remind him of a happier past. "Surprise" working parties visited his claim with spasmodic essays towards helping him, and great good humor and hilarity prevailed. It was not an unusual thing for an honest miner to arise from an idle gathering in some cabin and excuse himself with the remark that he "reckoned he'd put in an hour's work in Uncle Billy's tailings!" And yet, as before, it was very improbable if any of these reckless benefactors *really* believed in their own earnestness or in the gravity of the situation. Indeed, a kind of hopeful cynicism ran through their performances. "Like as not, Uncle Billy is still in ' cahoots ' [*i. e.*, shares] with his old pard, and is just laughin' at us as he's sendin' him accounts of our tomfoolin'."

And so the winter passed and the rains, and the days of cloudless skies and chill starlit nights began. There were still freshets from the snow reservoirs piled high in the Sierran passes, and the Bar was flooded, but that passed too, and only the sunshine remained. Monotonous as the seasons were, there was a faint movement in the camp with the stirring of the sap in the pines and cedars. And then, one day, there was a strange excitement on the Bar. Men were seen running hither and thither, but mainly gathering in a crowd on Uncle Billy's claim, that still retained the old partners' names in "The Fall and Foster." To add to the excitement, there was the quickly repeated report of a revolver, to all appearance aimlessly exploded in the air by some one on the outskirts of the assemblage. As the crowd opened, Uncle Billy appeared, pale, hysterical, breathless, and staggering a little under the back-slapping and hand-shaking of the whole camp. For Uncle Billy had "struck it rich" — had just discovered a "pocket," roughly estimated to be worth fifteen thousand dollars!

Although in that supreme moment he missed the face of his old partner, he could not help seeing the unaffected delight and happiness shining in the eyes of all who surrounded him. It was characteristic of

that sanguine but uncertain life that success
and good fortune brought no jealousy nor
envy to the unfortunate, but was rather a
promise and prophecy of the fulfillment of
their own hopes. The gold was there —
Nature but yielded up her secret. There
was no prescribed limit to her bounty. So
strong was this conviction that a long-suffer-
ing but still hopeful miner, in the enthusiasm of the moment, stooped down and patted
a large boulder with the apostrophic "Good
old gal!"

Then followed a night of jubilee, a next
morning of hurried consultation with a mining expert and speculator lured to the camp
by the good tidings; and then the very next
night — to the utter astonishment of Cedar
Camp — Uncle Billy, with a draft for twenty
thousand dollars in his pocket, started for
San Francisco, and took leave of his claim
and the camp forever!

. . . . . . . .

When Uncle Billy landed at the wharves
of San Francisco he was a little bewildered.
The Golden Gate beyond was obliterated by
the incoming sea-fog, which had also roofed
in the whole city, and lights already glittered along the gray streets that climbed the

grayer sand - hills. As a Western man,
brought up by inland rivers, he was fascinated and thrilled by the tall-masted sea-
going ships, and he felt a strange sense of
the remoter mysterious ocean, which he
had never seen. But he was impressed and
startled by smartly dressed men and women,
the passing of carriages, and a sudden conviction that he was strange and foreign to
what he saw. It had been his cherished intention to call upon his old partner in his
working clothes, and then clap down on the
table before him a draft for ten thousand
dollars as *his* share of their old claim. But
in the face of these brilliant strangers a sudden and unexpected timidity came upon him.
He had heard of a cheap popular hotel,
much frequented by the returning gold-
miner, who entered its hospitable doors —
which held an easy access to shops — and
emerged in a few hours a gorgeous butterfly
of fashion, leaving his old chrysalis behind
him. Thence he inquired his way; hence
he afterwards issued in garments glaringly
new and ill fitting. But he had not sacri-
ficed his beard, and there was still something
fine and original in his handsome weak face
that overcame the cheap convention of his

clothes. Making his way to the post-office,
he was again discomfited by the great size
of the building, and bewildered by the array
of little square letter-boxes behind glass
which occupied one whole wall, and an equal
number of opaque and locked wooden ones
legibly numbered. His heart leaped; he
remembered the number, and before him
was a window with a clerk behind it. Uncle Billy leaned forward.

"Kin you tell me if the man that box
690 b'longs to is in?"

The clerk stared, made him repeat the
question, and then turned away. But he
returned almost instantly, with two or three
grinning heads besides his own, apparently
set behind his shoulders. Uncle Billy was
again asked to repeat his question. He
did so.

"Why don't you go and see if 690 is in
his box?" said the first clerk, turning with
affected asperity to one of the others.

The clerk went away, returned, and said
with singular gravity, "He was there a moment ago, but he's gone out to stretch his
legs. It's rather crampin' at first; and he
can't stand it more than ten hours at a time,
you know."

But simplicity has its limits. Uncle Billy had already guessed his real error in believing his partner was officially connected with the building; his cheek had flushed and then paled again. The pupils of his blue eyes had contracted into suggestive black points. "Ef you 'll let me in at that winder, young fellers," he said, with equal gravity, "I 'll show yer how I kin make *you* small enough to go in a box without crampin'! But I only wanted to know where Jim Foster *lived*."

At which the first clerk became perfunctory again, but civil. "A letter left in his box would get you that information," he said, "and here 's paper and pencil to write it now."

Uncle Billy took the paper and began to write, "Just got here. Come and see me at" — He paused. A brilliant idea had struck him; he could impress both his old partner and the upstarts at the window; he would put in the name of the latest "swell" hotel in San Francisco, said to be a fairy dream of opulence. He added "The Oriental," and without folding the paper shoved it in the window.

"Don't you want an envelope?" asked the clerk.

"Put a stamp on the corner of it," responded Uncle Billy, laying down a coin, "and she 'll go through." The clerk smiled, but affixed the stamp, and Uncle Billy turned away.

But it was a short-lived triumph. The disappointment at finding Uncle Jim's address conveyed no idea of his habitation seemed to remove him farther away, and lose his identity in the great city. Besides, he must now make good his own address, and seek rooms at the Oriental. He went thither. The furniture and decorations, even in these early days of hotel-building in San Francisco, were extravagant and overstrained, and Uncle Billy felt lost and lonely in his strange surroundings. But he took a handsome suite of rooms, paid for them in advance on the spot, and then, half frightened, walked out of them to ramble vaguely through the city in the feverish hope of meeting his old partner. At night his inquietude increased; he could not face the long row of tables in the pillared dining-room, filled with smartly dressed men and women; he evaded his bedroom, with its brocaded satin chairs and its gilt bedstead, and fled to his modest lodgings at the Good Cheer House, and appeased his hunger at its cheap restaurant, in the company of retired miners and freshly arrived Eastern emigrants. Two or three days passed thus in this quaint double existence. Three or four times a day he would enter the gorgeous Oriental with affected ease and carelessness, demand his key from the hotel-clerk, ask for the letter that did not come, go to his room, gaze vaguely from his window on the passing crowd below for the partner he could not find, and then return to the Good Cheer House for rest and sustenance. On the fourth day he received a short note from Uncle Jim; it was couched in his usual sanguine but brief and business-like style. He was very sorry, but important and profitable business took him out of town, but he trusted to return soon and welcome his old partner. He was also, for the first time, jocose, and hoped that Uncle Billy would not "see all the sights" before he, Uncle Jim, returned. Disappointing as this procrastination was to Uncle Billy, a gleam of hope irradiated it: the letter had bridged over that gulf which seemed to yawn between them at the post-office. His old partner had accepted his visit to San Francisco without question, and had alluded to a renewal

of their old intimacy. For Uncle Billy,
with all his trustful simplicity, had been tor-
tured by two harrowing doubts : one, whether
Uncle Jim in his new-fledged smartness as
a "city" man — such as he saw in the
streets — would care for his rough companionship; the other, whether he, Uncle Billy,
ought not to tell him at once of his changed
fortune. But, like all weak, unreasoning
men, he clung desperately to a detail — he
could not forego his old idea of astounding
Uncle Jim by giving him his share of the
"strike" as his first intimation of it, and
he doubted, with more reason perhaps, if
Jim would see him after he had heard of his
good fortune. For Uncle Billy had still a
frightened recollection of Uncle Jim's sudden stroke for independence, and that rigid
punctiliousness which had made him doggedly accept the responsibility of his extravagant stake at euchre.

With a view of educating himself for
Uncle Jim's company, he "saw the sights"
of San Francisco — as an overgrown and
somewhat stupid child might have seen them
— with great curiosity, but little contamina-
tion or corruption. But I think he was
chiefly pleased with watching the arrival of

the Sacramento and Stockton steamers at
the wharves, in the hope of discovering his
old partner among the passengers on the
gang-plank. Here, with his old superstitious tendency and gambler's instinct, he
would augur great success in his search that
day if any one of the passengers bore the
least resemblance to Uncle Jim, if a man or
woman stepped off first, or if he met a single
person's questioning eye. Indeed, this got
to be the real occupation of the day, which
he would on no account have omitted, and
to a certain extent revived each day in his
mind the morning's work of their old partnership. He would say to himself, "It's
time to go and look up Jim," and put off
what he was pleased to think were his pleasures until this act of duty was accomplished.

In this singleness of purpose he made very
few and no entangling acquaintances, nor
did he impart to any one the secret of his
fortune, loyally reserving it for his partner's
first knowledge. To a man of his natural
frankness and simplicity this was a great
trial, and was, perhaps, a crucial test of his
devotion. When he gave up his rooms at
the Oriental — as not necessary after his
partner's absence — he sent a letter, with

his humble address, to the mysterious lock-
box of his partner without fear or false
shame.  He would explain it all when they
met.  But he sometimes treated unlucky
and returning miners to a dinner and a visit
to the gallery of some theatre.  Yet while
he had an active sympathy with and understanding of the humblest, Uncle Billy, who
for many years had done his own and his
partner's washing, scrubbing, mending, and
cooking, and saw no degradation in it, was
somewhat inconsistently irritated by menial
functions in men, and although he gave ex-
travagantly to waiters, and threw a dollar
to the crossing-sweeper, there was always a
certain shy avoidance of them in his manner.
Coming from the theatre one night Uncle
Billy was, however, seriously concerned by
one of these crossing-sweepers turning hastily before them and being knocked down
by a passing carriage.  The man rose and
limped hurriedly away; but Uncle Billy was
amazed and still more irritated to hear from
his companion that this kind of menial occupation was often profitable, and that at some
of the principal crossings the sweepers were
already rich men.

But a few days later brought a more not-

able event to Uncle Billy. One afternoon
in Montgomery Street he recognized in one
of its smartly dressed frequenters a man
who had a few years before been a member
of Cedar Camp. Uncle Billy's childish delight at this meeting, which seemed to bridge
over his old partner's absence, was, however,
only half responded to by the ex-miner, and
then somewhat satirically. In the fullness
of his emotion, Uncle Billy confided to him
that he was seeking his old partner, Jim
Foster, and, reticent of his own good fortune, spoke glowingly of his partner's brilliant expectations, but deplored his inability
to find him. And just now he was away on
important business. "I reckon he's got
back," said the man dryly. "I didn't know
he had a lock-box at the post-office, but I
can give you his other address. He lives at
the Presidio, at Washerwoman's Bay." He
stopped and looked with a satirical smile at
Uncle Billy. But the latter, familiar with
Californian mining-camp nomenclature, saw
nothing strange in it, and merely repeated
his companion's words.

"You'll find him there! Good-by! So
long! Sorry I'm in a hurry," said the ex-
miner, and hurried away.

Uncle Billy was too delighted with the prospect of a speedy meeting with Uncle Jim to resent his former associate's supercilious haste, or even to wonder why Uncle Jim had not informed him that he had returned. It was not the first time that he had felt how wide was the gulf between himself and these others, and the thought drew him closer to his old partner, as well as his old idea, as it was now possible to surprise him with the draft. But as he was going to surprise him in his own boarding-house — probably a handsome one — Uncle Billy reflected that he would do so in a certain style.

He accordingly went to a livery stable and ordered a landau and pair, with a negro coachman. Seated in it, in his best and most ill-fitting clothes, he asked the coachman to take him to the Presidio, and leaned back in the cushions as they drove through the streets with such an expression of beaming gratification on his good-humored face that the passers-by smiled at the equipage and its extravagant occupant. To them it seemed the not unusual sight of the successful miner "on a spree." To the unsophisticated Uncle Billy their smiling seemed only a natural and kindly recognition of his hap-

piness, and he nodded and smiled back to
them with unsuspecting candor and innocent playfulness. "These yer 'Frisco fellers ain't *all* slouches, you bet," he added
to himself half aloud, at the back of the
grinning coachman.

Their way led through well-built streets
to the outskirts, or rather to that portion of
the city which seemed to have been over-
whelmed by shifting sand-dunes, from which
half-submerged fences and even low houses
barely marked the line of highway. The
resistless trade-winds which had marked this
change blew keenly in his face and slightly
chilled his ardor. At a turn in the road the
sea came in sight, and sloping towards it
the great Cemetery of Lone Mountain, with
white shafts and marbles that glittered in
the sunlight like the sails of ships waiting
to be launched down that slope into the Eternal Ocean. Uncle Billy shuddered. What
if it had been his fate to seek Uncle Jim
there!

"Dar's yar Presidio!" said the negro
coachman a few moments later, pointing
with his whip, "and dar's yar Wash'woman's Bay!"

Uncle Billy stared. A huge quadrangu-

lar fort of stone with a flag flying above its
battlements stood at a little distance, pressed
against the rocks, as if beating back the en-
croaching surges; between him and the fort
but farther inland was a lagoon with a number of dilapidated, rudely patched cabins or
cottages, like stranded driftwood around its
shore. But there was no mansion, no block
of houses, no street, not another habitation
or dwelling to be seen!

Uncle Billy's first shock of astonishment
was succeeded by a feeling of relief. He
had secretly dreaded a meeting with his old
partner in the "haunts of fashion;" whatever was the cause that made Uncle Jim
seek this obscure retirement affected him
but slightly; he even was thrilled with a
vague memory of the old shiftless camp
they had both abandoned. A certain instinct — he knew not why, or less still that
it might be one of delicacy — made him
alight before they reached the first house.
Bidding the carriage wait, Uncle Billy entered, and was informed by a blowzy Irish
laundress at a tub that Jim Foster, or
"Arkansaw Jim," lived at the fourth shanty
"beyant." He was at home, for "he'd
shprained his fut." Uncle Billy hurried

on, stopped before the door of a shanty scarcely less rude than their old cabin, and half timidly pushed it open. A growling voice from within, a figure that rose hurriedly, leaning on a stick, with an attempt to fly, but in the same moment sank back in a chair with an hysterical laugh — and Uncle Billy stood in the presence of his old partner! But as Uncle Billy darted forward, Uncle Jim rose again, and this time with outstretched hands. Uncle Billy caught them, and in one supreme pressure seemed to pour out and transfuse his whole simple soul into his partner's. There they swayed each other backwards and forwards and sideways by their still clasped hands, until Uncle Billy, with a glance at Uncle Jim's bandaged ankle, shoved him by sheer force down into his chair.

Uncle Jim was first to speak. "Caught, b' gosh! I mighter known you 'd be as big a fool as me! Look you, Billy Fall, do you know what you 've done? You 've druv me out er the streets whar I was makin' an honest livin', by day, on three crossin's! Yes," he laughed forgivingly, "you druv me out er it, by day, jest because I reckoned that some time I might run into your darned

fool face," — another laugh and a grasp of
the hand, — "and then, b' gosh! not content
with ruinin' my business *by day*, when I
took to it at night, *you* took to goin' out at
nights too, and so put a stopper on me there!
Shall I tell you what else you did? Well,
by the holy poker! I owe this sprained foot
to your darned foolishness and my own, for
it was getting away from *you* one night after
the theatre that I got run into and run over!

"Ye see," he went on, unconscious of
Uncle Billy's paling face, and with a *naïveté*,
though perhaps not a delicacy, equal to
Uncle Billy's own, "I had to play roots on
you with that lock-box business and these
letters, because I did not want you to know
what I was up to, for you might n't like it,
and might think it was lowerin' to the old
firm, don't yer see? I would n't hev gone
into it, but I was played out, and I don't
mind tellin' you *now*, old man, that when I
wrote you that first chipper letter from the
lock-box I hed n't eat anythin' for two days.
But it 's all right *now*," with a laugh. "Then
I got into this business — thinkin' it nothin'
— jest the very last thing — and do you
know, old pard, I could n't tell anybody but
*you* — and, in fact, I kept it jest to tell you

— I 've made nine hundred and fifty-six dollars! Yes, sir, *nine hundred and fifty-six dollars!* solid money, in Adams and Co.'s Bank, just out er my trade."

"Wot trade?" asked Uncle Billy.

Uncle Jim pointed to the corner, where stood a large, heavy crossing - sweeper's broom. "That trade."

"Certingly," said Uncle Billy, with a quick laugh.

"It 's an outdoor trade," said Uncle Jim gravely, but with no suggestion of awkwardness or apology in his manner; "and thar ain't much difference between sweepin' a crossin' with a broom and raking over tailing with a rake, *only — wot ye get* with a broom *you have handed to ye,* and ye don't have to *pick it up and fish it out er* the wet rocks and sluice-gushin'; and it 's a heap less tiring to the back."

"Certingly, you bet!" said Uncle Billy enthusiastically, yet with a certain nervous abstraction.

"I 'm glad ye say so; for yer see I did n't know at first how you 'd tumble to my doing it, until I 'd made my pile. And ef I had n't made it, I would n't hev set eyes on ye agin, old pard — never!"

"Do you mind my runnin' out a minit," said Uncle Billy, rising. "You see, I've got a friend waitin' for me outside — and I reckon " — he stammered — "I'll jest run out and send him off, so I kin talk comf'ble to ye."

"Ye ain't got anybody you're owin' money to," said Uncle Jim earnestly, "anybody follerin' you to get paid, eh? For I kin jest set down right here and write ye off a check on the bank!"

"No," said Uncle Billy. He slipped out of the door, and ran like a deer to the waiting carriage. Thrusting a twenty - dollar gold-piece into the coachman's hand, he said hoarsely, "I ain't wantin' that kerridge just now; ye ken drive around and hev a private jamboree all by yourself the rest of the afternoon, and then come and wait for me at the top o' the hill yonder."

Thus quit of his gorgeous equipage, he hurried back to Uncle Jim, grasping his ten-thousand dollar draft in his pocket. He was nervous, he was frightened, but he must get rid of the draft and his story, and have it over. But before he could speak he was unexpectedly stopped by Uncle Jim.

"Now, look yer, Billy boy!" said Uncle

Jim; "I got suthin' to say to ye — and I might as well clear it off my mind at once, and then we can start fair agin. Now," he went on, with a half laugh, "was n't it enough for *me* to go on pretendin' I was rich and doing a big business, and gettin' up that lock-box dodge so as ye could n't find out whar I hung out and what I was doin' — was n't it enough for *me* to go on with all this play-actin', but *you*, you long-legged or'nary cuss! must get up and go to lyin' and play-actin', too!"

"*Me* play-actin'? *Me* lyin'?" gasped Uncle Billy.

Uncle Jim leaned back in his chair and laughed. "Do you think you could fool *me?* Do you think I did n't see through your little game o' going to that swell Oriental, jest as if ye 'd made a big strike — and all the while ye was n't sleepin' or eatin' there, but jest wrastlin' yer hash and having a roll down at the Good Cheer! Do you think I did n't spy on ye and find that out? Oh, you long-eared jackass-rabbit!"

He laughed until the tears came into his eyes, and Uncle Billy laughed too, albeit until the laugh on his face became quite fixed, and he was fain to bury his head in his handkerchief.

"And yet," said Uncle Jim, with a deep breath, "gosh! I was frighted — jest for a minit! I thought, mebbe, you *had* made a big strike — when I got your first letter — and I made up my mind what I 'd do! And then I remembered you was jest that kind of an open sluice that could n't keep anythin' to yourself, and you 'd have been sure to have yelled it out to *me* the first thing. So I waited. And I found you out, you old sinner!" He reached forward and dug Uncle Billy in the ribs.

"What *would* you hev done?" said Uncle Billy, after an hysterical collapse.

Uncle Jim's face grew grave again. "I 'd hev — I 'd — hev cl'ared out! Out er 'Frisco! out er Californy! out er Ameriky! I could n't have stud it! Don't think I would hev begrudged ye yer luck! No man would have been gladder than me." He leaned forward again, and laid his hand caressingly upon his partner's arm — "Don't think I 'd hev wanted to take a penny of it — but I — thar! I *could n't* hev stood up under it! To hev had *you*, you that I left behind, comin' down here rollin' in wealth and new partners and friends, and arrive upon me — and this shanty — and " — he threw towards the corner of the room a terrible gesture, none the less terrible that it was illogical and inconsequent to all that had gone before — "and — and — *that broom!*"

There was a dead silence in the room. With it Uncle Billy seemed to feel himself again transported to the homely cabin at Cedar Camp and that fateful night, with his partner's strange, determined face before him as then. He even fancied that he heard the roaring of the pines without, and did not know that it was the distant sea.

But after a minute Uncle Jim resumed : —

"Of course you 've made a little raise somehow, or you would n't be here?"

"Yes," said Uncle Billy eagerly. "Yes! I 've got" — He stopped and stammered. "I 've got — a — few hundreds."

"Oh, oh!" said Uncle Jim cheerfully. He paused, and then added earnestly, "I say! You ain't got left, over and above your d—d foolishness at the Oriental, as much as five hundred dollars?"

"I 've got," said Uncle Billy, blushing a little over his first deliberate and affected lie, "I 've got at least five hundred and seventy-two dollars. Yes," he added tenta-

tively, gazing anxiously at his partner, "I 've
got at least that."

"Je whillikins!" said Uncle Jim, with a
laugh. Then eagerly, "Look here, pard!
Then we 're on velvet! I 've got *nine* hundred; put your *five* with that, and I know
a little ranch that we can get for twelve hundred. That 's what I 've been savin' up for
— that 's my little game! No more minin'
for *me*. It 's got a shanty twice as big as
our old cabin, nigh on a hundred acres, and
two mustangs. We can run it with two
Chinamen and jest make it howl! Wot yer
say — eh?" He extended his hand.

"I 'm in," said Uncle Billy, radiantly
grasping Uncle Jim's. But his smile faded,
and his clear simple brow wrinkled in two
lines.

Happily Uncle Jim did not notice it.
"Now, then, old pard," he said brightly,
"we 'll have a gay old time to-night — one
of our jamborees! I 've got some whiskey
here and a deck o' cards, and we 'll have
a little game, you understand, but not for
' keeps ' now! No, siree; we 'll play for
beans."

A sudden light illuminated Uncle Billy's
face again, but he said, with a grim despera-

tion, "Not to-night! I've got to go into town. That fren' o' mine expects me to go to the theayter, don't ye see? But I'll be out to-morrow at sun-up, and we'll fix up this thing o' the ranch."

"Seems to me you're kinder stuck on this fren'," grunted Uncle Jim.

Uncle Billy's heart bounded at his partner's jealousy. "No — but I *must*, you know," he returned, with a faint laugh.

"I say — it ain't a *her*, is it?" said Uncle Jim.

Uncle Billy achieved a diabolical wink and a creditable blush at his lie.

"Billy?"

"Jim!"

And under cover of this festive gallantry Uncle Billy escaped. He ran through the gathering darkness, and toiled up the shifting sands to the top of the hill, where he found the carriage waiting.

"Wot," said Uncle Billy in a low confidential tone to the coachman, "wot do you 'Frisco fellers allow to be the best, biggest, and riskiest gamblin'-saloon here? Suthin' high-toned, you know?"

The negro grinned. It was the usual case of the extravagant spendthrift miner, though perhaps he had expected a different question and order.

"Dey is de ' Polka,' de ' El Dorado,' and de ' Arcade ' saloon, boss," he said, flicking his whip meditatively. "Most .gents from de mines prefer de ' Polka,' for dey is dancing wid de gals frown in. But de real *prima facie* place for gents who go for buckin' agin de tiger and straight-out gamblin' is de ' Arcade.' "

"Drive there like thunder!" said Uncle Billy, leaping into the carriage.

.    .    .    .    .    .    .    .

True to his word, Uncle Billy was at his partner's shanty early the next morning. He looked a little tired, but happy, and had brought a draft with him for five hundred and seventy-five dollars, which he explained was the total of his capital. Uncle Jim was overjoyed. They would start for Napa that very day, and conclude the purchase of the ranch; Uncle Jim's sprained foot was a sufficient reason for his giving up his present vocation, which he could also sell at a small profit. His domestic arrangements were very simple; there was nothing to take with him — there was everything to leave behind. And that afternoon, at sunset, the two reunited partners were seated on the deck of the Napa boat as she swung into the stream.

Uncle Billy was gazing over the railing with a look of abstracted relief towards the Golden Gate, where the sinking sun seemed to be drawing towards him in the ocean a golden stream that was forever pouring from the Bay and the three-hilled city beside it. What Uncle Billy was thinking of, or what the picture suggested to him, did not transpire; for Uncle Jim, who, emboldened by his holiday, was luxuriating in an evening paper, suddenly uttered a long-drawn whistle, and moved closer to his abstracted partner. "Look yer," he said, pointing to a paragraph he had evidently just read, "just you listen to this, and see if we ain't lucky, you and me, to be jest wot we air — trustin' to our own hard work — and not thinkin' o' ' strikes ' and ' fortins.' Jest unbutton yer ears, Billy, while I reel off this yer thing I 've jest struck in the paper, and see what d—d fools some men kin make o' themselves. And that theer reporter wot wrote it — must hev seed it reely! "

Uncle Jim cleared his throat, and holding the paper close to his eyes read aloud slowly : —

" ' A scene of excitement that recalled the palmy days of '49 was witnessed last night at the Arcade Saloon. A stranger, who might have belonged to that reckless epoch, and who bore every evidence of being a successful Pike County miner out on a " spree," appeared at one of the tables with a negro coachman bearing two heavy bags of gold. Selecting a faro-bank as his base of operations, he began to bet heavily and with apparent recklessness, until his play excited the breathless attention of every one. In a few moments he had won a sum variously estimated at from eighty to a hundred thousand dollars. A rumor went round the room that it was a concerted attempt to " break the bank " rather than the drunken freak of a Western miner, dazzled by some successful strike. To this theory the man's careless and indifferent bearing towards his extraordinary gains lent great credence. The attempt, if such it was, however, was unsuccessful. After winning ten times in succession the luck turned, and the unfortunate " bucker " was cleared out not only of his gains, but of his original investment, which may be placed roughly at twenty thousand dollars. This extraordinary play was

witnessed by a crowd of excited players, who
were less impressed by even the magnitude
of the stakes than the perfect *sang-froid*
and recklessness of the player, who, it is
said, at the close of the game tossed a twenty-
dollar gold-piece to the banker and smilingly
withdrew.   The man was not recognized by
any of the habitués of the place.'

"There!" said Uncle Jim, as he hurriedly
slurred over the French substantive at the
close, "did ye ever see such God-forsaken
foolishness?'

Uncle Billy lifted his abstracted eyes
from the current, still pouring its unreturn-
ing gold into the sinking sun, and said, with
a deprecatory smile, "Never!"

Nor even in the days of prosperity that
visited the Great Wheat Ranch of "Fall
and Foster" did he ever tell his secret to
his partner.

# SEE YUP

I DON'T suppose that his progenitors ever gave him that name, or, indeed, that it was a *name* at all; but it was currently believed that — as pronounced "See *Up* " — it meant that lifting of the outer angle of the eye common to the Mongolian. On the other hand, I had been told that there was an old Chinese custom of affixing some motto or legend, or even a sentence from Confucius, as a sign above their shops, and that two or more words, which might be merely equivalent to "Virtue is its own reward," or "Riches are deceitful," were believed by the simple Californian miner to be the name of the occupant himself. Howbeit, "See Yup" accepted it with the smiling patience of his race, and never went by any other. If one of the tunnelmen always addressed him as "Brigadier-General," "Judge," or "Commodore," it was understood to be only the American fondness for ironic title, and was never used except in personal conversa-

tion. In appearance he looked like any
other Chinaman, wore the ordinary blue cotton blouse and white drawers of the Sampan
coolie, and, in spite of the apparent cleanliness and freshness of these garments, always
exhaled that singular medicated odor — half
opium, half ginger — which we recognized
as the common "Chinese smell."

Our first interview was characteristic of
his patient quality. He had done my washing for several months, but I had never yet
seen him. A meeting at last had become
necessary to correct his impressions regarding "buttons" — which he had seemed to
consider as mere excrescences, to be removed
like superfluous dirt from soiled linen. I
had expected him to call at my lodgings, but
he had not yet made his appearance. One
day, during the noontide recess of the little
frontier school over which I presided, I returned rather early. Two or three of the
smaller boys, who were loitering about the
school-yard, disappeared with a certain
guilty precipitation that I suspected for the
moment, but which I presently dismissed
from my mind. I passed through the empty
school-room to my desk, sat down, and began
to prepare the coming lessons. Presently I

heard a faint sigh. Looking up, to my intense concern, I discovered a solitary Chinaman whom I had overlooked, sitting in a rigid attitude on a bench with his back to the window. He caught my eye and smiled sadly, but without moving.

"What are you doing here?" I asked sternly.

"Me washee shilts; me talkee ' buttons.' "

"Oh! you 're See Yup, are you?"

"Allee same, John."

"Well, come here."

I continued my work, but he did not move.

"Come here, hang it! Don't you understand?"

"Me shabbee, ' comme yea.' But me no shabbee Mellican boy, who catchee me, allee same. *You* ' comme yea '—*you* shabbee?"

Indignant, but believing that the unfortunate man was still in fear of persecution from the mischievous urchins whom I had evidently just interrupted, I put down my pen and went over to him. Here I discovered, to my surprise and mortification, that his long pigtail was held hard and fast by the closed window behind him. which the young rascals had shut down upon it, after having

first noiselessly fished it outside with a hook
and line. I apologized, opened the window,
and released him. He did not complain, although he must have been fixed in that uncomfortable position for some minutes, but
plunged at once into the business that brought
him there.

"But *why* didn't you come to my lodgings?" I asked.

He smiled sadly but intelligently.

"Mishtel Bally [Mr. Barry, my landlord]
he owce me five dollee fo washee, washee.
He no payee me. He say he knock hellee
outee me allee time I come for payee. So
me no come *housee*, me come *schoolee*.
Shabbee? Mellican boy no good, but not
so big as Mellican man. No can hurtee
Chinaman so much. Shabbee?"

Alas! I knew that this was mainly true.
Mr. James Barry was an Irishman, whose
finer religious feelings revolted against paying money to a heathen. I could not find
it in my heart to say anything to See Yup
about the buttons; indeed, I spoke in complimentary terms about the gloss of my
shirts, and I think I meekly begged him to
come again for my washing. When I went
home I expostulated with Mr. Barry, but

succeeded only in extracting from him the conviction that I was one of "thim black Republican fellys that worshiped naygurs." I had simply made an enemy of him. But I did not know that, at the same time, I had made a friend of See Yup!

I became aware of this a few days later, by the appearance on my desk of a small pot containing a specimen of camellia japonica in flower. I knew the school-children were in the habit of making presents to me in this furtive fashion, — leaving their own nosegays of wild flowers, or perhaps a cluster of roses from their parents' gardens, — but I also knew that this exotic was too rare to come from them. I remembered that See Yup had a Chinese taste for gardening, and a friend, another Chinaman, who kept a large nursery in the adjoining town. But my doubts were set at rest by the discovery of a small roll of red rice-paper containing my washing-bill, fastened to the camellia stalk. It was plain that this mingling of business and delicate gratitude was clearly See Yup's own idea. As the finest flower was the topmost one, I plucked it for wearing, when I found, to my astonishment, that it was simply wired to the stalk. This led me to look

at the others, which I found also wired!
More than that, they seemed to be an inferior flower, and exhaled that cold, earthy
odor peculiar to the camellia, even, as I
thought, to an excess. A closer examination resulted in the discovery that, with the
exception of the first flower I had plucked,
they were one and all ingeniously constructed
of thin slices of potato, marvelously cut to
imitate the vegetable waxiness and formality
of the real flower. The work showed an infinite and almost pathetic patience in detail,
yet strangely incommensurate with the result, admirable as it was. Nevertheless,
this was also like See Yup. But whether
he had tried to deceive me, or whether he
only wished me to admire his skill, I could
not say. And as his persecution by my
scholars had left a balance of consideration
in his favor, I sent him a warm note of
thanks, and said nothing of my discovery.

As our acquaintance progressed, I became
frequently the recipient of other small presents from him: a pot of preserves of a
quality I could not purchase in shops, and
whose contents in their crafty, gingery dis-
simulation so defied definition that I never
knew whether they were animal, vegetable,

or mineral; two or three hideous Chinese idols, "for luckee," and a diabolical firework with an irregular spasmodic activity that would sometimes be prolonged until the next morning. In return, I gave him some apparently hopeless oral lessons in English, and certain sentences to be copied, which he did with marvelous precision. I remember one instance when this peculiar faculty of imitation was disastrous in result. In setting him a copy, I had blurred a word which I promptly erased, and then traced the letters more distinctly over the scratched surface. To my surprise, See Yup triumphantly produced *his* copy with the erasion itself carefully imitated, and, in fact, much more neatly done than mine.

In our confidential intercourse, I never seemed to really get nearer to him. His sympathy and simplicity appeared like his flowers — to be a good-humored imitation of my own. I am satisfied that his particularly soulless laugh was not derived from any amusement he actually felt, yet I could not say it was forced. In his accurate imitations, I fancied he was only trying to evade any responsibility of his own. *That* devolved upon his taskmaster! In the attention he displayed when new ideas were presented to him, there was a slight condescension, as if he were looking down upon them from his three thousand years of history.

"Don't you think the electric telegraph wonderful?" I asked one day.

"Very good for Mellican man," he said, with his aimless laugh; "plenty makee him jump!"

I never could tell whether he had confounded it with electro-galvanism, or was only satirizing our American haste and feverishness. He was capable of either. For that matter, we knew that the Chinese themselves possessed some means of secretly and quickly communicating with one another. Any news of good or ill import to their race was quickly disseminated through the settlement before *we* knew anything about it. An innocent basket of clothes from the wash, sent up from the river-bank, became in some way a library of information; a single slip of rice-paper, aimlessly fluttering in the dust of the road, had the mysterious effect of diverging a whole gang of coolie tramps away from our settlement.

When See Yup was not subject to the

persecutions of the more ignorant and brutal he was always a source of amusement to all, and I cannot recall an instance when he was ever taken seriously. The miners found diversions even in his alleged frauds and trickeries, whether innocent or retaliatory, and were fond of relating with great gusto his evasion of the Foreign Miners' Tax. This was an oppressive measure aimed principally at the Chinese, who humbly worked the worn-out "tailings" of their Christian fellow miners. It was stated that See Yup, knowing the difficulty — already alluded to — of identifying any particular Chinaman by *name*, conceived the additional idea of confusing recognition by intensifying the monotonous facial expression. Having paid his tax himself to the collector, he at once passed the receipt to his fellows, so that the collector found himself confronted in different parts of the settlement with the receipt and the aimless laugh of, apparently, See Yup himself. Although we all knew that there were a dozen Chinamen or more at work at the mines, the collector never was able to collect the tax from more than *two*, — See Yup and one See Yin, — and so great was *their* facial resemblance that the unfortunate official for a long time hugged himself with the conviction that he had made See Yup *pay twice*, and withheld the money from the government! It is very probable that the Californian's recognition of the sanctity of a joke, and his belief that "cheating the government was only cheating himself," largely accounted for the sympathies of the rest of the miners.

But these sympathies were not always unanimous.

One evening I strolled into the bar-room of the principal saloon, which, so far as mere upholstery and comfort went, was also the principal house in the settlement. The first rains had commenced; the windows were open, for the influence of the southwest trades penetrated even this far-off mountain mining settlement, but, oddly enough, there was a fire in the large central stove, around which the miners had collected, with their steaming boots elevated on a projecting iron railing that encircled it. They were not attracted by the warmth, but the stove formed a social pivot for gossip, and suggested that mystic circle dear to the gregarious instinct. Yet they were decidedly a despondent group. For some moments the silence was only broken by a gasp, a sigh, a muttered oath, or an impatient change of position. There was nothing in the fortunes of the settlement, nor in their own individual affairs to suggest this gloom. The singular truth was that they were, one and all, suffering from the pangs of dyspepsia.

Incongruous as such a complaint might seem to their healthy environment, — their outdoor life, their daily exercise, the healing balsam of the mountain air, their enforced temperance in diet, and the absence of all enervating pleasures, — it was nevertheless the incontestable fact. Whether it was the result of the nervous, excitable temperament which had brought them together in this feverish hunt for gold; whether it was the quality of the tinned meats or half-cooked provisions they hastily bolted, begrudging the time it took to prepare and to consume them; whether they too often supplanted their meals by tobacco or whiskey, the singular physiological truth remained that these young, finely selected adventurers, living the lives of the natural, aboriginal man, and looking the picture of health and strength, actually suffered more from indigestion than the pampered dwellers of the cities. The quantity of "patent medicines," "bitters," "pills," "panaceas," and "lozenges" sold in the settlement almost exceeded the amount of the regular provisions whose effects they were supposed to correct. The sufferers eagerly scanned advertisements and placards. There were occasional "runs" on new "specifics," and general conversation eventually turned into a discussion of their respective merits. A certain childlike faith and trust in each new remedy was not the least distressing and pathetic of the symptoms of these grown-up, bearded men.

"Well, gentlemen," said Cyrus Parker, glancing around at his fellow sufferers, "ye kin talk of your patent medicines, and I've tackled 'em all, but only the other day I struck suthin' that I'm goin' to hang on to, you bet."

Every eye was turned moodily to the speaker, but no one said anything.

"And I did n't get it out er advertisements, nor off of circulars. I got it out er my head, just by solid thinking," continued Parker.

"What was it, Cy?" said one unsophisticated and inexperienced sufferer.

Instead of replying, Parker, like a true artist, knowing he had the ear of his audi-

ence, dramatically flashed a question upon
them.

"Did you ever hear of a Chinaman having dyspepsy?"

"Never heard he had sabe enough to hev
*anything*," said a scorner.

"No, but *did* ye?" insisted Parker.

"Well, no!" chorused the group. They
were evidently struck with the fact.

"Of course you did n't," said Parker triumphantly. " 'Cos they *ain't*. Well, gentlemen, it did n't seem to me the square thing
that a pesky lot o' yellow-skinned heathens
should be built different to a white man, and
never know the tortur' that a Christian feels;
and one day, arter dinner, when I was just
a-lyin' flat down on the bank, squirmin',
and clutching the short grass to keep from
yellin', who should go by but that pizened
See Yup, with a grin on his face.

"' Mellican man plenty playee to him
Joss after eatin',' sez he; ' but Chinaman
smellee punk, allee same, and no hab got.'

"I knew the slimy cuss was just purtend-
in' he thought I was prayin' to my Joss, but
I was that weak I had n't stren'th, boys, to
heave a rock at him. Yet it gave me an
idea."

"What was it?" they asked eagerly.

"I went down to his shop the next day, when he was alone, and I was feeling mighty bad, and I got hold of his pigtail and I allowed I'd stuff it down his throat if he didn't tell me what he meant. Then he took a piece of punk and lit it, and put it under my nose, and, darn my skin, gentlemen, you migh'n't believe me, but in a minute I felt better, and after a whiff or two I was all right."

"Was it pow'ful strong, Cy?" asked the inexperienced one.

"No," said Parker, "and that's just what's got me. It was a sort o' dreamy, spicy smell, like a hot night. But as I couldn't go 'round 'mong you boys with a lighted piece o' punk in my hand, ez if I was settin' off Fourth of July firecrackers, I asked him if he couldn't fix me up suthin' in another shape that would be handier to use when I was took bad, and I'd reckon to pay him for it like ez I'd pay for any other patent medicine. So he fixed me up this."

He put his hand in his pocket, and drew out a small red paper which, when opened, disclosed a pink powder. It was gravely passed around the group.

"Why, it smells and tastes like ginger," said one.

"It is only ginger!" said another scornfully.

"Mebbe it is, and mebbe it isn't," returned Cy Parker stoutly. "Mebbe ut's only my fancy. But if it's the sort o' stuff to bring on that fancy, and that fancy *cures* me, it's all the same. I've got about two dollars' worth o' that fancy or that ginger, and I'm going to stick to it. You hear me!" And he carefully put it back in his pocket.

At which criticisms and gibes broke forth. If he (Cy Parker), a white man, was going to "demean himself" by consulting a Chinese quack, he'd better buy up a lot o' idols and stand 'em up around his cabin. If he had that sort o' confidences with See Yup, he ought to go to work with him on his cheap tailings, and be fumigated all at the same time. If he'd been smoking an opium pipe, instead of smelling punk, he ought to be man enough to confess it. Yet it was noticeable that they were all very anxious to examine the packet again, but Cy Parker was alike indifferent to demand or entreaty.

A few days later I saw Abe Wynford,

one of the party, coming out of See Yup's wash-house. He muttered something in passing about the infamous delay in sending home his washing, but did not linger long in conversation. The next day I met another miner *at* the wash-house, but *he* lingered so long on some trifling details that I finally left him there alone with See Yup. When I called upon Poker Jack of Shasta, there was a singular smell of incense in *his* cabin, which he attributed to the very resinous quality of the fir logs he was burning. I did not attempt to probe these mysteries by any direct appeal to See Yup himself: I respected his reticence; indeed, if I had not, I was quite satisfied that he would have lied to me. Enough that his wash-house was well patronized, and he was decidedly "getting on."

It might have been a month afterwards that Dr. Duchesne was setting a broken bone in the settlement, and after the operation was over, had strolled into the Palmetto Saloon. He was an old army surgeon, much respected and loved in the district, although perhaps a little feared for the honest roughness and military precision of his speech. After he had exchanged salutations with the

miners in his usual hearty fashion, and accepted their invitation to drink, Cy Parker,
with a certain affected carelessness which
did not, however, conceal a singular hesitation in his speech, began: —

"I 've been wantin' to ask ye a question,
Doc, — a sort o' darned fool question, ye
know, — nothing in the way of consultation,
don't you see, though it 's kin ˉer in the way
o' your purfeshun. Sabe?"

"Go on, Cy," said the doctor good-humoredly, "this is my dispensary hour."

"Oh! it ain't anything about symptoms,
Doc, and there ain't anything the matter
with me. It 's only just to ask ye if ye
happened to know anything about the medical practice of these yer Chinamen?"

"*I* don't know," said the doctor bluntly,
"and I don't know *anybody* who does."

There was a sudden silence in the bar,
and the doctor, putting down his glass, continued with slight professional precision: —

"You see, the Chinese know nothing of
anatomy from personal observation. Au-
topsies and dissection are against their
superstitions, which declare the human body
sacred, and are consequently never prac-
ticed."

There was a slight movement of inquiring interest among the party, and Cy Parker, after a meaning glance at the others, went on half aggressively, half apologetically: —

"In course, they ain't surgeons like you, Doc, but that don't keep them from having their own little medicines, just as dogs eat grass, you know. Now I want to put it to you, as a fa'r-minded man, if you mean ter say that, jest because those old women who sarve out yarbs and spring medicines in families don't know anything of anatomy, they ain't fit to give us their simple and nat'ral medicines?"

"But the Chinese medicines are not simple or natural," said the doctor coolly.

"Not simple?" echoed the party, closing round him.

"I don't mean to say," continued the doctor, glancing around at their eager, excited faces with an appearance of wonder, "that they are positively noxious, unless taken in large quantities, for they are not drugs at all, but I certainly should not call them ' simple.' Do *you* know what they principally are?"

"Well, no," said Parker cautiously, "per-haps not *exactly*."

"Come a little closer, and I 'll tell you."

Not only Parker's head but the others were bent over the counter. Dr. Duchesne uttered a few words in a tone inaudible to the rest of the company. There was a profound silence, broken at last by Abe Wynford's voice:—

"Ye kin pour me out about three fingers o' whiskey, Barkeep. I 'll take it straight."

"Same to me," said the others.

The men gulped down their liquor; two of them quietly passed out. The doctor wiped his lips, buttoned his coat, and began to draw on his riding-gloves.

"I 've heerd," said Poker Jack of Shasta, with a faint smile on his white face, as he toyed with the last drops of liquor in his glass, "that the darned fools sometimes smell punk as a medicine, eh?"

"Yes, *that* 's comparatively decent," said the doctor reflectively. "It 's only sawdust mixed with a little gum and formic acid."

"Formic acid? Wot 's that?"

"A very peculiar acid secreted by ants. It is supposed to be used by them offensively in warfare — just as the skunk, eh?"

But Poker Jack of Shasta had hurriedly declared that he wanted to speak to a man who was passing, and had disappeared. The doctor walked to the door, mounted his horse, and rode away. I noticed, however, that there was a slight smile on his bronzed, impassive face. This led me to wonder if he was entirely ignorant of the purpose for which he had been questioned, and the effect of his information. I was confirmed in the belief by the remarkable circumstances that nothing more was said of it; the incident seemed to have terminated there, and the victims made no attempt to revenge themselves on See Yup. That they had one and all, secretly and unknown to one another, patronized him, there was no doubt; but, at the same time, as they evidently were not sure that Dr. Duchesne had not hoaxed them in regard to the quality of See Yup's medicines, they knew that an attack on the unfortunate Chinaman would in either case reveal their secret and expose them to the ridicule of their brother miners. So the matter dropped, and See Yup remained master of the situation.

Meantime he was prospering. The coolie gang he worked on the river, when not engaged in washing clothes, were "picking over" the "tailings," or refuse of gravel, left on abandoned claims by successful miners. As there was no more expense attending this than in stone-breaking or rag-picking, and the feeding of the coolies, which was ridiculously cheap, there was no doubt that See Yup was reaping a fair weekly return from it; but, as he sent his receipts to San Francisco through coolie managers, after the Chinese custom, and did not use the regular Express Company, there was no way of ascertaining the amount. Again, neither See Yup nor his fellow countrymen ever appeared to have any money about them. In ruder times and more reckless camps, raids were often made by ruffians on their cabins or their traveling gangs, but never with any pecuniary result. This condition, however, it seemed was destined to change.

One Saturday See Yup walked into Wells, Fargo & Co.'s Express office with a package of gold-dust, which, when duly weighed, was valued at five hundred dollars. It was consigned to a Chinese company in San Francisco. When the clerk handed See Yup a receipt, he remarked casually: —

"Washing seems to pay, See Yup."

"Washee velly good pay. You wantee washee, John?" said See Yup eagerly.

"No, no," said the clerk, with a laugh. "I was only thinking five hundred dollars would represent the washing of a good many shirts."

"No leplesent washee shirts at all! Catchee gold-dust when washee tailings. Shabbee?"

The clerk *did* "shabbee," and lifted his eyebrows. The next Saturday See Yup appeared with another package, worth about four hundred dollars, directed to the same consignee.

"Didn't pan out quite so rich this week, eh?" said the clerk engagingly.

"No," returned See Yup impassively; "next time he payee more."

When the third Saturday came, with the appearance of See Yup and four hundred and fifty dollars' worth of gold-dust, the clerk felt he was no longer bound to keep the secret. He communicated it to others, and in twenty-four hours the whole settlement knew that See Yup's coolie company were taking out an average of four hundred dollars per week from the refuse and tailings of the old abandoned Palmetto claim!

The astonishment of the settlement was

profound. In earlier days jealousy and indignation at the success of these degraded heathens might have taken a more active and aggressive shape, and it would have fared ill with See Yup and his companions. But the settlement had become more prosperous and law-abiding; there were one or two Eastern families and some foreign capital already there, and its jealousy and indignation were restricted to severe investigation and legal criticism. Fortunately for See Yup, it was an old-established mining law that an abandoned claim and its tailings became the property of whoever chose to work it. But it was alleged that See Yup's company had in reality "struck a lead," — discovered a hitherto unknown vein or original deposit of gold, not worked by the previous company, — and having failed legally to declare it by preëmption and public registry, in their foolish desire for secrecy, had thus forfeited their right to the property. A surveillance of their working, however, did not establish this theory; the gold that See Yup had sent away was of the kind that might have been found in the tailings overlooked by the late Palmetto owners. Yet it was a very large yield for mere refuse.

"Them Palmetto boys were mighty keer-less after they 'd made their big ' strike ' and got to work on the vein, and I reckon they threw a lot of gold away," said Cy Parker, who remembered their large-handed recklessness in the "flush days." "On'y that *we* did n't think it was white man's work to rake over another man's leavin's, we might hev had what them derned China-men hev dropped into. Tell ye what, boys, we 've been a little too ' high and mighty,' and we 'll hev to climb down."

At last the excitement reached its climax, and diplomacy was employed to effect what neither intimidation nor espionage could se-cure. Under the pretense of desiring to buy out See Yup's company, a select com-mittee of the miners was permitted to exam-ine the property and its workings. They found the great bank of stones and gravel, representing the cast-out débris of the old claim, occupied by See Yup and four or five plodding automatic coolies. At the end of two hours the committee returned to the sa-loon bursting with excitement. They spoke under their breath, but enough was gathered to satisfy the curious crowd that See Yup's pile of tailings was rich beyond their expectations. The committee had seen with their own eyes gold taken out of the sand and gravel to the amount of twenty dollars in the two short hours of their examination. And the work had been performed in the stupidest, clumsiest, yet *patient* Chinese way. What might not white men do with better appointed machinery! A syndicate was at once formed. See Yup was offered twenty thousand dollars if he would sell out and put the syndicate in possession of the claim in twenty-four hours. The Chinaman received the offer stolidly. As he seemed inclined to hesitate, I am grieved to say that it was intimated to him that if he declined he might be subject to embarrassing and expensive legal proceedings to prove his property, and that companies would be formed to "prospect" the ground on either side of his heap of tailings. See Yup at last consented, with the proviso that the money should be paid in gold into the hands of a Chinese agent in San Francisco on the day of the delivery of the claim. The syndicate made no opposition to this characteristic precaution of the Chinaman. It was like them not to travel with money, and the implied uncomplimentary suspicion of danger

from the community was overlooked.   See
Yup departed the day that the syndicate
took possession.   He came to see me before
he went.   I congratulated him upon his good
fortune; at the same time, I was embarrassed by the conviction that he was unfairly
forced into a sale of his property at a figure
far below its real value.

I think differently now.

At the end of the week it was said that
the new company cleared up about three
hundred dollars.   This was not so much as
the community had expected, but the syndicate was apparently satisfied, and the new
machinery was put up.   At the end of the
next week the syndicate were silent as to
their returns.   One of them made a hurried
visit to San Francisco.   It was said that he
was unable to see either See Yup or the
agent to whom the money was paid.   It was
also noticed that there was no Chinaman
remaining in the settlement.   Then the fatal
secret was out.

The heap of tailings had probably never
yielded the See Yup company more than
twenty dollars a week, the ordinary wage of
such a company.   See Yup had conceived
the brilliant idea of "booming" it on a bor-

rowed capital of five hundred dollars in gold-dust, which he *openly* transmitted by express to his confederate and creditor in San Francisco, who in turn *secretly* sent it back to See Yup by coolie messengers, to be again openly transmitted to San Francisco. The package of gold-dust was thus passed backwards and forwards between debtor and creditor, to the grave edification of the Express Company and the fatal curiosity of the settlement. When the syndicate had gorged the bait thus thrown out, See Yup, on the day the self-invited committee inspected the claim, promptly "salted" the tailings by *conscientiously distributing the gold-dust over it* so deftly that it appeared to be its natural composition and yield.

I have only to bid farewell to See Yup, and close this reminiscence of a misunderstood man, by adding the opinion of an eminent jurist in San Francisco, to whom the facts were submitted: "So clever was this alleged fraud, that it is extremely doubtful if an action would lie against See Yup in the premises, there being no legal evidence of the ' salting,' and none whatever of his actual allegation that the gold-dust was the *ordinary* yield of the tailings, that implica-

tion resting entirely with the committee who
examined it under false pretense, and who
subsequently forced the sale by intimidation."

# THE DESBOROUGH CONNECTIONS

"THEN it isn't a question of property or next of kin?" said the consul.

"Lord! no," said the lady vivaciously. "Why, goodness me! I reckon old Desborough could, at any time before he died, have 'bought up' or 'bought out' the whole lot of his relatives on this side of the big pond, no matter what they were worth. No, it's only a matter of curiosity and just sociableness."

The American consul at St. Kentigorn felt much relieved. He had feared it was only the old story of delusive quests for imaginary estates and impossible inheritances which he had confronted so often in nervous wan-eyed enthusiasts and obstreperous claimants from his own land. Certainly there was no suggestion of this in the richly dressed and be-diamonded matron before him, nor in her pretty daughter, charming in a Paris frock, alive with the consciousness of beauty and admiration, and yet a little *ennuyé* from gratified indulgence. He knew the mother to be the wealthy widow of a New York millionaire, that she was traveling for pleasure in Europe, and a chance meeting with her at dinner a few nights before had led to this half-capricious, half-confidential appointment at the consulate.

"No," continued Mrs. Desborough; "Mr. Desborough came to America, when a small boy, with an uncle who died some years ago. Mr. Desborough never seemed to hanker much after his English relatives as long as I knew him, but now that I and Sadie are over here, why we guessed we might look 'em up and sort of sample 'em! 'Desborough' 's rather a good name," added the lady, with a complacency that, however, had a suggestion of query in it.

"Yes," said the consul; "from the French, I fancy."

"Mr. Desborough was English — very English," corrected the lady.

"I mean it may be an old Norman name," said the consul.

"Norman 's good enough for *me*," said the daughter, reflecting. "We 'll just settle it as Norman. I never thought about that *Des*."

"Only you may find it called ' Debborough' here, and spelt so," said the consul, smiling.

Miss Desborough lifted her pretty shoulders and made a charming grimace. "Then we won't acknowledge 'em. No Debborough for me!"

"You might put an advertisement in the papers, like the ' next of kin' notice, intimating, in the regular way, that they would ' hear of something to their advantage' — as they certainly would," continued the consul, with a bow. "It would be such a refreshing change to the kind of thing I 'm accustomed to, don't you know — this idea of one of my countrywomen coming over just to benefit English relatives! By Jove! I would n't mind undertaking the whole thing for you — it 's such a novelty." He was quite carried away with the idea.

But the two ladies were far from participating in this joyous outlook. "No," said Mrs. Desborough promptly, "that would n't do. You see," she went on with superb frankness, "that would be just giving ourselves away, and saying who *we* were before we found out what *they* were like. Mr. Desborough was all right in *his* way, but we don't know anything about his *folks!* We ain't here on a mission to improve the Desboroughs, nor to gather in any ' lost tribes.' "

It was evident that, in spite of the humor of the situation and the levity of the ladies, there was a characteristic national practicalness about them, and the consul, with a sigh, at last gave the address of one or two responsible experts in genealogical inquiry, as he had often done before. He felt it was impossible to offer any advice to ladies as thoroughly capable of managing their own affairs as his fair countrywomen, yet he was not without some curiosity to know the result of their practical sentimental quest. That he should ever hear of them again he doubted. He knew that after their first loneliness had worn off in their gregarious gathering at a London hotel they were not likely to consort with their own country people, who indeed were apt to fight shy of one another, and even to indulge in invidious criticism of one another when admitted in that society to which they were all equally strangers. So he took leave of them on their way back to London with the belief that their acquaintance terminated with that brief incident. But he was mistaken.

In the year following he was spending his autumn vacation at a country house. It was an historic house, and had always struck him as being — even in that country of historic seats — a singular example of the vicissitudes of English manorial estates and the mutations of its lords. His host in his prime had been recalled from foreign service to unexpectedly succeed to an uncle's title and estate. That estate, however, had come into the possession of the uncle only through his marriage with the daughter of an old family whose portraits still looked down from the walls upon the youngest and alien branch. There were likenesses, effigies, memorials, and reminiscences of still older families who had occupied it through forfeiture by war or the favoritism of kings, and in its stately cloisters and ruined chapel was still felt the dead hand of its evicted religious founders, which could not be shaken off.

It was this strange individuality that affected all who saw it. For, however changed were those within its walls, whoever were its inheritors or inhabiters, Scrooby Priory never changed nor altered its own character. However incongruous or ill-assorted the portraits that looked from its walls, — so ill met that they might have flown at one another's throats in the long nights when the family were away, — the great house itself was independent of them all. The be-wigged, belaced, and be-furbelowed of one day's gathering, the round-headed, steel-fronted, and prim-kerchiefed congregation of another day, and even the black-coated, bare-armed, and bare-shouldered assemblage of to-day had no effect on the austerities of the Priory. Modern houses might show the tastes and prepossessions of their dwellers, might have caught some passing trick of the hour, or have recorded the augmented fortunes or luxuriousness of the owner, but Scrooby Priory never! No one had dared even to disturb its outer rigid integrity; the breaches of time and siege were left untouched. It held its calm indifferent sway over all who passed its low-arched portals, and the consul was fain to believe that he — a foreign visitor — was no more alien to the house than its present owner.

"I'm expecting a very charming compatriot of yours to-morrow," said Lord Beverdale as they drove from the station together. "You must tell me what to show her."

"I should think any countrywoman of mine would be quite satisfied with the Priory," said the consul, glancing thoughtfully towards the pile dimly seen through the park.

"I should n't like her to be bored here," continued Beverdale. "Algy met her at Rome, where she was occupying a palace with her mother — they 're very rich, you know. He found she was staying with Lady Minever at Hedham Towers, and I went over and invited her with a little party. She 's a Miss Desborough."

The consul gave a slight start, and was aware that Beverdale was looking at him.

"Perhaps you know her?" said Beverdale.

"Just enough to agree with you that she is charming," said the consul. "I dined with them, and saw them at the consulate."

"Oh yes; I always forget you are a consul. Then, of course, you know all about them. I suppose they 're very rich, and in society over there?" said Beverdale in a voice that was quite animated.

It was on the consul's lips to say that the late Mr. Desborough was an Englishman, and even to speak playfully of their proposed quest, but a sudden instinct withheld

v. 13                                        E

him. After all, perhaps it was only a caprice, or idea, they had forgotten,— perhaps,
who knows? — that they were already
ashamed of. They had evidently "got on"
in English society, if that was their real intent, and doubtless Miss Desborough, by this
time, was quite as content with the chance
of becoming related to the Earl of Beverdale, through his son and heir, Algernon, as
if they had found a real Lord Desborough
among their own relatives. The consul knew
that Lord Beverdale was not a rich man,
that like most men of old family he was not
a slave to class prejudice; indeed, the consul had seen very few noblemen off the stage
or out of the pages of a novel who were.
So he said, with a slight affectation of authority, that there was as little doubt of the
young lady's wealth as there was of her personal attractions.

They were nearing the house through a
long avenue of chestnuts whose variegated
leaves were already beginning to strew the
ground beneath, and they could see the vista
open upon the mullioned windows of the
Priory, lighted up by the yellow October
sunshine. In that sunshine stood a tall,
clean-limbed young fellow, dressed in a

shooting-suit, whom the consul recognized at once as Lord Algernon, the son of his companion. As if to accent the graces of this vision of youth and vigor, near him, in the shadow, an old man had halted, hat in hand, still holding the rake with which he had been gathering the dead leaves in the avenue; his back bent, partly with years, partly with the obeisance of a servitor. There was something so marked in this contrast, in this old man standing in the shadow of the fading year, himself as dried and withered as the leaves he was raking, yet pausing to make his reverence to this passing sunshine of youth and prosperity in the presence of his coming master, that the consul, as they swept by, looked after him with a stirring of pain.

"Rather an old man to be still at work," said the consul.

Beverdale laughed. "You must not let him hear you say so; he considers himself quite as fit as any younger man in the place, and, by Jove! though he's nearly eighty, I'm inclined to believe it. He's not one of our people, however; he comes from the village, and is taken on at odd times, partly to please himself. His great aim is to be independent of his children, — he has a grand-daughter who is one of the maids at the Priory, — and to keep himself out of the workhouse. He does not come from these parts — somewhere farther north, I fancy. But he's a tough lot, and has a deal of work in him yet."

"Seems to be going a bit stale lately," said Lord Algernon, "and I think is getting a little queer in his head. He has a trick of stopping and staring straight ahead, at times, when he seems to go off for a minute or two. There!" continued the young man, with a light laugh. "I say! he's doing it now!" They both turned quickly and gazed at the bent figure — not fifty yards away — standing in exactly the same attitude as before. But, even as they gazed, he slowly lifted his rake and began his monotonous work again.

At Scrooby Priory, the consul found that the fame of his fair countrywoman had indeed preceded her, and that the other guests were quite as anxious to see Miss Desborough as he was. One of them had already met her in London; another knew her as one of the house party at the Duke of North-foreland's, where she had been a central fig-

ure. Some of her naïve sallies and frank
criticisms were repeated with great unction
by the gentlemen, and with some slight trep-
idation and a "fearful joy" by the ladies.
He was more than ever convinced that mother and daughter had forgotten their lineal
Desboroughs, and he resolved to leave any
allusion to it to the young lady herself.

She, however, availed herself of that privilege the evening after her arrival. "Who'd
have thought of meeting *you* here?" she
said, sweeping her skirts away to make room
for him on a sofa. "It's a coon's age since
I saw you — not since you gave us that letter
to those genealogical gentlemen in London."

The consul hoped that it had proved successful.

"Yes, but maw guessed we didn't care
to go back to Hengist and Horsa, and when
they let loose a lot of 'Debboroughs' and
'Daybrooks' upon us, maw kicked! We've
got a drawing ten yards long, that looks like
a sour apple tree, with lots of Desboroughs
hanging up on the branches like last year's
pippins, and I guess about as worm-eaten.
We took that well enough, but when it came
to giving us a map of straight lines and
dashes with names written under them like

an old Morse telegraph slip, struck by lightning, then maw and I guessed that it made us tired.

"You know," she went on, opening her clear gray eyes on the consul, with a characteristic flash of shrewd good sense through her quaint humor, "we never reckoned where this thing would land us, and we found we were paying a hundred pounds, not only for the Desboroughs, but all the people they'd *married*, and their *children*, and children's children, and there were a lot of outsiders we'd never heard of, nor wanted to hear of. Maw once thought she'd got on the trail of a Plantagenet, and followed it keen, until she found she had been reading the dreadful thing upside down. Then we concluded we wouldn't take any more stock in the family until it had risen."

During this speech the consul could not help noticing that, although her attitude was playfully confidential to him, her voice really was pitched high enough to reach the ears of smaller groups around her, who were not only following her with the intensest admiration, but had shamelessly abandoned their own conversation, and had even faced towards her. Was she really posing in her *naïveté?*

There was a certain mischievous, even aggressive, consciousness in her pretty eyelids. Then she suddenly dropped both eyes and voice, and said to the consul in a genuine aside, "I like this sort of thing much better."

The consul looked puzzled. "What sort of thing?"

"Why, all these swell people, don't you see? those pictures on the walls! this elegant room! everything that has come down from the past, all ready and settled for you, you know — ages ago! Something you have n't to pick up for yourself and worry over."

But here the consul pointed out that the place itself was not "ancestral" as regarded the present earl, and that even the original title of his predecessors had passed away from it. "In fact, it came into the family by one of those 'outsiders' you deprecate. But I dare say you 'd find the place quite as comfortable with Lord Beverdale for a host as you would if you had found out he were a cousin," he added.

"Better," said the young lady frankly.

"I suppose your mother participates in these preferences?" said the consul, with a smile.

"No," said Miss Desborough, with the same frankness, "I think maw's rather cut up at not finding a Desborough. She was invited down here, but *she*'s rather independent, you know, so she allowed I could take care of myself, while she went off to stay with the old Dowager Lady Mistowe, who thinks maw a very proper womanly person. I made maw mad by telling her that's just what old Lady Mistowe would say of her cook — for I can't stand these people's patronage. However, I shouldn't wonder if I was invited here as a ' most original person.' "

But here Lord Algernon came up to implore her to sing them one of "those plantation songs;" and Miss Desborough, with scarcely a change of voice or manner, allowed herself to be led to the piano. The consul had little chance to speak with her again, but he saw enough that evening to convince him not only that Lord Algernon was very much in love with her, but that the fact had been equally and complacently accepted by the family and guests. That her present visit was only an opportunity for a formal engagement was clear to every woman in the house — not excepting, I fear, even the fair subject of gossip herself. Yet she seemed so unconcerned and self-contained that the consul wondered if she really cared for Lord Algernon. And having thus wondered, he came to the conclusion that it did n't much matter, for the happiness of so practically organized a young lady, if she loved him or not.

It is highly probable that Miss Sadie Desborough had not even gone so far as to ask herself that question. She awoke the next morning with a sense of easy victory and calm satisfaction that had, however, none of the transports of affection. Her taste was satisfied by the love of a handsome young fellow, — a typical Englishman, — who, if not exactly original or ideal, was, she felt, of an universally accepted, "hall-marked" standard, the legitimate outcome of a highly ordered, carefully guarded civilization, whose repose was the absence of struggle or ambition; a man whose regular features were not yet differentiated from the rest of his class by any of those disturbing lines which people call character. Everything was made ready for her, without care or preparation; she had not even an ideal to realize or to modify. She could slip without any jar or

dislocation into this life which was just saved
from self-indulgence and sybaritic luxury by
certain conventional rules of activity and
the occupation of amusement which, as obli-
gations of her position, even appeared to
suggest the novel aspect of a *duty!* She
could accept all this without the sense of being an intruder in an unbroken lineage —
thanks to the consul's account of the Beverdales' inheritance. She already pictured
herself as the mistress of this fair domain,
the custodian of its treasures and traditions,
and the dispenser of its hospitalities, but —
as she conscientiously believed — without
pride or vanity, in her position; only an
intense and thoughtful appreciation of it.
Nor did she dream of ever displaying it ostentatiously before her less fortunate fellow
countrywomen; on the contrary, she looked
forward to their possible criticism of her
casting off all transatlantic ties with an uneasy consciousness that was perhaps her
nearest approach to patriotism. Yet, again,
she reasoned that, as her father was an Englishman, she was only returning to her old
home. As to her mother, she had already
comforted herself by noticing certain dis-
crepancies in that lady's temperament, which

led her to believe that she herself alone inherited her father's nature — for her mother was, of course, distinctly American! So little conscious was she of any possible snobbishness in this belief, that in her superb *naïveté* she would have argued the point with the consul, and employed a wit and dialect that were purely American.

She had slipped out of the Priory early that morning that she might enjoy alone, unattended and unciceroned, the aspect of that vast estate which might be hers for the mere accepting. Perhaps there was some instinct of delicacy in her avoiding Lord Algernon that morning; not wishing, as she herself might have frankly put it, "to take stock" of his inheritance in his presence. As she passed into the garden through the low postern door, she turned to look along the stretching façade of the main building, with the high stained windows of its banqueting-hall and the state chamber where a king had slept. Even in that crisp October air, and with the green of its ivied battlements against the gold of the distant wood, it seemed to lie in the languid repose of an eternal summer. She hurried on down the other terrace into the Italian garden, a

quaint survival of past grandeur, passed the
great orangery and numerous conservatories,
making a crystal hamlet in themselves —
seeing everywhere the same luxury. But
it was a luxury that she fancied was re-
deemed from the vulgarity of ostentation
by the long custom of years and generations,
so unlike the millionaire palaces of her own
land; and, in her enthusiasm, she even fancied it was further sanctified by the grim
monastic founders who had once been content with bread and pulse in the crumbling
and dismantled refectory. In the plenitude
of her feelings she felt a slight recognition
of some beneficent being who had rolled this
golden apple at her feet, and felt as if she
really should like to "do good" in her
sphere.

It so chanced that, passing through a
small gate in the park, she saw walking, a
little ahead of her, a young girl whom she
at once recognized as a Miss Amelyn, one
of the guests of the evening before. Miss
Desborough remembered that she played the
accompaniment of one or two songs upon the
piano, and had even executed a long solo
during the general conversation, without attention from the others, and apparently with

little irritation to herself, subsiding afterwards into an armchair, quite on the fringe of other people's conversation. She had been called "my dear" by one or two dowagers, and by her Christian name by the earl, and had a way of impalpably melting out of sight at times. These trifles led Miss Desborough to conclude that she was some kind of dependent or poor relation. Here was an opportunity to begin her work of "doing good." She quickened her pace and overtook Miss Amelyn.

"Let me walk with you," she said graciously.

The young English girl smiled assent, but looked her surprise at seeing the cynosure of last night's eyes unattended.

"Oh," said Sadie, answering the mute query, "I did n't want to be ' shown round ' by anybody, and I 'm not going to bore *you* with asking to see sights either. We 'll just walk together; wherever *you* 're going is good enough for me."

"I 'm going as far as the village," said Miss Amelyn, looking down doubtfully at Sadie's smart French shoes — "if you care to walk so far."

Sadie noticed that her companion was

more solidly booted, and that her straight, short skirts, although less stylish than her own, had a certain character, better fitted to the freer outdoor life of the country. But she only said, however, "The village will do," and gayly took her companion's arm.

"But I'm afraid you'll find it very uninteresting, for I am going to visit some poor cottages," persisted Miss Amelyn, with a certain timid ingenuousness of manner which, however, was as distinct as Miss Desborough's bolder frankness. "I promised the rector's daughter to take her place to-day."

"And I feel as if I was ready to pour oil and wine to any extent," said Miss Desborough, "so come along!"

Miss Amelyn laughed, and yet glanced around her timidly, as if she thought that Miss Desborough ought to have a larger and more important audience. Then she continued more confidentially and boldly, "But it isn't at all like ' slumming,' you know. These poor people here are not very bad, and are not at all extraordinary."

"Never mind," said Sadie, hurrying her along. After a pause she went on, "You know the Priory very well, I guess?"

"I lived there when I was a little girl,

with my aunt, the Dowager Lady Beverdale," said Miss Amelyn. "When my
cousin Fred, who was the young heir, died,
and the present Lord Beverdale succeeded,
— *he* never expected it, you know, for there
were two lives, his two elder brothers, besides
poor Fred's, between, but they both died, —
we went to live in the Dower House."

"The Dower House?" repeated Sadie.

"Yes, Lady Beverdale's separate property."

"But I thought all this property — the
Priory — came into the family through *her*."

"It did — this was the Amelyns' place;
but the oldest son or nearest male heir always succeeds to the property and title."

"Do you mean to say that the present
Lord Beverdale turned that old lady out?"

Miss Amelyn looked shocked. "I mean
to say," she said gravely, "Lady Beverdale
would have had to go when her own son became of age, had he lived." She paused,
and then said timidly, "Isn't it that way in
America?"

"Dear no!" Miss Desborough had a
faint recollection that there was something
in the Constitution or the Declaration of
Independence against primogeniture. "No!

the men have n't it *all* their own way *there*
— not much ! "

Miss Amelyn looked as if she did not care
to discuss this problem. After a few moments Sadie continued, "You and Lord
Algernon are pretty old friends, I guess?"

"No," replied Miss Amelyn. "He came
once or twice to the Priory for the holidays,
when he was quite a boy at Marlborough —
for the family were n't very well off, and
his father was in India. He was a very shy
boy, and of course no one ever thought of
him succeeding."

Miss Desborough felt half inclined to be
pleased with this, and yet half inclined to
resent this possible snubbing of her future
husband. But they were nearing the village, and Miss Amelyn turned the conversation to the object of her visit. It was a new
village — an unhandsome village, for all
that it stood near one of the gates of the
park. It had been given over to some mines
that were still worked in its vicinity, and
to the railway, which the uncle of the present
earl had resisted; but the railway had triumphed, and the station for Scrooby Priory
was there. There was a grim church, of a
blackened or weather-beaten stone, on the

hill, with a few grim Amelyns reposing cross-legged in the chancel, but the character of the village was as different from the Priory as if it were in another county. They stopped at the rectory, where Miss Amelyn provided herself with certain doles and gifts, which the American girl would have augmented with a five-pound note but for Miss Amelyn's horrified concern. "As many shillings would do, and they would be as grateful," she said. "More they wouldn't understand."

"Then keep it, and dole it out as you like," said Sadie quickly.

"But I don't think that — that Lord Beverdale would quite approve," hesitated Miss Amelyn.

The pretty brow of her companion knit, and her gray eyes flashed vivaciously. "What has *he* to do with it?" she said pertly; "besides, you say these are not *his* poor. Take that five-pound note — or — I'll *double it*, get it changed into sovereigns at the station, and hand 'em round to every man, woman, and child."

Miss Amelyn hesitated. The American girl looked capable of doing what she said; perhaps it was a national way of almsgiving! She took the note, with the mental reservation of making a full confession to the rector and Lord Beverdale.

She was right in saying that the poor of Scrooby village were not interesting. There was very little squalor or degradation; their poverty seemed not a descent, but a condition to which they had been born; the faces which Sadie saw were dulled and apathetic rather than sullen or rebellious; they stood up when Miss Amelyn entered, paying *her* the deference, but taking little note of the pretty butterfly who was with her, or rather submitting to her frank curiosity with that dull consent of the poor, as if they had lost even the sense of privacy, or a right to respect. It seemed to the American girl that their poverty was more indicated by what they were *satisfied* with than what she thought they *missed*. It is to be feared that this did not add to Sadie's sympathy; all the beggars she had seen in America wanted all they could get, and she felt as if she were confronted with an inferior animal.

"There's a wonderful old man lives here," said Miss Amelyn, as they halted before a stone and thatch cottage quite on the outskirts of the village. "We can't call him one of our poor, for he still works, although over eighty, and it 's his pride to keep out of the poorhouse, and, as he calls it, ' off ' the hands of his granddaughters. But we manage to do something for *them*, and we hope he profits by it. One of them is at the Priory; they 're trying to make a maid of her, but her queer accent — they 're from the north — is against her with the servants. I am afraid we won't see old Debs, for he 's at work again to-day, though the doctor has warned him."

"Debs! What a funny name!"

"Yes, but as many of these people cannot read or write, the name is carried by the ear, and not always correctly. Some of the railway navvies, who come from the north as he does, call him ' Debbers.' "

They were obliged to descend into the cottage, which was so low that it seemed to have sunk into the earth until its drooping eaves of thatch mingled with the straw heap beside it. Debs was not at home. But his granddaughter was there, who, after a preliminary "bob," continued the stirring of the pot before the fire in tentative silence.

"I am sorry to find that your grandfather has gone to work again in spite of the doctor's orders," said Miss Amelyn.

The girl continued to stir the pot, and then said without looking up, but as if also continuing a train of aggressive thoughts with her occupation: "Eay, but 'e 's so set oop in 'issen 'ee döan't take orders from nobbut — leastways doctor. Möinds 'em now moor nor a floy. Says 'ee knaws there nowt wrong wi' 'is 'eart. Mout be roight — how'siver, sarten sewer, 'is *'ead* 's a' in a muddle! Toims 'ee goes off stamrin' and starin' at nowt, as if 'ee a'nt a n'aporth o' sense. How'siver I be doing my duty by 'em — and 'ere 's 'is porritch when a' cooms — 'gin a' be sick or maad."

What the American understood of the girl's speech and manner struck her as having very little sympathy with either her aged relative or her present visitor. And there was a certain dogged selfish independence about her that Miss Desborough half liked and half resented. However, Miss Amelyn did not seem to notice it, and, after leaving a bottle of port for the grandfather, she took her leave and led Sadie away. As they passed into the village a carriage, returning to the Priory, filled with their fellow guests, dashed by, but was instantly pulled up at a word from Lord Algernon, who leaped from the vehicle, hat in hand, and implored the fair truant and her companion to join them.

"We 're just making a tour around Windover Hill, and back to luncheon," he said, with a rising color. "We missed you awfully! If we had known you were so keen on 'good works,' and so early at it, by Jove! we 'd have got up a ' slummin' party,' and all joined!"

"And you have n't seen half," said Lord Beverdale from the box. "Miss Amelyn 's too partial to the village. There 's an old drunken retired poacher somewhere in a hut in Crawley Woods, whom it 's death to approach, except with a large party. There 's malignant diphtheria over at the South Farm, eight down with measles at the keeper's, and an old woman who has been bedridden for years."

But Miss Desborough was adamant, though sparkling. She thanked him, but said she had just seen an old woman "who had been lying in bed for twenty years, and had n't spoken the truth once!" She proposed "going outside of Lord Beverdale's own preserves of grain-fed poor," and starting up her own game. She would return in time for luncheon — if she could; if not, she "should annex the gruel of the first kind incapable she met."

Yet, actually, she was far from displeased at being accidentally discovered by these people while following out her capricious whim of the morning. One or two elder ladies, who had fought shy of her frocks and her frankness the evening before, were quite touched now by this butterfly who was willing to forego the sunlight of society, and soil her pretty wings on the haunts of the impoverished, with only a single companion, — of her own sex! — and smiled approvingly. And in her present state of mind, remembering her companion's timid attitude towards Lord Beverdale's opinions, she was not above administering this slight snub to him in her presence.

When they had driven away, with many regrets, Miss Amelyn was deeply concerned. "I am afraid," she said, with timid conscientiousness, "I have kept you from going with them. And you must be bored with what you have seen, I know. I don't believe you really care one bit for it — and you are only doing it to please me."

"Trot out the rest of your show," said

Sadie promptly, "and we'll wind up by lunching with the rector."

"He'd be too delighted," said Miss Amelyn, with disaster written all over her girlish, truthful face, "but — but — you know — it really wouldn't be quite right to Lord Beverdale. You're his principal guest — you know, and — they'd think I had taken you off."

"Well," said Miss Desborough impetuously, "what's the matter with that inn — the Red Lion? We can get a sandwich there, I guess. I'm not *very* hungry."

Miss Amelyn looked horrified for a moment, and then laughed; but immediately became concerned again. "No! listen to me, *really* now! Let me finish my round alone! You'll have ample time if you go *now* to reach the Priory for luncheon. Do, please! It would be ever so much better for everybody. I feel quite guilty as it is, and I suppose I am already in Lord Beverdale's black books."

The trouble in the young girl's face was unmistakable, and as it suited Miss Desborough's purpose just as well to show her independence by returning, as she had set out, alone, she consented to go. Miss Amelyn

showed her a short cut across the park, and
they separated — to meet at dinner. In this
brief fellowship, the American girl had kept
a certain supremacy and half-fascination
over the English girl, even while she was
conscious of an invincible character in Miss
Amelyn entirely different from and superior
to her own. Certainly there was a difference in the two peoples. Why else this
inherited conscientious reverence for Lord
Beverdale's position, shown by Miss Amelyn, which she, an American alive to its
practical benefits, could not understand?
Would Miss Amelyn and Lord Algernon
have made a better match? The thought
irritated her, even while she knew that she
herself possessed the young man's affec-
tions, the power to marry him, and, as she
believed, kept her own independence in the
matter.

As she entered the iron gates at the lower
end of the park, and glanced at the inter-
woven cipher and crest of the Amelyns still
above, she was conscious that the wind was
blowing more chill, and that a few clouds
had gathered. As she walked on down the
long winding avenue, the sky became over-
cast, and, in one of those strange contrasts

of the English climate, the glory of the whole day went out with the sunshine. The woods suddenly became wrinkled and gray, the distant hills sombre, the very English turf beneath her feet grew brown; a mile and a half away, through the opening of the trees, the west part of the Priory looked a crumbling, ivy-eaten ruin. A few drops of rain fell. She hurried on. Suddenly she remembered that the avenue made a long circuit before approaching the house, and that its lower end, where she was walking, was but a fringe of the park. Consequently there must be a short cut across some fields and farm buildings to the back of the park and the Priory. She at once diverged to the right, presently found a low fence, which she clambered over, and again found a footpath which led to a stile. Crossing that, she could see the footpath now led directly to the Priory, — now a grim and austere looking pile in the suddenly dejected landscape, — and that it was probably used only by the servants and farmers. A gust of wind brought some swift needles of rain to her cheek; she could see the sad hills beyond the Priory already veiling their faces; she gathered her skirts and ran. The next field was a long one, but beside the further stile was a small clump of trees, the only ones between her and the park. Hurrying on to that shelter, she saw that the stile was already occupied by a tall but bent figure, holding a long stick in his hand, which gave him the appearance, against the horizon, of the figure of Time leaning on his scythe. As she came nearer she saw it was, indeed, an old man, half resting on his rake. He was very rugged and weather-beaten, and although near the shelter of the trees, apparently unmindful of the rain that was falling on his bald head, and the limp cap he was holding uselessly in one hand. He was staring at her, yet apparently unconscious of her presence. A sudden instinct came upon her — it was "Debs"!

She went directly up to him, and with that frank common sense which ordinarily distinguished her, took his cap from his hand and put it on his head, grasped his arm firmly, and led him to the shelter of the tree. Then she wiped the raindrops from his face with her handkerchief, shook out her own dress and her wet parasol, and, propping her companion against the tree, said: —

"There, Mr. Debs! I 've heard of people who did n't know enough to come in when it rained, but I never met one before."

The old man started, lifted his hairy, sinewy arm, bared to the elbow, and wiped his bare throat with the dry side of it. Then a look of intelligence — albeit half aggressive — came into his face. "Wheer bëest tha going?" he asked.

Something in his voice struck Sadie like a vague echo. Perhaps it was only the queer dialect — or some resemblance to his granddaughter's voice. She looked at him a little more closely as she said: —

"To the Priory."

"Whäat?"

She pointed with her parasol to the gray pile in the distance. It was possible that this demented peasant did n't even *understand* English.

"The hall. Oh, ay!" Suddenly his brows knit ominously as he faced her. "An' wassist tha doin' drest oop in this foinery? Wheer gettist thee that goawn? Thissen, or thy mäester? Nowt even a napron, fit for thy wark as mäaid at serviss; an' parson a gettin' tha plääce at Hall! So thou 'lt be high and moity will tha! thou 'lt not walk wi' mäaids, but traipse by thissen like a slut in the toon — dang tha!"

Although it was plain to Sadie that the old man, in his wandering perception, had mistaken her for his granddaughter in service at the Priory, there was still enough rudeness in his speech for her to have resented it. But, strange to say, there was a kind of authority in it that touched her with an uneasiness and repulsion that was stronger than any other feeling. "I think you have mistaken me for some one else," she said hurriedly, yet wondering why she had admitted it, and even irritated at the admission. "I am a stranger here, a visitor at the Priory. I called with Miss Amelyn at your cottage, and saw your other granddaughter; that's how I knew your name."

The old man's face changed. A sad, senile smile of hopeless bewilderment crept into his hard mouth; he plucked his limp cap from his head and let it hang submissively in his fingers, as if it were his sole apology. Then he tried to straighten himself, and said, "Naw offins, miss, naw offins! If tha knaws mea tha 'll knaw I'm grandfeyther to two galls as moight be tha owern age; tha 'll tell 'ee that old Debs at haaty

years 'as warked and niver lost a day as
man or boy; has niver coome oopen 'em
for n'aporth. An' 'e 'll keep out o' warkus
till he doy. An' 'ee 's put by enow to loy
wi' his own feythers in Lanksheer, an' not
liggen aloane in parson's choorchyard."

It was part of her uneasiness that, scarcely
understanding or, indeed, feeling any interest in these maundering details, she still
seemed to have an odd comprehension of
his character and some reminiscent knowledge of him, as if she were going through
the repetition of some unpleasant dream.
Even his wrinkled face was becoming familiar to her. Some weird attraction was holding her; she wanted to get away from it as
much as she wanted to analyze it. She
glanced ostentatiously at the sky, prepared
to open her parasol, and began to edge cautiously away.

"Then tha beant from these pearts?" he
said suddenly.

"No, no," she said quickly and emphati-
cally, — "no, I 'm an American."

The old man started and moved towards
her, eagerly, his keen eyes breaking through
the film that at times obscured them.
"'Merrikan! tha baist 'Merrikan? Then

tha knaws ma son John, 'ee war nowt but
a bairn when brether Dick took un to 'Mer-
riky! Naw! Now! that wor fifty years sen!
— niver wroate to his old feyther — niver
coomed back。 'Ee wor tall-loike, an' thea
said 'e feavored mea." He stopped, threw
up his head, and with his skinny fingers
drew back his long, straggling locks from
his sunken cheeks, and stared in her face.
The quick transition of fascination, repulsion, shock, and indefinable apprehension
made her laugh hysterically。 To her terror
he joined in it, and eagerly clasped her
wrists. "Eh, lass! tha knaws John — tha
coomes from un to ole grandfeyther.
Who-rr-u! Eay! but tha tho't to fool
mea, did tha, lass? Whoy, I knoawed tha
voice, for a' tha foine peacock feathers.
So tha be John's gell coom from Ameriky.
Dear! a dear! Coom neaur, lass! let's see
what tha's loike. Eh, but thou'lt kiss tha
grandfather, sewerly?"

A wild terror and undefined consternation
had completely overpowered her! But she
made a desperate effort to free her wrists,
and burst out madly : —

"Let me go! How dare you! I don't
know you or yours! I'm nothing to you or

your kin! My name is Desborough — do
you understand — do you hear me, Mr.
Debs? — *Desborough!* "

At the word the old man's fingers stiffened
like steel around her wrists, as he turned
upon her a hard, invincible face.

"So thou 'lt call thissen Des-borough, wilt
thä? Let me tell thä, then, that ' Debs,'
' Debban,' ' Debbrook,' and ' Des-borough '
are all a seame! Ay! thy feyther and thy
feyther's feyther! Thou 'lt be ä Des-borough, will thä? Dang thä! and look doon
on tha kin, and dress thissen in silks o'
shame! Tell 'ee thou 'rt an ass, gell!
Don't tha hear? An ass! for all tha bean
John's bairn! An ass! that 's what tha
beast!"

With flashing eyes and burning cheeks
she made one more supreme effort, lifting
her arms, freeing her wrists, and throwing
the old man staggering from her. Then she
leaped the stile, turned, and fled through
the rain. But before she reached the end
of the field she stopped! She had freed
herself — she was stronger than he · — what
had she to fear? He was crazy! Yes, he
*must* be crazy, and he had insulted her, but
he was an old man — and God knows what!

Her heart was beating rapidly, her breath was hurried, but she ran back to the stile.

He was not there. The field sloped away on either side of it. But she could distinguish nothing in the pouring rain above the wind-swept meadow. He must have gone home. Relieved for a moment she turned and hurried on towards the Priory.

But at every step she was followed, not by the old man's presence, but by what he had said to her, which she could not shake off as she had shaken off his detaining fingers. Was it the ravings of insanity, or had she stumbled unwittingly upon some secret — was it after all a *secret?* Perhaps it was something they all knew, or would know later. And she had come down here for this. For back of her indignation, back even of her disbelief in his insanity, there was an awful sense of truth! The names he had flung out, of "Debs," "Debban," and "Debbrook" now flashed upon her as something she had seen before, but had not understood. Until she satisfied herself of this, she felt she could not live or breathe! She loathed the Priory, with its austere exclusiveness, as it rose before her; she wished she had never entered it; but it contained that which she must know, and know at once! She entered the nearest door and ran up the grand staircase. Her flushed face and disordered appearance were easily accounted for by her exposure to the sudden storm. She went to her bedroom, sent her maid to another room to prepare a change of dress, and sinking down before her traveling-desk, groped for a document. Ah! there it was — the expensive toy that she had played with! She hastily ran over its leaves to the page she already remembered. And there, among the dashes and perpendicular lines she had jested over last night, on which she had thought was a collateral branch of the line, stood her father's name and that of Richard, his uncle, with the bracketed note in red ink, "see Debbrook, Daybrook, Debbers, and Debs." Yes! this gaunt, half-crazy, overworked peasant, content to rake the dead leaves before the rolling chariots of the Beverdales, was her grandfather; that poorly clad girl in the cottage, and even the menial in the scullery of this very house that might be *hers*, were her *cousins!* She burst into a laugh, and then refolded the document and put it away.

At luncheon she was radiant and sparkling. Her drenched clothes were an excuse
for a new and ravishing toilette. She had
never looked so beautiful before, and significant glances were exchanged between some
of the guests, who believed that the expected
proposal had already come. But those who
were of the carriage party knew otherwise,
and of Lord Algernon's disappointment.
Lord Beverdale contented himself with rallying his fair guest on the becomingness of
"good works." But he continued, "You're
offering a dreadful example to these ladies,
Miss Desborough, and I know I shall never
hereafter be able to content them with any
frivolous morning amusement at the Priory.
For myself, when I am grown gouty and
hideous, I know I shall bloom again as a
district visitor."

Yet under this surface sparkle and nervous exaltation Sadie never lost consciousness of the gravity of the situation. If her
sense of humor enabled her to see one side of
its grim irony; if she experienced a wicked
satisfaction in accepting the admiration and
easy confidence of the high-born guests,
knowing that her cousin had assisted in pre-
paring the meal they were eating, she had

never lost sight of the practical effect of the discovery she had made. And she had come to a final resolution. She should leave the Priory at once, and abandon all idea of a matrimonial alliance with its heir! Inconsistent as this might seem to her selfish, worldly nature, it was nevertheless in keeping with a certain pride and independence that was in her blood. She did not love Lord Algernon, neither did she love her grandfather; she was equally willing to sacrifice either or both; she knew that neither Lord Algernon nor his father would make her connections an objection, however they might wish to keep the fact a secret, or otherwise dispose of them by pensions or emigration, but she could not bear to *know it herself!* She never could be happy as the mistress of Scrooby Priory with that knowledge; she did not idealize it as a principle! Carefully weighing it by her own practical common sense, she said to herself that "it wouldn't pay." The highest independence is often akin to the lowest selfishness; she did not dream that the same pride which kept her grandfather from the workhouse and support by his daughters, and had even kept him from communicating with his own son, now kept her from acknowledging them, even for the gift of a title and domain. There was only one question before her: should she stay long enough to receive the proposal of Lord Algernon, and then decline it? Why should she not snatch that single feminine joy out of the ashes of her burnt-up illusion? She knew that an opportunity would be offered that afternoon. The party were to take tea at Broxby Hall, and Lord Algernon was to drive her there in his dog-cart. Miss Desborough had gone up to her bedroom to put on a warmer cloak, and had rung twice or thrice impatiently for her maid.

When the girl made her appearance, apologetic, voluble, and excited, Miss Desborough scarcely listened to her excuses, until a single word suddenly arrested her attention. It was "old Debs."

"What *are* you talking about?" said Sadie, pausing in the adjustment of her hat on her brown hair.

"Old Debs, miss, — that 's what they call him; an old park-keeper, just found dead in a pool of water in the fields; the grandfather of one of the servants here; and there 's such an excitement in the servants' hall. The gentlemen all knew it, too, for I heard Lord Algernon say that he was looking very queer lately, and might have had a fit; and Lord Beverdale has sent word to the coroner. And only think, the people here are such fools that they dare n't touch or move the poor man, and him lyin' there in the rain all the time, until the coroner comes!"

Miss Desborough had been steadily regarding herself in the glass to see if she had turned pale. She had. She set her teeth together until the color partly returned. But she kept her face away from the maid. "That 'll do," she said quietly. "You can tell me all later. I have some important news myself, and I may not go out after all. I want you to take a note for me." She went to her table, wrote a line in pencil, folded it, scribbled an address upon it, handed it to the girl, and gently pushed her from the room.

. . . . . . . .

The consul was lingering on the terrace beside one of the carriages; at a little distance a groom was holding the nervous thoroughbred of Lord Algernon's dog-cart. Suddenly he felt a touch on his shoulder, and

Miss Desborough's maid put a note in his hand. It contained only a line: —

Please come and see me in the library, but without making any fuss about it — at once.                        S. D.

The consul glanced around him; no one had apparently noticed the incident. He slipped back into the house and made his way to the library. It was a long gallery; at the further end Miss Desborough stood cloaked, veiled, and coquettishly hatted. She was looking very beautiful and animated. "I want you to please do me a great favor," she said, with an adorable smile, "as your own countrywoman, you know — for the sake of Fourth of July and Pumpkin Pie and the Old Flag! I don't want to go to this circus to-day. I am going to leave here to-night! I am! Honest Injin! I want *you* to manage it. I want you to say that as consul you've received important news for me: the death of some relative, if you like; or better, something *affecting my property*, you know," with a little satirical laugh. "I guess that would fetch 'em! So go at once."

"But really, Miss Desborough, do let us talk this over before you decide!" implored the bewildered consul. "Think what a disappointment to your host and these ladies. Lord Algernon expects to drive you there; he is already waiting! The party was got up for you!" Miss Desborough made a slight grimace. "I mean you ought to sacrifice something — but I trust there is really nothing serious — to them!"

"If *you* do not speak to them, I will!" said Miss Desborough firmly. "If you say what I tell you, it will come the more plausibly from you. Come! My mind is made up. One of us must break the news! Shall it be you or I?" She drew her cloak over her shoulders and made a step forwards.

The consul saw she was determined. "Then wait here till I return, but keep yourself out of sight," he said, and hurried away. Between the library and the terrace he conceived a plan. His perplexity lent him a seriousness which befitted the gravity of the news he had to disclose. "I am sorry to have to tell you," he said, taking Lord Beverdale aside, "that I was the unlucky bearer of some sad news to Miss Desborough this morning, through my consular letters —

some matter concerning the death of a relation of hers, and some wearisome question
of property. I thought that it was of little
importance, and that she would not take it
seriously, but I find I was mistaken. It
may even oblige her to catch the London
train to-night. I promised to make her excuses to you for the present, and I 'm afraid
I must add my own to them, as she wishes
me to stay and advise her in this matter,
which requires some prompt action."

Miss Desborough was right: the magic
word "property" changed the slight annoyance on the earl's face to a sympathetic
concern. "Dear me! I trust it is nothing
really serious," he said. "Of course you
will advise her, and, by the way, if my so-
licitor, Withers, who 'll be here to-morrow,
can do anything, you know, call him in. I
hope she 'll be able to see me later. It could
not be a *near* relation who died, I fancy;
she has no brothers or sisters, I understand."

"A cousin, I think; an old friend," said
the consul hastily. He heard Lord Beverdale say a few words to his companions, saw
with a tinge of remorse a cloud settle upon
Lord Algernon's fresh face, as he appealed
in a whisper to old Lady Mesthyn, who

leaned forward from the carriage, and said, "If the dear child thought *I* could be of any service, I should only be too glad to stay with her."

"I knew she would appreciate Lady Mesthyn's sympathy," said the ingenious consul quickly, "but I really think the question is more a business one — and " —

"Ah, yes," said the old lady, shaking her head, "it's dreadful, of course, but we must all think of *that!*"

As the carriage drove away, the consul hurried back a little viciously to his fair countrywoman. "There!" he said, "I have done it! If I have managed to convey either the idea that you are a penniless orphan, or that I have official information that you are suspected of a dynamite conspiracy, don't blame me! And now," he said, "as I have excused myself on the ground that I must devote myself to this dreadful business of yours, perhaps you'll tell me *what* it really is."

"Not a word more," said Miss Desborough; "except," she added, — checking her smile with a weary gesture, — "except that I want to leave this dreadful place at once! There! don't ask me any more!"

There could be no doubt of the girl's sin-

cerity. Nor was it the extravagant caprice
of a petted idol. What had happened? He
might have believed in a lovers' quarrel, but
he knew that she and Lord Algernon could
have had no private interview that evening.
He must perforce accept her silence, yet he
could not help saying: —

"You seemed to like the place so much
last night. I say, you have n't seen the
Priory ghost, have you?"

"The Priory ghost," she said quickly.
"What 's that?"

"The old monk who passes through the
cloisters with the sacred oil, the bell, and
the smell of incense whenever any one is to
die here. By Jove! it would have been a
good story to tell instead of this cock-and-
bull one about your property. And there *was*
a death here to-day. You 'd have added the
sibyl's gifts to your other charms."

"Tell me about that old man," she said,
looking past him out of the window. "I was
at his cottage this morning. But, no! first
let us go out. You can take me for a walk,
if you like. You see I am all ready, and
I 'm just stifling here."

They descended to the terrace together.
"Where would you like to go?" he asked.

"To the village. I may want to telegraph, you know."

They turned into the avenue, but Miss
Desborough stopped.

"Is there not a shorter cut across the
fields," she asked, "over there?"

"There is," said the consul.

They both turned into the footpath which
led to the farm and stile. After a pause
she said, "Did you ever talk with that poor
old man?"

"No."

"Then you don't know if he really was
crazy, as they think."

"No. But they may have thought an old
man's forgetfulness of present things and
his habit of communing with the past was
insanity. For all that he was a plucky, independent old fellow, with a grim purpose
that was certainly rational."

"I suppose in his independence he would
not have taken favors from these people, or
anybody?"

"I should think not."

"Don't you think it was just horrid —
their leaving him alone in the rain, when
he might have been only in a fit?"

"The doctor says he died suddenly of

heart disease," said the consul. "It might have happened at any moment and without warning."

"Ah, that was the coroner's verdict, then," said Miss Desborough quickly.

"The coroner did not think it necessary to have any inquest after Lord Beverdale's statement. It would n't have been very joyous for the Priory party. And I dare say he thought it might not be very cheerful for *you.*"

"How very kind!" said the young girl, with a quick laugh. "But do you know that it 's about the only thing human, original, and striking that has happened in this place since I 've been here! And so unexpected, considering how comfortably everything is ordered here beforehand."

"Yet you seemed to like that kind of thing very well, last evening," said the consul mischievously.

"That was last night," retorted Miss Desborough; "and you know the line, ' Colors seen by candlelight do not look the same by day.' But I 'm going to be very consistent to-day, for I intend to go over to that poor man's cottage again, and see if I can be of any service. Will you go with me?"

"Certainly," said the consul, mystified by his companion's extraordinary conduct, yet apparent coolness of purpose, and hoping for some further explanation. Was she only an inexperienced flirt who had found herself on the point of a serious entanglement she had not contemplated? Yet even then he knew she was clever enough to extricate herself in some other way than this abrupt and brutal tearing through the meshes. Or was it possible that she really had any intelligence affecting her property? He reflected that he knew very little of the Desboroughs, but on the other hand he knew that Beverdale knew them much better, and was a prudent man. He had no right to demand her confidence as a reward for his secrecy; he must wait her pleasure. Perhaps she would still explain; women seldom could resist the triumph of telling the secret that puzzled others.

When they reached the village she halted before the low roof of Debs's cottage. "I had better go in first," she said; "you can come in later, and in the meantime you might go to the station for me and find out the exact time that the express train leaves for the north."

"But," said the astonished consul, "I thought you were going to London?"

"No," said Miss Desborough quietly, "I am going to join some friends at Harrogate."

"But that train goes much earlier than the train south, and — and I 'm afraid Lord Beverdale will not have returned so soon."

"How sad!" said Miss Desborough, with a faint smile, "but we must bear up under it, and — I 'll write him. I will be here until you return."

She turned away and entered the cottage. The granddaughter she had already seen and her sister, the servant at the Priory, were both chatting comfortably, but ceased as she entered, and both rose with awkward respect. There was little to suggest that the body of their grandfather, already in a rough oak shell, was lying upon trestles beside them.

"You have carried out my orders, I see," said Miss Desborough, laying down her parasol.

"Ay, miss; but it was main haard gettin' et döoan so soon, and et cöoast " —

"Never mind the cost. I 've given you money enough, I think, and if I haven't, I guess I can give you more."

"Ay, miss! Abbut the pa'son 'ead gi' un a funeral for nowt."

"But I understood you to say," said Miss Desborough, with an impatient flash of eye, "that your grandfather wished to be buried with his kindred in the north?"

"Ay, miss," said the girl apologetically, "an naw 'ees savit th' munny. Abbut e 'd bean tickled 'ad 'ee knowed it! Dear! dear! 'ee niver thowt et 'ud be gi'en by stranger an' not 'es ownt fammaly."

"For all that, you need n't tell anybody it was given by *me*," said Miss Desborough. "And you 'll be sure to be ready to take the train this afternoon — without delay." There was a certain peremptoriness in her voice very unlike Miss Amelyn's, yet apparently much more effective with the granddaughter.

"Ay, miss. Then, if tha 'll excoose mëa, I 'll go streight to 'oory oop sexten."

She bustled away. "Now," said Miss Desborough, turning to the other girl, "I shall take the same train, and will probably see you on the platform at York to give my final directions. That 's all. Go and see if the gentleman who came with me has returned from the station."

The girl obeyed. Left entirely alone, Miss Desborough glanced around the room, and then went quietly up to the unlidded coffin. The repose of death had softened the hard lines of the old man's mouth and brow into a resemblance she now more than ever understood. She had stood thus only a few years before, looking at the same face in a gorgeously inlaid mahogany casket, smothered amidst costly flowers, and surrounded by friends attired in all the luxurious trappings of woe; yet it was the same face that was now rigidly upturned to the bare thatch and rafters of that crumbling cottage, herself its only companion. She lifted her delicate veil with both hands, and, stooping down, kissed the hard, cold forehead, without a tremor. Then she dropped her veil again over her dry eyes, readjusted it in the little, cheap, black-framed mirror that hung against the wall, and opened the door as the granddaughter returned. The gentleman was just coming from the station.

"Remember to look out for me at York," said Miss Desborough, extending her gloved hand. "Good-by till then." The young girl respectfully touched the ends of Miss

Desborough's fingers, dropped a curtsy, and Miss Desborough rejoined the consul.

"You have barely time to return to the Priory and see to your luggage," said the consul, "if you must go. But let me hope that you have changed your mind."

"I have not changed my mind," said Miss Desborough quietly, "and my baggage is already packed." After a pause, she said thoughtfully, "I 've been wondering" —

"What?" said the consul eagerly.

"I 've been wondering if people brought up to speak in a certain dialect, where certain words have their own significance and color, and are part of their own lives and experience — if, even when they understand another dialect, they really feel any sympathy with it, or the person who speaks it?"

"Apropos of" — asked the consul.

"These people I 've just left! I don't think I quite felt with them, and I guess they did n't feel with me."

"But," said the consul laughingly, "you know that we Americans speak with a decided dialect of our own, and attach the same occult meaning to it. Yet, upon my word, I think that Lord Beverdale — or shall I say Lord Algernon? — would not only understand that American word ' guess ' as you mean it, but would perfectly sympathize with you."

Miss Desborough's eyes sparkled even through her veil as she glanced at her companion and said, "I *guess not.*"

As the "tea" party had not yet returned, it fell to the consul to accompany Miss Desborough and her maid to the station. But here he was startled to find a collection of villagers upon the platform, gathered round two young women in mourning, and an ominous-looking box. He mingled for a moment with the crowd, and then returned to Miss Desborough's side.

"Really," he said, with a concern that was scarcely assumed, "I ought not to let you go. The omens are most disastrous! You came here to a death; you are going away with a funeral!"

"Then it 's high time I took myself off!" said the lady lightly.

"Unless, like the ghostly monk, you came here on a mission, and have fulfilled it."

"Perhaps I have. Good-by!"

.    .    .    .    .    .    .    .

In spite of the bright and characteristic letter which Miss Desborough left for her

host, — a letter which mingled her peculiar
shrewd sense with her humorous extravagance of expression, — the consul spent a
somewhat uneasy evening under the fire of
questions that assailed him in reference to
the fair deserter. But he kept loyal faith
with her, adhering even to the letter of her
instructions, and only once was goaded into
more active mendacity. The conversation
had turned upon "Debs," and the consul
had remarked on the singularity of the
name. A guest from the north observed,
however, that the name was undoubtedly a
contraction. "Possibly it might have been
'Debborough,' or even the same name as
our fair friend."

"But did n't Miss Desborough tell you
last night that she had been hunting up her
people, with a family tree, or something
like that?" said Lord Algernon eagerly.
"I just caught a word here and there, for
you were both laughing."

The consul smiled blandly. "You may
well say so, for it was all the most delightful piece of pure invention and utter extravagance. It would have amused her still more
if she had thought you were listening and
took it seriously!"

"Of course; I see!" said the young fellow, with a laugh and a slight rise of color. "I knew she was taking some kind of a rise out of *you*, and that remark reminded me of it."

Nevertheless, within a year, Lord Algernon was happily married to the daughter of a South African millionaire, whose bridal offerings alone touched the sum of half a million. It was also said that the mother was "impossible" and the father "unspeakable," the relations "inextinguishable;" but the wedding was an "occasion," and in the succeeding year of festivity it is presumed that the names of "Debs" and "Desborough" were alike forgotten.

But they existed still in a little hamlet near the edge of a bleak northern moor, where they were singularly exalted on a soaring shaft of pure marble above the submerged and moss-grown tombstones of a simple country churchyard. So great was the contrast between the modern and pretentious monument and the graves of the humbler forefathers of the village, that even the Americans who chanced to visit it were shocked at what they believed was the ostentatious and vulgar pride of one of their **own**

countrywomen. For on its pedestal was
inscribed : —

Sacred to the Memory
of
JOHN DEBS DESBOROUGH,
Formerly of this parish,
Who departed this life October 20th, 1892,
At Scrooby Priory,
At the age of eighty-two years.
This monument was erected as a loving testimony
by his granddaughter,
Sadie Desborough, of New York, U. S. A.

———

"And evening brings us home."

# SALOMY JANE'S KISS

ONLY one shot had been fired. It had
gone wide of its mark, — the ringleader of
the Vigilantes, — and had left Red Pete,
who had fired it, covered by their rifles and
at their mercy. For his hand had been
cramped by hard riding, and his eye distracted by their sudden onset, and so the
inevitable end had come. He submitted
sullenly to his captors; his companion fugitive and horse-thief gave up the protracted
struggle with a feeling not unlike relief.
Even the hot and revengeful victors were
content. They had taken their men alive.
At any time during the long chase they
could have brought them down by a rifle-
shot, but it would have been unsportsman-
like, and have ended in a free fight, instead
of an example. And, for the matter of
that, their doom was already sealed. Their
end, by a rope and a tree, although not
sanctified by law, would have at least the
deliberation of justice. It was the tribute

**paid** by the Vigilantes to that order which
they had themselves disregarded in the pursuit and capture. Yet this strange logic of
the frontier sufficed them, and gave a certain dignity to the climax.

"Ef you 've got anything to say to your
folks, say it *now*, and say it quick," said the
ringleader.

Red Pete glanced around him. He had
been run to earth at his own cabin in the
clearing, whence a few relations and friends,
mostly women and children, non-combat-
ants, had outflowed, gazing vacantly at the
twenty Vigilantes who surrounded them.
All were accustomed to scenes of violence,
blood-feud, chase, and hardship; it was only
the suddenness of the onset and its quick
result that had surprised them. They looked
on with dazed curiosity and some disappointment; there had been no fight to speak of
— no spectacle! A boy, nephew of Red
Pete, got upon the rain-barrel to view the
proceedings more comfortably; a tall, handsome, lazy Kentucky girl, a visiting neighbor, leaned against the doorpost, chewing
gum. Only a yellow hound was actively
perplexed. He could not make out if a
hunt were just over or beginning, and ran

eagerly backwards and forwards, leaping alternately upon the captives and the captors.

The ringleader repeated his challenge. Red Pete gave a reckless laugh and looked at his wife.

At which Mrs. Red Pete came forward. It seemed that she had much to say, incoherently, furiously, vindictively, to the ringleader. His soul would roast in hell for that day's work! He called himself a man, skunkin' in the open and afraid to show himself except with a crowd of other "Kiyi's" around a house of women and children. Heaping insult upon insult, inveighing against his low blood, his ancestors, his dubious origin, she at last flung out a wild taunt of his invalid wife, the insult of a woman to a woman, until his white face grew rigid, and only that Western-American fetich of the sanctity of sex kept his twitching fingers from the lock of his rifle. Even her husband noticed it, and with a half-authoritative "Let up on that, old gal," and a pat of his freed left hand on her back, took his last parting. The ringleader, still white under the lash of the woman's tongue, turned abruptly to the second cap-

tive. "And if *you*'ve got anybody to say
' good-by ' to, now 's your chance."

The man looked up. Nobody stirred or
spoke. He was a stranger there, being a
chance confederate picked up by Red Pete,
and known to no one. Still young, but an
outlaw from his abandoned boyhood, of
which father and mother were only a forgotten dream, he loved horses and stole them,
fully accepting the frontier penalty of life
for the interference with that animal on
which a man's life so often depended. But
he understood the good points of a horse, as
was shown by the one he bestrode — until a
few days before the property of Judge Boompointer. This was his sole distinction.

The unexpected question stirred him for a
moment out of the attitude of reckless indifference, for attitude it was, and a part of
his profession. But it may have touched
him that at that moment he was less than
his companion and his virago wife. However, he only shook his head. As he did so
his eye casually fell on the handsome girl
by the doorpost, who was looking at him.
The ringleader, too, may have been touched
by his complete loneliness, for *he* hesitated.
At the same moment he saw that the girl
was looking at his friendless captive.

A grotesque idea struck him.

"Salomy Jane, ye might do worse than come yere and say 'good-by' to a dying man, and him a stranger," he said.

There seemed to be a subtle stroke of poetry and irony in this that equally struck the apathetic crowd. It was well known that Salomy Jane Clay thought no small potatoes of herself, and always held off the local swain with a lazy nymph-like scorn. Nevertheless, she slowly disengaged herself from the doorpost, and, to everybody's astonishment, lounged with languid grace and outstretched hand towards the prisoner. The color came into the gray reckless mask which the doomed man wore as her right hand grasped his left, just loosed by his captors. Then she paused; her shy, fawn-like eyes grew bold, and fixed themselves upon him. She took the chewing-gum from her mouth, wiped her red lips with the back of her hand, by a sudden lithe spring placed her foot on his stirrup, and, bounding to the saddle, threw her arms about his neck and pressed a kiss upon his lips.

They remained thus for a hushed moment — the man on the threshold of death, the young woman in the fullness of youth and beauty — linked together. Then the crowd laughed; in the audacious effrontery of the girl's act the ultimate fate of the two men was forgotten. She slipped languidly to the ground; *she* was the focus of all eyes, — she only! The ringleader saw it and his opportunity. He shouted: "Time's up — Forward!" urged his horse beside his captives, and the next moment the whole cavalcade was sweeping over the clearing into the darkening woods.

Their destination was Sawyer's Crossing, the headquarters of the committee, where the council was still sitting, and where both culprits were to expiate the offense of which that council had already found them guilty. They rode in great and breathless haste, — a haste in which, strangely enough, even the captives seemed to join. That haste, possibly prevented them from noticing the singular change which had taken place in the second captive since the episode of the kiss. His high color remained, as if it had burned through his mask of indifference; his eyes were quick, alert, and keen, his mouth half open as if the girl's kiss still lingered there. And that haste had made them careless, for the horse of the man who

led him slipped in a gopher-hole, rolled
over, unseated his rider, and even dragged
the bound and helpless second captive from
Judge Boompointer's favorite mare. In an
instant they were all on their feet again,
but in that supreme moment the second captive felt the cords which bound his arms
had slipped to his wrists. By keeping his
elbows to his sides, and obliging the others
to help him mount, it escaped their notice.
By riding close to his captors, and keeping
in the crush of the throng, he further concealed the accident, slowly working his hands
downwards out of his bonds.

Their way lay through a sylvan wilder-
ness, mid-leg deep in ferns, whose tall fronds
brushed their horses' sides in their furious
gallop and concealed the flapping of the captive's loosened cords. The peaceful vista,
more suggestive of the offerings of nymph
and shepherd than of human sacrifice, was
in a strange contrast to this whirlwind rush
of stern, armed men. The westering sun
pierced the subdued light and the tremor of
leaves with yellow lances; birds started into
song on blue and dove-like wings, and on
either side of the trail of this vengeful storm
could be heard the murmur of hidden and

tranquil waters. In a few moments they
would be on the open ridge, whence sloped
the common turnpike to "Sawyer's," a mile
away. It was the custom of returning cavalcades to take this hill at headlong speed,
with shouts and cries that heralded their
coming. They withheld the latter that day,
as inconsistent with their dignity; but,
emerging from the wood, swept silently like
an avalanche down the slope. They were
well under way, looking only to their
horses, when the second captive slipped his
right arm from the bonds and succeeded in
grasping the reins that lay trailing on the
horse's neck. A sudden *vaquero* jerk,
which the well-trained animal understood,
threw him on his haunches with his forelegs
firmly planted on the slope. The rest of
the cavalcade swept on; the man who was
leading the captive's horse by the *riata*,
thinking only of another accident, dropped
the line to save himself from being dragged
backwards from his horse. The captive
wheeled, and the next moment was galloping
furiously up the slope.

It was the work of a moment; a trained
horse and an experienced hand. The cavalcade had covered nearly fifty yards before

they could pull up; the freed captive had
covered half that distance uphill. The road
was so narrow that only two shots could be
fired, and these broke dust two yards ahead
of the fugitive. They had not dared to fire
low; the horse was the more valuable animal. The fugitive knew this in his extrem-
ity also, and would have gladly taken a shot
in his own leg to spare that of his horse.
Five men were detached to recapture or kill
him. The latter seemed inevitable. But
he had calculated his chances; before they
could reload he had reached the woods
again; winding in and out between the pillared tree trunks, he offered no mark. They
knew his horse was superior to their own;
at the end of two hours they returned, for
he had disappeared without track or trail.
The end was briefly told in the "Sierra
Record:" —

"Red Pete, the notorious horse-thief, who
had so long eluded justice, was captured
and hung by the Sawyer's Crossing Vigilantes last week; his confederate, unfortunately, escaped on a valuable horse belong-
ing to Judge Boompointer. The judge had
refused one thousand dollars for the horse
only a week before. As the thief, who is

still at large, would find it difficult to dispose of so valuable an animal without detection, the chances are against either of them turning up again."

. . . . . . . . . .

Salomy Jane watched the cavalcade until it had disappeared. Then she became aware that her brief popularity had passed. Mrs. Red Pete, in stormy hysterics, had included her in a sweeping denunciation of the whole universe, possibly for simulating an emotion in which she herself was deficient. The other women hated her for her momentary exaltation above them; only the children still admired her as one who had undoubtedly "canoodled" with a man "a-going to be hung" — a daring flight beyond their wildest ambition. Salomy Jane accepted the change with charming unconcern. She put on her yellow nankeen sunbonnet, — a hideous affair that would have ruined any other woman, but which only enhanced the piquancy of her fresh brunette skin, — tied the strings, letting the blue-black braids escape below its frilled curtain behind, jumped on her mustang with a casual display of agile ankles in shapely white stockings, whistled to the hound, and waving her hand with a

"So long, sonny!" to the lately bereft but admiring nephew, flapped and fluttered away in her short brown holland gown.

Her father's house was four miles distant. Contrasted with the cabin she had just quitted, it was a superior dwelling, with a long "lean-to" at the rear, which brought the eaves almost to the ground and made it look like a low triangle. It had a long barn and cattle sheds, for Madison Clay was a "great" stock-raiser and the owner of a "quarter section." It had a sitting-room and a parlor organ, whose transportation thither had been a marvel of "packing." These things were supposed to give Salomy Jane an undue importance, but the girl's reserve and inaccessibility to local advances were rather the result of a cool, lazy temperament and the preoccupation of a large, protecting admiration for her father, for some years a widower. For Mr. Madison Clay's life had been threatened in one or two feuds, — it was said, not without cause, — and it is possible that the pathetic spectacle of her father doing his visiting with a shotgun may have touched her closely and somewhat prejudiced her against the neighboring masculinity. The thought that cattle, horses, and "quarter section" would one day be hers did not disturb her calm. As for Mr. Clay, he accepted her as housewifely, though somewhat "interfering," and, being one of "his own womankind," therefore not without some degree of merit.

"Wot's this yer I'm hearin' of your doin's over at Red Pete's? Honeyfoglin' with a horse-thief, eh?" said Mr. Clay two days later at breakfast.

"I reckon you heard about the straight thing, then," said Salomy Jane unconcernedly, without looking round.

"What do you kalkilate Rube will say to it? What are you goin' to tell *him?*" said Mr. Clay sarcastically.

"Rube," or Reuben Waters, was a swain supposed to be favored particularly by Mr. Clay. Salomy Jane looked up.

"I'll tell him that when *he*'s on his way to be hung, I'll kiss him, — not till then," said the young lady brightly.

This delightful witticism suited the paternal humor, and Mr. Clay smiled; but, nevertheless, he frowned a moment afterwards.

"But this yer hoss-thief got away arter all, and that's a hoss of a different color," he said grimly.

G

Salomy Jane put down her knife and
fork. This was certainly a new and different phase of the situation. She had never
thought of it before, and, strangely enough,
for the first time she became interested in
the man. "Got away?" she repeated.
"Did they let him off?"

"Not much," said her father briefly.
"Slipped his cords, and going down the
grade pulled up short, just like a *vaquero*
agin a lassoed bull, almost draggin' the
man leadin' him off his hoss, and then
skyuted up the grade. For that matter, on
that hoss o' Judge Boompointer's he mout
have dragged the whole posse of 'em down
on their knees ef he liked! Sarved 'em
right, too. Instead of stringin' him up
afore the door, or shootin' him on sight,
they must allow to take him down afore the
hull committee ' for an example.' ' Example ' be blowed! Ther' 's example enough
when some stranger comes unbeknownst slap
onter a man hanged to a tree and plugged
full of holes. *That*'s an example, and *he*
knows what it means. Wot more do ye
want? But then those Vigilantes is allus
clingin' and hangin' onter some mere scrap
o' the law they 're pretendin' to despise. It

makes me sick! Why, when Jake Myers shot your ole Aunt Viney's second husband, and I laid in wait for Jake afterwards in the Butternut Hollow, did *I* tie him to his hoss and fetch him down to your Aunt Viney's cabin ' for an example ' before I plugged him? No!" in deep disgust. "No! Why, I just meandered through the wood, careless-like, till he comes out, and I just rode up to him, and I said " —

But Salomy Jane had heard her father's story before. Even one's dearest relatives are apt to become tiresome in narration. "I know, dad," she interrupted; "but this yer man, — this hoss-thief, — did *he* get clean away without gettin' hurt at all?"

"He did, and unless he's fool enough to sell the hoss he kin keep away, too. So ye see, ye can't ladle out purp stuff about a ' dyin' stranger ' to Rube. He won't swaller it."

"All the same, dad," returned the girl cheerfully, "I reckon to say it, and say *more;* I'll tell him that ef *he* manages to get away too, I'll marry him — there! But ye don't ketch Rube takin' any such risks in gettin' ketched, or in gettin' away arter!"

Madison Clay smiled grimly, pushed back

his chair, rose, dropped a perfunctory kiss on his daughter's hair, and, taking his shotgun from the corner, departed on a peaceful Samaritan mission to a cow who had dropped a calf in the far pasture. Inclined as he was to Reuben's wooing from his eligibility as to property, he was conscious that he was sadly deficient in certain qualities inherent in the Clay family. It certainly would be a kind of *mésalliance*.

Left to herself, Salomy Jane stared a long while at the coffee-pot, and then called the two squaws who assisted her in her household duties, to clear away the things while she went up to her own room to make her bed. Here she was confronted with a possible prospect of that proverbial bed she might be making in her willfulness, and on which she must lie, in the photograph of a somewhat serious young man of refined features — Reuben Waters — stuck in her window-frame. Salomy Jane smiled over her last witticism regarding him and enjoyed it, like your true humorist, and then, catching sight of her own handsome face in the little mirror, smiled again. But wasn't it funny about that horse-thief getting off after all? Good Lordy! Fancy Reuben hearing he

was alive and going round with that kiss of
hers set on his lips! She laughed again, a
little more abstractedly. And he had returned it like a man, holding her tight and
almost breathless, and he going to be hung
the next minute! Salomy Jane had been
kissed at other times, by force, chance, or
stratagem. In a certain ingenuous forfeit
game of the locality known as "I'm a-pin-
in'," many had "pined" for a "sweet kiss"
from Salomy Jane, which she had yielded
in a sense of honor and fair play. She had
never been kissed like this before — she
would never again; and yet the man was
alive! And behold, she could see in the
mirror that she was blushing!

She should hardly know him again. A
young man with very bright eyes, a flushed
and sunburnt cheek, a kind of fixed look in
the face, and no beard; no, none that she
could feel. Yet he was not at all like Reuben, not a bit. She took Reuben's picture
from the window, and laid it on her work-
box. And to think she did not even know
this young man's name! That was queer.
To be kissed by a man whom she might
never know! Of course he knew hers. She
wondered if he remembered it and her. But

of course he was so glad to get off with his life that he never thought of anything else. Yet she did not give more than four or five minutes to these speculations, and, like a sensible girl, thought of something else. Once again, however, in opening the closet, she found the brown holland gown she had worn on the day before; thought it very unbecoming, and regretted that she had not worn her best gown on her visit to Red Pete's cottage. On such an occasion she really might have been more impressive.

When her father came home that night she asked him the news. No, they had *not* captured the second horse-thief, who was still at large. Judge Boompointer talked of invoking the aid of the despised law. It remained, then, to see whether the horse-thief was fool enough to try to get rid of the animal. Red Pete's body had been delivered to his widow. Perhaps it would only be neighborly for Salomy Jane to ride over to the funeral. But Salomy Jane did not take to the suggestion kindly, nor yet did she explain to her father that, as the other man was still living, she did not care to undergo a second disciplining at the widow's hands. Nevertheless, she contrasted her situation with that of the widow with a new and singular satisfaction. It might have been Red Pete who had escaped. But he had not the grit of the nameless one. She had already settled his heroic quality.

"Ye ain't harkenin' to me, Salomy."

Salomy Jane started.

"Here I'm askin' ye if ye 've see that hound Phil Larrabee sneaking by yer to-day?"

Salomy Jane had not. But she became interested and self-reproachful, for she knew that Phil Larrabee was one of her father's enemies. "He would n't dare to go by here unless he knew you were out," she said quickly.

"That 's what gets me," he said, scratching his grizzled head. "I 've been kind o' thinkin' o' him all day, and one of them Chinamen said he saw him at Sawyer's Crossing. He was a kind of friend o' Pete's wife. That 's why I thought yer might find out ef he 'd been there." Salomy Jane grew more self-reproachful at her father's self-interest in her "neighborliness." "But that ain't all," continued Mr. Clay. "Thar was tracks over the far pasture that warn't mine. I followed them, and they went round and

round the house two or three times, ez ef
they mout hev bin prowlin', and then I lost
'em in the woods again. It's just like that
sneakin' hound Larrabee to hev bin lyin'
in wait for me and afraid to meet a man
fair and square in the open."

"You just lie low, dad, for a day or two
more, and let me do a little prowlin'," said
the girl, with sympathetic indignation in her
dark eyes. "Ef it's that skunk, I'll spot
him soon enough and let you know whar
he's hiding."

"You'll just stay where ye are, Salomy,"
said her father decisively. "This ain't no
woman's work — though I ain't sayin' you
haven't got more head for it than some
men I know."

Nevertheless, that night, after her father
had gone to bed, Salomy Jane sat by the
open window of the sitting-room in an apparent attitude of languid contemplation,
but alert and intent of eye and ear. It was
a fine moonlit night. Two pines near the
door, solitary pickets of the serried ranks of
distant forest, cast long shadows like paths
to the cottage, and sighed their spiced breath
in the windows. For there was no frivol-
ity of vine or flower round Salomy Jane's

bower. The clearing was too recent, the life too practical for vanities like these. But the moon added a vague elusiveness to everything, softened the rigid outlines of the sheds, gave shadows to the lidless windows, and touched with merciful indirectness the hideous débris of refuse gravel and the gaunt scars of burnt vegetation before the door. Even Salomy Jane was affected by it, and exhaled something between a sigh and a yawn with the breath of the pines. Then she suddenly sat upright.

Her quick ear had caught a faint "click, click," in the direction of the wood; her quicker instinct and rustic training enabled her to determine that it was the ring of a horse's shoe on flinty ground; her knowledge of the locality told her it came from the spot where the trail passed over an outcrop of flint scarcely a quarter of a mile from where she sat, and within the clearing. It was no errant "stock," for the foot was *shod* with iron; it was a mounted trespasser by night, and boded no good to a man like Clay.

She rose, threw her shawl over her head, more for disguise than shelter, and passed out of the door. A sudden impulse made her seize her father's shotgun from the corner where it stood, — not that she feared any danger to herself, but that it was an excuse. She made directly for the wood, keeping in the shadow of the pines as long as she could. At the fringe she halted; whoever was there must pass her before reaching the house.

Then there seemed to be a suspense of all nature. Everything was deadly still — even the moonbeams appeared no longer tremulous; soon there was a rustle as of some stealthy animal among the ferns, and then a dismounted man stepped into the moonlight. It was the horse - thief — the man she had kissed!

For a wild moment a strange fancy seized her usually sane intellect and stirred her temperate blood. The news they had told her was *not* true; he had been hung, and this was his ghost! He looked as white and spirit-like in the moonlight, dressed in the same clothes, as when she saw him last. He had evidently seen her approaching, and moved quickly to meet her. But in his haste he stumbled slightly; she reflected suddenly that ghosts did not stumble, and a feeling of relief came over her. And it was no assassin of her father that had been prowl-

ing around — only this unhappy fugitive.
A momentary color came into her cheek;
her coolness and hardihood returned; it was
with a tinge of sauciness in her voice that
she said: —

"I reckoned you were a ghost."

"I mout have been," he said, looking at
her fixedly; "but I reckon I'd have come
back here all the same."

"It's a little riskier comin' back alive,"
she said, with a levity that died on her lips,
for a singular nervousness, half fear and
half expectation, was beginning to take the
place of her relief of a moment ago. "Then
it was *you* who was prowlin' round and
makin' tracks in the far pasture?"

"Yes; I came straight here when I got
away."

She felt his eyes were burning her, but
did not dare to raise her own. "Why," she
began, hesitated, and ended vaguely. "*How*
did you get here?"

"You helped me!"

"I?"

"Yes. That kiss you gave me put life
into me — gave me strength to get away. I
swore to myself I'd come back and thank
you, alive or dead."

Every word he said she could have anticipated, so plain the situation seemed to her
now.   And every word he said she knew
was the truth.   Yet her cool common sense
struggled against it.

"What's the use of your escaping, ef
you're comin' back here to be ketched
again?" she said pertly.

He drew a little nearer to her, but seemed
to her the more awkward as she resumed her
self-possession.   His voice, too, was broken,
as if by exhaustion, as he said, catching his
breath at intervals: —

"I'll tell you.   You did more for me than
you think.   You made another man o' me.
I never had a man, woman, or child do to
me what you did.   I never had a friend —
only a pal like Red Pete, who picked me up
' on shares.'   I want to quit this yer —
what I'm doin'.   I want to begin by doin'
the square thing to you" —   He stopped,
breathed hard, and then said brokenly, "My
hoss is over thar, staked out.   I want to
give him to you.   Judge Boompointer will
give you a thousand dollars for him.   I
ain't lyin'; it's God's truth!   I saw it on
the handbill agin a tree.   Take him, and
I'll get away afoot.   Take him.   It's the

only thing I can do for you, and I know it
don't half pay for what you did. Take it;
your father can get a reward for you, if you
can't."

Such were the ethics of this strange locality that neither the man who made the offer
nor the girl to whom it was made was
struck by anything that seemed illogical or
indelicate, or at all inconsistent with justice
or the horse-thief's real conversion. Salomy
Jane nevertheless dissented, from another
and weaker reason.

"I don't want your hoss, though I reckon
dad might; but you 're just starvin'. I 'll
get suthin'." She turned towards the house.

"Say you 'll take the hoss first," he said,
grasping her hand. At the touch she felt
herself coloring and struggled, expecting
perhaps another kiss. But he dropped her
hand. She turned again with a saucy gesture, said, "Hol' on; I 'll come right back,"
and slipped away, the mere shadow of a coy
and flying nymph in the moonlight, until
she reached the house.

Here she not only procured food and
whiskey, but added a long dust-coat and hat
of her father's to her burden. They would
serve as a disguise for him and hide that

heroic figure, which she thought everybody must now know as she did. Then she rejoined him breathlessly. But he put the food and whiskey aside.

"Listen," he said; "I 've turned the hoss into your corral. You 'll find him there in the morning, and no one will know but that he got lost and joined the other hosses."

Then she burst out. "But you — *you* — what will become of you? You 'll be ketched!"

"I 'll manage to get away," he said in a low voice, "ef — ef " —

"Ef what?" she said tremblingly.

"Ef you 'll put the heart in me again, — as you did!" he gasped.

She tried to laugh — to move away. She could do neither. Suddenly he caught her in his arms, with a long kiss, which she returned again and again. Then they stood embraced as they had embraced two days before, but no longer the same. For the cool, lazy Salomy Jane had been transformed into another woman — a passionate, clinging savage. Perhaps something of her father's blood had surged within her at that supreme moment. The man stood erect and determined.

"Wot 's your name?" she whispered quickly. It was a woman's quickest way of defining her feelings.

"Dart."

"Yer first name?"

"Jack."

"Let me go now, Jack. Lie low in the woods till to-morrow sunup. I 'll come again."

He released her. Yet she lingered a moment. "Put on those things," she said, with a sudden happy flash of eyes and teeth, "and lie close till I come." And then she sped away home.

But midway up the distance she felt her feet going slower, and something at her heartstrings seemed to be pulling her back. She stopped, turned, and glanced to where he had been standing. Had she seen him then, she might have returned. But he had disappeared. She gave her first sigh, and then ran quickly again. It must be nearly ten o'clock! It was not very long to morning!

She was within a few steps of her own door, when the sleeping woods and silent air appeared to suddenly awake with a sharp "crack!"

She stopped, paralyzed. Another "crack!" followed, that echoed over to the far corral. She recalled herself instantly and dashed off wildly to the woods again.

As she ran she thought of one thing only. He had been "dogged" by one of his old pursuers and attacked. But there were two shots, and he was unarmed. Suddenly she remembered that she had left her father's gun standing against the tree where they were talking. Thank God! she may again have saved him. She ran to the tree; the gun was gone. She ran hither and thither, dreading at every step to fall upon his lifeless body. A new thought struck her; she ran to the corral. The horse was not there! He must have been able to regain it, and escaped, *after* the shots had been fired. She drew a long breath of relief, but it was caught up in an apprehension of alarm. Her father, awakened from his sleep by the shots, was hurriedly approaching her.

"What's up now, Salomy Jane?" he demanded excitedly.

"Nothin'," said the girl with an effort. "Nothin', at least, that *I* can find." She was usually truthful because fearless, and a lie stuck in her throat; but she was no longer fearless, thinking of *him*. "I was n't abed; so I ran out as soon as I heard the shots fired," she answered in return to his curious gaze.

"And you 've hid my gun somewhere where it can't be found," he said reproachfully. "Ef it was that sneak Larrabee, and he fired them shots to lure me out, he might have potted me, without a show, a dozen times in the last five minutes."

She had not thought since of her father's enemy! It might indeed have been he who had attacked Jack. But she made a quick point of the suggestion. "Run in, dad, run in and find the gun; you 've got no show out here without it." She seized him by the shoulders from behind, shielding him from the woods, and hurried him, half expostulating, half struggling, to the house.

But there no gun was to be found. It was strange; it must have been mislaid in some corner! Was he sure he had not left it in the barn? But no matter now. The danger was over; the Larrabee trick had failed; he must go to bed now, and in the morning they would make a search together. At the same time she had inwardly resolved to rise before him and make another search of the wood, and perhaps — fearful joy as she recalled her promise! — find Jack alive and well, awaiting her!

Salomy Jane slept little that night, nor did her father. But towards morning he fell into a tired man's slumber until the sun was well up the horizon. Far different was it with his daughter: she lay with her face to the window, her head half lifted to catch every sound, from the creaking of the sun-warped shingles above her head to the far-off moan of the rising wind in the pine trees. Sometimes she fell into a breathless, half-ecstatic trance, living over every moment of the stolen interview; feeling the fugitive's arm still around her, his kisses on her lips; hearing his whispered voice in her ears — the birth of her new life! This was followed again by a period of agonizing dread — that he might even then be lying, his life ebbing away, in the woods, with her name on his lips, and she resting here inactive, until she half started from her bed to go to his succor. And this went on until a pale opal glow came into the sky, followed by a still paler pink on the summit of the white Sierras, when she rose and hurriedly began to dress. Still so sanguine was her hope of meeting him, that she lingered yet a moment to select the brown holland skirt and yellow sunbonnet she had worn when she first saw him. And she had only seen him twice! Only *twice!* It would be cruel, too cruel, not to see him again!

She crept softly down the stairs, listening to the long-drawn breathing of her father in his bedroom, and then, by the light of a guttering candle, scrawled a note to him, begging him not to trust himself out of the house until she returned from her search, and leaving the note open on the table, swiftly ran out into the growing day.

Three hours afterwards Mr. Madison Clay awoke to the sound of loud knocking. At first this forced itself upon his consciousness as his daughter's regular morning summons, and was responded to by a grunt of recognition and a nestling closer in the blankets. Then he awoke with a start and a muttered oath, remembering the events of last night, and his intention to get up early, and rolled out of bed. Becoming aware by this time that the knocking was at the outer door, and hearing the shout of a familiar voice, he hastily pulled on his boots, his jean trousers, and fastening a single sus-

pender over his shoulder as he clattered
downstairs, stood in the lower room. The
door was open, and waiting upon the threshold was his kinsman, an old ally in many a
blood-feud — Breckenridge Clay!

"You *are* a cool one, Mad!" said the
latter in half-admiring indignation.

"What's up?" said the bewildered Madison.

"*You* ought to be, and scootin' out o'
this," said Breckenridge grimly. "It's all
very well to ' know nothin';' but here Phil
Larrabee's friends hev just picked him up,
drilled through with slugs and deader nor a
crow, and now they're lettin' loose Larrabee's two half-brothers on you. And you
must go like a derned fool and leave these
yer things behind you in the bresh," he
went on querulously, lifting Madison Clay's
dust-coat, hat, and shotgun from his horse,
which stood saddled at the door. "Luckily
I picked them up in the woods comin' here.
Ye ain't got more than time to get over the
state line and among your folks thar afore
they'll be down on you. Hustle, old man!
What are you gawkin' and starin' at?"

Madison Clay had stared amazed and bewildered — horror-stricken. The incidents

of the past night for the first time flashed
upon him clearly — hopelessly! The shot;
his finding Salomy Jane alone in the woods;
her confusion and anxiety to rid herself of
him; the disappearance of the shotgun; and
now this new discovery of the taking of his
hat and coat for a disguise! *She* had killed
Phil Larrabee in that disguise, after pro-
voking his first harmless shot! She, his
own child, Salomy Jane, had disgraced herself by a man's crime; had disgraced him by
usurping his right, and taking a mean advantage, by deceit, of a foe!

"Gimme that gun," he said hoarsely.

Breckenridge handed him the gun in wonder and slowly gathering suspicion. Madison examined nipple and muzzle; one barrel
had been discharged. It was true! The
gun dropped from his hand.

"Look here, old man," said Breckenridge, with a darkening face, "there's bin
no foul play here. Thar's bin no hiring of
men, no deputy to do this job. *You* did it
fair and square — yourself?"

"Yes, by God!" burst out Madison Clay
in a hoarse voice. "Who says I did n't?"

Reassured, yet believing that Madison
Clay had nerved himself for the act by an

over-draught of whiskey, which had affected his memory, Breckenridge said curtly, "Then wake up and 'lite' out, ef ye want me to stand by you."

"Go to the corral and pick me out a hoss," said Madison slowly, yet not without a certain dignity of manner. "I 've suthin' to say to Salomy Jane afore I go." He was holding her scribbled note, which he had just discovered, in his shaking hand.

Struck by his kinsman's manner, and knowing the dependent relations of father and daughter, Breckenridge nodded and hurried away. Left to himself, Madison Clay ran his fingers through his hair, and straightened out the paper on which Salomy Jane had scrawled her note, turned it over, and wrote on the back: —

You might have told me you did it, and not leave your ole father to find it out how you disgraced yourself and him, too, by a low-down, underhanded, woman's trick! I 've said I done it, and took the blame myself, and all the sneakiness of it that folks suspect. If I get away alive — and I don't care much which — you need n't foller. The house and stock are yours; but you ain't

any longer the daughter of your disgraced
father, MADISON CLAY.

He had scarcely finished the note when,
with a clatter of hoofs and a led horse,
Breckenridge reappeared at the door elate
and triumphant. "You're in nigger luck,
Mad! I found that stole hoss of Judge
Boompointer's had got away and strayed
among your stock in the corral. Take him
and you're safe; he can't be outrun this
side of the state line."

"I ain't no hoss-thief," said Madison
grimly.

"Nobody sez ye are, but you'd be wuss
— a fool — ef you didn't take him. I'm
testimony that you found him among your
hosses; I'll tell Judge Boompointer you've
got him, and ye kin send him back when
you're safe. The judge will be mighty
glad to get him back, and call it quits. So
ef you've writ to Salomy Jane, come."

Madison Clay no longer hesitated. Salomy Jane might return at any moment, — it
would be part of her "fool womanishness,"
— and he was in no mood to see her before
a third party. He laid the note on the
table, gave a hurried glance around the

house, which he grimly believed he was leaving forever, and, striding to the door, leaped on the stolen horse, and swept away with his kinsman.

But that note lay for a week undisturbed on the table in full view of the open door. The house was invaded by leaves, pine cones, birds, and squirrels during the hot, silent, empty days, and at night by shy, stealthy creatures, but never again, day or night, by any of the Clay family. It was known in the district that Clay had flown across the state line, his daughter was believed to have joined him the next day, and the house was supposed to be locked up. It lay off the main road, and few passed that way. The starving cattle in the corral at last broke bounds and spread over the woods. And one night a stronger blast than usual swept through the house, carried the note from the table to the floor, where, whirled into a crack in the flooring, it slowly rotted.

But though the sting of her father's reproach was spared her, Salomy Jane had no need of the letter to know what had happened. For as she entered the woods in the dim light of that morning she saw the figure of Dart gliding from the shadow of a pine towards her. The unaffected cry of joy that rose from her lips died there as she caught sight of his face in the open light.

"You are hurt," she said, clutching his arm passionately.

"No," he said. "But I would n't mind that if " —

"You 're thinkin' I was afeard to come back last night when I heard the shootin', but I *did* come," she went on feverishly. "I ran back here when I heard the two shots, but you were gone. I went to the corral, but your hoss was n't there, and I thought you 'd got away."

"I *did* get away," said Dart gloomily. "I killed the man, thinkin' he was huntin' *me*, and forgettin' I was disguised. He thought I was your father."

"Yes," said the girl joyfully, "he was after dad, and *you* — you killed him." She again caught his hand admiringly.

But he did not respond. Possibly there were points of honor which this horse-thief felt vaguely with her father. "Listen," he said grimly. "Others think it was your father killed him. When *I* did it — for he fired at me first — I ran to the corral again and took my hoss, thinkin' I might be follered. I made a clear circuit of the house, and when I found he was the only one, and no one was follerin', I come back here and took off my disguise. Then I heard his friends find him in the wood, and I know they suspected your father. And then another man come through the woods while I was hidin' and found the clothes and took them away." He stopped and stared at her gloomily.

But all this was unintelligible to the girl. "Dad would have got the better of him ef you had n't," she said eagerly, "so what 's the difference?"

"All the same," he said gloomily, "I must take his place."

She did not understand, but turned her head to her master. "Then you 'll go back with me and tell him *all?*" she said obediently.

"Yes," he said.

She put her hand in his, and they crept out of the wood together. She foresaw a thousand difficulties, but, chiefest of all, that he did not love as she did. *She* would not have taken these risks against their happiness.

But alas for ethics and heroism. As

they were issuing from the wood they heard
the sound of galloping hoofs, and had barely
time to hide themselves before Madison
Clay, on the stolen horse of Judge Boompointer, swept past them with his kinsman.

Salomy Jane turned to her lover.

.    .    .    .    .    .    .    .

And here I might, as a moral romancer,
pause, leaving the guilty, passionate girl
eloped with her disreputable lover, destined
to lifelong shame and misery, misunderstood
to the last by a criminal, fastidious parent.
But I am confronted by certain facts, on
which this romance is based.  A month later
a handbill was posted on one of the sentinel
pines, announcing that the property would
be sold by auction to the highest bidder by
Mrs. John Dart, daughter of Madison Clay,
Esq., and it was sold accordingly.  Still
later — by ten years — the chronicler of
these pages visited a certain "stock" or
"breeding farm," in the "Blue Grass Country," famous for the popular racers it has
produced.  He was told that the owner was
the "best judge of horse-flesh in the country."
"Small wonder," added his informant, "for
they say as a young man out in California
he was a horse-thief, and only saved himself

by eloping with some rich farmer's daughter. But he's a straight-out and respectable man now, whose word about horses can't be bought; and as for his wife, *she*'s a beauty! To see her at the ' Springs,' rigged out in the latest fashion, you'd never think she had ever lived out of New York or wasn't the wife of one of its millionaires."

# THE MAN AND THE MOUNTAIN

HE was such a large, strong man that, when he first set foot in the little parallelogram I called my garden, it seemed to shrink to half its size and become preposterous. But I noticed at the same time that he was holding in the open palm of his huge hand the roots of a violet, with such infinite tenderness and delicacy that I would have engaged him as my gardener on the spot. But this could not be, as he was already the proud proprietor of a market-garden and nursery on the outskirts of the suburban Californian town where I lived. He would, however, come for two days in the week, stock and look after my garden, and impart to my urban intellect such horticultural hints as were necessary. His name was "Rütli," which I presumed to be German, but which my neighbors rendered as "Rootleigh," possibly from some vague connection with his occupation. His own knowledge of English was oral and phonetic. I have a delightful recollection of a bill of his in which I was charged for "fioletz," with the vague addition of "maine cains." Subsequent explanation proved it to be "many kinds."

Nevertheless, my little garden bourgeoned and blossomed under his large, protecting hand. I became accustomed to walk around his feet respectfully when they blocked the tiny paths, and to expect the total eclipse of that garden-bed on which he worked, by his huge bulk. For the tiniest and most reluctant rootlet seemed to respond to his caressing paternal touch; it was a pretty sight to see his huge fingers tying up some slender stalk to its stick with the smallest thread, and he had a reverent way of laying a bulb or seed in the ground, and then gently shaping and smoothing a small mound over it, which made the little inscription on the stick above more like an affecting epitaph than ever. Much of this gentleness may have been that apology for his great strength, common with large men; but his face was distinctly amiable, and his very light blue eyes were at times wistful and doglike in their kindliness. I was soon to learn, however, that placability was not entirely his nature.

The garden was part of a fifty *vara* lot of land, on which I was simultaneously erecting a house. But the garden was finished before the house was, through certain circumstances very characteristic of that epoch and civilization. I had purchased the Spanish title, the only *legal* one, to the land, which, however, had been in *possession* of a "squatter." But he had been unable to hold that possession against a "jumper," — another kind of squatter who had entered upon it covertly, fenced it in, and marked it out in building sites. Neither having legal rights, they could not invoke the law; the last man held possession. There was no doubt that in due course of litigation and time both these ingenuous gentlemen would have been dispossessed in favor of the real owner, — myself, — but that course would be a protracted one. Following the usual custom of the locality, I paid a certain sum to the jumper to yield up peaceably *his* possession of the land, and began to build upon it. It might be reasonably supposed that the question was settled. But it was not. The house was nearly finished when, one morning, I was called out of my editorial sanctum by a pallid painter, looking even more white-

leaded than usual, who informed me that
my house was in the possession of five armed
men! The entry had been made peaceably
during the painters' absence to dinner under
a wayside tree. When they returned, they
had found their pots and brushes in the
road, and an intimation from the windows
that their reëntrance would be forcibly resisted as a trespass.

I honestly believe that Rütli was more
concerned than myself over this disposses-
sion. While he loyally believed that I would
get back my property, he was dreadfully
grieved over the inevitable damage that
would be done to the garden during this interval of neglect and carelessness. I even
think he would have made a truce with my
enemies, if they would only have let him
look after his beloved plants. As it was,
he kept a passing but melancholy surveillance of them, and was indeed a better spy
of the actions of the intruders than any I
could have employed. One day, to my astonishment, he brought me a moss-rose bud
from a bush which had been trained against
a column of the veranda. It appeared that
he had called, from over the fence, the attention of one of the men to the neglected

condition of the plant, and had obtained permission to "come in and tie it up." The men, being merely hirelings of the chief squatter, had no personal feeling, and I was not therefore surprised to hear that they presently allowed Rütli to come in occasionally and look after his precious "slips." If they had any suspicions of his great strength, it was probably offset by his peaceful avocation and his bland, childlike face. Meantime, I had begun the usual useless legal proceeding, but had also engaged a few rascals of my own to be ready to take advantage of any want of vigilance on the part of my adversaries. I never thought of Rütli in that connection any more than they had.

A few Sundays later I was sitting in the little tea-arbor of Rütli's nursery, peacefully smoking with him. Presently he took his long china-bowled pipe from his mouth, and, looking at me blandly over his yellow mustache, said: —

"You vonts sometimes to go in dot house, eh?"

I said, "Decidedly."

"Mit a revolver, and keep dot house dose men out?"

"Yes!"

H

"Vell! I put you in dot house — to-day!"

"Sunday?"

"Shoost so! It is a goot day! On der Suntay *dree* men vill out go to valk mit demselluffs, and visky trinken. *Two*," holding up two gigantic fingers, apparently only a shade or two smaller than his destined victims, "stay dere. Dose I lift de fence over."

I hastened to inform him that any violence attempted against the parties *while in possession*, although that possession was illegal, would, by a fatuity of the law, land him in the county jail. I said I would not hear of it.

"But suppose dere vos no fiolence? Suppose dose men vos villin', eh? How vos dot for high?"

"I don't understand."

"So! You shall *not* understand! Dot is better. Go away now and dell your men to coom dot house arount at halluff past dree. But *you* coom, mit yourselluff alone, shoost as if you vos *spazieren gehen*, for a valk, by dat fence at dree! Ven you shall dot front door vide open see, go in, and dere you vos! You vill der rest leef to me!"

It was in vain that I begged Rütli to divulge his plan, and pointed out again the danger of his technically breaking the law. But he was firm, assuring me that I myself would be a witness that no assault would be made. I looked into his clear, good-humored eyes, and assented. I had a burning desire to right my wrongs, but I think I also had considerable curiosity.

I passed a miserable quarter of an hour after I had warned my partisans, and then walked alone slowly down the broad leafy street towards the scene of contest. I have a very vivid recollection of my conflicting emotions. I did not believe that I would be killed; I had no distinct intention of killing any of my adversaries; but I had some considerable concern for my loyal friend Rütli, whom I foresaw might be in some peril from the revolver in my unpracticed hand. If I could only avoid shooting *him*, I would be satisfied. I remember that the bells were ringing for church, — a church of which my enemy, the chief squatter, was a deacon in good standing, — and I felt guiltily conscious of my revolver in my hip-pocket, as two or three church-goers passed me with their hymn-books in their hands. I walked leisurely, so as not to attract attention, and to appear at the exact time, a not very easy task in my youthful excitement. At last I reached the front gate with a beating heart. There was no one on the high veranda, which occupied three sides of the low one-storied house, nor in the garden before it. But the front door was open; I softly passed through the gate, darted up the veranda and into the house. A single glance around the hall and bare, deserted rooms, still smelling of paint, showed me it was empty, and with my pistol in one hand and the other on the lock of the door, I stood inside, ready to bolt it against any one but Rütli. But where was *he?*

The sound of laughter and a noise like skylarking came from the rear of the house and the back yard. Then I suddenly heard Rütli's heavy tread on the veranda, but it was slow, deliberate, and so exaggerated in its weight that the whole house seemed to shake with it. Then from the window I beheld an extraordinary sight! It was Rütli, swaying from side to side, but steadily carrying with outstretched arms two of the squatter party, his hands tightly grasping their collars. Yet I believe his touch was as gentle as with the violets. His face was preternaturally grave; theirs, to my intense astonishment, while they hung passive from his arms, wore that fatuous, imbecile smile seen on the faces of those who lend themselves to tricks of acrobats and strong men in the arena. He slowly traversed the whole length of one side of the house, walked down the steps to the gate, and then gravely deposited them *outside*. I heard him say, "Dot vins der pet, ain't it?" and immediately after the sharp click of the gate-latch.

Without understanding a thing that had happened, I rightly conceived this was the cue for my appearance with my revolver at the front door. As I opened it I still heard the sound of laughter, which, however, instantly stopped at a sentence from Rütli, which I could not hear. There was an oath, the momentary apparition of two furious and indignant faces over the fence; but these, however, seemed to be instantly extinguished and put down by the enormous palms of Rütli clapped upon their heads. There was a pause, and then Rütli turned around and quietly joined me in the doorway. But the gate was not again opened until the arrival of my partisans, when the house was clearly in my possession.

Safe inside with the door bolted, I turned

eagerly to Rütli for an explanation. It
then appeared that during his occasional
visits to the garden he had often been an
object of amusement and criticism to the
men on account of his size, which seemed to
them ridiculously inconsistent with his great
good humor, gentleness, and delicacy of
touch. They had doubted his strength and
challenged his powers. He had responded
once or twice before, lifting weights or even
carrying one of his critics at arm's length
for a few steps. But he had reserved his
final feat for this day and this purpose. It
was for a bet, which they had eagerly accepted, secure in their belief in his simplicity, the sincerity of his motives in coming
there, and glad of the opportunity of a little
Sunday diversion. In their security they
had not locked the door when they came
out, and had not noticed that *he* had opened
it. This was his simple story. His only
comment, "I haf von der pet, but I dinks
I shall nod gollect der money." The two
men did not return that afternoon, nor did
their comrades. Whether they wisely conceived that a man who was so powerful in
play might be terrible in earnest; whether
they knew that his act, in which they had

been willing performers, had been witnessed by passing citizens, who supposed it was skylarking; or whether their employer got tired of his expensive occupation, I never knew. The public believed the latter; Rütli, myself, and the two men he had evicted alone kept our secret.

From that time Rütli and I became firm friends, and, long after I had no further need of his services in the recaptured house, I often found myself in the little tea-arbor of his prosperous nursery. He was frugal, sober, and industrious; small wonder that in that growing town he waxed rich, and presently opened a restaurant in the main street, connected with his market-garden, which became famous. His relations to me never changed with his changed fortunes; he was always the simple market-gardener and florist who had aided my first house-keeping, and stood by me in an hour of need. Of all things regarding himself he was singularly reticent; I do not think he had any confidants or intimates, even among his own countrymen, whom I believed to be German. But one day he quite acciden-tally admitted he was a Swiss. As a youth-ful admirer of the race I was delighted, and

told him so, with the enthusiastic addition
that I could now quite understand his independence, with his devoted adherence to another's cause. He smiled sadly, and astonished me by saying that he had not heard
from Switzerland since he left six years
ago. He did not want to hear anything;
he even avoided his countrymen lest he
should. I was confounded.

"But," I said, "surely you have a long,
ing to return to your country; all Swiss
have! You will go back some day just to
breathe the air of your native mountains."

"I shall go back some days," said Rütli,
"after I have made mooch, mooch money,
but not for dot air."

"What for, then?"

"For revenge — to get efen."

Surprised, and for a moment dismayed as
I was, I could not help laughing. "Rütli
and revenge!" Impossible! And to make
it the more absurd, he was still smoking
gently and regarding me with soft, compla-
cent eyes. So unchanged was his face and
manner that he might have told me he was
going back to be married.

"You do not oonderstand," he said forgivingly. "Some days I shall dell to you

id. Id is a story. You shall make it yourselluff for dose babers dot you write. It is
not bretty, berhaps, ain't it, but it is droo.
And de endt is not yet."

Only that Rütli never joked, except in a
ponderous fashion with many involved sentences, I should have thought he was taking
a good-humored rise out of me. But it was
not funny. I am afraid I dismissed it from
my mind as a revelation of something weak
and puerile, quite inconsistent with his practical common sense and strong simplicity,
and wished he had not alluded to it. I
never asked him to tell me the story. It
was a year later, and only when he had invited me to come to the opening of a new
hotel, erected by him at a mountain spa of
great resort, that he himself alluded to it.

The hotel was a wonderful affair, even
for those days, and Rütli's outlay of capital
convinced me that by this time he must
have made the "mooch money" he coveted.
Something of this was in my mind when we
sat by the window of his handsomely furnished private office, overlooking the pines
of a Californian cañon. I asked him if the
scenery was like Switzerland.

"Ach! no!" he replied; "but I vill puild
a hotel shoost like dis dare."

"Is that a part of your revenge?" I asked, with a laugh.

"Ah! so! a bart."

I felt relieved; a revenge so practical did not seem very malicious or idiotic. After a pause he puffed contemplatively at his pipe, and then said, "I dell you somedings of dot story now."

He began. I should like to tell it in his own particular English, mixed with American slang, but it would not convey the simplicity of the narrator. He was the son of a large family who had lived for centuries in one of the highest villages in the Bernese Oberland. He attained his size and strength early, but with a singular distaste to use them in the rough regular work on the farm, although he was a great climber and mountaineer, and, what was at first overlooked as mere boyish fancy, had an insatiable love and curious knowledge of plants and flowers. He knew the haunts of Edelweiss, Alpine rose, and blue gentian, and had brought home rare and unknown blossoms from under the icy lips of glaciers. But as he did this when his time was supposed to be occupied in looking after the cows in the higher pastures and making cheeses, there was trou-

ble in that hard-working, practical family.
A giant with the tastes and disposition of a
schoolgirl was an anomaly in a Swiss village. Unfortunately again, he was not studious; his record in the village school had
been on a par with his manual work, and
the family had not even the consolation of
believing that they were fostering a genius.
In a community where practical industry
was the highest virtue, it was not strange,
perhaps, that he was called "lazy" and
"shiftless;" no one knew the long climbs
and tireless vigils he had undergone in remote solitudes in quest of his favorites, or,
knowing, forgave him for it. Abstemious,
frugal, and patient as he was, even the
crusts of his father's table were given him
grudgingly. He often went hungry rather
than ask the bread he had failed to earn.
How his great frame was nurtured in those
days he never knew; perhaps the giant
mountains recognized some kin in him and
fed and strengthened him after their own
fashion. Even his gentleness was confounded with cowardice. "Dot vos de hardt-
est," he said simply; "it is not goot to be
opligit to half crush your brudder, ven he
would make a laugh of you to your sweet-

heart." The end came sooner than he expected, and, oddly enough, through this sweetheart. "Gottlieb," she said to him one day, "the English *Fremde* who stayed here last night met me when I was carrying some of those beautiful flowers you gave me. He asked me where they were to be found, and I told him only *you* knew. He wants to see you; go to him. It may be luck to you." Rütli went. The stranger, an English Alpine climber of scientific tastes, talked with him for an hour. At the end of that time, to everybody's astonishment, he engaged this hopeless idler as his personal guide for three months, at the sum of five francs a day! It was inconceivable, it was unheard of! The Englander was as mad as Gottlieb, whose intellect had always been under suspicion! The schoolmaster pursed up his lips, the pastor shook his head; no good could come of it; the family looked upon it as another freak of Gottlieb's, but there was one big mouth less to feed and more room in the kitchen, and they let him go. They parted from him as ungraciously as they had endured his presence.

Then followed two months of sunshine in Rütli's life — association with his beloved

plants, and the intelligent sympathy and
direction of a cultivated man. Even in al-
titudes so dangerous that they had to take
other and more experienced guides, Rütli
was always at his master's side. That sa-
vant's collection of Alpine flora excelled all
previous ones; he talked freely with Rütli
of further work in the future, and relaxed
his English reserve so far as to confide to
him that the outcome of their collection and
observation might be a book. He gave a
flower a Latin name, in which even the ignorant and delighted Rütli could distinguish
some likeness to his own. But the book
was never compiled. In one of their later
and more difficult ascents they and their two
additional guides were overtaken by a sudden storm. Swept from their feet down an
ice-bound slope, Rütli alone of the roped-
together party kept a foothold on the treacherous incline. Here this young Titan, with
bleeding fingers clenched in a rock cleft,
sustained the struggles and held up the lives
of his companions by that precious thread
for more than an hour. Perhaps he might
have saved them, but in their desperate efforts to regain their footing the rope slipped
upon a jagged edge of outcrop and parted as

if cut by a knife. The two guides passed without an outcry into obscurity and death; Rütli, with a last despairing exertion, dragged to his own level his unconscious master, crippled by a broken leg.

Your true hero is apt to tell his tale simply. Rütli did not dwell upon these details, nor need I. Left alone upon a treacherous ice slope in benumbing cold, with a helpless man, eight hours afterwards he staggered, half blind, incoherent, and inarticulate, into a "shelter" hut, with the dead body of his master in his stiffened arms. The shelter-keepers turned their attention to Rütli, who needed it most. Blind and delirious, with scarce a chance for life, he was sent the next day to a hospital, where he lay for three months, helpless, imbecile, and unknown. The dead body of the Englishman was identified, and sent home; the bodies of the guides were recovered by their friends; but no one knew aught of Rütli, even his name. While the event was still fresh in the minds of those who saw him enter the hut with the body of his master, a paragraph appeared in a Berne journal recording the heroism of this nameless man. But it could not be corroborated nor explained by the demented hero, and was presently forgotten. Six months from the day he had left his home he was discharged cured. He had not a kreutzer in his pocket; he had never drawn his wages from his employer; he had preferred to have it in a lump sum that he might astonish his family on his return. His eyes were still weak, his memory feeble; only his great physical strength remained through his long illness. A few sympathizing travelers furnished him the means to reach his native village, many miles away. He found his family had heard of the loss of the Englishman and the guides, and had believed he was one of them. Already he was forgotten.

"Ven you vos once peliefed to be det," said Rütli, after a philosophic pause and puff, "it vos not goot to ondeceif beoples. You oopset somedings, soomdimes always. Der hole dot you hef made in der grount, among your frients and your family, vos covered up alretty. You are loocky if you vill not fint some vellars shtanding upon id! My frent, ven you vos *dink* det, *shtay* det, *be* det, and you vill lif happy!"

"But your sweetheart?" I said eagerly.

A slight gleam of satire stole into Rütli's

light eyes. "My sweetheart, ven I vos dinks det, is der miller engaged do bromply! It is mooch better dan to a man dot vos boor and plint and grazy! So! Vell, der next day I pids dem goot-py, und from der door I say, ' I am det now; but ven I next comes pack alife, I shall dis village py! der lants, der houses all togedders. And den for yourselluffs look oudt! ' "

"Then that's your revenge? That is what you really intend to do?" I said, half laughing, yet with an uneasy recollection of his illness and enfeebled mind.

"Yes. Look here! I show you some-dings." He opened a drawer of his desk and took out what appeared to be some dia-grams, plans, and a small water-colored map, like a surveyor's tracing. "Look," he said, laying his finger on the latter, "dat is a map from my fillage. I hef myselluff made it out from my memory. Dot," point-ing to a blank space, "is der mountain side high up, so far. It is no goot until I vill a tunnel make or der grade lefel. Dere vas mine fader's house, dere vos der church, der schoolhouse, dot vos de burgomaster's house," he went on, pointing to the respec-tive plots in this old curving parallelogram of the mountain shelf. "So was the fillage when I leave him on the 5th of March, eighteen hundred and feefty. Now you shall see him shoost as I vill make him ven I go back." He took up another plan, beautifully drawn and colored, and evidently done by a professional hand. It was a practical, yet almost fairylike transformation of the same spot! The narrow mountain shelf was widened by excavation, and a boulevard stretched on either side. A great hotel, not unlike the one in which we sat, stood in an open terrace, with gardens and fountains — the site of his father's house. Blocks of pretty dwellings, shops, and cafés filled the intermediate space. I laid down the paper.

"How long have you had this idea?"

"Efer since I left dere, fifteen years ago."

"But your father and mother may be dead by this time?"

"So, but dere vill be odders. Und der blace — it vill remain."

"But all this will cost a fortune, and you are not sure" —

"I know shoost vot id vill gost, to a cend."

"And you think you can ever afford to carry out your idea?"

"I *vill* affort id. Ven you shall make yet some moneys and go to Europe, you shall see. I *vill* infite you dere first. Now coom and look der house around."

.  .  .  .  .  .  .  .

I did *not* make "some moneys," but I *did* go to Europe. Three years after this last interview with Rütli I was coming from Interlaken to Berne by rail. I had not heard from him, and I had forgotten the name of his village, but as I looked up from the paper I was reading, I suddenly recognized him in the further end of the same compartment I occupied. His recognition of me was evidently as sudden and unexpected. After our first hand-grasp and greeting, I said: —

"And how about our new village?"

"Dere is no fillage."

"What! You have given up the idea?"

"Yes. There is no fillage, olt or new."

"I don't understand."

He looked at me a moment. "You have not heard?"

"No."

He gently picked up a little local guide-book that lay in my lap, and turning its leaves, pointed to a page, and read as follows: —

"5 M. beyond, the train passes a curve R.,
where a fine view of the lake may be seen.
A little to the R. rises the steep slopes of
the ——, the scene of a terrible disaster.
At three o'clock on March 5, 1850, the little village of ——, lying midway of the
slope, with its population of 950 souls, was
completely destroyed by a landslip from the
top of the mountain. So sudden was the
catastrophe that not a single escape is recorded. A large portion of the mountain
crest, as will be observed when it is seen in
profile, descended to the valley, burying the
unfortunate village to a depth variously estimated at from 1000 ft. to 1800 ft. The
geological causes which produced this extraordinary displacement have been fully
discussed, but the greater evidence points
to the theory of subterranean glaciers.
5 M. beyond —— the train crosses the R.
bridge."

I laid down the guide-book in breathless
astonishment.

"And you never heard of this in all these
years?"

"Nefer! I asked no questions, I read
no pooks. I have no ledders from home."

"And yet you" — I stopped, I could not

call him a fool; neither could I, in the face of his perfect composure and undisturbed eyes, exhibit a concern greater than his own. An uneasy recollection of what he confessed had been his mental condition immediately after his accident came over me. Had he been the victim of a strange hallucination regarding his house and family all these years? Were these dreams of revenge, this fancy of creating a new village, only an outcome of some shock arising out of the disaster itself, which he had long since forgotten?

He was looking from the window. "Coom," he said, "ve are near der blace. I vill show id to you." He rose and passed out to the rear platform. We were in the rear car, and a new panorama of the lake and mountains flashed upon us at every curve of the line. I followed him. Presently he pointed to what appeared to be a sheer wall of rock and stunted vegetation towering two or three thousand feet above us, which started out of a gorge we were passing. "Dere it vos!" he said. I saw the vast stretch of rock face rising upward and onward, but nothing else. No débris, no ruins, nor even a swelling or rounding of the mountain flank over that awful tomb. Yet, stay! as we dashed across the gorge, and the face of the mountain shifted, high up, the sky-line was slightly broken as if a few inches, a mere handful, of the crest was crumbled away. And then — both gorge and mountain vanished.

I was still embarrassed and uneasy, and knew not what to say to this man at my side, whose hopes and ambition had been as quickly overthrown and buried, and whose life-dream had as quickly vanished. But he himself, taking his pipe from his lips, broke the silence.

"It vos a narrow esgabe!"

"What was?"

"Vy, dis dings. If I had stayed in my fader's house, I vould haf been det for goot, and perried too! Somedimes dose dings cooms oudt apout right, don't id?"

Unvanquished philosopher! As we stood there looking at the flying landscape and sinking lesser hills, one by one the great snow peaks slowly arose behind them, lifting themselves, as if to take a last wondering look at the man they had triumphed over, but had not subdued.

# THE PASSING OF ENRIQUEZ

WHEN Enriquez Saltillo ran away with
Miss Mannersley, as already recorded in
these chronicles,[1] her relatives and friends
found it much easier to forgive that ill-
assorted union than to understand it. For,
after all, Enriquez was the scion of an old
Spanish-Californian family, and in due time
would have his share of his father's three
square leagues, whatever incongruity there
was between his lively Latin extravagance
and Miss Mannersley's Puritan precision
and intellectual superiority. They had gone
to Mexico; Mrs. Saltillo, as was known,
having an interest in Aztec antiquities, and
he being utterly submissive to her wishes.
For myself from my knowledge of Enriquez's nature, I had grave doubts of his
entire subjugation, although I knew the
prevailing opinion was that Mrs. Saltillo's
superiority would speedily tame him. Since

[1] See "The Devotion of Enriquez," in *Barker's Luck,
and Other Stories.*

**his** brief and characteristic note apprising
me of his marriage, I had not heard from
him. It was, therefore, with some surprise,
a good deal of reminiscent affection, and a
slight twinge of reproach that, two years
after, I looked up from some proofs, in the
sanctum of the "Daily Excelsior," to recognize his handwriting on a note that was
handed to me by a yellow Mexican boy.

A single glance at its contents showed me
that Mrs. Saltillo's correct Bostonian speech
had not yet subdued Enriquez's peculiar
Spanish-American slang: —

"Here we are again, — right side up with
care, — at 1110 Dupont Street, Telegraph
Hill. Second floor from top. ' Ring and
push.' ' No book agents need apply.'
How's your royal nibs? I kiss your hand!
Come at six, — the band shall play at seven,
— and regard your friend ' Mees Boston,'
who will tell you about the little old nigger
boys, and your old Uncle 'Ennery."

Two things struck me: Enriquez had not
changed; Mrs. Saltillo had certainly yielded
up some of her peculiar prejudices. For
the address given, far from being a fashion-
able district, was known as the "Spanish
quarter," which, while it still held some old

Spanish families, was chiefly given over to
half-castes and obscurer foreigners. Even
poverty could not have driven Mrs. Saltillo
to such a refuge against her will; nevertheless, a good deal of concern for Enriquez's
fortune mingled with my curiosity, as I impatiently waited for six o'clock to satisfy it.

It was a breezy climb to 1110 Dupont
Street; and although the street had been
graded, the houses retained their airy eleva-
tion, and were accessible only by successive
flights of wooden steps to the front door,
which still gave perilously upon the street,
sixty feet below. I now painfully appre-
ciated Enriquez's adaptation of the time-
honored joke about the second floor. An
invincible smell of garlic almost took my
remaining breath away as the door was
opened to me by a swarthy Mexican woman,
whose loose *camisa* seemed to be slipping
from her unstable bust, and was held on
only by the mantua-like shawl which sup-
plemented it, gripped by one brown hand.
Dizzy from my ascent to that narrow perch,
which looked upon nothing but the distant
bay and shores of Contra Costa, I felt as
apologetic as if I had landed from a balloon;
but the woman greeted me with a languid

Spanish smile and a lazy display of white teeth, as if my arrival was quite natural. Don Enriquez, "of a fact," was not himself in the *casa*, but was expected "on the instant." "Donna Urania" was at home.

"Donna Urania"? For an instant I had forgotten that Mrs. Saltillo's first name was Urania, so pleasantly and spontaneously did it fall from the Spanish lips. Nor was I displeased at this chance of learning something of Don Enriquez's fortunes and the Saltillo ménage before confronting my old friend. The servant preceded me to the next floor, and, opening a door, ushered me into the lady's presence.

I had carried with me, on that upward climb, a lively recollection of Miss Mannersley as I had known her two years before. I remembered her upright, almost stiff, slight figure, the graceful precision of her poses, the faultless symmetry and taste of her dress, and the atmosphere of a fastidious and wholesome cleanliness which exhaled from her. In the lady I saw before me, half reclining in a rocking-chair, there was none of the stiffness and nicety. Habited in a loose gown of some easy, flexible, but rich material, worn with that peculiarly indolent slouch of the Mexican woman, Mrs. Saltillo had parted with half her individuality. Even her arched feet and thin ankles, the close-fitting boots or small slippers of which were wont to accent their delicacy, were now lost in a short, low-quartered kid shoe of the Spanish type, in which they moved loosely. Her hair, which she had always worn with a certain Greek simplicity, was parted at one side. Yet her face, with its regularity of feature, and small, thin, red-lipped mouth, was quite unchanged; and her velvety brown eyes were as beautiful and inscrutable as ever.

With the same glance I had taken in her surroundings, quite as incongruous to her former habits. The furniture, though of old and heavy mahogany, had suffered from careless alien hands, and was interspersed with modern and unmatchable makeshifts, yet preserving the distinctly scant and formal attitude of furnished lodgings. It was certainly unlike the artistic trifles and delicate refinements of her uncle's drawing-room, which we all knew her taste had dictated and ruled. The black and white engravings, the outlined heads of Minerva and Diana, were excluded from the walls for

two cheap colored Catholic prints, — a soulless Virgin, and the mystery of the Bleeding
Heart. Against the wall, in one corner,
hung the only object which seemed a me-
mento of their travels, — a singular-looking
upright Indian "papoose-case" or cradle,
glaringly decorated with beads and paint,
probably an Aztec relic. On a round table,
the velvet cover of which showed marks of
usage and abusage, there were scattered
books and writing materials; and my editorial instinct suddenly recognized, with a
thrill of apprehension, the loose leaves of an
undoubted manuscript. This circumstance,
taken with the fact of Donna Urania's hair
being parted on one side, and the general
negligée of her appearance, was a disturbing
revelation.

My wandering eye apparently struck her,
for after the first greeting she pointed to
the manuscript with a smile.

"Yes; that is *the* manuscript. I suppose
Enriquez told you all about it? He said he
had written."

I was dumfounded. I certainly had not
understood *all* of Enriquez's slang; it was
always so decidedly his own, and peculiar.
Yet I could not recall any allusion to this.

"He told me something of it, but very vaguely," I ventured to say deprecatingly; "but I am afraid that I thought more of seeing my old friend again than of anything else."

"During our stay in Mexico," continued Mrs. Saltillo, with something of her old precision, "I made some researches into Aztec history, a subject always deeply interesting to me, and I thought I would utilize the result by throwing it on paper. Of course it is better fitted for a volume of reference than for a newspaper, but Enriquez thought you might want to use it for your journal."

I knew that Enriquez had no taste for literature, and had even rather depreciated it in the old days, with his usual extravagance; but I managed to say very pleasantly that I was delighted with his suggestion and should be glad to read the manuscript. After all, it was not improbable that Mrs. Saltillo, who was educated and intelligent, should write well, if not popularly. "Then Enriquez does not begrudge you the time that your work takes from him," I added laughingly. "You seem to have occupied your honeymoon practically."

"We quite comprehend our respective duties," said Mrs. Saltillo dryly; "and have from the first. We have our own lives to live, independent of my uncle and Enriquez's father. We have not only accepted the responsibility of our own actions, but we both feel the higher privilege of creating our own conditions without extraneous aid from our relatives."

It struck me that this somewhat exalted statement was decidedly a pose, or a return of Urania Mannersley's old ironical style. I looked quietly into her brown, near-sighted eyes; but, as once before, my glance seemed to slip from their moist surface without penetrating the inner thought beneath. "And what does Enriquez do for *his* part?" I asked smilingly.

I fully expected to hear that the energetic Enriquez was utilizing his peculiar tastes and experiences by horse-breaking, stock-raising, professional bull-fighting, or even horse-racing, but was quite astonished when she answered quietly: —

"Enriquez is giving himself up to geology and practical metallurgy, with a view to scientific, purely scientific, mining."

Enriquez and geology! In that instant

all I could remember of it were his gibes at the "geologian," as he was wont to term Professor Dobbs, a former admirer of Miss Mannersley's. To add to my confusion Mrs. Saltillo at the same moment absolutely voiced my thought.

"You may remember Professor Dobbs," she went on calmly, "one of the most eminent scientists over here, and a very old Boston friend. He has taken Enriquez in hand. His progress is most satisfactory; we have the greatest hopes of him."

"And how soon do you both hope to have some practical results of his study?" I could not help asking a little mischievously; for I somehow resented the plural pronoun in her last sentence.

"Very soon," said Mrs. Saltillo, ignoring everything but the question. "You know Enriquez's sanguine temperament. Perhaps he is already given to evolving theories without a sufficient basis of fact. Still, he has the daring of a discoverer. His ideas of the oölitic formation are not without originality, and Professor Dobbs says that in his conception of the Silurian beach there are gleams that are distinctly precious."

I looked at Mrs. Saltillo, who had reinforced her eyes with her old piquant *pince-nez*, but could detect no irony in them. She was prettily imperturbable, that was all. There was an awkward silence. Then it was broken by a bounding step on the stairs, a wide-open fling of the door, and Enriquez pirouetted into the room: Enriquez, as of old, unchanged from the crown of his smooth, coal-black hair to the tips of his small, narrow Arabian feet; Enriquez, with his thin, curling mustache, his dancing eyes set in his immovable face, just as I had always known him!

He affected to lapse against the door for a minute, as if staggered by a resplendent vision. Then he said : —

"What do I regard? Is it a dream, or have I again got them — thees jimjams? My best friend and my best — I mean my *only* — wife! Embrace me!"

He gave me an enthusiastic embrace and a wink like sheet-lightning, passed quickly to his wife, before whom he dropped on one knee, raised the toe of her slipper to his lips, and then sank on the sofa in simulated collapse, murmuring, "Thees is too mooch of white stone for one day!"

Through all this I saw his wife regarding

him with exactly the same critically amused expression with which she had looked upon him in the days of their strange courtship. She evidently had not tired of his extravagance, and yet I feel as puzzled by her manner as then. She rose and said: "I suppose you have a good deal to say to each other, and I will leave you by yourselves." Turning to her husband, she added, "I have already spoken about the Aztec manuscript."

The word brought Enriquez to his feet again. "Ah! The little old nigger — you have read?" I began to understand. "My wife, my best friend, and the little old nigger, all in one day. Eet is perfect!" Nevertheless, in spite of this ecstatic and overpowering combination, he hurried to take his wife's hand; kissing it, he led her to a door opening into another room, made her a low bow to the ground as she passed out, and then rejoined me.

"So these are the little old niggers you spoke of in your note," I said, pointing to the manuscript. "Deuce take me if I understood you!"

"Ah, my leetle brother, it is *you* who have changed!" said Enriquez dolorously. "Is it that you no more understand Ameri-

can, or have the ' big head ' of the editor?
Regard me! Of these Aztecs my wife have
made study. She have pursued the little
nigger to his cave, his grotto, where he is
dead a thousand year. I have myself assist,
though I like it not, because thees mummy,
look you, Pancho, is not lively. And the
mummy who is not dead, believe me! even
the young lady mummy, you shall not take
to your heart. But my wife " — he stopped,
and kissed his hand toward the door whence
she had flitted — "ah, *she* is wonderful!
She has made the story of them, the peecture
of them, from the life and on the instant!
You shall take them, my leetle brother, for
your journal; you shall announce in the big
letter: ' Mooch Importance. The Aztec,
He is Found.' ' How He Look and Lif.'
' The Everlasting Nigger.' You shall sell
many paper, and Urania shall have scoop in
much spondulics and rocks. Hoop-la! For
— you comprehend? — my wife and I have
settled that she shall forgif her oncle; I
shall forgif my father; but from them we
take no cent, not a red, not a scad! We
are independent! Of ourselves we make a
Fourth of July. United we stand; divided
we shall fall over! There you are! *Bueno!* "

It was impossible to resist his wild, yet perfectly sincere, extravagance, his dancing black eyes and occasional flash of white teeth in his otherwise immovable and serious countenance. Nevertheless, I managed to say : —

"But how about yourself, Enriquez, and this geology, you know?"

His eyes twinkled. "Ah, you shall hear. But first you shall take a drink. I have the very old Bourbon. He is not so old as the Aztec, but, believe me, he is very much liflier. Attend! Hol' on!" He was already rummaging on a shelf, but apparently without success; then he explored a buffet, with no better results, and finally attacked a large drawer, throwing out on the floor, with his old impetuosity, a number of geological specimens, carefully labeled. I picked up one that had rolled near me. It was labeled "Conglomerate sandstone." I picked up another: it had the same label.

"Then you are really collecting?" I said, with astonishment.

" *Ciertamente*," responded Enriquez, — "what other fool shall I look? I shall relate of this geology when I shall have found this beast of a bottle. Ah, here he have

hide!'" He extracted from a drawer a bottle nearly full of spirits, — tippling was not
one of Enriquez's vices. "You shall say
' when.' 'Ere's to our noble selfs!'"

When he had drunk, I picked up another
fragment of his collection. It had the same
label. "You are very rich in ' conglomerate sandstone,'" I said. "Where do you
find it?"

"In the street," said Enriquez, with great
calmness.

"In the street?" I echoed.

"Yes, my friend! He ees call the ' cob-
blestone,' also the ' pouding-stone,' when he
ees at his home in the country. He ees also
a small ' boulder.' I pick him up; I crack
him; he made three separate piece of conglomerate sandstone. I bring him home
to my wife in my pocket. She rejoice; we
are happy. When comes the efening, I sit
down and make him a label; while my wife,
she sit down and write of the Aztec. Ah,
my friend, you shall say of the geology it
ees a fine, a *beautiful* study; but the study
of the wife, and what shall please her, believe me, ees much finer! Believe your old
Uncle 'Ennery every time! On thees question he gets there; he gets left, nevarre!'"

"But Professor Dobbs, your geologian, what does *he* say to this frequent recurrence of the conglomerate sandstone period in your study?" I asked quickly.

"He say nothing. You comprehend? He ees a profound geologian, but he also has the admiration excessif for my wife Urania." He stopped to kiss his hand again toward the door, and lighted a cigarette. "The geologian would not that he should break up the happy efening of his friends by thees small detail. He put aside his head — so; he say, ' A leetle freestone, a leetle granite, now and then, for variety; they are building in Montgomery Street.' I take the hint, like a wink to the horse that has gone blind. I attach to myself part of the edifice that is erecting himself in Montgomery Street. I crack him; I bring him home. I sit again at the feet of my beautiful Urania, and I label him ' Freestone,' ' Granite;' but I do not say ' from Parrott's Bank ' — eet is not necessary for our happiness."

"And you do this sort of thing only because you think it pleases your wife?" I asked bluntly.

"My friend," rejoined Enriquez, perching

himself on the back of the sofa, and caressing his knees as he puffed his cigarette
meditatively, "you have ask a conundrum.
Gif to me an easier one! It is of truth that
I make much of these thing to please Urania.
But I shall confess all. Behold, I appear to
you, my leetle brother, in my *camisa* — my
shirt! I blow on myself; I gif myself away."

He rose gravely from the sofa, and drew
a small box from one of the drawers of the
wardrobe. Opening it, he discovered several specimens of gold-bearing quartz, and
one or two scales of gold. "Thees," he
said, "friend Pancho, is my own geology;
for thees I am what you see. But I say
nothing to Urania; for she have much disgust of mere gold, — of what she calls ' vulgar mining,' — and believe me, a fear of the
effect of ' speculation ' upon my *tempera-
mento* — you comprehend my complexion, my
brother? Reflect upon it, Pancho! *I*, who
am the *filosofo*, if that I am anything!" He
looked at me with great levity of eye and
supernatural gravity of demeanor. "But
eet ees the jealous affection of the wife, my
friend, for which I make play to her with
the humble leetle pouding-stone rather than
the gold quartz that affrights."

"But what do you want with them, if you have no shares in anything and do not speculate?" I asked.

"Pardon! That ees where you slip up, my leetle friend." He took from the same drawer a clasped portfolio, and unlocked it, producing half a dozen prospectuses and certificates of mining shares. I stood aghast as I recognized the names of one or two extravagant failures of the last ten years, — "played-out" mines that had been galvanized into deceptive life in London, Paris, and New York, to the grief of shareholders abroad and the laughter of the initiated at home. I could scarcely keep my equanimity. "You do not mean to say that you have any belief or interest in this rubbish?" I said quickly.

"What you call ' rubbish,' my good Pancho, ees the rubbish that the American speculator have dump himself upon them in the shaft, the rubbish of the advertisement, of the extravagant expense, of the salary, of the assessment, of the ' freeze-out.' For thees, look you, is the old Mexican mine. My grandfather and hees father have both seen them work before you were born, and the American knew not there was gold in California."

I knew he spoke truly. One or two were original silver mines in the south, worked by peons and Indian slaves, a rope windlass, and a venerable donkey.

"But those were silver mines," I said suspiciously, "and these are gold specimens."

"They are from the same mother," said the imperturbable Enriquez, — "the same mine. The old peons worked him for *silver*, the precious dollar that buy everything, that he send in the galleon to the Philippines for the silk and spice! *That* is good enough for *him!* For the gold he made nothing, even as my leetle wife Urania. And regard me here! There ees a proverb of my father's which say that ' it shall take a gold mine to work a silver mine,' so mooch more he cost. You work him, you are lost! *Naturalmente*, if you turn him round, if it take you only a silver mine to work a gold mine, you are gain. Thees ees logic! "

The intense gravity of his face at this extraordinary deduction upset my own. But as I was never certain that Enriquez was not purposely mystifying me, with some ulterior object, I could not help saying a little wickedly: —

"Yes, I understand all that; but how

about this geologian? Will he not tell your wife? You know he was a great admirer of hers."

"That shall show the great intelligence of him, my Pancho. He will have the four 'S's,' especially the *secreto!*"

There could be no serious discussion in his present mood. I gathered up the pages of his wife's manuscript, said lightly that, as she had the first claim upon my time, I should examine the Aztec material and report in a day or two. As I knew I had little chance in the hands of these two incomprehensibles together, I begged him not to call his wife, but to convey my adieus to her, and, in spite of his embraces and protestations, I managed to get out of the room. But I had scarcely reached the front door when I heard Enriquez's voice and his bounding step on the stairs. In another moment his arm was round my neck.

"You must return on the instant! Mother of God! I haf forget, *she* haf forget, *we* all haf forget! But you have not seen him!"

"Seen whom?"

"*El niño*, the baby! You comprehend, pig! The *criaturica*, the leetle child of ourselfs!"

"The baby?" I said confusedly. "*Is* there — is there a *baby?*"

"You hear him?" said Enriquez, sending an appealing voice upward. "You hear him, Urania? You comprehend. This beast of a leetle brother demands if there ees one!"

"I beg your pardon," I said, hurriedly reascending the stairs. On the landing I met Mrs. Saltillo, but as calm, composed, and precise as her husband was extravagant and vehement. "It was an oversight of Enriquez's," she said quietly, reëntering the room with us; "and was all the more strange, as the child was in the room with you all the time."

She pointed to the corner of the wall, where hung what I had believed to be an old Indian relic. To my consternation, it *was* a bark "papoose-case," occupied by a *living* child, swathed and bandaged after the approved Indian fashion. It was asleep, I believe, but it opened a pair of bright huckleberry eyes, set in the smallest of features, that were like those of a carved ivory idol, and uttered a "coo" at the sound of its mother's voice. She stood on one side with unruffled composure, while Enriquez threw himself into an attitude before it, with clasped hands, as if it had been an image of the Holy Child. For myself, I was too astounded to speak; luckily, my confusion was attributed to the inexperience of a bachelor.

"I have adopted," said Mrs. Saltillo, with the faintest touch of maternal pride in her manner, "what I am convinced is the only natural and hygienic mode of treating the human child. It may be said to be a reversion to the aborigine, but I have yet to learn that it is not superior to our civilized custom. By these bandages the limbs of the infant are kept in proper position until they are strong enough to support the body, and such a thing as malformation is unknown. It is protected by its cradle, which takes the place of its incubating-shell, from external injury, the injudicious coddling of nurses, the so-called ' dancings ' and pernicious rockings. The supine position, as in the adult, is imposed only at night. By the aid of this strap it may be carried on long journeys, either by myself or by Enriquez, who thus shares with me, as he fully recognizes, its equal responsibility and burden."

"It — certainly does not — cry," I stammered.

"Crying," said Mrs. Saltillo, with a curve of her pretty red lip, "is the protest of the child against insanitary and artificial treatment. In its upright, unostentatious cradle it is protected against that injudicious fondling and dangerous promiscuous osculation to which, as an infant in human arms, it is so often subjected. Above all, it is kept from that shameless and mortifying publicity so unjust to the weak and unformed animal. The child repays this consideration by a gratifying silence. It cannot be expected to understand our thoughts, speech, or actions; it cannot participate in our pleasures. Why should it be forced into premature contact with them, merely to feed our vanity or selfishness? Why should we assume our particular parental accident as superior to the common lot? If we do not give our offspring that prominence before our visitors so common to the young wife and husband, it is for that reason solely; and this may account for what seemed the forgetfulness of Enriquez in speaking of it or pointing it out to you. And I think his action in calling you back to see it was somewhat precipitate. As one does not usually introduce an unknown and inferior stranger without some previous introduction, he might have asked you if you wished to see the baby before he recalled you."

I looked from Urania's unfathomable eyes to Enriquez's impenetrable countenance. I might have been equal to either of them alone, but together they were invincible. I looked hopelessly at the baby. With its sharp little eyes and composed face, it certainly was a marvelous miniature of Enriquez. I said so.

"It would be singular if it was not," said Mrs. Saltillo dryly; "and as I believe it is by no means an uncommon fact in human nature, it seems to me strange that people should insist upon it as a discovery. It is an inheritance, however, that in due time progress and science will no doubt interrupt, to the advancement of the human race. I need not say that both Enriquez and myself look forward to it with confident tranquillity."

There was clearly nothing for me to do now but to shake hands again and take my leave. Yet I was so much impressed with the unreality of the whole scene that when I reached the front door I had a strong impulse to return suddenly and fall in upon

them in their relaxed and natural attitudes.
They could not keep up this pose between
themselves; and I half expected to see their
laughing faces at the window, as I glanced
up before wending my perilous way to the
street.

I found Mrs. Saltillo's manuscript well
written and, in the narrative parts, even
graphic and sparkling. I suppressed some
general remarks on the universe, and some
correlative theories of existence, as not ap-
pertaining particularly to the Aztecs, and as
not meeting any unquenchable thirst for information on the part of the readers of the
"Daily Excelsior." I even promoted my
fair contributor to the position of having
been commissioned, at great expense, to
make the Mexican journey especially for the
"Excelsior." This, with Mrs. Saltillo's
somewhat precise preraphaelite drawings and
water-colors, vilely reproduced by woodcuts,
gave quite a sensational air to her production, which, divided into parts, for two or
three days filled a whole page of the paper.
I am not aware of any particular service that
it did to ethnology; but, as I pointed out
in the editorial column, it showed that the
people of California were not given over by

material greed to the exclusion of intellectual research; and as it was attacked instantly in long communications from one or two scientific men, it thus produced more copy.

Briefly, it was a boom for the author and the "Daily Excelsior." I should add, however, that a rival newspaper intimated that it was also a boom for Mrs. Saltillo's *husband*, and called attention to the fact that a deserted Mexican mine, known as "El Bolero," was described graphically in the Aztec article among the news, and again appeared in the advertising columns of the same paper. I turned somewhat indignantly to the file of the "Excelsior," and, singularly enough, found in the elaborate prospectus of a new gold-mining company the description of the El Bolero mine as a *quotation* from the Aztec article, with extraordinary inducements for the investment of capital in the projected working of an old mine. If I had had any difficulty in recognizing in the extravagant style the flamboyant hand of Enriquez in English writing, I might have read his name plainly enough displayed as president of the company. It was evidently the prospectus of one of the ventures he had shown me. I was more amused than indignant at the little trick he had played upon my editorial astuteness. After all, if I had thus bene-fited the young couple I was satisfied. I had not seen them since my first visit, as I was very busy, — my communications with Mrs. Saltillo had been carried on by letters and proofs, — and when I did finally call at their house, it was only to find that they were visiting at San José. I wondered whether the baby was still hanging on the wall, or, if he was taken with them, who carried him.

A week later the stock of El Bolero was quoted at par. More than that, an incom-prehensible activity had been given to all the deserted Mexican mines, and people be-gan to look up scrip hitherto thrown aside as worthless. Whether it was one of those extraordinary fevers which attacked Califor-nian speculation in the early days, or whether Enriquez Saltillo had infected the stock-market with his own extravagance, I never knew; but plans as wild, inventions as fan-tastic, and arguments as illogical as ever emanated from his own brain, were set forth "on 'Change" with a gravity equal to his own. The most reasonable hypothesis was

that it was the effect of the well-known fact
that the Spanish Californian hitherto had
not been a mining speculator, nor connected
in any way with the gold production on his
native soil, deeming it inconsistent with his
patriarchal life and landed dignity, and that
when a "son of one of the oldest Spanish
families, identified with the land and its peculiar character for centuries, lent himself
to its mineral exploitations," — I beg to say
that I am quoting from the advertisement
in the "Excelsior," — "it was a guerdon of
success." This was so far true that in a
week Enriquez Saltillo was rich, and in a
fair way to become a millionaire.

It was a hot afternoon when I alighted
from the stifling Wingdam coach, and stood
upon the cool, deep veranda of the Carquinez Springs Hotel. After I had shaken
off the dust which had lazily followed us, in
our descent of the mountain road, like a red
smoke, occasionally overflowing the coach
windows, I went up to the room I had engaged for my brief holiday. I knew the
place well, although I could see that the
hotel itself had lately been redecorated and
enlarged to meet the increasing requirements

of fashion. I knew the forest of enormous redwoods where one might lose one's self in a five minutes' walk from the veranda. I knew the rocky trail that climbed the mountain to the springs, twisting between giant boulders. I knew the arid garden, deep in the wayside dust, with its hurriedly planted tropical plants, already withering in the dry autumn sunshine, and washed into fictitious freshness, night and morning by the hydraulic irrigating-hose. I knew, too, the cool, reposeful night winds that swept down from invisible snow-crests beyond, with the hanging out of monstrous stars, that too often failed to bring repose to the feverish guests. For the overstrained neurotic workers who fled hither from the baking plains of Sacramento, or from the chill sea-fogs of San Francisco, never lost the fierce unrest that had driven them here. Unaccustomed to leisure, their enforced idleness impelled them to seek excitement in the wildest gayeties; the bracing mountain air only reinvigorated them to pursue pleasure as they had pursued the occupations they had left behind. Their sole recreations were furious drives over break-neck roads; mad, scampering cavalcades through the sedate woods;

gambling parties in private rooms, where large sums were lost by capitalists on leave; champagne suppers; and impromptu balls that lasted through the calm, reposeful night to the first rays of light on the distant snow-line.   Unimaginative men, in their temporary sojourn they more often outraged or dispossessed nature in her own fastnesses than courted her for sympathy or solitude. There were playing-cards left lying behind boulders, and empty champagne bottles forgotten in forest depths.

I remembered all this when, refreshed by a bath, I leaned from the balcony of my room and watched the pulling up of a brake, drawn by six dusty, foam-bespattered horses, driven by a noted capitalist.   As its hot, perspiring, closely veiled yet burning-faced fair occupants descended, in all the dazzling glory of summer toilets, and I saw the gentlemen consult their watches with satisfaction, and congratulate their triumphant driver, I knew the characteristic excitement they had enjoyed from a "record run," probably for a bet, over a mountain road in a burning sun.

"Not bad, eh?   Forty-four minutes from the summit!"

The voice seemed at my elbow. I turned quickly, to recognize an acquaintance, a young San Francisco broker, leaning from the next balcony to mine. But my attention was just then preoccupied by the face and figure, which seemed familiar to me, of a woman who was alighting from the brake.

"Who is that?" I asked; "the straight slim woman in gray, with the white veil twisted round her felt hat?"

"Mrs. Saltillo," he answered; "wife of 'El Bolero' Saltillo, don't you know. Mighty pretty woman, if she is a little stiffish and set up."

Then I had not been mistaken! "Is Enriquez — is her husband — here?" I asked quickly.

The man laughed. "I reckon not. This is the place for other people's husbands, don't you know."

Alas! I *did* know; and as there flashed upon me all the miserable scandals and gossip connected with this reckless, frivolous caravansary, I felt like resenting his suggestion. But my companion's next words were more significant: —

"Besides, if what they say is true, Saltillo wouldn't be very popular here."

"I don't understand," I said quickly.

"Why, after all that row he had with the El Bolero Company."

"I never heard of any row," I said, in astonishment.

The broker laughed incredulously. "Come! and *you* a newspaper man! Well, maybe they *did* try to hush it up, and keep it out of the papers, on account of the stock. But it seems he got up a reg'lar shindy with the board, one day; called 'em thieves and swindlers, and allowed he was disgracing himself as a Spanish hidalgo by having anything to do with 'em. Talked, they say, about Charles V. of Spain, or some other royal galoot, giving his ancestors the land in trust! Clean off his head, I reckon. Then shunted himself off the company, and sold out. You can guess he wouldn't be very popular around here, with Jim Bestley, there," pointing to the capitalist who had driven the brake, "who used to be on the board with him. No, sir. He was either lying low for something, or was off his head. Think of his throwing up a place like that!"

"Nonsense!" I said indignantly. "He is mercurial, and has the quick impulsiveness of his race, but I believe him as sane

**as** any who sat with him on the board. There must be some mistake, or you have n't got the whole story." Nevertheless, I did not care to discuss an old friend with a mere acquaintance, and I felt secretly puzzled to account for his conduct, in the face of his previous cleverness in manipulating the El Bolero, and the undoubted fascination he had previously exercised over the stock-holders. The story had, of course, been garbled in repetition. I had never before imagined what might be the effect of Enriquez's peculiar eccentricities upon matter-of-fact people, — I had found them only amusing, — and the broker's suggestion annoyed me. However, Mrs. Saltillo was here in the hotel, and I should, of course, meet her. Would she be as frank with me?

I was disappointed at not finding her in the drawing-room or on the veranda; and the heat being still unusually oppressive, **I** strolled out toward the redwoods, hesitating for a moment in the shade before I ran the fiery gauntlet of the garden. To my surprise, I had scarcely passed the giant sentinels on its outskirts before I found that, from some unusual condition of the atmosphere, the cold undercurrent of air which generally drew through these pillared aisles was withheld that afternoon; it was absolutely hotter than in the open, and the wood was charged throughout with the acrid spices of the pine. I turned back to the hotel, reascended to my bedroom, and threw myself in an armchair by the open window. My room was near the end of a wing; the corner room at the end was next to mine, on the same landing. Its closed door, at right angles to my open one, gave upon the staircase, but was plainly visible from where I sat. I remembered being glad that it was shut, as it enabled me without offense to keep my own door open.

The house was very quiet. The leaves of a catalpa, across the roadway, hung motionless. Somebody yawned on the veranda below. I threw away my half-finished cigar, and closed my eyes. I think I had not lost consciousness for more than a few seconds before I was awakened by the shaking and thrilling of the whole building. As I staggered to my feet, I saw the four pictures hanging against the wall swing outwardly from it on their cords, and my door swing back against the wall. At the same moment, acted upon by the same potential impulse, the door of the end room in the hall, opposite the stairs, also swung open. In that brief moment I had a glimpse of the interior of the room, of two figures, a man and a woman, the latter clinging to her companion in abject terror. It was only for an instant, for a second thrill passed through the house, the pictures clattered back against the wall, the door of the end room closed violently on its strange revelation, and my own door swung back also. Apprehensive of what might happen, I sprang toward it, but only to arrest it an inch or two before it should shut, when, as my experience had taught me, it might stick by the subsidence of the walls. But it did stick ajar, and remained firmly fixed in that position. From the clattering of the knob of the other door, and the sound of hurried voices behind it, I knew that the same thing had happened there when that door had fully closed.

I was familiar enough with earthquakes to know that, with the second shock or subsidence of the earth, the immediate danger was passed, and so I was able to note more clearly what else was passing. There was the usual sudden stampede of hurrying feet, the solitary oath and scream, the half-hyster-

ical laughter, and silence. Then the tumult
was reawakened to the sound of high voices,
talking all together, or the impatient calling
of absentees in halls and corridors. Then I
heard the quick swish of female skirts on
the staircase, and one of the fair guests
knocked impatiently at the door of the end
room, still immovably fixed. At the first
knock there was a sudden cessation of the
hurried whisperings and turning of the door-
knob.

"Mrs. Saltillo, are you there? Are you
frightened?" she called.

"Mrs. Saltillo"! It was *she*, then, who
was in the room! I drew nearer my door,
which was still fixed ajar. Presently a voice,
— Mrs. Saltillo's voice,— with a constrained
laugh in it, came from behind the door:
"Not a bit. I'll come down in a minute."

"Do," persisted the would-be intruder.
"It's all over now, but we're all going out
into the garden; it's safer."

"All right," answered Mrs. Saltillo.
"Don't wait, dear. I'll follow. Run
away, now."

The visitor, who was evidently still nervous, was glad to hurry away, and I heard
her retreating step on the staircase. The

rattling of the door began again, and at last
it seemed to yield to a stronger pull, and
opened sufficiently to allow Mrs. Saltillo to
squeeze through. I withdrew behind my
door. I fancied that it creaked as she
passed, as if, noticing it ajar, she had laid
an inquiring hand upon it. I waited, but
she was not followed by any one. I wondered if I had been mistaken. I was going
to the bell-rope to summon assistance to
move my own door when a sudden instinct
withheld me. If there was any one still in
that room, he might come from it just as
the servant answered my call, and a public discovery would be unavoidable. I was
right. In another instant the figure of a
man, whose face I could not discern, slipped
out of the room, passed my door, and went
stealthily down the staircase.

Convinced of this, I resolved not to call
public attention to my being in my own
room at the time of the incident; so I did
not summon any one, but, redoubling my
efforts, I at last opened the door sufficiently
to pass out, and at once joined the other
guests in the garden. Already, with characteristic recklessness and audacity, the
earthquake was made light of; the only dic-

tate of prudence had resolved itself into a hilarious proposal to "camp out" in the woods all night, and have a "torch-light picnic." Even then preparations were being made for carrying tents, blankets, and pillows to the adjacent redwoods; dinner and supper, cooked at campfires, were to be served there on stumps of trees and fallen logs. The convulsion of nature had been used as an excuse for one of the wildest freaks of extravagance that Carquinez Springs had ever known. Perhaps that quick sense of humor which dominates the American male in exigencies of this kind kept the extravagances from being merely bizarre and grotesque, and it was presently known that the hotel and its ménage were to be appropriately burlesqued by some of the guests, who, attired as Indians, would personate the staff, from the oracular hotel proprietor himself down to the smart hotel clerk.

During these arrangements I had a chance of drawing near Mrs. Saltillo. I fancied she gave a slight start as she recognized me; but her greetings were given with her usual precision. "Have you been here long?" she asked.

"I have only just come," I replied laughingly; "in time for the shock."

"Ah, you felt it, then? I was telling these ladies that our eminent geologist, Professor Dobbs, assured me that these seismic disturbances in California have a very remote centre, and are seldom serious."

"It must be very satisfactory to have the support of geology at such a moment," I could not help saying, though I had not the slightest idea whose the figure was that I had seen, nor, indeed, had I recognized it among the guests. She did not seem to detect any significance in my speech, and I added: "And where is Enriquez? He would enjoy this proposed picnic to-night."

"Enriquez is at Salvatierra Rancho, which he lately bought from his cousin."

"And the baby? Surely, here is a chance for you to hang him up on a redwood to-night, in his cradle."

"The boy," said Mrs. Saltillo quickly, "is no longer in his cradle; he has passed the pupa state, and is now free to develop his own perfected limbs. He is with his father. I do not approve of children being submitted to the indiscriminate attentions of a hotel. I am here myself only for that supply of ozone indicated for brain exhaustion."

She looked so pretty and prim in her gray dress, so like her old correct self, that I could not think of anything but her mental attitude, which did not, by the way, seem much like mental depressio. Yet I was aware that I was getting no information of Enriquez's condition or affairs, unless the whole story told by the broker was an exaggeration. I did not, however, dare to ask more particularly.

"You remember Professor Dobbs?" she asked abruptly.

This recalled a suspicion awakened by my vision, so suddenly that I felt myself blushing. She did not seem to notice it, and was perfectly composed.

"I do remember him. Is he here?"

"He is; that is what makes it so particularly unfortunate for me. You see, after that affair of the board, and Enriquez's withdrawal, although Enriquez may have been a little precipitate in his energetic way, I naturally took my husband's part in public; for although we preserve our own independence inviolable, we believe in absolute confederation as against society."

"But what has Professor Dobbs to do with the board?" I interrupted.

"The professor was scientific and geological adviser to the board, and it was upon some report or suggestion of his that Enriquez took issue, against the sentiment of the board. It was a principle affecting Enriquez's Spanish sense of honor."

"Do tell me all about it," I said eagerly; "I am very anxious to know the truth."

"As I was not present at the time," said Mrs. Saltillo, rebuking my eagerness with a gentle frigidity, "I am unable to do so. Anything else would be mere hearsay, and more or less *ex parte*. I do not approve of gossip."

"But what did Enriquez tell you? You surely know that."

"*That*, being purely confidential, as between husband and wife, — perhaps I should say partner and partner, — of course you do not expect me to disclose. Enough that *I* was satisfied with it. I should not have spoken to you about it at all, but that, through myself and Enriquez, you are an acquaintance of the professor's, and I might save you the awkwardness of presenting yourself with him. Otherwise, although you are a friend of Enriquez, it need not affect your acquaintance with the professor."

"Hang the professor!" I ejaculated. "I don't care a rap for *him*."

"Then I differ with you," said Mrs. Saltillo, with precision. "He is distinctly an able man, and one cannot but miss the contact of his original mind and his liberal teachings."

Here she was joined by one of the ladies, and I lounged away. I dare say it was very mean and very illogical, but the unsatisfactory character of this interview made me revert again to the singular revelation I had seen a few hours before. I looked anxiously for Professor Dobbs; but when I did meet him, with an indifferent nod of recognition, I found I could by no means identify him with the figure of her mysterious companion. And why should I suspect him at all, in the face of Mrs. Saltillo's confessed avoidance of him? Who, then, could it have been? I had seen them but an instant, in the opening and the shutting of a door. It was merely the shadowy bulk of a man that flitted past my door, after all. Could I have imagined the whole thing? Were my perceptive faculties — just aroused from slumber, too

— sufficiently clear to be relied upon? Would I not have laughed had Urania, or even Enriquez himself, told me such a story?

As I reëntered the hotel the clerk handed me a telegram. "There's been a pretty big shake all over the country," he said eagerly. "Everybody is getting news and inquiries from their friends. Anything fresh?" He paused interrogatively as I tore open the envelope. The dispatch had been redirected from the office of the "Daily Excelsior." It was dated, "Salvatierra Rancho," and contained a single line: "Come and see your old uncle 'Ennery."

There was nothing in the wording of the message that was unlike Enriquez's usual light-hearted levity, but the fact that he should have *telegraphed* it to me struck me uneasily. That I should have received it at the hotel where his wife and Professor Dobbs were both staying, and where I had had such a singular experience, seemed to me more than a mere coincidence. An instinct that the message was something personal to Enriquez and myself kept me from imparting it to Mrs. Saltillo. After worrying half the night in our bizarre camp in

the redwoods, in the midst of a restless festivity which was scarcely the repose I had
been seeking at Carquinez Springs, I resolved to leave the next day for Salvatierra
Rancho. I remembered the rancho, — a
low, golden-brown, adobe-walled quadrangle,
sleeping like some monstrous ruminant in
a hollow of the Contra Costa Range. I recalled, in the midst of this noisy picnic, the
slumberous coolness of its long corridors and
soundless courtyard, and hailed it as a relief. The telegram was a sufficient excuse
for my abrupt departure. In the morning
I left, but without again seeing either Mrs.
Saltillo or the professor.

It was late the next afternoon when I rode
through the *cañada* that led to the rancho.
I confess my thoughts were somewhat
gloomy, in spite of my escape from the noisy
hotel; but this was due to the sombre scenery through which I had just ridden, and
the monotonous russet of the leagues of wild
oats. As I approached the rancho, I saw
that Enriquez had made no attempt to mod-
ernize the old *casa*, and that even the garden was left in its lawless native luxuriance,
while the rude tiled sheds near the walled
corral contained the old farming implements,

unchanged for a century, even to the ox-carts, the wheels of which were made of a single block of wood. A few peons, in striped shirts and velvet jackets, were sunning themselves against a wall, and near them hung a half-drained *pellejo*, or goat-skin water-bag. The air of absolute shift-lessness must have been repellent to Mrs. Saltillo's orderly precision, and for a moment I pitied her. But it was equally in-consistent with Enriquez's enthusiastic ideas of American progress, and the extravagant designs he had often imparted to me of the improvements he would make when he had a fortune. I was feeling uneasy again, when I suddenly heard the rapid clack of unshod hoofs on a rocky trail that joined my own. At the same instant a horseman dashed past me at full speed. I had barely time to swerve my own horse aside to avoid a colli-sion, yet in that brief moment I recognized the figure of Enriquez. But his face I should have scarcely known. It was hard and fixed. His upper lip and thin, pen-ciled mustache were drawn up over his teeth, which were like a white gash in his dark face. He turned into the courtyard of the rancho. I put spurs to my horse,

J

and followed, in nervous expectation. He
turned in his saddle as I entered. But the
next moment he bounded from his horse,
and, before I could dismount, flew to my
side and absolutely lifted me from the saddle to embrace me. It was the old Enriquez again; his face seemed to have utterly
changed in that brief moment.

"This is all very well, old chap," I said;
"but do you know that you nearly ran me
down, just now, with that infernal half-
broken mustang? Do you usually charge
the *casa* at that speed?"

"Pardon, my leetle brother! But here
you shall slip up. The mustang is not *half-*
broken; he is not broke at all! Look at his
hoof — never have a shoe been there. For
myself — attend me! When I rride alone,
I think mooch; when I think mooch I think
fast; my idea he go like a cannon-ball!
Consequent, if I ride not thees horse like
the cannon-ball, my thought *he* arrive first,
and where are you? You get left! Believe
me that I fly thees horse, thees old Mexican
plug, and your de' uncle 'Ennery and his
leetle old idea arrive all the same time, and
on the instant."

It *was* the old Enriquez! I perfectly un-

derstood his extravagant speech and illustra-
tion, and yet for the first time I wondered
if others did.

"Tak'-a-drink!" he said, all in one word.
"You shall possess the old Bourbon or the
rhum from the Santa Cruz! Name your
poison, gentlemen!"

He had already dragged me up the steps
from the *patio* to the veranda, and seated
me before a small round table still covered
with the chocolate equipage of the morning.
A little dried-up old Indian woman took it
away, and brought the spirits and glasses.

"*Mirar* the leetle old one!" said Enriquez, with unflinching gravity. "Consider
her, Pancho, to the bloosh! She is not
truly an Aztec, but she is of years one hundred and one, and *lifs!* Possibly she haf
not the beauty which ravishes, which devas-
tates. But she shall attent you to the hot
water, to the bath. Thus shall you be protect, my leetle brother, from scandal."

"Enriquez," I burst out suddenly, "tell
me about yourself. Why did you leave the
El Bolero board? What was the row
about?"

Enriquez's eyes for a moment glittered;
then they danced as before.

"Ah," he said, "you have heard?"

"Something; but I want to know the truth from you."

He lighted a cigarette, lifted himself backward into a grass hammock, on which he sat, swinging his feet. Then, pointing to another hammock, he said: "Tranquillize yourself there. I will relate; but, truly, it ees nothing."

He took a long pull at his cigarette, and for a few moments seemed quietly to exude smoke from his eyes, ears, nose, even his finger-ends — everywhere, in fact, but his mouth. That and his mustache remained fixed. Then he said slowly, flicking away the ashes with his little finger: —

"First you understand, friend Pancho, that *I* make no row. The other themself make the row, the shindig. They make the dance, the howl, the snap of the finger, the oath, the 'Helen blazes,' the 'Wot the devil,' the 'That be d—d,' the bad language; they themselves finger the revolver, advance the bowie-knife, throw off the coat, square off, and say 'Come on.' I remain as you see me now, little brother — tranquil." He lighted another cigarette, made his position more comfortable in the ham-

mock, and resumed: "The Professor Dobbs,
who is the geologian of the company, made
a report for which he got two thousand
dollar. But thees report — look you, friend
Pancho — he is not good for the mine. For
in the hole in the ground the Professor
Dobbs have found a ' hoss.' "

"A what?" I asked.

"A hoss," repeated Enriquez, with infinite gravity. "But not, leetle Pancho, the
hoss that run, the hoss that buck-jump, but
what the miner call a ' hoss,' a something
that rear up in the vein and stop him. You
pick around the hoss; you pick under him;
sometimes you find the vein, sometimes you
do not. The hoss rear up, and remain!
Eet ees not good for the mine. The board
say, ' D—— the hoss!' ' Get rid of the
hoss.' ' Chuck out the hoss.' Then they
talk together, and one say to the Professor
Dobbs: ' Eef you cannot thees hoss remove
from the mine, you can take him out of the
report.' He look to me, thees professor.
I see nothing; I remain tranquil. Then the
board say: ' Thees report with the hoss in
him is worth two thousand dollar, but *without* the hoss he is worth five thousand dollar. For the stockholder is frighted of the

rearing hoss. It is of a necessity that the stockholder should remain tranquil. Without the hoss the report is good; the stock shall errise; the director shall sell out, and leave the stockholder the hoss to play with.' The professor he say, ' Al-right;' he scratch out the hoss, sign his name, and get a check for three thousand dollar."

"Then I errise — so!" He got up from the hammock, suiting the action to the word, and during the rest of his narrative, I honestly believe, assumed the same attitude and deliberate intonation he had exhibited at the board. I could even fancy I saw the reckless, cynical faces of his brother directors turned upon his grim, impassive features. "I am tranquil· I smoke my cigarette. I say that for three hundred year my family have held the land of thees mine; that it pass from father to son, and from son to son; it pass by gift, it pass by grant, but that *nevarre there pass a lie with it!* I say it was a gift by a Spanish Christian king to a Christian hidalgo for the spread of the gospel, and not for the cheat and the swindle! I say that this mine was worked by the slave, and by the mule, by the ass, but never by the cheat and swindler. I say that if they have struck the hoss in the mine, they have struck a hoss *in the land*, a Spanish hoss; a hoss that have no bridle worth five thousand dollar in his mouth, but a hoss to rear, and a hoss that cannot be struck out by a Yankee geologian; and that hoss is Enriquez Saltillo!'"

He paused, and laid aside his cigarette. "Then they say, ' Dry up,' and ' Sell out;' and the great bankers say, ' Name your own price for your stock, and resign.' And I say, ' There is not enough gold in your bank, in your San Francisco, in the mines of California, that shall buy a Spanish gentleman. When I leave, I leave the stock at my back; I shall take it, nevarre!' Then the banker he say, ' And you will go and blab, I suppose?' And then, Pancho, I smile, I pick up my mustache — so! and I say: ' Pardon, señor, you haf mistake. The Saltillo haf for three hundred year no stain, no blot upon him. Eet is not now — the last of the race — who shall confess that he haf sit at a board of disgrace and dishonor!' And then it is that the band begin to play, and the animals stand on their hind leg and waltz, and behold, the row he haf begin!'"

I ran over to him, and fairly hugged him. But he put me aside with a gentle and philosophical calm. "Ah, eet is nothing, Pancho. It is, believe me, all the same a hundred years to come, and where are you, then? The earth he turn round, and then come *el temblor*, the earthquake, and there you are! Bah! eet is not of the board that I have asked you to come; it is something else I would tell you. Go and wash yourself of thees journey, my leetle brother, as I have " — looking at his narrow, brown, well-bred hands — "wash myself of the board. Be very careful of the leetle old woman, Pancho; do not wink to her of the eye! Consider, my leetle brother, for one hundred and one year she haf been as a nun, a saint! Disturb not her tranquillity."

Yes, it was the old Enriquez; but he seemed graver, — if I could use that word of one of such persistent gravity; only his gravity heretofore had suggested a certain irony rather than a melancholy which I now fancied I detected. And what was this "something else" he was to "tell me later"? Did it refer to Mrs. Saltillo? I had purposely waited for him to speak of her, before I should say anything of my visit to

Carquinez Springs. I hurried through my
ablutions in the hot water, brought in a
bronze jar on the head of the centenarian
handmaid; and even while I was smiling
over Enriquez's caution regarding this aged
Ruth, I felt I was getting nervous to hear
his news.

I found him in his sitting-room, or study,
— a long, low apartment with small, deep
windows like embrasures in the outer adobe
wall, but glazed in lightly upon the veranda.
He was sitting quite abstractedly, with a
pen in his hand, before a table, on which
a number of sealed envelopes were lying.
He looked *so* formal and methodical for
Enriquez.

"You like the old *casa*, Pancho?" he
said in reply to my praise of its studious
and monastic gloom. "Well, my leetle brother, some day that is fair — who knows? —
it may be at your *disposicion;* not of our
politeness, but of a truth, friend Pancho.
For, if I leave it to my wife " — it was the
first time he had spoken of her — "for my
leetle child," he added quickly, "I shall
put in a bond, an *obligacion*, that my friend
Pancho shall come and go as he will."

"The Saltillos are a long-lived race," I

laughed. "I shall be a gray-haired man, with a house and family of my own by that time." But I did not like the way he had spoken.

"*Quien sabe?*" he only said, dismissing the question with the national gesture. After a moment he added: "I shall tell you something that is strrange, so strrange that you shall say, like the banker say, 'Thees Enriquez, he ees off his head; he ees a crank, a *lunatico;*' but it ees a *fact;* believe me, I have said!"

He rose, and, going to the end of the room, opened a door. It showed a pretty little room, femininely arranged in Mrs. Saltillo's refined taste. "Eet is pretty; eet is the room of my wife. *Bueno!* attend me now." He closed the door, and walked back to the table. "I have sit here and write when the earthquake arrive. I have feel the shock, the grind of the walls on themselves, the tremor, the stagger, and — that — door — he swing open!"

"The door?" I said, with a smile that I felt was ghastly.

"Comprehend me," he said quickly; "it ees not *that* which ees strrange. The wall lift, the lock slip, the door he fell open; it is frequent; it comes so ever when the earth-quake come. But eet is not my wife's room I see; it is *another room*, a room I know not. My wife Urania, she stand there, of a fear, of a tremble; she grasp, she cling to some one. The earth shake again; the door shut. I jump from my table; I shake and tumble to the door. I fling him open. *Maravilloso!* it is the room of my wife again. She is *not* there; it is empty; it is nothing!"

I felt myself turning hot and cold by turns. I was horrified, and — and I blundered. "And who was the other figure?" I gasped.

"Who?" repeated Enriquez, with a pause, a fixed look at me, and a sublime gesture. "Who *should* it be, but myself, Enriquez Saltillo?"

A terrible premonition that this was a chivalrous *lie*, that it was *not* himself he had seen, but that our two visions were identical, came upon me. "After all," I said, with a fixed smile, "if you could imagine you saw your wife, you could easily imagine you saw yourself too. In the shock of the moment you thought of *her* naturally, for then she would as naturally seek your protection. You have written for news of her?"

"No," said Enriquez quietly.

"No?" I repeated amazedly.

"You understand, Pancho! Eef it was the trick of my eyes, why should I affright her for the thing that is not? If it is the truth, and it arrive to *me*, as a warning, why shall I affright her before it come?"

"Before *what* comes? What is it a warning of?" I asked impetuously.

"That we shall be separated! That *I* go, and she do not."

To my surprise, his dancing eyes had a slight film over them. "I don't understand you," I said awkwardly.

"Your head is not of a level, my Pancho. Thees earthquake he remain for only ten seconds, and he fling open the door. If he remain for twenty seconds, he fling open the wall, the hoose toomble, and your friend Enriquez is feenish."

"Nonsense!" I said. "Professor — I mean the geologists — say that the centre of disturbance of these Californian earthquakes is some far-away point in the Pacific and there never will be any serious convulsions here."

"Ah, the geologist," said Enriquez gravely, "understand the hoss that rear in the mine, and the five thousand dollar, believe me, no more. He haf lif here three year. My family haf lif here three hundred. My grandfather saw the earth swallow the church of San Juan Baptista."

I laughed, until, looking up, I was shocked to see for the first time that his dancing eyes were moist and shining. But almost instantly he jumped up, and declared that I had not seen the garden and the corral, and, linking his arm in mine, swept me like a whirlwind into the *patio*. For an hour or two he was in his old invincible spirits. I was glad I had said nothing of my visit to Carquinez Springs and of seeing his wife; I determined to avoid it as long as possible; and as he did not again refer to her, except in the past, it was not difficult. At last he infected me with his extravagance, and for a while I forgot even the strangeness of his conduct and his confidences. We walked and talked together as of old. I understood and enjoyed him perfectly, and it was not strange that in the end I began to believe that this strange revelation was a bit of his extravagant acting,

got up to amuse me. The coincidence of
his story with my own experience was not,
after all, such a wonderful thing, considering what must have been the nervous and
mental disturbance produced by the earthquake. We dined together, attended only
by Pedro, an old half-caste body-servant.
It was easy to see that the household was
carried on economically, and, from a word
or two casually dropped by Enriquez, it
appeared that the rancho and a small sum
of money were all that he retained from his
former fortune when he left the El Bolero.
The stock he kept intact, refusing to take
the dividend upon it until that collapse of
the company should occur which he confidently predicted, when he would make good
the swindled stockholders. I had no reason
to doubt his perfect faith in this.

The next morning we were up early for a
breezy gallop over the three square miles
of Enriquez's estate. I was astounded,
when I descended to the *patio*, to find Enriquez already mounted, and carrying before
him, astride of the horn of his saddle, a
small child, — the identical papoose of my
memorable first visit. But the boy was no
longer swathed and bandaged, although, for

security, his plump little body was engirt by the same sash that encircled his father's own waist. I felt a stirring of self-reproach; I had forgotten all about him! To my suggestion that the exercise might be fatiguing to him, Enriquez shrugged his shoulders: —

"Believe me, no! He is ever with me when I go on the *pasear*. He is not too yonge. For he shall learn 'to rride, to shoot, and to speak the truth,' even as the Persian chile. Eet ees all I can gif to him."

Nevertheless, I think the boy enjoyed it, and I knew he was safe with such an accomplished horseman as his father. Indeed, it was a fine sight to see them both careering over the broad plain, Enriquez with jingling spurs and whirling *riata*, and the boy, with a face as composed as his father's, and his tiny hand grasping the end of the flapping rein with a touch scarcely lighter than the skillful rider's own. It was a lovely morning; though warm and still, there was a faint haze — a rare thing in that climate — on the distant range. The sun-baked soil, arid and thirsty from the long summer drought, and cracked into long fissures, broke into puffs of dust, with a slight deto-

nation like a pistol-shot, at each stroke of
our pounding hoofs.  Suddenly my horse
swerved in full gallop, almost lost his footing, "broke," and halted with braced fore
feet, trembling in every limb.  I heard a
shout from Enriquez at the same instant,
and saw that he too had halted about a hundred paces from me, with his hand uplifted
in warning, and between us a long chasm in
the dry earth, extending across the whole
field.  But the trembling of the horse continued until it communicated itself to me.
*I* was shaking, too, and, looking about for
the cause, when I beheld the most weird
and remarkable spectacle I had ever witnessed.  The whole *llano*, or plain, stretching to the horizon-line, was *distinctly undu-
lating !*  The faint haze of the hills was
repeated over its surface, as if a dust had
arisen from some grinding displacement of
the soil.  I threw myself from my horse,
but the next moment was fain to cling to
him, as I felt the thrill under my very feet.
Then there was a pause, and I lifted my
head to look for Enriquez.  He was nowhere to be seen !  With a terrible recollection of the fissure that had yawned between
us, I sprang to the saddle again, and spurred

the frightened beast toward that point. *But it was gone, too!* I rode backward and forward repeatedly along the line where I had seen it only a moment before. The plain lay compact and uninterrupted, without a crack or fissure. The dusty haze that had arisen had passed as mysteriously away; the clear outline of the valley returned; the great field was empty!

Presently I was aware of the sound of galloping hoofs. I remembered then — what I had at first forgotten — that a few moments before we had crossed an *arroyo*, or dried bed of a stream, depressed below the level of the field. How foolish that I had not remembered! He had evidently sought that refuge; there were his returning hoofs. I galloped toward it, but only to meet a frightened *vaquero*, who had taken that avenue of escape to the rancho.

"Did you see Don Enriquez?" I asked impatiently.

I saw that the man's terror was extreme, and his eyes were staring in their sockets. He hastily crossed himself: —

"Ah, God, yes!"

"Where is he?" I demanded.

"Gone!"

"Where?"

He looked at me with staring, vacant eyes, and, pointing to the ground, said in Spanish: "He has returned to the land of his fathers!"

We searched for him that day and the next, when the country was aroused and his neighbors joined in a quest that proved useless. Neither he nor his innocent burden was ever seen again of men. Whether he had been engulfed by mischance in some unsuspected yawning chasm in that brief moment, or had fulfilled his own prophecy by deliberately erasing himself for some purpose known only to himself, no one ever knew. His country-people shook their heads and said "it was like a Saltillo." And the few among his retainers who knew him and loved him, whispered still more ominously: "He will yet return to his land to confound the *Americanos*."

Yet the widow of Enriquez did *not* marry Professor Dobbs. But she too disappeared from California, and years afterward I was told that she was well known to the ingenuous Parisians as the usual wealthy widow "from South America."

THE ARGONAUTS OF NORTH LIBERTY

# THE ARGONAUTS OF NORTH LIBERTY.

## PART I

## CHAPTER I

THE bell of the North Liberty Second Presbyterian Church had just ceased ringing. North Liberty, Connecticut, never on any day a cheerful town, was always bleaker and more cheerless on the seventh, when the Sabbath sun, after vainly trying to coax a smile of reciprocal kindliness from the drawn curtains and half-closed shutters of the austere dwellings and the equally sealed and hard-set churchgoing faces of the people, at last settled down into a blank stare of stony astonishment. On this chilly March evening of the year 1850, that stare had kindled into an of-

fended sunset and an angry night that
furiously spat sleet and hail in the faces
of the worshippers, and made them fight
their way to the church, step by step, with
bent heads and fiercely compressed lips,
until they seemed to be carrying its forbidding portals at the point of their umbrellas.

Within that sacred but graceless edifice,
the rigors of the hour and occasion reached
their climax. The shivering gas-jets lit up
the austere pallor of the bare walls, and
the hollow, shell-like sweep of colorless
vacuity behind the cold communion table.
The chill of despair and hopeless renuncia-
tion was in the air, untempered by any
glow from the sealed air-tight stove that
seemed only to bring out a lukewarm ex-
halation of wet clothes and cheaply dyed
umbrellas. Nor did the presence of the
worshippers themselves impart any life to
the dreary apartment. Scattered throughout the white pews, in dull, shapeless,
neutral blotches, rigidly separated from
each other, they seemed only to accent the
colorless church and the emptiness of all
things. A few children, who had huddled
together for warmth in one of the back
benches and who had became glutinous

and adherent through moisture, were labo-
riously drawn out and painfully picked
apart by a watchful deacon.

The dry, monotonous disturbance of the
bell had given way to the strain of a bass
viol, that had been apparently pitched to
the key of the east wind without, and the
crude complaint of a new harmonium that
seemed to bewail its limited prospect of
ever becoming seasoned or mellowed in its
earthly tabernacle, and then the singing began. Here and there a human voice soared
and struggled above the narrow text and the
monotonous cadence with a cry of individual
longing, but was borne down by the dull,
trampling precision of the others' formal
chant. This and a certain muffled raking
of the stove by the sexton brought the tem-
perature down still lower. A sermon, in
keeping with the previous performance, in
which the chill east wind of doctrine was
not tempered to any shorn lamb within that
dreary fold, followed. A spark of human
and vulgar interest was momentarily kindled by the collection and the simultaneous
movement of reluctant hands towards their
owners' pockets; but the coins fell on the
baize-covered plates with a dull thud, like

clods on a coffin, and the dreariness returned. Then there was another hymn and
a prolonged moan from the harmonium, to
which mysterious suggestion the congregation rose and began slowly to file into the
aisle. For a moment they mingled; there
was the silent grasping of damp woollen
mittens and cold black gloves, and the whispered interchange of each other's names
with the prefix of "Brother" or "Sister,"
and an utter absence of fraternal geniality,
and then the meeting slowly dispersed.

The few who had waited until the minister had resumed his hat, overcoat, and
overshoes, and accompanied him to the
door, had already passed out; the sexton
was turning out the flickering gas jets one
by one, when the cold and austere silence
was broken by a sound—the unmistakable
echo of a kiss of human passion.

As the horror-stricken official turned angrily, the figure of a man glided from the
shadow of the stairs below the organ loft,
and vanished through the open door. Before the sexton could follow, the figure of a
woman slipped out of the same portal and
with a hurried glance after the first retreating figure, turned in the opposite di-

rection and was lost in the darkness. By the time the indignant and scandalized custodian had reached the portal, they had both melted in the troubled sea of tossing umbrellas already to the right and left of him, and pursuit and recognition were hopeless.

## CHAPTER II

The male figure, however, after mingling with his fellow-worshippers to the corner of the block, stopped a moment under the lamp-post as if uncertain as to the turning, but really to cast a long, scrutinizing look towards the scattered umbrellas now almost lost in the opposite direction. He was still gazing and apparently hesitating whether to retrace his steps, when a horse and buggy rapidly driven down the side street passed him. In a brief glance he evidently recognized the driver, and stepping over the curbstone called in a brief authoritative voice:

"Ned!"

The occupant of the vehicle pulled up suddenly, leaned from the buggy, and said in an astonished tone:

"Dick Demorest! Well! I declare! Hold on, and I'll drive up to the curb."

"No; stay where you are."

The speaker approached the buggy, jumped in beside the occupant, refastened the apron, and coolly taking the reins from his companion's hand, started the horse forward. The action was that of an habitually imperious man; and the only recognition he made of the other's ownership was the question:

"Where were you going?"

"Home—to see Joan," replied the other. "Just drove over from Warensboro Station. But what on earth are *you* doing here?"

Without answering the question, Demorest turned to his companion with the same good-natured, half humorous authority. "Let your wife wait; take a drive with me. I want to talk to you. She'll be just as glad to see you an hour later, and it's her fault if I can't come home with you now."

"I know it," returned his companion, in a tone of half-annoyed apology. "She still sticks to her old compact when we first married, that she shouldn't be obliged to receive my old worldly friends. And, see here, Dick, I thought I'd talked her out of it as regards *you* at least, but Parson Thomas has been raking up all the old stories about you—you know that affair of the Fall River widow, and that breaking off of Garry Spofferth's match—and about your horse-racing—until—you know, she's more set than ever against knowing you."

"That's not a bad sort of horse you've got there," interrupted Demorest, who usually conducted conversation without reference to alien topics suggested by others. "Where did you get him? He's good yet for a spin down the turnpike and over the bridge. We'll do it, and I'll bring you home safely to Mrs. Blandford inside the hour."

Blandford knew little of horseflesh, but like all men he was not superior to this implied compliment to his knowledge. He resigned himself to his companion as he had been in the habit of doing, and Demorest hurried the horse at a rapid gait down the street until they left the lamps behind, and were fully on the dark turnpike. The sleet rattled against the hood and leathern apron of the buggy, gusts of fierce wind filled the vehicle and seemed to hold it

back, but Demorest did not appear to mind
it. Blandford thrust his hands deeply into
his pockets for warmth, and contracted his
shoulders as if in dogged patience. Yet,
in spite of the fact that he was tired, cold,
and anxious to see his wife, he was conscious of a secret satisfaction in submitting
to the caprices of this old friend of his
boyhood. After all, Dick Demorest knew
what he was about, and had never led him
astray by his autocratic will. It was safe
to let Dick have his way. It was true it
was generally Dick's own way—but he
made others think it was theirs too—or
would have been theirs had they had the
will and the knowledge to project it. He
looked up comfortably at the handsome,
resolute profile of the man who had taken
selfish possession of him. Many women
had done the same.

"Suppose if you were to tell your wife I
was going to reform," said Demorest, "it
might be different, eh? She'd want to take
me into the church—'another sinner saved,'
and all that, eh?"

"No," said Blandford, earnestly. "Joan
isn't as rigid as all that, Dick. What she's
got against you is the common report of

your free way of living, and that—come
now, you know yourself, Dick, that isn't
exactly the thing a woman brought up in
her style can stand. Why, she thinks I'm
unregenerate, and—well, a man can't
carry on business always like a class meeting. But are you thinking of reforming?"
he continued, trying to get a glimpse of his
companion's eyes.

"Perhaps. It depends. Now—there's
a woman I know—"

"What, another? and you call this going
to reform?" interrupted Blandford, yet
not without a certain curiosity in his
manner.

"Yes; that's just why I think of reforming. For this one isn't exactly like any
other—at least as far as I know."

"That means you don't know anything
about her."

"Wait, and I'll tell you." He drew the
reins tightly to accelerate the horse's
speed, and, half turning to his companion,
without, however, moving his eyes from
the darkness before him, spoke quickly
between the blasts: "I've seen her only
half a dozen times. Met her first in 6.40
train out from Boston last fall. She sat

next to me. Covered up with wraps and
veils; never looked twice at her. She
spoke first—kind of half bold, half frightened way. Then got more comfortable
and unwound herself, you know, and I
saw she was young and not bad-looking.
Thought she was some school-girl out for
a lark—but rather new at it. Inexperienced, you know, but quite able to take
care of herself, by George! and although
she looked and acted as if she'd never
spoken to a stranger all her life, didn't
mind the kind of stuff I talked to her.
Rather encouraged it; and laughed—such
a pretty little odd laugh, as if laughing
wasn't in her usual line, either, and she
didn't know how to manage it. Well, it
ended in her slipping out at one end of
the car when we arrived, while I was looking out for a cab for her at the other."
He stopped to recover from a stronger gust
of wind. "I—I thought it a good joke on
me, and let the thing drop out of my mind,
although, mind you, she'd promised to
meet me a month afterwards at the same
time and place. Well, when the day came
I happened to be in Boston, and went to
the station. Don't know why I went, for

I didn't for a moment think she'd keep her appointment. First, I couldn't find her in the train, but after we'd started she came along out of some seat in the corner, prettier than ever, holding out her hand." He drew a long inspiration. "You can bet your life, Ned, I didn't let go that little hand the rest of the journey."

His passion, or what passed for it, seemed to impart its warmth to the vehicle, and even stirred the chilled pulses of the man beside him.

"Well, who and what was she?"

"Didn't find out; don't know now. For the first thing she made me promise was not to follow her, nor to try to know her name. In return she said she would meet me again on another train near Hartford. She did—and again and again—but always on the train for about an hour, going or coming. Then she missed an appointment. I was regularly cut up, I tell you, and swore as she hadn't kept her word, I wouldn't keep mine, and began to hunt for her. In the midst of it I saw her accidentally; no matter where; I followed her to—well, that's no matter to you, either. Enough that I saw her again—

and, well, Ned, such is the influence of that girl over me that, by George! she made me make the same promise again!"

Blandford, a little disappointed at his friend's dogmatic suppression of certain material facts, shrugged his shoulders.

"If that's all your story," he said, "I must say I see no prospect of your reforming. It's the old thing over again, only this time you are evidently the victim. She's some designing creature who will have you if she hasn't already got you completely in her power."

"You don't know what you're talking about, Ned, and you'd better quit," returned Demorest, with cheerful authoritativeness. "I tell you that that's the sort of girl I'm going to marry, if I can, and settle down upon. You can make a memorandum of that, old man, if you like."

"Then I don't really see why you want to talk to *me* about it. And if you are thinking that such a story would go down for a moment with Joan as an evidence of your reformation, you're completely out, Dick. Was that your idea?"

"Yes—and I can tell you, you're wrong again, Ned. You don't know anything

about women. You do just as I say—do
you understand?—and don't interfere
with your own wrong-headed opinions of
what other people will think, and I'll take
the risks of Mrs. Blandford giving me
good advice. Your wife has got a heap
more sense on these subjects than you have,
you bet. You just tell her that I want to
marry the girl and want her to help me—
that I mean business, this time—and
you'll see how quick she'll come down.
That's all I want of you. Will you or
won't you?"

With an outward expression of sceptical
consideration and an inward suspicion of
the peculiar force of this man's dogmatic
insight, Blandford assented, with, I fear,
the mental reservation of telling the story
to his wife in his own way. He was surprised when his friend suddenly drew the
horse up sharply, and after a moment's
pause began to back him, cramp the wheels
of the buggy and then skilfully, in the
almost profound darkness, turn the vehicle
and horse completely round to the opposite
direction.

"Then you are not going over the
bridge?" said Blandford.

K

Demorest made an imperative gesture of silence. The tumultuous rush and roar of swollen and rapid water came from the darkness behind them. "There's been another break-out somewhere, and I reckon the bridge has got all it can do to-night to keep itself out of water without taking us over. At least, as I promised to set you down at your wife's door inside of the hour, I don't propose to try." As the horse now travelled more easily with the wind behind him, Demorest, dismissing abruptly all other subjects, laid his hand with brusque familiarity on his companion's knee, and as if the hour for social and confidential greeting had only just then arrived, said: "Well, Neddy, old boy, how are you getting on?"

"So, so," said Blandford, dubiously. "You see," he began, argumentatively, "in my business there's a good deal of competition, and I was only saying this morning—"

But either Demorest was already familiar with his friend's arguments, or had as usual exhausted his topic, for without paying the slightest attention to him, he again demanded abruptly, "Why don't you go to California? Here everything's played out. That's the country for a young man like you—just starting into life, and without incumbrances. If I was free and fixed in my family affairs like you I'd go to-morrow."

There was such an occult positivism in Demorest's manner that for an instant Blandford, who had been married two years, and was transacting a steady and fairly profitable manufacturing business in the adjacent town, actually believed he was more fitted for adventurous speculation than the grimly erratic man of energetic impulses and pleasures beside him. He managed to stammer hesitatingly:

"But there's Joan—she—"

"Nonsense! Let her stay with her mother; you sell out your interest in the business, put the money into an assorted cargo, and clap it and yourself into the first ship out of Boston—and there you are. You've been married going on two years now, and a little separation until you've built up a business out there, won't do either of you any harm."

Blandford, who was very much in love with his wife, was not, however, above putting the onus of embarrassing affection upon *her*. "You don't know, Joan, Dick," he replied. "She'd never consent to a separation, even for a short time."

"Try her. She's a sensible woman—a deuced sight more than you are. You don't understand women, Ned. That's what's the matter with you."

It required all of Blandford's fond memories of his wife's conservative habits, Puritan practicality, religious domesticity, and strong family attachments, to withstand Demorest's dogmatic convictions. He smiled, however, with a certain complacency, as he also recalled the previous autumn when the first news of the California gold discovery had penetrated North Liberty, and he had expressed to her his belief that it would offer an outlet to Demorest's adventurous energy. She had received it with ill-disguised satisfaction, and the remark that if this exodus of Mammon cleared the community of the godless and unregenerate it would only be another proof of God's mysterious providence.

With the tumultuous wind at their backs it was not long before the buggy rattled once more over the cobble-stones of the town. Under the direction of his friend, Demorest, who still retained possession of the reins, drove briskly down a side street of more pretentious dwellings, where Blandford lived. One or two wayfarers looked up.

"Not so fast, Dick."

"Why? I want to bring you up to your door in style."

"Yes—but—it's Sunday. That's my house, the corner one."

They had stopped before a square, two-storied brick house, with an equally square wooden porch suported by two plain, rigid wooden columns, and a hollow sweep of dull concavity above the door, evidently of the same architectural order as the church. There was no corner or projection to break the force of the wind that swept its smooth glacial surface; there was no indication of light or warmth behind its six closed windows.

"There seems to be nobody at home," said Demorest, briefly. "Come along with me to the hotel."

"Joan sits in the back parlor, Sundays," explained the husband.

"Shall I drive round to the barn and leave the horse and buggy there while you go in?" continued Demorest, good-humoredly, pointing to the stable gate at the side.

"No, thank you," returned Blandford, "it's locked, and I'll have to open it from the other side after I go in. The horse will stand until then. I think I'll have to say good-night, now," he added, with a sudden half-ashamed consciousness of the forbidding aspect of the house, and his own inhospitality. "I'm sorry I can't ask you in—but you understand why."

"All right," returned Demorest, stoutly, turning up his coat-collar, and unfurling his umbrella. "The hotel is only four blocks away—you'll find me there to-morrow morning if you call. But mind you tell your wife just what I told you—and no meandering of your own—you hear! She'll strike out some idea with her woman's wits, you bet. Good-night, old man!" He reached out his hand, pressed Blandford's strongly and potentially, and strode down the street.

Blandford hitched his steaming horse to a sleet-covered horse block with a quick sigh of impatient sympathy over the animal and himself, and after fumbling in his pocket for a latchkey, opened the front door. A vista of well-ordered obscurity with shadowy trestle-like objects against the walls, and an odor of chill decorum, as if of a damp but respectable funeral, greeted him on entering. A faint light, like a cold dawn, broke through the glass pane of a door leading to the kitchen. Blandford paused in the mid-darkness and hesitated. Should he first go to his wife in the back parlor, or pass silently through the kitchen, open the back gate, and mercifully bestow his sweating beast in the stable? With the reflection that an immediate conjugal greeting, while his horse was still exposed to the fury of the blast in the street, would necessarily be curtailed and limited, he compromised by quickly passing through the kitchen into the stable yard, opening the gate, and driving horse and vehicle under the shed to await later and more thorough ministration. As he entered the back door, a faint hope that his wife might have heard him and would be waiting for him in the hall for an instant thrilled him; but he re-

membered it was Sunday, and that she
was probably engaged in some devotional
reading or exercise. He hesitatingly
opened the back-parlor door with a consciousness of committing some unreason-
able trespass, and entered.

She was there, sitting quietly before a
large, round, shining centre-table, whose
sterile emptiness was relieved only by a
shaded lamp and a large black and gilt
open volume. A single picture on the
opposite wall—the portrait of an elderly
gentleman stiffened over a corresponding
volume, which he held in invincible mort-
main in his rigid hand, and apparently defied posterity to take from him—seemed
to offer a not uncongenial companionship.
Yet the greenish light of the shade fell
upon a young and pretty face, despite the
color it extracted from it, and the hand
that supported her low white forehead
over which her full hair was simply parted,
like a brown curtain, was slim and gentle-
womanly. In spite of her plain lustreless
silk dress, in spite of the formal frame of
sombre heavy horsehair and mahogany
furniture that seemed to set her off, she
diffused an atmosphere of cleanly grace

and prim refinement through the apartment. The priestess of this ascetic temple, the femininity of her closely covered arms, her pink ears, and a little serviceable morocco house-shoe that was visible lower down, resting on the carved lion's paw that upheld the centre-table, appeared to be only the more accented. And the precisely rounded but softly heaving bosom, that was pressed upon the edges of the open book of sermons before her, seemed to assert itself triumphantly over the rigors of the volume.

At least so her husband and lover thought, as he moved tenderly towards her. She met his first kiss on her forehead; the second, a supererogatory one, based on some supposed inefficiency in the first, fell upon a shining band of her hair, beside her neck. She reached up her slim hands, caught his wrists firmly, and, slightly putting him aside, said:

"There, Edward?"

"I drove out from Warensboro, so as to get here to-night, as I have to return to the city on Tuesday. I thought it would give me a little more time with you, Joan," he said, looking around him, and, at last, hesitatingly drawing an apparently reluctant chair from its formal position at the window. The remembrance that he had ever dared to occupy the same chair with her, now seemed hardly possible of credence.

"If it was a question of your travelling on the Lord's Day, Edward, I would rather you should have waited until to-morrow," she said, with slow precision.

"But—I—I thought I'd get here in time for the meeting," he said, weakly.

"And instead, you have driven through the town, I suppose, where everybody will see you and talk about it. But," she added, raising her dark eyes suddenly to his, "where else have you been? The train gets into Warensboro at six, and it's only half an hour's drive from there. What have you been doing, Edward?"

It was scarcely a felicitous moment for the introduction of Demorest's name, and he would have avoided it. But he reflected that he had been seen, and he was naturally truthful. "I met Dick Demorest near the church, and as he had something to tell me, we drove down the turnpike a

little way—so as to be out of the town,
you know, Joan—and—and—"

He stopped. Her face had taken upon
itself that appalling and exasperating
calmness of very good people who never
get angry, but drive others to frenzy by the
simple occlusion of an adamantine veil between their own feelings and their oppo-
nents'. "I'll tell you all about it after I've
put up the horse," he said hurriedly, glad
to escape until the veil was lifted again.
"I suppose the hired man is out."

"I should hope he was in church, Edward, but I trust *you* won't delay taking
care of that poor dumb brute who has been
obliged to minister to your and Mr. Demorest's Sabbath pleasures."

Blandford did not wait for a further
suggestion. When the door had closed behind him, Mrs. Blandford went to the
mantel-shelf, where a grimly allegorical
clock cut down the hours and minutes of
men with a scythe, and consulted it with
a slight knitting of her pretty eyebrows.
Then she fell into a vague abstraction,
standing before the open book on the
centre-table. Then she closed it with a
snap, and methodically putting it exactly

in the middle of the top of a black cabinet in the corner, lifted the shaded lamp in her hand and passed slowly with it up the stairs to her bedroom, where her light steps were heard moving to and fro. In a few moments she reappeared, stopping for a moment in the hall with the lighted lamp as if to watch and listen for her husband's return. Seen in that favorable light, her cheeks had caught a delicate color, and her dark eyes shone softly. Putting the lamp down in exactly the same place as before, she returned to the cabinet for the book, brought it again to the table, opened it at the page where she had placed her perforated cardboard book-marker, sat down beside it, and with her hands in her lap and her eyes on the page began abstractedly to tear a small piece of paper into tiny fragments. When she had reduced it to the smallest shreds, she scraped the pieces out of her silk lap and again collected them in the pink hollow of her little hand, kneeling down on the scrupulously well-swept carpet to peck up with a bird-like action of her thumb and forefinger an escaped atom here and there. These and the contents of her hand she poured into the

chilly cavity of a sepulchral-looking ala-
baster vase that stood on the *etagère*. Returning to her old seat, and making a nest
for her clasped fingers in the lap of her
dress, she remained in that attitude, her
shoulders a little narrowed and bent forward, until her husband returned.

"I've lit the fire in the bedroom for you
to change your clothes by," she said, as he
entered; then evading the caress which this
wifely attention provoked, by bending still
more primly over her book, she added, "Go
at once. You're making everything quite
damp here."

He returned in a few moments in his
slippers and jacket, but evidently found
the same difficulty in securing a conjugal
and confidential contiguity to his wife.
There was no apparent social centre or
nucleus of comfort in the apartment; its
fireplace, sealed by an iron ornament like
a monumental tablet over dead ashes, had
its functions superseded by an air-tight
drum in the corner, warmed at second-hand
from the dining-room below, and offered no
attractive seclusion; the sofa against the
wall was immovable and formally repellent. He was obliged to draw a chair

beside the table, whose every curve seemed to facilitate his wife's easy withdrawal from side-by-side familiarity.

"Demorest has been urging me very strongly to go to California, but, of course, I spoke of you," he said, stealing his hand into his wife's lap, and possessing himself of her fingers.

Mrs. Blandford slowly lifted her fingers enclosed in his clasping hand and placed them in shameless publicity on the volume before her. This implied desecration was too much for Blandford; he withdrew his hand.

"Does that man propose to go with you?" asked Mrs. Blandford, coldly.

"No; he's preoccupied with other matters that he wanted me to talk to you about," said her husband, hesitatingly. "He is—"

"Because"—continued Mrs. Blandford in the same measured tone, "if he does not add his own evil company to his advice, it is the best he has ever given yet. I think he might have taken another day than the Lord's to talk about it, but we must not despise the means nor the hour whence the truth comes. Father wanted me to take some reasonable moment to prepare you to consider it seriously, and I thought of talking to you about it to-morrow. He thinks it would be a very judicious plan. Even Deacon Truesdail——"

"Having sold his invoice of damaged sugar kettles for mining purposes, is converted," said Blandford, goaded into momentary testiness by his wife's unexpected acquiescence and a sudden recollection of Demorest's prophecy. "You have changed your opinion, Joan, since last fall, when you couldn't bear to think of my leaving you," he added reproachfully.

"I couldn't bear to think of your joining the mob of lawless and sinful men who use that as an excuse for leaving their wives and families. As for my own feelings, Edward, I have never allowed them to stand between me and what I believed best for our home and your Christian welfare. Though I have no cause to admire the influence that I find this man, Demorest, still holds over you, I am willing to acquiesce, as you see, in what he advises for your good. You can hardly reproach *me,* Edward, for worldly or selfish motives."

Blandford felt keenly the bitter truth of

his wife's speech. For the moment he would gladly have exchanged it for a more illogical and selfish affection, but he reflected that he had married this religious girl for the security of an affection which he felt was not subject to the temptations of the world—or even its own weakness— as was too often the case with the giddy maidens whom he had known through Demorest's companionship. It was, therefore, more with a sense of recalling this distinctive quality of his wife than any loyalty to Demorest that he suddenly resolved to confide to her the latter's fatuous folly.

"I know it, dear," he said, apologetically, "and we'll talk it over to-morrow, and it may be possible to arrange it so that you shall go with me. But, speaking of Demorest, I think you don't quite do *him* justice. He really respects *your* feelings and your knowledge of right and wrong more than you imagine. I actually believe he came here to-night merely to get me to interest you in an extraordinary love affair of his. I mean, Joan," he added hastily, seeing the same look of dull repression come over her face, "I mean, Joan

—that is, you know, from all I can judge —it is something really serious this time. He intends to reform. And this is because he has become violently smitten with a young woman whom he has only seen half a dozen times, at long intervals, whom he first met in a railway train, and whose name and residence he don't even know."

There was an ominous silence—so hushed that the ticking of the allegorical clock came like a grim monitor. "Then," said Mrs. Blandford, in a hard, dry voice that her alarmed husband scarcely recognized, "he proposed to insult your wife by taking her into his shameful confidence."

"Good heavens! Joan, no—you don't understand. At the worst, this is some virtuous but silly school-girl, who, though she may be intending only an innocent flirtation with him, has made this man actually and deeply in love with her. Yes; it is a fact, Joan. I know Dick Demorest, and if ever there was a man honestly in love, it is he."

"Then you mean to say that this man— an utter stranger to me—a man whom I've never laid my eyes on—whom I wouldn't

know if I met in the street—expects me to
advise him—to—to—" She stopped.
Blandford could scarcely believe his senses.
There were tears in her eyes—this woman
who never cried; her voice trembled—she
who had always controlled her emotions.

He took advantage of this odd but oppor-
tune melting. He placed his arm around
her shoulders. She tried to escape it, but
with a coy, shy movement, half hysterical,
half girlish, unlike her usual stony, moral
precision. "Yes, Joan," he repeated,
laughingly, "but whose fault is it? Not
*his,* remember! And I firmly believe he
thinks you can do him good."

"But he has never seen me," she continued, with a nervous little laugh, "and
probably considers me some old Gorgon—
like—like—Sister Jemima Skerret."

Blandford smiled with the complacency
of far-reaching masculine intuition. Ah!
that shrewd fellow, Demorest, was right.
Joan, dear Joan, was only a woman
after all.

"Then he'll be the more agreeably astonished," he returned, gayly, "and I think
*you* will, too, Joan. For Dick isn't a bad-
looking fellow; most women like him. It's

true," he continued, much amused at the novelty of the perfectly natural toss and grimace with which Mrs. Blandford received this statement.

"I think he's been pointed out to me somewhere," she said, thoughtfully, "he's a tall, dark, dissipated-looking man."

"Nothing of the kind," laughed her husband. "He's middle-sized and as blond as your cousin Joe, only he's got a long yellow moustache, and has a quick, abrupt way of talking. He isn't at all fancy-looking; you'd take him for an energetic business man or a doctor, if you didn't know him. So you see, Joan, this correct little wife of mine has been a little, just a little, prejudiced."

He drew her again gently backwards and nearer his seat, but she caught his wrists in her slim hands, and rising from the chair at the same moment, dexterously slipped from his embrace with her back towards him. "I do not know why I should be unprejudiced by anything you've told me," she said, sharply closing the book of sermons, and, with her back still to her husband, reinstating it formally in its place on the cabinet. "It's probably one of his

many scandalous pursuits of defenceless
and believing women, and he, no doubt,
goes off to Boston, laughing at you for
thinking him in earnest; and as ready to
tell his story to anybody else and boast of
his double deceit." Her voice had a touch
of human asperity in it now, which he
had never before noticed, but recognizing,
as he thought, the human cause, it was far
from exciting his displeasure.

"Wrong again, Joan; he's waiting here
at the Independence House for me to see
him to-morrow," he returned, cheerfully.
"And I believe him so much in earnest that
I would be ready to swear that not another
person will ever know the story but you
and I and he. No, it is a real thing with
him; he's dead in love, and it's your duty
as a Christian to help him."

There was a moment of silence. Mrs.
Blandford remained by the cabinet,
methodically arranging some small articles
displaced by the return of the book.
"Well," she said, suddenly, "you don't tell
me what mother had to say. Of course, as
you came home earlier than you expected,
you had time to stop *there*—only four
doors from this house."

"Well, no, Joan," replied Blandford, in awkward discomfiture. "You see I met Dick first, and then—then I hurried here to you—and—and—I clean forgot it. I'm very sorry," he added, dejectedly.

"And *I* more deeply so," she returned, with her previous bloodless moral precision, "for she probably knows by this time, Edward, why you have omitted your usual Sabbath visit, and with *whom* you were."

"But I can pull on my boots again and run in there for a moment," he suggested, dubiously, "if you think it necessary. It won't take me a moment."

"No," she said, positively; "it is so late now that your visit would only show it to be a second thought. I will go myself—it will be a call for us both."

"But shall I go with you to the door? It is dark and sleeting," suggested Blandford, eagerly.

"No," she replied, peremptorily. "Stay where you are, and when Ezekiel and Bridget come in send them to bed, for *I* have made everything fast in the kitchen. Don't wait up for me."

She left the room, and in a few moments returned, wrapped from head to foot in an

enormous plaid shawl. A white woollen
scarf thrown over her bare brown head,
and twice rolled around her neck, almost
concealed her face from view. When she
had parted from her husband, and reached
the darkened hall below, she drew from
beneath the folds of her shawl a thick blue
veil, with which she completely enveloped
her features. As she opened the front door
and peered out into the night, her own
husband would have scarcely recognized
her.

With her head lowered against the keen
wind she walked rapidly down the street
and stopped for an instant at the door of
the fourth house. Glancing quickly back
at the house she had left and then at the
closed windows of the one she had halted
before, she gathered her skirts with one
hand and sped away from both, never
stopping until she reached the door of the
Independence Hotel.

## CHAPTER III

MRS. BLANDFORD entered the side door
boldly. Luckily for her, the austerities of

the Sabbath were manifest even here; the
bar-room was closed, and the usual loungers in the passages were absent. Without
risking the recognition of her voice in an
inquiry to the clerk, she slipped past the
office, still muffled in her veil, and quickly
mounted the narrow staircase. For an
instant she hesitated before the public
parlor, and glanced dubiously along the
half-lit corridor. Chance befriended her;
the door of a bedroom opened at that moment, and Richard Demorest, with his
overcoat and hat on, stepped out in the
hall.

With a quick and nervous gesture of her
hand she beckoned him to approach. He
came towards her leisurely, with an
amused curiosity that suddenly changed
to utter astonishment as she hurriedly
lifted her veil, dropped it, turned, and
glided down the staircase into the street
again. He followed rapidly, but did not
overtake her until she had reached the
corner, when she slackened her pace an
instant for him to join her.

"Lulu," he said eagerly; "is it you?"

"Not a word here," she said, breathlessly. "Follow me at a distance."

She started forward again in the direction of her own house. He followed her at a sufficient interval to keep her faintly distinguishable figure in sight until she had crossed three streets, and near the end of the next block glided up the steps of a house not far from the one where he remembered to have left Blandford. As he joined her, she had just succeeded in opening the door with a pass-key, and was awaiting him. With a gesture of silence she took his hand in her cold fingers, and leading him softly through the dark hall and passage, quickly entered the kitchen. Here she lit a candle, turned, and faced him. He could see that the outside shutters were bolted, and the kitchen evidently closed for the night.

As she removed the veil from her face he made a movement as if to regain her hand again, but she drew it away.

"You have forced this upon me," she said hurriedly, "and it may be ruin to us both. Why have you betrayed me?"

"Betrayed you, Lulu—Good God! what do you mean?"

She looked him full in the eye, and then

said slowly, "Do you mean to say that you have told no one of our meetings ?"

"Only one—my old friend Blandford, who lives— Ah, yes! I see it now. You are neighbors. He has betrayed me. This house is—"

"My father's!" she replied boldly.

The momentary uneasiness passed from Demorest's resolute face. His old self-sufficiency returned. "Good," he said, with a frank laugh, "that will do for me. Open the door there, Lulu, and take me to him. I'm not ashamed of anything I've done, my girl, nor need you be. I'll tell him my real name is Dick Demorest, as I ought to have told you before, and that I want to marry you, fairly and squarely, and let him make the conditions. I'm not a vagabond nor a thief, Lulu, if I have met you on the sly. Come, dear, let us end this now. Come—"

But she had thrown herself before him and placed her hand upon his lips. "Hush! are you mad ? Listen to me, I tell you—please—oh, do—no you must not!" He had covered her hand with kisses and was drawing her face towards his own. "No— not again, it was wrong then, it is mon-

strous now. I implore you, listen, if you
love me, stop."

He released her. She sank into a chair
by the kitchen-table, and buried her flushed
face in her hands.

He stood for a moment motionless before
her. "Lulu, if that is your name," he said
slowly, but gently, "tell me all now. Be
frank with me, and trust me. If there is
anything stands in the way, let me know
what it is and I can overcome it. If it is
my telling Ned Blandford, don't let that
worry you, he's as loyal a fellow as ever
breathed, and I'm a dog to ever think he
willingly betrayed us. His wife, well,
she's one of those pious saints—but no, she
would not be such a cursed hypocrite and
bigot as this."

"Hush, I tell you! *Will* you hush," she
said, in a frantic whisper, springing to her
feet and grasping him convulsively by the
lapels of his overcoat. "Not a word more,
or I'll kill myself. Listen! Do you know
what I brought you here for? why I left
my—this house and dragged you out of
your hotel? Well, it was to tell you that
you must leave me, leave *here*—go out of
this house and out of this town at once, to-

night! And never look on it or me again!
There! you have said we must end this
now. It is ended, as only it could and ever
would end. And if you open that door except to go, or if you attempt to—to touch
me again, I'll do something desperate.
There!"

She threw him off again and stepped
back, strangely beautiful in the loosened
shackles of her long repressed human emotion. It was as if the passion-rent robes of
the priestess had laid bare the flesh of the
woman dazzling and victorious. Demorest
was fascinated and frightened.

"Then you do not love me?" he said
with a constrained smile, "and I am a
fool?"

"Love you!" she repeated. "Love you,"
she continued, bowing her brown head over
her hanging arms and clasped hands.
"What then has brought me to this? Oh,"
she said suddenly, again seizing him by his
two arms, and holding him from her with
a half-prudish, half-passionate gesture,
"why could you not have left things as
they were; why could we not have met in
the same old way we used to meet, when I
was so foolish and so happy? Why could

you spoil that one dream I have clung to? Why didn't you leave me those few days of my wretched life when I was weak, silly, vain, but not the unhappy woman I am now. You were satisfied to sit beside me and talk to me then. You respected my secret, my reserve. My God! I used to think you loved me as I loved you—for *that!* Why did you break your promise and follow me here? I believed you the first day we met, when you said there was no wrong in my listening to you; that it should go no further; that you would never seek to renew it without my consent. You tell me I don't love you, and I tell you now that we must part, that frightened as I was, foolish as I was, that day was the first day I had ever lived and felt as other women live and feel. If I ran away from you then it was because I was running away from my old self too. Don't you understand me? Could you not have trusted me as I trusted you?"

"I broke my promise only when you broke yours. When you would not meet me I followed you here, because I loved you."

"And that is why you must leave me

now," she said, starting from his outstretched arms again. "Do not ask me
why, but go, I implore you. You must
leave this town to-night, to-morrow will be
too late."

He cast a hurried glance around him, as
if seeking to gather some reason for this
mysterious haste, or a clue for future
identification. He saw only the Sabbath-
sealed cupboards, the cold white china on
the dresser, and the flicker of the candle
on the partly-opened glass transom above
the door. "As you wish," he said, with
quiet sadness. "I will go now, and leave
the town to-night; but"—his voice struck
its old imperative note—"this shall not end
here, Lulu. There will be a next time, and
I am bound to win you yet, in spite of all
and everything."

She looked at him with a half-frightened, half-hysterical light in her eyes.
"God knows!"

"And you will be frank with me then,
and tell me all?"

"Yes, yes, another time; but go now."
She had extinguished the candle, turned
the handle of the door noiselessly, and was
holding it open. A faint light stole

through the dark passage. She drew back
hastily. "You have left the front door
open," she said in a frightened voice. "I
thought you had shut it behind me," he returned quickly. "Good night." He drew
her towards him. She resisted slightly.
They were for an instant clasped in a passionate embrace; then there was a sudden
collapse of the light and a dull jar. The
front door had swung to.

With a desperate bound she darted into
the passage and through the hall, dragging
him by the hand, and threw the front door
open. Without, the street was silent and
empty.

"Go," she whispered frantically.

Demorest passed quickly down the steps
and disappeared. At the same moment a
voice came from the banisters of the landing above. "Who's there?"

"It's I, mother."

"I thought so. And it's like Edward to
bring you and sneak off in that fashion."

Mrs. Blandford gave a quick sigh of relief. Demorest's flight had been mistaken
for her husband's habitual evasion. Knowing that her mother would not refer to the
subject again, she did not reply, but slowly

mounted the dark staircase with an assumption of more than usual hesitating precaution, in order to recover her equanimity.

The clocks were striking eleven when she left her mother's house and reëntered her own. She was surprised to find a light burning in the kitchen, and Ezekiel, their hired man, awaiting her in a dominant and nasal key of religious and practical disapprobation. "Pity you wern't tu hum afore, ma'am, considerin' the doins that's goin' on in perfessed Christians' houses arter meetin' on the Sabbath Day."

"What's the difficulty now, Ezekiel?" said Mrs. Blandford, who had regained her rigorous precision once more under the decorous security of her own roof.

"Wa'al, here comes an entire stranger axin for Squire Blandford. And when I tells he warn't tu hum—"

"Not at home?" interrupted Mrs. Blandford, with a slight start. "I left him here." "Mebbee so, but folks nowadays don't 'pear to keer much whether they break the Sabbath or not, trapsen' raound town in and arter meetin' hours, ez if

'twor gin'ral tranin' day—and hez gone
out agin.''

"Go on," said Mrs. Blandford, curtly.

"Wa'al, the stranger sez, sez he, 'Show
me the way to the stables,' sez he, and without taken' no for an answer, ups and mean-
ders through the hall, outer the kitchen
inter the yard, ez if he was justice of the
peace; and when he gets there he sez,
'Fetch out his hoss and harness up, and be
blamed quick about it, and tell Ned Blandford that Dick Demorest hez got to leave
town to-night, and ez ther ain't a blamed
puritanical shadbelly in this hull town ez
would let a hoss go on hire Sunday night,
he guesses he'll hev to borry his.' And
afore I could say Jack Robinson, he tack-
les the hoss up and drives outer the yard,
flinging this two-dollar-and-a-half-piece
behind him ez if I wur a Virginia slave
and he was John C. Calhoun hisself. I'd
a chucked it after him if it hadn't been
the Lord's Day, and it mout hev provoked
disturbance.''

"Mr. Demorest is worldly, but one of
Edward's old friends," said Mrs. Blandford, with a slight kindling of her eyes,
"and he would not have refused to aid

him in what might be an errand of grace or necessity. You can keep the money, Ezekiel, as a gift, not as a wage. And go to bed. I will sit up for Mr. Blandford."

She passed out and up the staircase into her bedroom, pausing on her way to glance into the empty back parlor and take the lamp from the table. Here she noticed that her husband had evidently changed his clothes again and taken a heavier overcoat from the closet. Removing her own wraps she again descended to the lower apartment, brought out the volume of sermons, placed it and the lamp in the old position, and with her abstracted eyes on the page fell into her former attitude. Every suggestion of the passionate, half-frenzied woman in the kitchen of the house only four doors away, had vanished; one would scarcely believe she had ever stirred from the chair in which she had formally received her husband two hours before. And yet she was thinking of herself and Demorest in that kitchen.

His prompt and decisive response to her appeal, as shown in this last bold and characteristic action, relieved, while it half piqued her. But the overruling destiny

which had enabled her to bring him from
his hotel to her mother's house unnoticed,
had protected them while there, had arrested a dangerous meeting between him
and herself and her husband in her own
house, impressed her more than all. It
imparted to her a hideous tranquillity born
of the doctrines of her youth—Predestination! She reflected with secret exultation
that her moral resolution to fly from him
and her conscientiously broken promise
had been the direct means of bringing him
there; that step by step circumstances not
in themselves evil or to be combated had
led her along; that even her husband and
mother had felt it their duty to assist
towards this fateful climax! If Edward
had never kept up his worldly friendship,
if she had never been restricted and com-
passed in her own; if she had ever known
the freedom of other girls,—all this might
not have happened. She had been elected
to share with Demorest and her husband
the effects of their ungodliness. She was
no longer a free agent; what availed her
resolutions? To Demorest's imperious
hope, she had said, "God knows." What
more could she say? Her small red lips

grew white and compressed; her face rigid,
her eyes hollow and abstracted; she looked
like the genius of asceticism as she sat
there, grimly formulating a dogmatic explanation of her lawless and unlicensed
passion.

The wind had risen to a gale without,
and stirred even the sealed sepulchre of the
fireplace with dull rumblings and muffled
moans. At times the hot-air drum in the
corner seemed to expand as with some
pent-up emotion. Strange currents of air
crossed the empty room like the passage of
unseen spirits, and she even fancied she
heard whispers at the window. This
caused her to rise and open it, when she
found that the sleet had given way to a
dry feathery snow that was swarming
through the slits of the shutter; a faint
reflection from the already whitened fences
glimmered in the panes. She shut the
window hastily, with a little shiver of cold.
Where was Demorest in this storm?
Would it stop him? She thought with
pride now of the dominant energy that had
frightened her, and knew it would not.
But her husband?—what kept him? It
was twelve o'clock; he had seldom stayed

out so late before. During the first half
hour of her reflections she had been relieved by his absence; she had even believed that he had met Demorest in the
town, and was not alarmed by it, for she
knew that the latter would avoid any further confidence, and cut short any return
to it. But why had not Edward returned?
For an instant the terrible thought that
something had happened, and that they
might both return together, took possession
of her, and she trembled. But no; Demorest, who had already taken such extreme
measures, could not consistently listen to
any suggestion for delay. As her only
danger lay in Demorest's presence, the absence of her husband caused her more undefinable uneasiness than actual alarm.

The room had become cold with the
dying out of the dining-room fire that
warmed the drum. She would go to bed.
She nevertheless arranged the room again
with a singular impression that she was
doing it for the last time in her present
existing circumstances, and placing the
lamp on the table in the hall, went up to
her own room. By the light of a single
candle she undressed herself hastily, said

her prayers punctiliously, and got into bed, with an unexpected relief at finding herself still occupying it alone. Then she fell asleep and dreamed of Demorest.

## CHAPTER IV

WHEN Edward Blandford found himself alone after his wife had undertaken to fulfil his abandoned filial duty at her parents' house, he felt a slight twinge of self-reproach. He could not deny that this was not the first time he had evaded the sterile Sabbath evenings at his mother-in-law's, or that even at other times he was not in accord with the cold and colorless sanctity of the family. Yet he remembered that when he picked out from the budding womanhood of North Liberty this pure, scentless blossom, he had endured the privations of its surroundings with a sense of security in inhaling the atmosphere in which it grew, and knowing the integrity of its descent. There was a certain pleasure also in invading this seclusion with human passion; the first pressure of her hand when they were kneeling together at family prayers had the zest without the sin of a forbidden pleasure; the first kiss he had given her with their heads over the family Bible had fairly intoxicated him in the thin, rarefied air of their surroundings. In transplanting this blossom to his own home with the fond belief that it would eventually borrow the hues and color of his own passion, he had no further interest in the house he had left behind. When he found, however, that the ancestral influence was stronger than he expected, that the young wife, instead of assimilating to his conditions, had imported into their little household the rigors of her youthful home, he had been chilled and disappointed. But he could not help also remembering that his own boyhood had been spent in an atmosphere like her own in everything but its sincerity and deep conviction. His father had recognized the business value of placating the narrow tyranny of the respectable well-to-do religious community, and had become a conscious hypocrite and a popular citizen. He had himself been under that influence, and it was partly a conviction of this that had drawn him towards her as something genuine and real. It occurred to him now for the first time, as he looked around upon that compromise of their two lives in this chilly artificial home, that it was only natural that she would prefer the more truthful austerities of her mother's house. Had she detected the sham, and did she despise him for it?

These were questions which seemed to bring another self-accusing doubt in his own mind, although, without his being conscious of it, they had been really the outcome of that doubt. He could not help dwelling on the singular human interest she had taken in Demorest's love affair, and the utterly unexpected emotion she had shown. He had never seen her as charmingly illogical, capricious, and be-witchingly feminine. Had he not made a radical mistake in not giving her a frequent provocation for this innocent emotion—in fact, in not taking her out into a world of broader sympathies and experiences? What a household they might have had—if necessary in some other town—away from those cramped prejudices and limitations! What friends she might have been with Dick and his other worldly

acquaintances; what social pleasures—
guiltless amusements for her pure mind
—in theatres, parties, and concerts!
Would she have objected to them?—had
he ever seriously proposed them to her?
No! if she had objected there would have
been time enough to have made this present compromise; she would have at least
respected and understood his sacrifice—
and his friends.

Even the artificial externals of his
household had never before so visibly
impressed him. Now that she was no
longer in the room it did not even bear
a trace of her habitation, it certainly bore
no suggestion of his own. Why had he
bought that hideous horsehair furniture?
To remind her of the old provincial heir-
looms of her father's sitting-room. Did
it remind her of it? The stiff and stony
emptiness of this room had been fashioned
upon the decorous respectability of his
own father's parlor—in which his father,
who usually spent his slippered leisure in
the family sitting-room, never entered except on visits from the minister. It had
chilled his own youthful soul—why had
he perpetuated it here?

He could only answer these questions by moodily wandering about the house, and regretting he had not gone with her. After a vain attempt to establish social and domestic relations with the hot-air drum by putting his feet upon it—after an equally futile attempt to extract interest from the book of sermons by opening its pages at random—he glanced at the clock and suddenly resolved to go and fetch her. It would remind him of the old times when he used to accompany her from church, and, after her parents had retired, spend a blissful half-hour alone with her. With what a mingling of fear and childish curiosity she used to accept his equally timid caresses! Yes, he would go and fetch her; and he would recall it to her in a whisper while they were there.

Filled with this idea, when he changed his clothes again he put on a certain heavy beaver overcoat, on whose shaggy sleeve her little hand had so often rested when he escorted her from meeting; and he even selected the gray muffler she had knit for him in the old ante-nuptial days. It was lying in the half-opened drawer from where she had not long before taken her disguising veil.

It was still blowing in sudden, capricious gusts; and when he opened the front door the wind charged fiercely upon him, as if to drive him back. When he had finally forced his way into the street, a return current closed the door as suddenly and sharply behind him as if it had ejected him from his home for ever.

He reached the fourth house quickly, and as quickly ran up the steps; his hand was upon the bell when his eye suddenly caught sight of his wife's pass-key still in the lock. She had evidently forgotten it. Here was a chance to mischievously banter that habitually careful little woman! He slipped it into his pocket and quietly entered the dark but perfectly familiar hall. He reached the staircase without a stumble and began to ascend softly. Half-way up he heard the sound of his wife's hurried voice and another that startled him. He ascended hastily two steps, which brought him to the level of the half-opened transom of the kitchen. A candle was burning on the kitchen table; he could see everything that passed in the room; he could hear distinctly every word that was uttered.

He did not utter a cry or sound; he did not even tremble. He remained so rigid and motionless, clutching the banisters with his stiffened fingers, that when he did attempt to move, all life, as well as all that had made life possible to him, seemed to have died from him for ever. There was no nervous illusion, no dimming of his senses; he saw everything with a hideous clarity of perception. By some diabolical instantaneous photography of the brain, little actions, peculiarities, touches of gesture, expression and attitude never before noted by him in his wife, were clearly fixed and bitten in his consciousness. He saw the color of his friend's overcoat, the reddish tinge of his wife's brown hair, till then unnoticed; in that supreme moment he was aware of a sudden likeness to her mother; but more terrible than all, there seemed to be a nameless sympathetic resemblance that the guilty pair had to each other in gesture and movement as of some unhallowed relationship beyond his ken. He knew not how long he stood there without breath,

without reflection, without one connected
thought. He saw her suddenly put her
hand on the handle of the door. He knew
that in another moment they would pass
almost before him. He made a convulsive
effort to move, with an inward cry to God
for support, and succeeded in staggering
with outstretched palms against the wall,
down the staircase, and blindly forward
through the hall to the front door. As
yet he had been able to formulate only
one idea—to escape before them, for it
seemed to him that their contact meant
the ruin of them both, of that house, of
all that was near to him—a catastrophe
that struck blindly at his whole visible
world. He had reached the door and
opened it at the moment that the handle
of the kitchen-door was turned. He mechanically fell back behind the open door
that hid him, while it let the cruel light
glimmer for a moment on their clasped
figures. The door slipped from his nerve-
less fingers and swung to with a dull
sound. Crouching still in the corner, he
heard the quick rush of hurrying feet in
the darkness, saw the door open and Demorest glide out—saw her glance hurriedly

after him, close the door, and involve herself and him in the blackness of the hall. Her dress almost touched him in his corner; he could feel the near scent of her clothes, and the air stirred by her figure retreating towards the stairs; could hear the unlocking of a door above and the voice of her mother from the landing, his wife's reply, the slow fading of her footsteps on the stairs and overhead, the closing of a door, and all was quiet again. Still stooping, he groped for the handle of the door, opened it, and the next moment reeled like a drunken man down the steps into the street.

It was well for him that a fierce onset of wind and sleet at that instant caught him savagely—stirred his stagnated blood into action, and beat thought once more into his brain. He had mechanically turned towards his own home; his first effort of recovering will hurried him furiously past it and into a side street. He walked rapidly, but undeviatingly on to escape observation and secure some solitude for his returning thoughts. Almost before he knew it he was in the open fields.

The idea of vengeance had never crossed

his mind. He was neither a physical nor a moral coward, but he had never felt the merely animal fury of disputed animal possession which the world has chosen to recognize as a proof of outraged sentiment, nor had North Liberty accepted the ethics that an exchange of shots equalized a transferred affection. His love had been too pure and too real to be moved like the beasts of the field, to seek in one brutal passion compensation for another. Killing—what was there to kill? All that he had to live for had been already slain. With the love that was in him—in them —already dead at his feet, what was it to him whether these two hollow lives moved on and passed him, or mingled their emptiness elsewhere? Only let them henceforth keep out of his way!

For in his first feverish flow of thought —the reaction to his benumbed will within and the beating sleet without—he believed Demorest as treacherous as his wife. He recalled his sudden and unexpected intrusion into the buggy only a few hours before, his mysterious confidences, his assurance of Joan's favorable reception of his secret, and her consent to the Californian trip. What had all this meant if not that Demorest was using him, the husband, to assist his intrigue, and carry the news of his presence in the town to her? And this boldness, this assurance, this audacity of conception was like Demorest! While only certain passages of the guilty meeting he had just seen and overheard were distinctly impressed on his mind, he remembered now, with hideous and terrible clearness, all that had gone before. It was part of the disturbed and unequal exaltation of his faculties that he dwelt more upon this and his wife's previous deceit and manifest hypocrisy, than upon the actual evidence he had witnessed of her unfaithfulness. The corroboration of the fact was stronger to him than the fact itself. He understood the coldness, the uncongeniality now—the simulated increase of her aversion to Demorest—her journeys to Boston and Hartford to see her relatives, her acquiescence to his frequent absences; not an incident, not a characteristic of her married life was inconsistent with her guilt and her deceit. He went even back to her maidenhood: how did he know this was not the legitimate sequence of other secret schoolgirl escapades. The bitter worldly light that had been forced upon his simple ingenuous nature had dazzled and blinded him. He passed from fatuous credulity to equally fatuous distrust.

He stopped suddenly with the roaring of water before him. In the furious following of his rapid thought through storm and darkness he had come, he knew not how, upon the bank of the swollen river, whose endangered bridge Demorest had turned from that evening. A few steps more and he would have fallen into it. He drew nearer and looked at it with vague curiosity. Had he come there with any definite intention? The thought sobered without frightening him. There was always *that* culmination possible, and to be considered coolly.

He turned and began to retrace his steps. On his way thither he had been fighting the elements step by step; now they seemed to him to have taken possession of him and were hurrying him quickly away. But where? and to what? He was always thinking of the past. He had wandered he knew not how long, always

thinking of that. It was the future he
had to consider. What was to be done?

He had heard of such cases before; he
had read of them in newspapers and talked
of them with cold curiosity. But they
were of worldly, sinful people, of disso-
lute men whose characters he could not
conceive—of silly, vain, frivolous, and
abandoned women whom he had never
even met. But Joan—O God! It was
the first time since his mute prayer on the
staircase that the Divine name had been
wrested from his lips. It came with his
wife's—and his first tears! But the wind
swept the one away and dried the others
upon his hot cheeks.

It had ceased to rain, and the wind,
which was still high, had shifted more
to the north and was bitterly cold. He
could feel the roadway stiffening under
his feet. When he reached the pavement
of the outskirts once more he was obliged
to take the middle of the street, to avoid
the treacherous films of ice that were beginning to glaze the sidewalks. Yet this
very inclemency, added to the usual Sabbath seclusion, had left the streets deserted. He was obliged to proceed more

slowly, but he met no one and could pursue his bewildering thoughts unchecked. As he passed between the lines of cold, colorless houses, from which all light and life had vanished, it seemed to him that their occupants were dead as his love, or had fled their ruined houses as he had. Why should he remain? Yet what was his duty now as a man—as a Christian? His eye fell on the hideous façade of the church he was passing—her church! He gave a bitter laugh and stumbled on again.

With one of the gusts he fancied he heard a familiar sound—the rattling of buggy wheels over the stiffening road. Or was it merely the fanciful echo of an idea that only at that moment sprung up in his mind? If it was real it came from the street parallel with the one he was in. Who could be driving out at this time? what other buggy than his own could be found to desecrate this Christian Sabbath? An irresistible thought impelled him at the risk of recognition to quicken his pace and turn the corner as Richard Demorest drove up to the Independence Hotel, sprang from his buggy, throwing the reins over the dashboard, and disappeared into the hotel!

Blandford stood still, but for an instant only. He had been wandering for an hour aimlessly, hopelessly, without consecutive idea, coherent thought or plan of action; without the faintest inspiration or suggestion of escape from his bewildering torment, without—he had begun to fear— even the power to conceive or the will to execute; when a wild idea flashed upon him with the rattle of his buggy wheels. And even as Demorest disappeared into the hotel, he had conceived his plan and executed it. He crossed the street swiftly, leaped into his buggy, lifted the reins and brought down the whip simultaneously, and the next instant was dashing down the street in the direction of the Warensboro turnpike. So sudden was the action that by the time the astonished hall porter had rushed into the street, horse and buggy had already vanished in the darkness.

Presently it began to snow. So lightly at first that it seemed a mere passing whisper to the ear, the brush of some viewless insect upon the cheek, or the soft tap of unseen fingers on the shoulders. But by the time the porter returned from his hope-

less and invisible chase of the "runaway,"
he came in out of a swarming cloud of
whirling flakes, blinded and whitened.
There was a hurried consultation with the
landlord, the exhibition of much imperious energy and some bank-notes from
Demorest, and with a glance at the clock
that marked the expiring limit of the
Puritan Sabbath, the landlord at last consented. By the time the falling snow had
muffled the street from the indiscreet
clamor of Sabbath-breaking hoofs, the
landlord's noiseless sledge was at the door
and Demorest had departed.

The snow fell all that night; with fierce
gusts of wind that moaned in the chimneys
of North Liberty and sorely troubled the
Sabbath sleep of its decorous citizens;
with deep, passionless silences, none the
less fateful, that softly precipitated a spot-
less mantle of merciful obliteration equally
over their precise or their straying foot-
prints, that would have done them good
to heed and to remember; and when morning broke upon a world of week-day labor,
it was covered as far as their eyes could
reach as with a clear and unwritten tablet,
on which they might record their lives

anew. Near the wreck of the broken bridge on the Warensboro turnpike an overturned buggy lay imbedded in the drift and débris of the river hurrying silently towards the sea, and a horse with fragments of broken and icy harness still clinging to him was found standing before the stable-door of Edward Blandford. But to any further knowledge of the fate of its owner, North Liberty awoke never again.

# PART II

## CHAPTER I

THE last note of the Angelus had just rung out of the crumbling fissures in the tower of the mission chapel of San Buenaventura. The sun which had beamed that day and indeed every day for the whole dry season over the red-tiled roofs of that old and happily ventured pueblo seemed to broaden to a smile as it dipped below the horizon, as if in undiminished enjoyment of its old practical joke of suddenly plunging the Southern California coast in darkness without any preliminary twilight. The olive and fig trees at once lost their characteristic outlines in formless masses of shadow; only the twisted trunks of the old pear trees in the mission garden retained their grotesque shapes and became gruesome in the gathering gloom. The encircling pines beyond closed up

372

their serried files; a cool breeze swept down from the coast range and, passing through them, sent their day-long heated spices through the town.

If there was any truth in the local belief that the pious incantation of the Angelus bell had the power of excluding all evil influence abroad at that perilous hour within its audible radius, and comfortably keeping all unbelieving wickedness at a distance, it was presumably ineffective as regarded the innovating stage-coach from Monterey that twice a week at that hour brought its question-asking, revolver-persuading and fortune-seeking load of passengers through the sleepy Spanish town. On the night of the 3d of August, 1856, it had not only brought but set down at the Posada one of those passengers. It was a Mr. Ezekiel Corwin, formerly known to these pages as "hired man" to the late Squire Blandford, of North Liberty, Connecticut, but now a shrewd, practical, self-sufficient, and self-asserting unit of the more cautious later Californian immigration. As the stage rattled away again with more or less humorous and open disparagement of the town and the Posada from its "out-siders," he lounged with lazy but systematic deliberation towards Mateo Morez, the proprietor.

"I guess that some of your folks here couldn't direct me to Dick Demorest's house, could ye ?"

The Señor Mateo Morez was at once perplexed and pained. Pained at the ignorance thus forced upon him by a caballero; perplexed as to its intention. Between the two he smiled apologetically but gravely, and said: "No sabe, Señor. I 'ave not understood."

"No more hev I," returned Ezekiel, with patronizing recognition of his obtuseness. "I guess ez heow you ain't much on American. You folks orter learn the language if you kalkilate to keep a hotel."

But the momentary vision of a waistless woman with a shawl gathered over her head and shoulders at the back door attracted his attention. She said something to Mateo in Spanish, and the yellowish-white of Mateo's eyes glistened with intelligent comprehension.

"Ah, *posiblemente;* it is Don Ricardo Demorest you wish ?"

Mr. Ezekiel's face and manner expressed a mingling of grateful curiosity and some scorn at the discovery. "Wa'al," he said, looking around as if to take the entire Posada into his confidence, "way up in North Liberty, where I kem from, he was allus known as Dick Demorest, and didn't tack any forrin titles to his name. Et wouldn't hev gone down there, I reckon, 'mongst free-born Merikin citizens, no mor'n *aliases* would in court—and I kinder guess for the same reason. But folks get peart and sassy when they're way from hum, and put on ez many airs as a buck nigger. And so he calls hisself Don Ricardo here, does he ?"

"The Señor knows Don Ricardo ?" said Mateo politely.

"Ef you mean me—wa'al, yes—I should say so. He was a partiklar friend of a man I've known since he was knee-high to a grasshopper."

Ezekiel had actually never seen Demorest but once in his life. He would have scorned to lie, but strict accuracy was not essential with an ignorant foreign audience.

He took up his carpet-bag.

"I reckon I kin find his house, ef it's anyway handy."

But the Señor Mateo was again politely troubled. The house of Don Ricardo was of a truth not more than a mile distant. It was even possible that the Señor had observed it above a wall and vineyard as he came into the pueblo. But it was late—it was also dark, as the Señor would himself perceive—and there was still to-morrow. To-morrow—ah, it was always there! Meanwhile there were beds of a miraculous quality at the Posada, and a supper such as a caballero might order in his own house. Health, discretion, solicitude for oneself—all pointed clearly to to-morrow.

What part of this speech Ezekiel understood affected him only as an innkeeper's bid for custom, and as such to be steadily exposed and disposed of. With the remark that he guessed Dick Demorest's was "a good enough hotel for *him*," and that he'd better be "getting along there," he walked down the steps, carpet-bag in hand, and coolly departed, leaving Mateo pained, but smiling, on the doorstep.

"An animal with a pig's head—without doubt," said Mateo, sententiously.

"Clearly a brigand with the liver of a chicken," responded his wife.

The subject of this ambiguous criticism, happily oblivious, meantime walked doggedly back along the road the stage-coach had just brought him. It was badly paved and hollowed in the middle with the worn ruts of a century of slow undeviating ox carts, and the passage of water during the rainy season. The low adobe houses on each side, with bright cinnamon-colored tiles relieving their dark-brown walls, had the regular outlines of their doors and windows obliterated by the crumbling of years, until they looked as if they had been afterthoughts of the builder, rudely opened by pick and crowbar, and finished by the gentle auxiliary architecture of birds and squirrels. Yet these openings at times permitted glimpses of a picturesque past in the occasional view of a lace-edged pillow or silken counterpane, striped hangings, or dyed Indian rugs, the flitting of a flounced petticoat or flower-covered head, or the indolent leaning figure framed in a doorway of a man in wide velvet trousers and crimson-barred serape, whose brown face was partly hidden in a yellow nimbus of

cigarette smoke. Even in the semi-darkness, Ezekiel's penetrating and impertinent
eyes took eager note of these facts with
superior complacency, quite unmindful,
after the fashion of most critical travellers,
of the hideous contrast of his own long
shapeless nankeen duster, his stiff half-
clerical brown straw hat, his wisp of
gingham necktie, his dusty boots, his out-
rageous carpet-bag, and his straggling
goat-like beard. A few looked at him in
grave, discreet wonder. Whether they recognized in him the advent of a civilization
that was destined to supplant their own
ignorant, sensuous, colorful life with austere intelligence and rigid practical im-
provement, did not appear. He walked
steadily on. As he passed the low arched
door of the mission church and saw a faint
light glimmering from the side windows,
he had indeed a weak human desire to go
in and oppose in his own person a debased
and idolatrous superstition with some happily chosen question that would necessarily
make the officiating priest and his congregation exceedingly uncomfortable. But he
resisted; partly in the hope of meeting
some idolater on his way to Benediction,

and, in the guise of a stranger seeking information, dropping a few unpalatable truths; and partly because he could unbosom himself later to Demorest, who he was not unwilling to believe had embraced Popery with his adoption of a Spanish surname and title.

It had become quite dark when he reached the long wall that enclosed Demorest's premises. The wall itself excited his resentment, not only as indicating an exclusiveness highly objectionable in a man who had emigrated from a free State, but because he, Ezekiel Corwin, had difficulty in discovering the entrance. When he succeeded, he found himself before an iron gate, happily open, but savoring offensively of feudalism and tyrannical proprietorship, and passed through and entered an avenue of trees scarcely distinguishable in the darkness, whose mysterious shapes and feathery plumes were unknown to him. Numberless odors equally vague and mysterious were heavy in the air, strange and delicate plants rose dimly on either hand; enormous blossoms, like ghostly faces, seemed to peer at him from the shadows. For an instant Ezekiel succumbed to an unprofitable sense of beauty, and acquiesced in this reckless extravagance of Nature that was so unlike North Liberty. But the next moment he recovered himself, with the reflection that it was probably unhealthy, and doggedly approached the house. It was a long, one-storied structure, apparently all roof, vine, and pillared veranda. Every window and door was open; the two or three grass hammocks swung emptily between the columns; the bamboo chairs and settees were vacant; his heavy footsteps on the floor had summoned no attendant; not even a dog had barked as he approached the house. It was shiftless, it was sinful—it boded no good to the future of Demorest.

He put down his carpet-bag on the veranda and entered the broad hall, where an old-fashioned lantern was burning on a stand. Here, too, the doors of the various apartments were open, and the rooms themselves empty of occupants. An opportunity not to be lost by Ezekiel's inquiring mind thus offered itself. He took the lantern and deliberately examined the several apartments, the furniture, the bedding, and even the small articles that were on the tables and mantels. When he had completed the round—including a corridor opening on a dark courtyard, which he did not penetrate—he returned to the hall, and set down the lantern again.

"Well," said a voice in his own familiar vernacular, "I hope you like it."

Ezekiel was surprised, but not disconcerted. What he had taken in the shadow for a bundle of *serapes* lying on the floor of the veranda, was the recumbent figure of a man who now raised himself to a sitting posture.

"Ez to that," drawled Ezekiel, with unshaken self-possession, "whether I like it or not ez only a question betwixt kempany manners and truth-telling. Beggars hadn't oughter be choosers, and transient visitors like myself needn't allus speak their mind. But if you mean to signify that with every door and window open and universal shiftlessness lying round everywhere temptin' Providence, you ain't lucky in havin' a feller-citizen of yours drop in on ye instead of some Mexican thief, I don't agree with ye—that's all."

The man laughed shortly and rose up. In spite of his careless yet picturesque

Mexican dress, Ezekiel instantly recognized Demorest. With his usual instincts he was naturally pleased to observe that he looked older and more careworn. The softer, sensuous climate had perhaps imparted a heaviness to his figure and a deliberation to his manner that was quite unlike his own potential energy.

"That don't tell me who you are, and what you want," he said, coldly.

"Wa'al then, I'm Ezekiel Corwin of North Liberty, ez used to live with my friend and *yours* too, I guess—seein' how the friendship was swapped into relationship—Squire Blandford."

A slight shade passed over Demorest's face. "Well," he said, impatiently, "I don't remember you; what then ?"

"You don't remember me; that's likely," returned Ezekiel imperturbably, combing his straggling chin beard with three fingers, "but whether it's *nat'ral* or not, considerin' the sukumstances when we last met, ez a matter of op-pinion. You got me to harness up the hoss and buggy the night Squire Blandford left home, and never was heard of again. It's true that it kem out on enquiry that the hoss and buggy ran away from the hotel, and that you had to go out to Warensboro in a sleigh, and the theory is that poor Squire Blandford must have stopped the hoss and buggy somewhere, got in and got run away agin, and pitched over the bridge. But seein' your relationship to both Squire and Mrs. Blandford, and all the sukumstances, I reckoned you'd remember it."

"I heard of it in Boston a month afterwards," said Demorest, dryly, "but I don't think I'd have recognized you. So you were the hired man who gave me the buggy. Well, I don't suppose they discharged you for it."

"No," said Ezekiel, with undisturbed equanimity. "I kalkilate Joan would have stopped that. Considerin', too, that I knew her when she was Deacon Salisbury's darter, and our fam'lies waz thick az peas. She knew me well enough when I met her in Frisco the other day."

"Have you seen Mrs. Demorest already?" said Demorest, with sudden vivacity. "Why didn't you say so before?" It was wonderful how quickly his face had lighted up with an earnestness that was not, however, without some undefinable uneasiness. The alert Ezekiel noticed it and observed that it was as totally unlike the irresistible dominance of the man of five years ago as it was different from the heavy abstraction of the man of five minutes before.

"I reckon you didn't ax me," he returned coolly. "She told me where you were, and as I had business down this way she guessed I might drop in."

"Yes, yes—it's all right, Mr. Corwin; glad you did," said Demorest, kindly but half nervously. "And you saw Mrs. Demorest? Where did you see her, and how did you think she was looking? As pretty as ever, eh?"

But the coldly literal Ezekiel was not to be beguiled into polite or ambiguous fiction. He even went to the extent of insulting deliberation before he replied. "I've seen Joan Salisbury lookin' healthier and ez far ez I kin judge doin' more credit to her stock and raisin' gin'rally," he said, thoughtfully combing his beard, "and I've seen her when she was too poor to get the silks and satins, furbelows, fineries and vanities she's flauntin' in now, and that was in Squire Blandford's time, too, I reckon. Ez to her purtiness, that's a matter of taste. You think her purty, and I guess them fellows ez was escortin' and squirin' her round Frisco thought so too, or *she* thought they did to hev allowed it."

"You are not very merciful to your townsfolk, Mr. Corwin," said Demorest, with a forced smile; "but what can I do for you?"

It was the turn for Ezekiel's face to brighten, or rather to break up, like a cold passionless mirror suddenly cracked, into various amusing but distorted reflections on the person before him. "Townies ain't to be fooled by other townies, Mr. Demorest; at least that ain't my idea o' marcy, he-he! But seen you're pressin', I don't mind tellen you *my* business. I'm the only agent of Seventeen Patent Medicine Proprietors in Connecticut represented by the firm of Dilworth & Dusenberry, of San Francisco. Mebbe you heard of 'em afore—A1 druggists and importers. Wa'al, I'm openin' a field for 'em and spreadin' 'em gin'rally through these air benighted and onhealthy districts, havin' the contract for the hull State—especially for Wozun's Universal Injin

Panacea ez cures everything—bein' had from a recipe given by a Sachem to Dr. Wozun's gran'ther. That bag—leavin' out a dozen paper collars and socks—is all the rest samples. That's me, Ezekiel Corwin —only agent for Californy, and that's my mission."

"Very well; but look here, Corwin," said Demorest, with a slight return of his old off-hand manner,—"I'd advise you to adopt a little more caution, and a little less criticism in your speech to the people about here, or I'm afraid you'll need the Universal Panacea for yourself. Better men than you have been shot in my presence for half your freedom."

"I guess you've just hit the bull's-eye there," replied Ezekiel, coolly, "for it's that *half*-freedom and *half*-truth that doesn't pay. I kalkilate gin'rally to speak my hull mind—and I *do*. Wot's the consequence? Why, when folks find I ain't afeard to speak my mind on their affairs, they kinder guess I'm tellin' the truth about my own. Folks don't like the man that truckles to 'em, whether it's in the sellin' of a box of pills or a principle. When they re-cognize Ezekiel Corwin

ain't goin' to lie about 'em to curry favor
with 'em, they're ready to believe he ain't
goin' to lie about Jones' Bitters or Wozun's Panacea. And, wa'al, I've been on
the road just about a fortnit, and I haven't
yet discovered that the original independent style introduced by Ezekiel Corwin
ever broke anybody's bones or didn't
pay."

And he told the truth. That remark-
ably unfair and unpleasant spoken man
had actually frozen Hanley's Ford into
icy astonishment at his audacity, and he
had sold them an invoice of the Panacea
before they had recovered; he had insulted
Chipitas into giving an extensive order
in bitters; he had left Hayward's Creek
pledged to Burne's pills—with drawn re-
volvers still in their hands.

At another time Demorest might have
been amused at his guest's audacity, or
have combated it with his old imperiousness, but he only remained looking at him
in a dull sort of way as if yielding to his
influence. It was part of the phenomenon
that the two men seemed to have changed
character since they last met, and when
Ezekiel said confidentially: "I reckon

you're goin' to show me what room I ken stow these duds o' mine in," Demorest replied hurriedly, "Yes, certainly," and taking up his guest's carpet-bag preceded him through the hall to one of the apartments.

"I'll send Manuel to you presently," he said, putting down the bag mechanically; "the servants are not back from church, it's some saint's festival to-day."

"And so you keep a pack of lazy idolaters to leave your house to take care of itself, whilst they worship graven images," said Ezekiel, delighted at this opportunity to improve the occasion.

"If my memory isn't bad, Mr. Corwin," said Demorest dryly, "when I accompanied Mr. Blandford home the night he returned from his journey, we found *you* at church, and he had to put up his horse himself."

"But that was the Sabbath—the seventh day of the command," retorted Ezekiel.

"And here the Sabbath doesn't consist of only *one* day to serve God in," said Demorest, sententiously.

Ezekiel glanced under his white lashes at Demorest's thoughtful face. His fondest fears appeared to be confirmed; Demo-rest had evidently become a Papist. But that gentleman stopped any theological discussion by the abrupt inquiry:

"Did Mrs. Demorest say when she thought of returning?"

"She allowed she mout kem to-morrow —but—" added Ezekiel dubiously.

"But what."

"Wa'al, wot with her enjyments of the vanities of this life and the kempany she keeps, I reckon she's in no hurry," said Ezekiel, cheerfully.

The entrance of Manuel here cut short any response from Demorest, who after a few directions in Spanish to the *peon,* left his guest to himself.

He walked to the veranda with the same dull preoccupation that Ezekiel had noticed as so different from his old deci-sive manner, and remained for a few mo-ments abstractedly gazing into the dark garden. The strange and mystic shapes which had impressed even the practical Ezekiel, had become even more weird and ghost-like in the faint radiance of a rising moon.

What memories evoked by his rude

guest seemed to take form and outline in
that dreamy and unreal expanse!

He saw his wife again, standing as she
had stood that night in her mother's house,
with the white muffler around her head,
and white face, imploring him to fly; he
saw himself again hurrying through the
driving storm to Warensboro, and reaching the train that bore him swiftly and
safely miles away—that same night when
her husband was perishing in the swollen
river. He remembered with what strangely
mingled sensations he had read the account
of Blandford's death in the newspapers,
and how the loss of his old friend was forgotten in the associations conjured up by
his singular meeting that very night with
the mysterious woman he had loved. He
remembered that he had never dreamed
how near and fateful were these associations; and how he had kept his promise
not to seek her without her permission,
until six months after, when she appointed
a meeting, and revealed to him the whole
truth. He could see her now, as he had
seen her then, more beautiful and fas-
cinating than ever in her black dress, and
the pensive grace of refined suffering and

restrained passion in her delicate face. He remembered, too, how the shock of her disclosure—the knowledge that she had been his old friend's wife—seemed only to accent her purity and suffering and his own wilful recklessness, and how it had stirred all the chivalry, generosity, and affection of his easy nature to take the whole responsibility of this innocent but compromising intrigue on his own shoulders. He had had no self-accusing sense of disloyalty to Blandford in his practical nature; he had never suspected the shy, proper girl of being his wife; he was willing to believe now, that had he known it, even that night, he would never have seen her again; he had been very foolish; he had made this poor woman participate in his folly; but he had never been dishonest or treacherous in thought or action. If Blandford had lived, even he would have admitted it. Yet he was guiltily conscious of a material satisfaction in Blandford's death, without his wife's religious conviction of the saving graces of predestination.

They had been married quietly when the two years of her widowhood had expired; his former relations with her husband and

the straitened circumstances in which
Blandford's death had left her having
been deemed sufficient excuse in the eyes
of North Liberty for her more worldly
union. They had come to California at
her suggestion "to begin life anew," for
she had not hesitated to make this dislocation of all her antecedent surroundings
as a reason as well as a condition of this
marriage. She wished to see the world
of which he had been a passing glimpse;
to expand under his protection beyond the
limits of her fettered youth. He had
bought this old Spanish estate, with its
near vineyard and its outlying leagues
covered with wild cattle, partly from
that strange contradictory predilection for
peaceful husbandry common to men who
have led a roving life, and partly as a
check to her growing and feverish desire
for change and excitement. He had at
first enjoyed with an almost parental
affection her childish unsophisticated delight in that world he had already wearied
of, and which he had been prepared to
gladly resign for her. But as the months
and even years had passed without any
apparent diminution in her zest for these

pleasures, he tried uneasily to resume his old interest in them, and spent ten months with her in the chaotic freedom of San Francisco hotel life. But to his discomfiture he found that they no longer diverted him; to his horror he discovered that those easy gallantries in which he had spent his youth, and in which he had seen no harm, were intolerable when exhibited to his wife, and he trembled between inquietude and indignation at the copies of his former self, whom he met in hotel parlors, at theatres, and in public conveyances. The next time she visited some friends in San Francisco he did not accompany her. Though he fondly cherished his experience of her power to resist even stronger temptation, he was too practical to subject himself to the annoyance of witnessing it. In her absence he trusted her completely; his scant imagination conjured up no disturbing picture of possibilities beyond what he actually knew. In his recent questions of Ezekiel he did not expect to learn anything more. Even his guest's uncomfortable comments added no sting that he had not already felt.

With these thoughts called up by the

unlooked-for advent of Ezekiel under his
roof, he continued to gaze moodily into
the garden. Near the house were scattered
several uncouth varieties of cacti which
seemed to have lost all semblance of vegetable growth, and had taken rude likeness
to beasts and human figures. One high-
shouldered specimen, partly hidden in the
shadow, had the appearance of a man with
a cloak or *serape* thrown over his left
shoulder. As Demorest's wandering eyes
at last became fixed upon it, he fancied
he could trace the faint outlines of a pale
face, the lower part of which was hidden
by the folds of the *serape*. There certainly was the forehead, the curve of the
dark eyebrows, the shadow of a nose, and
even as he looked more steadily, a glistening of the eyes upturned to the moonlight. A sudden chill seized him. It was
a horrible fancy, but it looked as might
have looked the dead face of Edward
Blandford! He started and ran quickly
down the steps of the veranda. A slight
wind at the same moment moved the long
leaves and tendrils of a vine nearest him
and sent a faint wave through the garden.
He reached the cactus; its fantastic bulk

stood plainly before him, but nothing more.

"Whar are ye runnin' to ?" said the inquiring voice of Ezekiel from the veranda.

"I thought I saw some one in the garden," returned Demorest, quietly, satisfied of the illusion of his senses, "but it was a mistake."

"It mout and it moutn't," said Ezekiel, dryly. "Thar's nothin' to keep any one out. It's only a wonder that you ain't overrun with thieves and sich like."

"There are usually servants about the place," said Demorest, carelessly.

"Ef they're the same breed ez that Manuel, I reckon I'd almost as leave take my chances in the road. Ef it's all the same to you I kalkilate to put a paytent fastener to my door and winder to-night. I allus travel with them." Seeing that Demorest only shrugged his shoulders without replying, he continued, "Et ain't far from here that some folks allow is the headquarters of that cattle-stealing gang. The driver of the coach went ez far ez to say that some of these high and mighty Dons hereabouts knows more of it than they keer to tell."

"That's simply a yarn for greenhorns," said Demorest, contemptuously. "I know all the ranch proprietors for twenty leagues around, and they've lost as many cattle and horses as I have."

"I wanter know," said Ezekiel, with grim interest. "Then you've already had consid'ble losses, eh? I kalkilate them cattle are vally'ble—about wot figger do you reckon yer out and injured?"

"Three or four thousand dollars, I suppose, altogether," replied Demorest, shortly.

"Then you don't take any stock in them yer yarns about the gang being run and protected by some first-class men in Frisco?" said Ezekiel, regretfully.

"Not much," responded Demorest, dryly; "but if people choose to believe this bluff gotten up by the petty thieves themselves to increase their importance and secure their immunity—they can. But here's Manuel to tell us supper is ready."

He led the way to the corridor and courtyard which Ezekiel had not penetrated on account of its obscurity and solitude, but which now seemed to be peopled with peons and household servants of both sexes. At the end of a long low-ceilinged room a table was spread with omelettes, *chupa,* cakes, chocolate, grapes, and melons, around which half a dozen attendants stood gravely in waiting. The size of the room, which to Ezekiel's eyes looked as large as the church at North Liberty, the profusion of the viands, the six attendants for the host and solitary guest, deeply impressed him. Morally rebelling against this feudal display and extravagance, he, who had disdained to even assist the Blandfords' servant-in-waiting at table and had always made his solitary meal on the kitchen dresser, was not above feeling a material satisfaction in sitting on equal terms with his master's friend and being served by these menials he despised. He did full justice to the victuals of which Demorest partook in sparing abstraction, and particularly to the fruit, which Demorest did not touch at all. Observant of his servants' eyes fixed in wonder on the strange guest who had just disposed of a second melon at supper, Demorest could not help remarking that he would lose credit as a *medico* with the natives unless he restrained a public exhibition of his tastes.

"Ez ha'aw?" queried Ezekiel.

"They have a proverb here that fruit is gold in the morning, silver at noon, and lead at night."

"That'll do for lazy stomicks," said the unabashed Ezekiel. "When they're once fortified by Jones' bitters and hard work, they'll be able to tackle the Lord's nat'ral gifts of the airth at any time."

Declining the cigarettes offered him by Demorest for a quid of tobacco, which he gravely took from a tin box in his pocket, and to the astonished eyes of the servants apparently obliterated any further remembrance of the meal, he accompanied his host to the veranda again, where, tilting his chair back and putting his feet on the railing, he gave himself up to unwonted and silent rumination.

The silence was broken at last by Demorest, who, half-reclining on a settee, had once or twice glanced towards the misshapen cactus.

"Was there any trace discovered of Blandford, other than we knew before we left the States?"

"Wa'al, no," said Ezekiel, thoughtfully. "The last idea was that he'd got control

of the hoss after passin' the bridge, and
had managed to turn him back, for there
was marks of buggy wheels on the snow
on the far side, and that fearin' to trust
the hoss or the bridge he tried to lead him
over when the bridge gave way, and he
was caught in the wreck and carried off
down stream. That would account for his
body not bein' found; they do tell that
chunks of that bridge were picked up on
the Sound beach near the mouth o' the
river, nigh unto sixty miles away. That's
about the last idea they had of it at North
Liberty." He paused and then cleverly
directing a stream of tobacco juice at an
accurate curve over the railing, wiped
his lips with the back of his hand, and
added, slowly: "Thar's another idea—but
I reckon it's only mine. Leastways I ain't
heard it argued by anybody."

"What is that?" asked Demorest.

"Wa'al, it ain't exakly complimentary
to E. Blandford, Esq., and it mout be
orkard for *you*."

"I don't think you're in the habit of
letting such trifles interfere with your
opinion," said Demorest, with a slightly
forced laugh; "but what is your idea?"

"That thar wasn't any accident."

"No accident?" replied Demorest, raising himself on his elbow.

"Nary accident," continued Ezekiel, deliberately, "and, if it comes to that, not much of a dead body either."

"What the devil do you mean?" said Demorest, sitting up.

"I mean," said Ezekiel, with momentous deliberation, "that E. Blandford, of the Winnipeg Mills, was in March, '50, ez nigh bein' bust up ez any man kin be without actually failin'; that he'd been down to Boston that day to get some extensions; that old Deacon Salisbury knew it, and had been pesterin' Mrs. Blandford to induce him to sell out and leave the place; and that the night he left he took about two hundred and fifty dollars in bank bills that they allus kept in the house, and Mrs. Blandford was in the habit o' hidin' in the breast-pocket of one of his old overcoats hangin' up in the closet. I mean that that air money and that air overcoat went off with him, ez Mrs. Blandford knows, for I heard her tell her ma about it. And when his affairs were wound up and his debts paid, I reckon that the two hundred and fifty was all there was left—and he scooted with it. It's orkard for you—ez I said afore—but I don't see wot on earth you need get riled for. Ef he ran off on account of only two hundred and fifty dollars he ain't goin' to run back again for the mere matter o' your marrying Joan. Ef he had—he'd a done it afore this. It's orkard ez I said—but the only orkardness is your feelin's. I reckon Joan's got used to hers."

Demorest had risen angrily to his feet. But the next moment the utter impossibility of reaching this man's hidebound moral perception by even physical force hopelessly overcame him. It would only impress him with the effect of his own disturbing power, that to Ezekiel was equal to a proof of the truth of his opinions. It might even encourage him to repeat this absurd story elsewhere with his own construction upon his reception of it. After all it was only Ezekiel's opinion— an opinion too preposterous for even a moment's serious consideration. Blandford alive, and a petty defaulter! Blandford above the earth and complacently abandoning his wife and home to another!

Blandford—perhaps a sneaking, cowardly Nemesis—hiding in the shadow for future —impossible! It really was enough to make him laugh.

He did laugh, albeit with an uneasy sense that only a few years ago he would have struck down the man who had thus traduced his friend's memory.

"You've been overtaxing your brain in patent-medicine circulars, Corwin," he said in a roughly rallying manner, "and you've got rather too much highfalutin and bitters mixed with your opinions. After that yarn of yours you must be dry. What'll you take? I haven't got any New England rum, but I can give you some ten-year-old *aguardiente* made on the place."

As he spoke he lifted a decanter and glass from a small table which Manuel had placed in the veranda.

"I guess not," said Ezekiel dryly. "It's now goin' on five years since I've been a consistent temperance man."

"In everything but melons, and criticism of your neighbor, eh?" said Demorest, pouring out a glass of the liquor.

"I hev my convictions," said Ezekiel with affected meekness.

"And I have mine," said Demorest, tossing off the fiery liquor at a draft, "and it's that this is devilish good stuff. Sorry you can't take some. I'm afraid I'll have to get you to excuse me for a while. I have to take a ride over the ranch before turning in, to see if everything's right. The house is 'at your disposition,' as we say here. I'll see you later."

He walked away with a slight exaggeration of unconcern. Ezekiel watched him narrowly with colorless eyes beneath his white lashes. When he had gone he examined the thoroughly emptied glass of *aguardiente,* and, taking the decanter, sniffed critically at its sharp and potent contents. A smile of gratified discernment followed. It was clear to him that Demorest was a heavy drinker.

Contrary to his prognostication, however, Mrs. Demorest *did* arrive the next day. But although he was to depart from Buenaventura by the same coach that had set her down at the gate of the *casa,* he had already left the house armed with some letters of introduction which Demorest had generously given him, to certain small traders in the pueblo and along the route. Demorest was not displeased to part with him before the arrival of his wife, and thus spare her the awkwardness of a repetition of Ezekiel's effrontery in her presence. Nor was he willing to have the impediment of a guest in the house to any explanation he might have to seek from her, or to the confidences that hereafter must be fuller and more mutual. For with all his deep affection for his wife, Richard Demorest unconsciously feared her. The strong man whose dominance over men and women alike had been his salient characteristic, had begun to feel an undefinable sense of some unrecognized quality in the woman he loved. He had once or twice detected it in a tone of her voice, in a remembered and perhaps even once idolized gesture, or in the accidental lapse of some bewildering word. With the generosity of a large nature he had put the thought aside, referring it to some selfish weakness of his own, or— more fatuous than all—to a possible diminution of his own affection.

He was standing on the steps ready to receive her. Few of her appreciative sex could have remained indifferent to the

tender and touching significance of his
silent and subdued welcome. He had that
piteous wistfulness of eye seen in some
dogs and the husbands of many charming
women—the affection that pardons beforehand the indifference it has learned to
expect. She approached him smiling in
her turn, meeting the sublime patience of
being unloved with the equally resigned
patience of being loved, and feeling that
comforting sense of virtue which might
become a bore, but never a self-reproach.
For the rest, she was prettier than ever;
her five years of expanded life had slightly
rounded the elongated oval of her face,
filled up the ascetic hollows of her temples,
and freed the repression of her mouth and
chin. A more genial climate had quickened the circulation that North Liberty
had arrested, and suffused the transparent
beauty of her skin with eloquent life. It
seemed as if the long, protracted northern spring of her youth had suddenly burst
into a summer of womanhood under those
gentle skies; and yet enough of her puritan precision of manner, movement, and
gesture remained to temper her fuller and
more exuberant life and give it repose.

In a community of pretty women more or less given to the license and extravagance of the epoch, she always looked like a lady.

He took her in his arms and half-lifted her up the last step of the veranda. She resisted slightly with her characteristic action of catching his wrists in both her hands and holding him off with an awkward primness, and almost in the same tone that she had used to Edward Blandford five years before, said:

"There, Dick, that will do."

## CHAPTER II

DEMOREST'S dream of a few days' conjugal seclusion and confidences with his wife was quickly dispelled by that lady. "I came down with Rosita Pico, whose father, you know, once owned this property," she said. "She's gone on to her cousins at Los Osos Rancho to-night, but comes here to-morrow for a visit. She knows the place well; in fact, she once had a romantic love affair here. But she is very entertaining. It will be a little change for us," she added, naively.

Demorest kept back a sigh, without changing his gentle smile. "I'm glad for your sake, dear. But is she not a little flighty and inclined to flirt a good deal? I think I've heard so."

"She's a young girl who has been severely tried, Richard, and perhaps is not to blame for endeavoring to forget it in such distraction as she can find," said Mrs. Demorest, with a slight return of her old manner. *"I* can understand her feelings perfectly." She looked pointedly at her husband as she spoke, it being one of her late habits to openly refer to their ante-nuptial acquaintance as a natural reaction from the martyrdom of her first marriage, with a quiet indifference that seemed almost an indelicacy. But her husband only said: "As you like, dear," vaguely remembering Doña Rosita as the alleged heroine of a forgotten romance with some earlier American adventurer who had disappeared, and trying vainly to reconcile his wife's sentimental description of her with his own recollection of the buxom, pretty, laughing, but dangerous-eyed Spanish girl he had, however, seen but once.

She arrived the next day, flying into a

protracted embrace of Joan, which included a smiling recognition of Demorest
with an unoccupied blue eye, and a shake
of her fan over his wife's shoulder. Then
she drew back and seemed to take in the
whole veranda and garden in another long
caress of her eyes. "Ah—yess! I have
recog-nized it, mooch. It es ze same. Of
no change—not even of a leetle. No, she
ess always—esso." She stopped, looked
unutterable things at Joan, pressed her fan
below a spray of roses on her full bodice
as if to indicate some thrilling memory
beneath it, shook her head again, suddenly
caught sight of Demorest's serious face,
said: "Ah, that brigand of our husband
laughs himself at me," and then herself
broke into a charming ripple of laughter.

"But I was not laughing, Doña Rosita,"
said Demorest, smiling sadly, however, in
spite of himself.

She made a little grimace, and then
raised her elbows, slightly lifting her
shoulders. "As it shall please you, Señor.
But he is gone—thees passion. Yess—
what you shall call thees sentiment of lof
—zo—as he came!" She threw her fingers in the air as if to illustrate the

volatile and transitory passage of her af-
fections, and then turned again to Joan
with her back towards Demorest.

"Do please go on—Doña Rosita," said
he. "I never heard the real story. If
there is any romance about my house, I'd
like to know it," he added with a faint
sigh.

Doña Rosita wheeled upon him with an
inquiring little look. "Ah, you have the
sentiment, and *you,*" she continued, taking
Joan by the arms, "*you* have not. Eet ess
good so. When a—the wife," she continued boldly, hazarding an extended English
abstraction, "he has the sentimente and the
hoosband he has nothing, eet is not good—
for a-him—ze wife," she concluded triumphantly.

"But I have great appreciation and I
am dying to hear it," said Demorest, trying to laugh.

"Well, poor one, you look so. But you
shall lif till another time," said Doña Rosita, with a mock courtesy, gliding with
Joan away.

The "other time" came that evening
when chocolate was served on the veranda,
where Doña Rosita, mantilla-draped

against the dry, clear, moonlit air, sat at the feet of Joan on the lowest step. Demorest, uneasily observant of the influence of the giddy foreigner on his wife, and conscious of certain confidences between them from which he was excluded, leaned against a pillar of the porch in half abstracted resignation; Joan, under the tutelage of Rosita, lit a cigarette; Demorest gazed at her wonderingly, trying to recall, in her fuller and more animated face, some memory of the pale, refined profile of the Puritan girl he had first met in the Boston train, the faint aurora of whose cheek in that northern clime seemed to come and go with his words. Becoming conscious at last of the eyes of Doña Rosita watching him from below, with an effort he recalled his duty as her host and gallantly reminded her that moonlight and the hour seemed expressly fitted for her promised love story.

"Do tell it," said Joan, "I don't mind hearing it again."

"Then you know it already?" said Demorest, surprised.

Joan took the cigarette from her lips, laughed complacently, and exchanged a fa-

miliar glance with Rosita. "She told it
me a year ago, when we first knew each
other," she replied. "Go on, dear," to
Rosita.

Thus encouraged, Doña Rosita began,
addressing herself first in Spanish to Demorest, who understood the language better
than his wife, and lapsing into her characteristic English as she appealed to them
both. It was really very little to interest
Don Ricardo—this story of a silly *mucha-
cha* like herself and a strange *caballero.*
He would go to sleep while she was talking,
and to-night he would say to his wife,
"Mother of God! why have you brought
here this chattering parrot who speaks but
of one thing?" But she would go on always like the windmill, whether there was
grain to grind or no. "It was four years
ago. Ah! Don Ricardo did not remember
the country then—it was when the first
Americans came—now it is different.
Then there were no coaches—in truth one
travelled very little, and always on horseback, only to see one's neighbors. And suddenly, as if in one day, it was changed;
there were strange men on the roads, and
one was frightened, and one shut the gates

of the pateo and drove the horses into the
corral. One did not know much of the
Americans then—for why? They were always going, going—never stopping, hurrying on to the gold mines, hurrying away
from the gold mines, hurrying to look for
other gold mines: but always going on foot,
on horseback, in queer wagons—hurrying,
pushing everywhere. Ah, it took away the
breath. All, except one 'American—he
did not hurry, he did not go with the
others, he came and stayed here at Buenaventura. He was very quiet, very civil,
very sad, and very discreet. He was not
like the others, and always kept aloof from
them. He came to see Don Andreas Pico,
and wanted to beg a piece of land and an
old *vaquero's* hut near the road for a trifle.
Don Andreas would have given it, or a
better house, to him, or have had him live
at the *casa* here; but he would not. He
was very proud and shy, so he took the
*vaquero's* hut, a mere adobe affair, and
lived in it, though a *caballero* like yourself,'
with white hands that knew not labor, and
small feet that had seldom walked. In
good time he learned to ride like the best
*vaquero,* and helped Don Andreas to find

the lost mustangs, and showed him how to
improve the old mill. And his pride and
his shyness wore off, and he would come to
the *casa* sometimes. And Don Andreas got
to love him very much, and his daughter,
Doña Rosita—ah, well, yes truly—a leetle.

"But he had strange moods and ways,
this American, and at times they would
have thought him a *lunatico* had they not
believed it to be an American fashion. He
would be very kind and gentle like one of
the family, coming to the *casa* every day,
playing with the children, advising Don
Andreas and—yes—having a devotion—
very discreet, very ceremonious, for Doña
Rosita. And then, all in a moment, he
would become as ill, without a word or gesture, until he would stalk out of the house,
gallop away furiously, and for a week not ·
be heard of. The first time it happened,
Doña Rosita was piqued by his rudeness,
Don Andreas was alarmed, for it was on
an evening like the present, and Doña Rosita was teaching him a little song on the
guitar when the fit came on him. And he
snapped the guitar strings like thread and
threw it down, and got up like a bear and
walked away without a word."

"I see it all," said Demorest, half seriously: "you were coquetting with him, and he was jealous."

But Doña Rosita shook her head and turned impetuously, and said in English to Joan:

"No, it was *astutcia*—a trick, a ruse. Because when my father have arrived at his house, he is agone. And so every time. When he have the fit he goes not to his house. No. And it ees not until after one time when he comes back never again, that we have comprehend what he do at these times. And what do you think? I shall tell to you."

She composed herself comfortably, with her plump elbows on her knees, and her fan crossed on the palm of her hand before her, and began again:

"It is a year he has gone, and the stage-coach is attack of brigands. Tiburcio, our *vaquero,* have that night made himself a *pasear* on the road, and he have seen *him.* He have seen, one, two, three men came from the wood with something on the face, and *he* is of them. He has nothing on his face, and Tiburcio have recognize him. We have laugh at Tiburcio. We believe

him not. It is improbable that this Señor
Huanson—"

"Senor who?" said Demorest.

"Huanson—eet is the name of him.
Ah, Carr!—posiblemente it is nothing—a
Don Fulano—or an *apodo*—Huanson."

"Oh, I see, *Johnson,* very likely."

"We have said it is not possible that this
good man, who have come to the house and
ride on his back the children, is a thief and
a brigand. And one night my father have
come from the Monterey in the coach, and
it was stopped. And the brigands have
take from the passengers the money, the
rings from the finger, and the watch—and
my father was of the same. And my
father, he have great dissatisfaction and
anguish, for his watch is given to him of
an old friend, and it is not like the other
watch. But the watch he go all the same.
And then when the robbers have made a
finish comes to the window of the coach a
*mascara* and have say, 'Who is the Don
Andreas Pico?' And my father have say,
'It is I who am Don Andreas Pico.' And
the mask have say, 'Behold, your watch is
restore!' and he gif it to him. And my
father say, 'To whom have I the dis-

tinguished honor to thank?' And the mask say—"

"Johnson," interrupted Demorest.

"No," said Doña Rosita in grave triumph, "he say Essmith. For this Essmith is like Huanson—an *apodo*—nothing."

"Then you really think this man was your old friend?" asked Demorest.

"I think."

"And that he was a robber even when living here—and that it was not your cruelty that really drove him to take the road?"

Doña Rosita shrugged her plump shoulders. "You will not comprehend. It was because of his being a brigand that he stayed not with us. My father would not have object if he have present himself to me for marriage in these times. I would not have object, for I was young, and we have knew nothing. It was he who have object. For why? Inside of his heart he have feel he was a brigand."

"But you might have reformed him in time," said Demorest.

She again shrugged her shoulders. *"Quien sabe."* After a pause she added with infinite gravity: "And before he have reform, it is bad for the menage. I should invite to my house some friend. They arrive, and one say, 'I have not the watch of my pocket,' and another, 'The ring of my finger, he is gone,' and another, 'My earrings, she is loss.' And I am obliged to say, 'They reside now in the pocket of my hoosband; patience! a little while—perhaps to-morrow—he will restore.' No," she continued, with an air of infinite conviction, "it is not good for the menage—the necessity of those explanation."

"You told me he was handsome," said Joan, passing her arm carelessly around Doña Rosita's comfortable waist. "How did he look?"

"As an angel! He have long curls to his back. His moustache was as silk, for he have had never a barber to his face. And his eyes—Santa Maria!—so soft and so—so melankoly. When he smile it is like the moonlight. But," she added, rising to her feet and tossing the end of her lace mantilla over her shoulder with a little laugh—"it is finish—*Adelante!* Dr-r-rive on!"

"I don't want to destroy your belief in the connection of your friend with the road agents," said Demorest grimly, "but if he belongs to their band it is in an inferior capacity. Most of them are known to the authorities, and I have heard it even said that their leader or organizer is a very unromantic speculator in San Francisco."

But this suggestion was received coldly by the ladies, who superciliously turned their backs upon it and the suggester. Joan dropped her voice to a lower tone and turned to Doña Rosita. "And you have never seen him since?"

"Never."

"*I* should—at least, I wouldn't have let it end in *that* way," said Joan in a positive whisper.

"Eh?" said Doña Rosita, laughing. "So eet is *you,* Juanita, that have the romance —eh? Ah, *bueno!* 'you have the house— so I gif to you the lover also.' I place him at your disposition." She made a mock gesture of elaborate and complete abnegation. "But," she added in Joan's ear, with a quick glance at Demorest, "do not let our hoosband eat him. Even now he have the look to strangle *me*. Make to him a little lof, quickly, when I shall walk in the gar- den." She turned away with a pretty wave of her fan to Demorest, and calling out, "I go to make an assignation with my memory," laughed again, and lazily passed into the shadow. An ominous silence on the veranda followed, broken finally by Mrs. Demorest.

"I don't think it was necessary for you to show your dislike to Doña Rosita quite so plainly," she said, coldly, slightly accenting the Puritan stiffness, which any conjugal *tête-à-tête* lately revived in her manner.

"I show dislike of Doña Rosita?" stammered Demorest, in surprise. "Come, Joan," he added, with a forgiving smile, "you don't mean to imply that I dislike her because I couldn't get up a thrilling interest in an old story I've heard from every gossip in the *pueblo* since I can remember."

"It's not an old story to *her*," said Joan, dryly, "and even if it were, you might reflect that all people are not as anxious to forget the past as you are."

Demorest drew back to let the shaft glance by. "The story is old enough, at least for her to have had a dozen flirtations, as you know, since then," he returned gently, "and I don't think she herself seriously believes in it. But let that pass. I am sorry I offended her. I had no idea of doing so. As a rule, I think she is not so easily offended. But I shall apologize to her." He stopped and approached nearer his wife in a half-timid, half-tentative affection. "As to my forgetfulness of the past, Joan, even if it were true, I have had little cause to forget it lately. Your friend, Corwin—"

"I must insist upon your not calling him *my* friend, Richard," interrupted Joan, sharply, "considering that it was through *your* indiscretion in coming to us for the buggy that night, that he suspected—"

She stopped suddenly, for at that moment a startled little shriek, quickly subdued, rang through the garden. Demorest ran hurriedly down the steps in the direction of the outcry. Joan followed more cautiously. At the first turning of the path Doña Rosita almost fell into his arms. She was breathless and trembling, but broke into a hysterical laugh.

"I have such a fear come to me—I cry out! I think I have seen a man; but it

was nothing—nothing! I am a fool. It is
no one here."

"But where did you see anything?" said
Joan, coming up.

Rosita flew to her side. "Where? Oh,
here!—everywhere! Ah, I am a fool!"
She was laughing now, albeit there were
tears glistening on her lashes when she laid
her head on Joan's shoulder.

"It was some fancy—some resemblance
you saw in that queer cactus," said Demorest, gently. "It is quite natural, I was
myself deceived the other night. But I'll
look around to satisfy you. Take Doña
Rosita back to the veranda, Joan. But
don't be alarmed, dear—it was only an
illusion."

He turned away. When his figure was
lost in the entwining foliage, Doña Rosita
seized Joan's shoulder and dragged her
face down to a level with her own.

"It was something!" she whispered
quickly.

"Who?"

"It was—*Him!*"

"Nonsense," groaned Joan, nevertheless
casting a hurried glance around her.

"Have no fear," said Doña Rosita

quickly, "he is gone—I saw him pass away —so! But it was *He*—Huanson. I recognize him. I forget him never."

"Are you sure?"

"Have I the eyes? the memory? *Madre de Dios!* Am I a lunatico too? Look! He have stood there—so."

"Then you think he knew you were here?"

*"Quien sabe?"*

"And that he came here to see you?"

Doña Rosita caught her again by the shoulders, and with her lips to Joan's ear, said with the intensest and most deliberate of emphasis:

"NO!"

"What in Heaven's name brought him here then?"

*"You!"*

"Are you crazy?"

"You! you! *you!*" repeated Doña Rosita, with crescendo energy. "I have come upon him here; where he stood and look at the veranda, absorrrb of *you.* You move —he fly."

"Hush!"

"Ah, yes! I have said I give him to you. And he came, *Bueno,*" murmured

Doña Rosita, with a half-resigned, half-superstitious gesture.

*"Will* you be quiet!"

It was the sound of Demorest's feet on the gravel path, returning from his fruitless search. He had seen nothing. It must have been Doña Rosita's fancy.

"She was just saying she thought she had been mistaken," said Joan, quietly. "Let us go in—it is rather chilly here, and I begin to feel creepy too."

Nevertheless, as they entered the house again, and the light of the hall lantern fell upon her face, Demorest thought he had never but once before seen her look so nervously and animatedly beautiful.

## CHAPTER III

The following day, when Mr. Ezekiel Corwin had delivered his letters of introduction, and thoroughly canvassed the scant mercantile community of San Buenaventura with considerable success, he deposited his carpet-bag at the stage office in the *posada,* and found to his chagrin that he had still two hours to wait before the

coach arrived. After a vain attempt to
impart cheerful but disparaging criticism
of the *pueblo* and its people to Señor
Mateo and his wife—whose external
courtesy had been visibly increased by a
line from Demorest, but whose confidence
towards the stranger had not been extended in the same proportion—he gave it
up, and threw himself lazily on a wooden
bench in the veranda, already hacked with
the initials of his countrymen, and drawing
a jack-knife from his pocket, he began to
add to that emblazonry the trade-mark of
the Panacea—as a casual advertisement.
During its progress, however, he was
struck by the fact that while no one seemed
to enter the *posada* through the stage office,
the number of voices in the adjoining room
seemed to increase, and the ministrations
of Mateo and his wife became more feverishly occupied with their invisible guests.
It seemed to Ezekiel that consequently
there must be a second entrance which he
had not seen, and this added to the circumstance that one or two lounging figures who
had been approaching unaccountably disappeared before reaching the veranda,
induced him to rise and examine the lo-

cality. A few paces beyond was an alley, but it appeared to be already blocked by several cigarette-smoking, short-jacketed men who were leaning against its walls, and showed no inclination to make way for him. Checked, but not daunted, Ezekiel coolly returned to the stage office, and taking the first opportunity when Mateo passed through the rear door, followed him. As he expected, the innkeeper turned to the left and entered a large room filled with tobacco smoke and the local habitués of the *posada*. But Ezekiel, shrewdly surmising that the private entrance must be in the opposite direction, turned to the right along the passage until he came unexpectedly upon the corridor of the usual courtyard, or *patio,* of every Mexican hostelry, closed at one end by a low adobe wall, in which there was a door. The free passage around the corridor was interrupted by wide partitions, fitted up with tables and benches, like stalls, opening . upon the courtyard where a few stunted fig and orange trees still grew. As the courtyard seemed to be the only communication between the passage he had left and the door in the wall, he was about to cross it, when the voices of two men in the compartment struck his ears. Although one was evidently an American's, Ezekiel was instinctively convinced that they were speaking in English only for greater security against being understood by the frequenters of the *posada*. It is unnecessary to say that this was an innocent challenge to the curiosity of Ezekiel that he instantly accepted. He drew back carefully into the shadow of the partition as one of the voices asked—

"Wasn't that Johnson just come in?"

There was a movement as if some one had risen to look over the compartment, but the gathering twilight completely hid Ezekiel.

"No!"

"He's late. Suppose he don't come— or back out?"

The other man broke into a grim laugh. "I reckon you don't know Johnson yet, or you'd understand this yer little game o' his is just the one idea o' his life. He's been two years on that man's track, and he ain't goin' to back out now that he's got a dead sure thing on him."

"But why is he so keen about it, any-

way? It don't seem nat'ral for a business
man built after Johnson's style, and a rich
man to boot, to go into this detective business. It ain't the reward, we know that.
Is it an old grudge?"

"You bet!" The speaker paused, and
then in a lower voice, which taxed Ezekiel's keen ear to the uttermost, resumed:
"It's said up in Frisco that Cherokee Bob
knew suthin' agin Johnson way back in the
States; anyhow, I believe it's understood
that they came across the plains together
in '50—and Bob hounded Johnson and
blackmailed him here where he was livin',
even to the point of makin' him help him
on the road or give information, until one
day Johnson bucked against it—kicked
over the traces—and swore he'd be re-
venged on Bob, and then just settled himself down to that business. Wotever he'd
been and done himself he made it all right
with the sheriff here; and I've heard ez it
wasn't anything criminal or that sort, but
that it was o' some private trouble that
he'd confided to that hound Bob, and Bob
had threatened to tell agen him. That's
the grudge they say Johnson has, and
that's why he's allowed to be the head

devil in this yer affair. It's an understood thing, too, that the sheriff and the
police ain't goin' to interfere if Johnson
accidentally blows the top of Bob's head
off in the scrimmage of a capter."

"And I reckon Bob wouldn't hesitate to
do the same thing to him when he finds
out that Johnson has given him away?"

"I reckon," said the other, sententiously,
"for it's Johnson's knowledge of the country and the hoss-stealers that are in with
Bob's gang of road agents that made it easy
for him to buy up and win over Bob's
friends here, so that they'd help to trap
him."

"It's pretty rough on Bob to be sold out
in that way," said the second speaker, sym-
pathizingly.

"If they were white men, p'rhaps," returned his companion, contemptuously,
"but this yer's a case of Injin agen Injin,
ez the men are Mexican half-breeds just
as Bob's a half Cherokee. The sooner that
kind o' cross cattle exterminate each other
the better it'll be for the country. It takes
a white man like Johnson to set 'em by
the ears."

A silence followed. Ezekiel, beginning

to be slightly bored with his cheaply ac-
quired but rather impractical information,
was about to slip back into the passage
again when he was arrested by a laugh
from the first speaker.

"What's the matter?" growled the other.
"Do you want to bring the whole *posada*
out here?"

"I was only thinkin' what a skeer them
innocent greenhorn passengers will get just
ez they're snoozing off for the night, ten
miles from here," responded his friend,
with a chuckle. "Wonder ef anybody's
goin' up from here besides that patent
medicine softy."

Ezekiel stopped as if petrified.

"Ef the —— fools keep quiet they
won't be hurt, for our men will be ready
to chip in the moment of the attack. But
we've got to let the attack be made for the
sake of the evidence. And if we warn off
the passengers from going this trip, and
let the stage go up empty, Bob would
suspect something and *vamose*. But here's
Johnson!"

The door in the adobe wall had suddenly opened, and a figure in a *serape*
entered the patio. Ezekiel, whose curios-

ity was whetted with indignation at the ignominious part assigned to him in this comedy, forgot even his risk of detection by the newcomer, who advanced quickly towards the compartment. When he had reached it he said, in a tone of bitterness:

"The game is up, gentlemen, and the whole thing is blown. The scoundrel has got some confederate here—for he's been seen openly on the road near Demorest's ranch, and the band have had warning and dispersed. We must find out the traitor, and take our precautions for the next time. Who is that there? I don't know him."

He was pointing to Ezekiel, who had started eagerly forward at the first sound of his voice. The two occupants of the compartment rose at the same moment, leaped into the courtyard, and confronted Ezekiel. Surrounded by the three menacing figures he did not quail, but remained intently gazing upon the newcomer. Then his mouth opened, and he drawled lazily:

"Wa'al, ef it ain't Squire Blandford, of North Liberty, Connecticut, I'm a treed coon. Squire Blandford, how *do* you do?"

The stranger drew back in undisguised amazement; the two men glanced hurriedly at each other; Ezekiel alone remained cool, smiling, imperturbable, and triumphant.

"Who are *you,* sir? I do not know you," demanded the newcomer, roughly.

"Like ez not," said Corwin dryly, "it's a matter o' four year sense I lived in your house. Even Dick Demorest—you knew Dick?—didn't know me; but I reckon that Mrs. Blandford as used to be—"

"That's enough," said Blandford—for it was he—suddenly mastering both himself and Corwin by a supreme emphasis of will and gesture. "Wait!" Then turning to the two others who were discreetly regarding the blank adobe wall before them, he said: "Excuse me for a few minutes, gentlemen. There is no hurry now. I will see you later;" and with an imperative wave of his hand motioned Ezekiel to precede him into the passage, and followed him.

He did not speak until they entered the stage office, when, passing through it, he said peremptorily: "Follow me." The few loungers, who seemed to recognize him,

made way for him with a singular deference that impressed Ezekiel, already dom-
inated by his manner. The first perception in his mind was that Blandford had
in some strange way succeeded to Demorest's former imperious character. There
was no trace left of the old, gentle subjec-
tion to Joan's prim precision. Ezekiel
followed him out of the office as unresist-
ingly as he had followed Demorest into
the stables on that eventful night. They
passed down the narrow street until Blandford suddenly stopped short and turned
into the crumbling doorway of one of the
low adobe buildings and entered an apartment. It seemed to be the ordinary living-
room of the house, made more domestic
by the presence of a silk counterpaned bed
in one corner, a *prie Dieu* and crucifix,
and one or two articles of bedchamber furniture. A woman was sitting in desha-
bille by the window; a man was smoking
on a lounge against the wall. Blandford,
in the same peremptory manner, addressed
a command in Spanish to the inmates, who
immediately abandoned the apartment to
the seeming trespasser.

Motioning his companion to a seat on

the lounge just vacated, Blandford folded his arms and stood erect before him.

"Well," he said, with quick, business conciseness, "what do you want?"

Ezekiel was staggered out of his complacency.

"Wa'al," he stammered, "I only reckoned to ask the news, ez we are old friends —I—"

"How much do you want?" repeated Blandford, impatiently.

Ezekiel was mystified, yet expectant. "I can't say ez I exakly understand," he began.

"How — much — money — do — you — want," continued Blandford, with frigid accuracy, "to get up and get out of this place?"

"Wa'al, consideren ez I'm travellin' here ez the only authorized agent of a first-class Frisco Drug House," said Ezekiel, with a mingling of mortification, pride, and hopefulness, "unless you're travellin' in the opposition business, I don't see what's that to you."

Blandford regarded him searchingly for an instant. "Who sent you here?"

"Dilworth & Dusenberry, Battery Street,

San Francisco. Hev their card ?" said Ezekiel, taking one from his waistcoat pocket.

"Corwin," said Blandford, sternly,
"whatever your business is here you'll
find it will pay you better, a —— sight,
to be frank with me and stop this Yankee
shuffling. You say you have been with
Demorest—what has *he* got to do with
your business here ?"

"Nothin'," said Ezekiel. "I reckon he
wos ez astonished to see me ez you are."

"And didn't he send you here to seek
me ?" said Blandford, impatiently.

"Considerin' he believes you a dead
man, I reckon not."

Blandford gave a hard, constrained
laugh. After a pause, still keeping his
eyes fixed on Ezekiel, he said:

"Then your recognition of me was
accidental ?"

"Wa'al, yes. And ez I never took much
stock in the stories that you were washed
off the Warensboro Bridge, I ain't much
astonished at finding you agin."

"What did you believe happened to
me ?" said Blandford, less brusquely.

Ezekiel noticed the softening; he felt
his own turn coming. "I kalkilated you

had reasons for going off, leaving no address behind you," he drawled.

"What reasons?" asked Blandford, with a sudden relapse of his former harshness.

"Wa'al, Squire Blandford, sens you wanter know—I reckon your business wasn't payin', and there was a matter of two hundred and fifty dollars ye took with ye, that your creditors would hev liked to hev back."

"Who dare say that?" demanded Blandford, angrily.

"Your wife that was—Mrs. Demorest ez is—told it to her mother," returned Ezekiel, lazily.

The blow struck deeper than even Ezekiel's dry malice imagined. For an instant, Blandford remained stupefied. In the five years' retrospect of his resolution on that fatal night, whatever doubt of its wisdom might have obtruded itself upon him, he had never thought of *this*. He had been willing to believe that his wife had quietly forgotten him as well as her treachery to him, he had passively acquiesced in the results of that forgetfulness and his own silence; he had been conscious

that his wound had healed sooner than he
expected, but if this consciousness had
enabled him to extend a certain passive
forgiveness to his wife and Demorest, it
was always with the conviction that his
mysterious effacement had left an inex-
plicable shadow upon them which their
consciences alone could explain. But
for this unjust, vulgar, and degrading
interpretation of his own act of expia-
tion, he was totally unprepared. It completely crushed whatever sentiment remained of that act in the horrible irony
of finding himself put upon his defence
before the world, without being able now
to offer the real cause. The anguish of
that night had gone forever; but the ridiculous interpretation of it had survived,
and would survive it. In the eyes of the
man before him he was not a wronged
husband, but an absconding petty defaulter, whom he had just detected!

His mind was quickly made up. In
that instant he had resolved upon a step
as fateful as his former one, and a fitting
climax to its results. For five years he
had clearly misunderstood his attitude
towards his treacherous wife and perjured

friend. Thanks to this practical, selfish machine before him, he knew it now.

"Look here, Corwin," he said, turning upon Ezekiel a colorless face, but a steady, merciless eye. "I can guess, without your telling me, what lies may be circulated about me by the man and woman who know that I have only to declare myself alive to convict them of infamy—perhaps even of criminality before the law. You are not *my* friend, or you would not have believed them; if you are *theirs,* you have two courses open to you now. Keep this meeting to yourself and trust to my mercy to keep it a secret also; or, tell Mrs. Demorest that you have seen Mr. Johnson, who is not afraid to come forward at any moment and proclaim that he is Edward Blandford, her only lawful husband. Choose which course you like—it is nothing more to me."

"Wa'al, I reckon that, as far as I know Mrs. Demorest," said Ezekiel, dryly, "it don't make the least difference to her either; but if you want to know my opinion o' this matter, it is that neither you nor Demorest exactly understand that woman. I've known Joan Salisbury since

she was so high, but if ye expected me
to tell you wot she was goin' to do next,
I'd be able to tell ye where the next flash
o' lightnin' would strike. It's wot you
don't expect of Joan Salisbury that she
does. And the best proof of it is that
she filed papers for a divorce agin you in
Chicago and got it by default a few weeks
afore she married Demorest — and you
don't know it."

Blandford recoiled. "Impossible," he
said, but his voice too plainly showed how
clearly its possibility struck him now.

"It's so, but it was kept secret by Deacon
Salisbury. I overheerd it. Wa'al, that's
a proof that *you* don't understand Joan,
I reckon. And considerin' that Demorest
*himself* don't know it, ez I found out only
the other day in talking to him, I kalkilate I'm safe in sayin' that you're neither
o' you quite up to Deacon Salisbury's darter in nat'ral cuteness. I don't like to
obtrude my opinion, Squire Blandford, ez
we're old friends, but I do say, that wot
with Demorest's prematooriness and yer
own hangfiredness, it's a good thing that
you two worldly men hev got Joan Salisbury to stand up for North Liberty and

keep it from bein' scandalized by the ungodly. Ef it hadn't been for her smartness, whar y'd both be landed now?
There's a heap in Christian bringin' up,
and a power in grace, Squire Blandford."

His hard, dry face was for an instant
transfigured by a grim fealty and the dull
glow of some sectarian clannishness. Or
was it possible that this woman's person-
ality had in some mysterious way disturbed his rooted selfishness?

During his speech Blandford had
walked to the window. When Corwin
had ceased speaking, Blandford turned
towards him with an equally changed face
and cold imperturbability that astonished
him, and held out his hand. "Let bygones be bygones, Corwin—whether we
ever meet again or not. Yet if I can do
anything for you for the sake of old times,
I am ready to do it. I have some power
here and in San Francisco," he continued,
with a slight touch of pride, "that isn't dependent upon the mere name I may travel
under. I have a purpose in coming here."

"I know it," said Ezekiel, dryly. "I
heard it all from your two friends. You're
huntin' some man that did you an injury."

"I'm hunting down a dog who, suspecting I had some secret in emigrating here, tried to blackmail and ruin me," said Blandford, with a sudden expression of hatred that seemed inconsistent with anything that Ezekiel had ever known of his old master's character—"a scoundrel who tried to break up my new life as another had broken up the old." He stopped and recovered himself with a short laugh. "Well, Ezekiel, I don't know as his opinion of me was any worse than yours or *hers*. And until I catch *him* to clear my name again, I let the other slanderers go."

"Wa'al, I reckon you might lay hands on that devil yet, and not far away, either. I was up at Demorest's to-day, and I heard Joan and a skittish sort o' Mexican young lady talkin' about some tramp that had frightened her. And Miss Pico said—"

"What! Who did you say?" demanded Blandford, with a violent start.

"Wa'al, I reckoned I heerd the first name too—Rosita."

A quick flush crossed Blandford's face, and left it glowing like a boy's.

"Is *she* there?"

"Wa'al, I reckon she's visitin' Joan," said Ezekiel, narrowly attentive of Blandford's strange excitement ; "but wot of it ?"

But Blandford had utterly forgotten Ezekiel's presence. He had remained speechless and flushed. And then, as if suddenly dazzled by an inspiration, he abruptly dashed from the room. Ezekiel heard him call to his passive host with a Spanish oath, but before he could follow, they had both hurriedly left the house.

Ezekiel glanced around him and contemplatively ran his fingers through his beard. "It ain't Joan Salisbury nor Dick Demorest ez giv' him that start! Humph! Wa'al—I wanter know!"

## CHAPTER IV

MRS. DEMOREST was so fascinated by the company of Doña Rosita Pico and her romantic memories, that she prevailed upon that heart-broken but scarcely attenuated young lady to prolong her visit beyond the fortnight she had allotted to communion with the past. For a day or

two following her singular experience in
the garden, Mrs. Demorest plied her with
questions regarding the apparition she had
seen, and finally extorted from her the
admission that she could not positively
swear to its being the real Johnson, or
even a perfectly consistent shade of that
faithless man. When Joan pointed out
to her that such masculine perfections as
curling raven locks, long silken mustachios,
and dark eyes, were attributes by no means
exclusive to her lover, but were occasionally seen among other less favored and
even equally dangerous Americans, Doña
Rosita assented with less objection than
Joan anticipated. "Besides, dear," said
Joan, eying her with feline watchfulness,
"it is four years since you've seen him,
and surely the man has either shaved
since, or else he took a ridiculous vow
never to do it, and then he would be more
fully bearded."

But Doña Rosita only shook her pretty
head. "Ah, but he have an air—a something I know not what you call—so." She
threw her shawl over her left shoulder, and
as far as a pair of soft blue eyes and comfortably pacific features would admit, en-

deavored to convey an idea of wicked and gloomy abstraction.

"You child," said Joan,—"that's nothing; they all of them do that. Why, there was a stranger at the Oriental Hotel whom I met twice when I was there—just as mysterious, romantic, and wicked-looking. And in fact they hinted terrible things about him. Well! so much so, that Mr. Demorest was quite foolish about my being barely civil to him—you understand—and—" She stopped suddenly, with a heightened color under the fire of Rosita's laughing eyes.

"Ah—so—Doña Discretion! Tell to me all. Did our hoosband eat him?"

Joan's features suddenly tightened to their old puritan rigidity. "Mr. Demorest has reasons—abundant reasons—to thoroughly understand and trust me," she replied in an austere voice.

Rosita looked at her a moment in mystification and then shrugged her shoulders. The conversation dropped. Nevertheless, it is worthy of being recorded that from that moment the usual familiar allusions, playful and serious, to Rosita's mysterious visitor began to diminish in frequency and finally ceased. Even the news brought by Demorest of some vague rumor in the *pueblo* that an intended attack on the stage-coach had been frustrated by the authorities, and that the vicinity had been haunted by incognitos of both parties, failed to revive the discussion.

Meantime the slight excitement that had stirred the sluggish life of the *pueblo* of San Buenaventura had subsided. The *posada* of Señor Mateo had lost its feverish and perplexing dual life; the alley behind it no longer was congested by lounging cigarette smokers; the compartment looking upon the silent *patio* was unoccupied, and its chairs and tables were empty. The two deputy sheriffs, of whom Señor Mateo presumably knew very little, had fled; and the mysterious Señor Johnson, of whom he —still presumably—knew still less, had also disappeared. For Señor Mateo's knowledge of what transpired in and about his *posada,* and of the character and purposes of those who frequented it, was tinctured by grave and philosophical doubts. This courteous and dignified scepticism generally took the formula of *quien sabe* to all frivolous and mundane

inquiry. He would affirm with strict
verity that his omelettes were unap-
proachable, his beds miraculous, his *aguardiente* supreme, his house was even as your
own. Beyond these were questions with
which the simply finite and always discreet
human intellect declined to grapple.

The disturbing effect of Señor Corwin
upon a mind thus gravely constituted may
be easily imagined. Besides Ezekiel's in-
ordinate capacity for useless or indiscreet
information, it was undeniable that his patent medicines had effected a certain peaceful revolutionary movement in San Buenaventura. A simple and superstitious
community that had steadily resisted the
practical domestic and agricultural American improvements, succumbed to the occult
healing influences of the Panacea and
Jones's Bitters. The virtues of a mysterious balsam, more or less illuminated
with a colored mythological label, deeply
impressed them; and the exhibition of a
circular, whereon a celestial visitant was
represented as descending with a gross of
Rogers' Pills to a suffering but admiring
multitude, touched their religious sympathies to such an extent that the good

Padre José was obliged to warn them from
the pulpit of the diabolical character of
their heresies of healing—with the natural
result of yet more dangerously advertising
Ezekiel. There were those too who spoke
under their breath of the miraculous ef-
ficacy of these nostrums. Had not Don
Victor Arguello, whose respectable diges-
tion, exhausted by continuous pepper and
garlic, failed him suddenly, received an unexpected and pleasurable stimulus from the
New England rum, which was the basis of
the Jones Bitters? Had not the baker,
tremulous from excessive *aguardiente,* been
soothed and sustained by the invisible mor-
phia, judiciously hidden in Blogg's Nerve
Tonic? Nor had the wily Ezekiel forgotten the weaker sex in their maiden and
maternal requirements. Unguents, that
made silken their black but somewhat
coarsely fibrous tresses, opened charming
possibilities to the Señoritas; while sooth-
ing syrups lent a peaceful repose to many
a distracted mother's household. The
success of Ezekiel was so marked as to
justify his return at the end of three weeks
with a fresh assortment and an undiminished audacity.

It was on his second visit that the sceptical, non-committal policy of Señor Mateo was sorely tried. Arriving at the *posada* one night, Ezekiel became aware that his host was engaged in some mysterious conference with a visitor who had entered through the ordinary public room. The view which the acute Ezekiel managed to get of the stranger, however, was productive of no further discovery than that he bore a faint and disreputable resemblance to Blandford, and was handsome after a conscious, reckless fashion, with an air of mingled bravado and conceit. But an hour later, as Corwin was taking the cooler air of the veranda before retiring to one of the miraculous beds of the *posada,* he was amazed at seeing what was apparently Blandford himself emerge on horseback from the alley, and after a quick glance towards the veranda, canter rapidly up the street. Ezekiel's first impression was to call to him, but the sudden recollection that he parted from his old master on confidential terms only three days before in San Francisco, and that it was impossible for him to be in the *pueblo,* stopped him with his fingers meditatively in his

O

beard. Then he turned in to the *posada,* and hastily summoned Mateo.

The gentleman presented himself in a state of such profound scepticism that it seemed to have already communicated itself to his shoulders, and gave him the appearance of having shrugged himself into the room.

"Ha'ow long ago did Mr. Johnson get here?" asked Corwin, lazily.

"Ah—possibly—then there has been a Mr. Johnson?" This is a polite doubt of his own perceptions and a courteous acceptance of his questioner's.

"Wa'al, I guess so. Considerin' I jest saw him with my own eyes," returned Ezekiel.

"Ah!" Mateo was relieved. Might he congratulate the Señor Corwin, who must be also relieved, and shake his respected hand. *Bueno.* And then he had met this Señor Johnson? doubtless a friend? And he was well? and all were happy?

"Look yer, Mattayo! What I wanter know ez *this.* When did that man, who has just ridden out of your alley, come here? *Sabe* that—it's a plain question."

Ah surely, of the clearest comprehension.

*Bueno.* It may have been last week—
or even this week—or perhaps yesterday—or of a possibility to-day. The Señor
Corwin, who was wise and omniscient,
would comprehend that the difficulty lay
in deciding *who* was that man. Perhaps
a friend of the Señor Corwin—perhaps
only one who *looked* like him. There existed—might Mateo point out—a doubt.

Ezekiel regarded Mateo with a certain
grim appreciation. "Wa'al, is there anybody here who looks like Johnson?"

Again there were the difficulty of ascertaining perfectly how the Señor Johnson
looked. If the Señor Johnson was *Ameri-
cano,* doubtless there were other *Americanos* who had resembled him. It was
possible. The Señor Corwin had doubtless observed for a little space a *caballero*
who was here, as it were, in the instant of
the appearance of Señor Johnson? Possibly there was a resemblance, and yet—

Corwin had certainly noticed this resemblance, but it did not suit his cautious
intellect to fall in with any prevailing
scepticism of his host. Satisfied in his
mind that Mateo was concealing something
from him, and equally satisfied that he

would sooner or later find it out, he grinned diabolically in the face of that worthy man, and sought the meditation of his miraculous couch. When he had departed, the sceptic turned to his wife:

"This animal has been sniffing at the trail."

"Truly—but Mother of God—where is the discretion of our friend. If he will continue to haunt the *pueblo* like a lovesick chicken, he will get his neck wrung yet."

Following out an ingenious idea of his own, Ezekiel called the next day on the Demorests, and in some occult fashion obtained an invitation to stay under their hospitable roof during his sojourn in Buenaventura. Perfectly aware that he owed this courtesy more to Joan than to her husband, it is probable that his grim enjoyment was not diminished by the fact; while Joan, for reasons of her own, preferred the constraint which the presence of another visitor put upon Demorest's uxoriousness. Of late, too, there were times when Doña Rosita's naive intelligence, which was not unlike the embarrassing perceptions of a bright and half-

spoiled child, was in her way, and she
would willingly have shared the young
lady's company with her husband had
Demorest shown any sympathy for the girl.
It was in the faint hope that Ezekiel
might in some way beguile Rosita's wandering attention that she had invited him.
The only difficulty lay in his uncouthness,
and in presenting to the heiress of the
Picos a man who had been formerly her
own servant. Had she attempted to conceal that fact she was satisfied that
Ezekiel's independence and natural predilection for embarrassing situations
would have inevitably revealed it. She
had even gone so far as to consider the
propriety of investing him with a poor
relationship to her family, when Doña
Rosita herself happily stopped all further
trouble. On her very first introduction to
him, that charming young lady at once accepted him as a lunatic whose brains were
turned by occult, scientific, and medical
study! Ah! she, Rosita, had heard of
such cases before. Had not a paternal
ancestor of hers, one Don Diego Castro,
believed he had discovered the elixir of
youth. Had he not to that end refused

even to wash him the hand, to cut him the nail of the finger and the hair of the head! Exalted by that discovery, had he not been unsparingly uncomplimentary to all humanity, especially to the weaker sex? Even as the Señor Corwin!

Far from being offended at this ingenious interpretation of his character, Ezekiel exhibited a dry gratification over it, and even conceived an unwholesome admiration of the fair critic; he haunted her presence and preoccupied her society far beyond Joan's most sanguine expectations. He sat in open-mouthed enjoyment of her at the table, he waylaid her in the garden, he attempted to teach her English. Doña Rosita received these extraordinary advances in a no less extraordinary manner. In the scant masculine atmosphere of the house, and the somewhat rigid New England reserve that still pervaded it, perhaps she languished a little, and was not averse to a slight flirtation, even with a madman. Besides, she assumed the attitude of exercising a wholesome restraint over him. "If we are not found dead in our bed one morning, and extracted of our blood for a cordial, you shall thank to me for it," she said to Joan. "Also for the not empoisoning of the coffee!"

So she permitted him to carry a chair or hammock for her into the garden, to fetch the various articles which she was continually losing, and which he found with his usual penetration; and to supply her with information, in which, however, he exercised an unwonted caution. On the other hand, certain naive recollections and admissions, which in the quality of a voluble child she occasionally imparted to this "madman" in return, were in the proportion of three to one.

It had been a hot day, and even the usual sunset breeze had failed that evening to rock the tops of the outlying pine-trees or cool the heated tiles of the *pueblo* roofs. There was a hush and latent expectancy in the air that reacted upon the people with feverish unrest and uneasiness; even a lull in the faintly whispering garden around the Demorests' *casa* had affected the spirits of its inmates, causing them to wander about in vague restlessness. Joan had disappeared; Doña Rosita, under an olive-tree in one of the deserted paths, and attended by the faithful Ezekiel, had said it was "earthquake weather," and recalled, with a sign of the cross, a certain dreadful day of her childhood, when *el temblor* had shaken down one of the Mission towers. "You shall see it now, as he have left it so it has remain always," she added with superstitious gravity.

"That's just the lazy shiftlessness of your folks," responded Ezekiel with prompt ungallantry. "It ain't no wonder the Lord Almighty hez to stir you up now and then to keep you goin'."

Doña Rosita gazed at him with simple childish pity. "Poor man; it have affect you also in the head, this weather. So! It was even so with the uncle of my father. Hush up yourself, and bring to me the box of chocolates of my table. I will gif to you one. You shall for one time have something pleasant on the end of your tongue, even if you must swallow him after."

Ezekiel grinned. "Ye ain't afraid o' bein' left alone with the ghost that haunts the garden, Miss Rosita?"

"After *you*—never-r-r."

"I'll find Mrs. Demorest and send her to ye," said Ezekiel, hesitatingly.

"Eh, to attract here the ghost? Thank you, no, very mooch."

Ezekiel's face contracted until nothing but his bright peering gray eyes could be seen. "Attract the ghost!" he echoed. "Then you kalkilate that it's—" he stopped, insinuatingly.

Rosita brought her fan sharply over his knuckles, and immediately opened it again over her half-embarrassed face. "I comprehend not anything to 'ekalkilate.' *Will* you go, Don Fantastico; or is it for me to bring to you?"

Ezekiel flew. He quickly found the chocolates and returned, but was disconcerted on arriving under the olive-tree to find Doña Rosita no longer in the hammock. He turned into a by-path, where an extraordinary circumstance attracted his attention. The air was perfectly still, but the leaves of a *manzanita* bush near the misshapen cactus were slightly agitated. Presently Ezekiel saw the stealthy figure of a man emerge from behind it and approach the cactus. Reaching his hand cautiously towards the plant, the stranger detached something from one of its thorns, and instantly disappeared. The quick

eyes of Ezekiel had seen that it was a
letter, his unerring perception of faces
recognized at the same moment that the
intruder was none other than the handsome, reckless-looking man he had seen the
other day in conference with Mateo.

But Ezekiel was not the only witness of
this strange intrusion. A few paces from
him, Doña Rosita, unconscious of his return, was gazing in a half-frightened,
breathless absorption in the direction of
the stranger's flight.

"Wa'al!" drawled Ezekiel lazily.

She started and turned towards him.
Her face was pale and alarmed, and yet
to the critical eye of Ezekiel it seemed to
wear an expression of gratified relief. She
laughed faintly.

"Ef that's the kind o' ghost you hev
about yer, it's a healthy one," drawled Ezekiel. He turned and fixed his keen eyes
on Rosita's face. "I wonder what kind o'
fruit grows on the cactus that he's so fond
of ?"

Either she had not seen the abstraction
of the letter, or his acting was perfect, for
she returned his look unwaveringly. "The
fruit, eh ? I have not comprehend."

"Wa'al, I reckon I will," said Ezekiel. He walked towards the cactus; there was nothing to be seen but its thorny spikes. He was confronted, however, by the sudden apparition of Joan from behind the *manzanita* at its side. She looked up and glanced from Ezekiel to Doña Rosita with an agitated air.

"Oh, you saw him too?" she said eagerly.

"I reckon," answered Ezekiel, with his eyes still on Rosita. "I was wondering what on airth he was so taken with that air cactus for."

Rosita had become slightly pale again in the presence of her friend. Joan quietly pushed Ezekiel aside and put her arm around her. "Are you frightened again?" she asked, in a low whisper.

"Not mooch," returned Rosita, without lifting her eyes.

"It was only some *peon,* trespassing to pick blossoms for his sweetheart," she said significantly, with a glance towards Ezekiel. "Let us go in."

She passed her hand through Rosita's passive arm and led her towards the house, Ezekiel's penetrating eyes still following

Rosita with an expression of gratified doubt.

For once, however, that astute observer was wrong. When Mrs. Demorest had reached the house she slipped into her own room, and, bolting the door, drew from her bosom a letter which *she* had picked from the cactus thorn, and read it with a flushed face and eager eyes.

It may have been the effect of the phenomenal weather, but the next day a malign influence seemed to pervade the Demorest household. Doña Rosita was confined to her room by an attack of languid nerves, superinduced, as she was still voluble enough to declare, by the narcotic effect of some unknown herb which the lunatic Ezekiel had no doubt mysteriously administered to her with a view of experimenting on its properties. She even avowed that she must speedily return to Los Osos, before Ezekiel should further compromise her reputation by putting her on a colored label in place of the usual Celestial Distributer of the Panacea. Ezekiel himself, who had been singularly abstracted and reticent, and had absolutely foregone one or two opportunities of disagreeable criticism, had gone to the *pueblo* early that morning. The house was comparatively silent and deserted when Demorest walked into his wife's boudoir.

It was a pretty room, looking upon the garden, furnished with a singular mingling of her own inherited formal tastes and the more sensuous coloring and abandon of her new life. There were a great many rugs and hangings scattered in disorder around the room, and apparently purposeless, except for color; there was a bamboo lounge as large as a divan, with two or three cushions disposed on it, and a low chair that seemed the incarnation of indolence. Opposed to this, on the wall, was the rigid picture of her grandfather, who had apparently retired with his volume further into the canvas before the spectacle of this ungodly opulence; a large Bible on a funereal trestle-like stand, and the primmest and barest of writing-tables, before which she was standing as at a sacrificial altar. With an almost mechanical movement she closed her portfolio as her husband entered, and also shut the lid of a small box with a slight snap. This suggested exclusion of him from her previous occupation, what-

ever it might have been, caused a faint
shadow of pain to pass across his loving
eyes. He cast a glance at his wife as if
mutely asking her to sit beside him, but
she drew a chair to the table, and with
her elbow resting on the box, resignedly
awaited his speech.

"I don't mean to disturb you, darling,"
he said, gently, "but as we were alone, I
thought we might have one of our old-
fashioned talks, and—"

"Don't let it be so old-fashioned as to
include North Liberty again," she interrupted, wearily. "We've had quite enough
of that since I returned."

"I thought you found fault with me then
for forgetting the past. But let that pass,
dear; it is not *our* affairs I wanted to talk
to you about now," he said, stifling a sigh,
"it's about your friend. Please don't
misunderstand what I am going to say;
nor that I interpose except from necessity."

She turned her dark brown eyes in his
direction, but her glance passed abstractedly over his head into the garden.

"It's a matter perfectly well known to
me—and, I fear, to all our servants also—

that somebody is making clandestine visits to our garden. I would not trouble you before, until I ascertained the object of these visits. It is quite plain to me now that Doña Rosita is that object, and that communications are secretly carried on between her and some unknown stranger. He has been here once or twice before; he was here again yesterday. Ezekiel saw him and saw her."

"Together?" asked Mrs. Demorest, sharply.

"No; but it was evident that there was some understanding, and that some communication passed between them."

"Well?" said Mrs. Demorest, with repressed impatience.

"It is equally evident, Joan, that this stranger is a man who does not dare to approach your friend in her own house, nor more openly in this; but who, with her connivance, uses us to carry on an intrigue which may be perfectly innocent, but is certainly compromising to all concerned. I am quite willing to believe that Doña Rosita is only romantic and reckless, but that will not prevent her from becoming a dupe of some rascal who dare not face us openly, and who certainly does not act as her equal."

"Well, Rosita is no chicken, and you are not her guardian."

There was a vague heartlessness, more in her voice than in her words, that touched him as her cold indifference to himself had never done, and for an instant stung his crushed spirit to revolt. "No," he said, sternly, "but I am her father's *friend,* and I shall not allow his daughter to be compromised under my roof."

Her eyes sprang up to meet his in hatred as promptly as they once had met in love. "And since when, Richard Demorest, have you become so particular?" she began, with dry asperity. "Since you lured *me* from the side of my wedded husband? Since you met *me* clandestinely in trains and made love to *me* under an assumed name? Since you followed *me* to my house under the pretext of being my husband's friend, and forced me—yes, forced me—to see you secretly under my mother's roof? Did you think of compromising *me* then? Did you think of ruining my reputation, of driving my husband from his home in despair? Did you call yourself a rascal then? Did you—"

"Stop!" he said, in a voice that shook the rafters; "I command you, stop!"

She had gradually worked herself from a deliberately insulting precision into an hysterical, and it is to be feared a virtuous, conviction of her wrongs. Beginning only with the instinct to taunt and wound the man before her, she had been led by a secret consciousness of something else he did not know to anticipate his reproach and justify herself in a wild feminine abandonment of emotion. But she stopped at his words. For a moment she was even thrilled again by the strength and imperiousness she had loved.

They were facing each other after five years of mistaken passion, even as they had faced each other that night in her mother's kitchen. But the grave of that dead passion yawned between them. It was Joan who broke the silence, that after her single outburst seemed to fill and oppress the room.

"As far as Rosita is concerned," she said, with affected calmness, "she is going to-night. And you probably will not be troubled any longer by your mysterious visitor."

Whether he heeded the sarcastic significance of her last sentence, or even heard her at all, he did not reply. For a moment he turned his blazing eyes full upon her, and then without a word strode from the room.

She walked to the door and stood uneasily listening in the passage until she heard the clatter of hoofs in the paved patio, and knew that he had ordered his horse. Then she turned back relieved to her room.

It was already sunset when Demorest drew rein again at the entrance of the *corral,* and the last stroke of the Angelus was ringing from the Mission tower. He looked haggard and exhausted, and his horse was flecked with foam and dirt. Wherever he had been, or for what object, or whether, objectless and dazed, he had simply sought to lose himself in aimlessly wandering over the dry yellow hills or in careering furiously among his own wild cattle on the arid, brittle plain; whether he had beaten all thought from his brain with the jarring leap of his horse, or whether he had pursued some vague and elusive determination to his own door, is not essential to this brief chronicle. Enough that when he dismounted he drew a pistol from his holster and replaced it in his pocket.

He had just pushed open the gate of the *corral* as he led in his horse by the bridle, when he noticed another horse tethered among some cotton woods that shaded the outer wall of his garden. As he gazed, the figure of a man swung lightly from one of the upper boughs of a cotton-wood on the wall and disappeared on the other side. It was evidently the clandestine visitor. Demorest was in no mood for trifling. Hurriedly driving his horse into the enclosure with a sharp cut of his *riata,* he closed the gate upon him, slipped past the intervening space into the patio, and then unnoticed into the upper part of the garden. Taking a narrow by-path in the direction of the cotton woods that could be seen above the wall, he presently came in sight of the object of his search moving stealthily towards the house. It was the work of a moment only to dash forward and seize him, to find himself engaged in a sharp wrestle, to half draw his pistol as he struggled with his captive in the open. But once in the clearer light, he started, his grasp of the stranger relaxed, and he fell back in bewildered terror.

"Edward Blandford! Good God!"

The pistol had dropped from his hand as he leaned breathless against a tree. The stranger kicked the weapon contemptuously aside. Then quietly adjusting his disordered dress, and picking the brambles from his sleeve, he said with the same air of disdain, "Yes! Edward Blandford, whom you thought dead! There! I'm not a ghost—though you tried to make me one this time," he said, pointing to the pistol.

Demorest passed his hand across his white face. "Then it's you—and you have come here for—for—Joan?"

"For Joan?" echoed Blandford, with a quick scornful laugh, that made the blood flow back into Demorest's face as from a blow, and recalled his scattered senses. "For Joan," he repeated. "Not much!"

The two men were facing each other in irreconcilable yet confused antagonism. Both were still excited and combative from their late physical struggle, but with feelings so widely different that it would have been impossible for either to have comprehended the other. In the figure that had apparently risen from the dead to confront him, Demorest only saw the man he had unconsciously wronged—the man who had it in his power to claim Joan and exact a terrible retribution! But it was part of this monstrous and irreconcilable situation that Blandford had ceased to contemplate it, and in his preoccupation only saw the actual interference of a man whom he no longer hated, but had begun to pity and despise.

He glanced coolly around him. "Whatever we've got to say to each other," he said deliberately, "had better not be overheard. At least what *I* have got to say to you."

## CHAPTER V

DEMOREST, now as self-possessed as his adversary, haughtily waved his hand towards the path. They walked on in silence, without even looking at each other, until they reached a small summer-house that stood in the angle of the wall. Demorest entered. "We cannot he heard here," he said curtly.

"And we can see what is going on. Good," said Blandford, coolly following him. The summer-house contained a bench and a table. Blandford seated himself on the bench. Demorest remained standing beside the table. There was a moment's silence.

"I came here with no desire to see you or avoid you," said Blandford, with cold indifference. "A few weeks ago I might perhaps have avoided you, for your own sake. But since then I have learned that among the many things I owe to—to your wife is the fact that five years ago she secretly *divorced me,* and that consequently my living presence could neither be a danger nor a menace to you. I see," he added, dryly, with a quick glance at Demorest's horror-stricken face, "that I was also told the truth when they said you were as ignorant of the divorce as I was."

He stopped, half in pity of his adversary's shame, half in surprise of his own calmness. Five years before, in the tumultuous consciousness of his wrongs, he would have scarcely trusted himself face to face with the cooler and more self-controlled Demorest. He wondered at and partly admired his own coolness now, in the presence of his enemy's confusion.

"As your mind is at rest on that point," he continued, sarcastically, "I don't suppose you care to know what became of *me* when I left North Liberty. But as it happens to have something to do with my being here to-night, and is a part of my business with you, you'll have to listen to it. Sit down! Very well, then—stand up! It's your own house."

His half cynical, wholly contemptuous ignoring of the real issue between them was more crushing to Demorest than the keenest reproach or most tragic outburst. He did not lift his eyes as Blandford resumed in a dry, business-like way:

"When I came across the plains to California, I fell in with a man about my own age—an emigrant also. I suppose I looked and acted like a crazy fool through all the journey, for he satisfied himself that I had some secret reason for leaving the States, and suspected that I was, like himself—a criminal. I afterwards learned that he was an escaped thief and assassin.

Well, he played upon me all the way here,
for I didn't care to reveal my real trouble
to him, lest it should get back to North
Liberty—" He interrupted himself with
a sarcastic laugh. "Of course, you understand that all this while Joan was getting
her divorce unknown to me, and you were
marrying her—yet as *I* didn't know anything about it I let him compromise me to
save her. But"—he stopped, his eye
kindled, and, losing his self-control in what
to Demorest seemed some incoherent passion, went on excitedly: "that man continued his persecution *here*—yes, *here,* in
this very house, where I was a trusted and
honored guest, and threatened to expose
me to a pure, innocent, simple girl who
had taken pity on me—unless I helped
him in a conspiracy of cattle-stealers and
road agents, of which he was chief. I was
such a cursed sentimental fool then, that
believing him capable of doing this, believing myself still the husband of that
woman, your wife, and to spare that innocent girl the shame of thinking me a villain, I purchased his silence by consenting.
May God curse me for it!"

He had started to his feet with flashing

eyes, and the indication of an overmaster-
ing passion that to Demorest, absorbed
only in the stupefying revelation of his
wife's divorce and the horrible doubt it
implied, seemed utterly vacant and un-
meaning.

He had often dreamed of Blandford
as standing before him, reproachful,
indignant, and even desperate over his
wife's unfaithfulness; but this insane folly
and fury over some trivial wrong done to
that plump, baby-faced, flirting Doña Rosita, crushed him by its unconscious but
degrading obliteration of Joan and himself more than the most violent denunciation. Dazed and bewildered, yet with the
instinct of a helpless man, he clung only
to that part of Blandford's story which indicated that he had come there for Rosita,
and *not* to separate him from Joan, and
even turned to his former friend with a
half-embarrassed gesture of apology as he
stammered—

"Then it was *you* who were Rosita's
lover, and you who have been here to see
her. Forgive me, Ned—if I had only
known it." He stopped and timidly extended his hand. But Blandford put it

aside with a cold gesture and folded his arms.

"You have forgotten all you ever knew of me, Demorest! *I* am not in the habit of making clandestine appointments with helpless women whose natural protectors I dare not face. *I* have never pursued an innocent girl to the house I dared not enter. When I found that I could not honorably retain Doña Rosita's affection, I fled her roof. When I believed that even if I broke with this scoundrel—as I did—I was still legally if not morally tied to your wife, and could not marry Rosita, I left her never to return. And I tore my heart out to do it."

The tears were standing in his eyes. Demorest regarded him again with vacant wonder. Tears!—not for Joan's unfaithfulness to him—but for this silly girl's transitory sentimentalism. It was horrible!

And yet what was Joan to Blandford now? Why should he weep for the woman who had never loved him—whom he loved no longer? The woman who had deceived him—who had deceived them *both*. Yes! for Joan must have suspected that Blandford was living to have sought her secret divorce—and yet she had never told him— *him*—the man for whom she got it. Ah! he must not forget *that!* It was to marry him that she had taken that step. It was perhaps a foolish caution—a mistaken reservation; but it was the folly—the mistake of a loving woman. He hugged this belief the closer, albeit he was conscious at the same time of following Blandford's story of his alienated affection with a feeling of wonder and envy.

"And what was the result of this touching sacrifice?" continued Blandford, trying to resume his former cynical indifference. "I'll tell you. This scoundrel set himself about to supplant me. Taking advantage of my absence, his knowledge that her affection for me was heightened by the mystery of my life, and trusting to profit by a personal resemblance he is said to bear to me, he began to haunt her. Lately he has grown bolder, and he dared even to communicate with her here. For it is he," he continued, again giving way to his passion, "this dog, this sneaking coward, who visits the place unknown to you, and thinks to entrap the poor girl through her memory of me. And it is he that I came here to prevent, to expose—if necessary to kill! Don't misunderstand me. I have made myself a deputy of the law for that purpose. I've a warrant in my pocket, and I shall take him, this mongrel, half-breed Cherokee Bob, by fair means or foul!"

The energy and presence of his passion was so infectious that it momentarily swept away Demorest's doubts of the past. "And I will help you, before God, Blandford," he said eagerly. "And Joan shall, too. She will find out from Rosita how far—"

"Thank you," interrupted Blandford, dryly; "but your wife has already interfered in this matter, to my cost. It is to her, I believe, I owe this wretch's following Rosita here. She already knows this man —has met him twice in San Francisco; he even boasts of *your* jealousy. You know best how far he lied."

But Demorest had braced himself against the chill sensation that had begun to creep over him as Blandford spoke. He nerved himself and said, proudly, "I forbade her knowing him on account of his reputation solely. I have no reason to believe she has ever even wished to disobey me."

A smile of scorn that had kindled in Blandford's eyes, darkened with a swift shadow of compassion as he glanced at Demorest's hard, ashen face. He held out his hand with a sudden impulse. "Enough, I accept your offer, and shall put it to the test this very night. I know—if you do not—that Rosita is to leave here for Los Osos an hour from now in a private carriage, which your wife has ordered especially for her. The same information tells me that this villain and another of his gang will be in wait for the carriage three miles out of the *pueblo* to attack it and carry off the young girl."

"Are you mad!" said Demorest, in unfeigned amazement. "Do you believe them capable of attacking a private carriage and carrying off a solitary, defenceless woman? Come, Blandford, this is a school-girl romance—not an act of mercenary highwaymen—least of all Cherokee Bob and his gang. This is some madness of Rosita's, surely," he continued with a forced laugh.

"Does this mean that you think better of your promise?" asked Blandford, dryly.

"I said I was at your service," said Demorest, reproachfully.

"Then hear my plan to prevent it, and yet take that dog in the act," said Blandford. "But we must first wait here till the last moment to ascertain if he makes any signal to show that his plan is altered, or that he has discovered he is watched." He turned, and in his preoccupation laid his hand for an instant upon Demorest's shoulder with the absent familiarity of old days. Unconscious as the action was, it thrilled them both—from its very unconsciousness—and impelled them to throw themselves into the new alliance with such feverish and excited activity in order to preclude any dangerous alien reflection, that when they rose a few moments later and cautiously left the garden arm-in-arm through the outer gates, no one would have believed they had ever been estranged, least of all the clever woman who had separated them.

It was nearly nine o'clock when the two friends, accompanied by the sheriff of the county, left San Buenaventura turnpike and turned into a thicket of alders to wait

the coming of the carriage they were to
henceforth follow cautiously and unseen in
a parallel trail to the main road. The
moon had risen, and with it the long withheld wind that now swept over the distant
stretch of gleaming road and partly veiled
it at times with flying dust unchecked by
any dew from the clear cold sky. Demorest shivered even with his ready hand on
his revolver. Suddenly the sheriff uttered
an exclamation of disgust.

"Blasted if thar ain't some one in the
road between us and their ambush."

"It's one of their gang—scouting. Lie
close."

"Scout be darned. Look at him buck-
ing round there in the dust. He can't even
ride! It's some blasted greenhorn taking
a *pasear* on a hoss for the first time. Dam-
nation! he's ruined everything. They'll
take the alarm."

"I'll push on and clear him out," said
Blandford, excitedly. "Even if they're
off, I may yet get a shot at the Cherokee."

"Quick then," said Demorest, "for here
comes the carriage." He pointed to a dark
spot on the road occasionally emerging
from the driven dust clouds.

In another moment Blandford was at the heels. of the awkward horseman, who wheeled clumsily at his approach and revealed the lank figure of Ezekiel Corwin!

"You here!" said Blandford, in stupefied fury.

"Wa'al, yes, squire," said Ezekiel lazily, in spite of his uneasy seat. "I kalkilated ef there was suthin' goin' on, I'd like to see it."

"You cursed prying fool! you've spoiled all. There!" he shouted despairingly, as the quick clatter of hoofs rang from the *arroyo* behind them, "there they go! That's your work, blockhead! Out of my way, or by God—" but the sentence was left unfinished as, joined by the sheriff, who had galloped up at the sound of the robbers' flight, he darted past the unconcerned Ezekiel. Demorest would have followed, but Blandford, with a warning cry to him to remain and protect the carriage, halted him at the side of Corwin as the vehicle now rapidly approached.

But Ezekiel was before him even then, and as the driver pulled up, that inquiring man tumbled from his horse, ran to the door and opened it. Demorest rode up, glanced into the carriage, and fell back in blank amazement.

It was his wife who was sitting there alone, pale, erect, and beautiful. By some illusion of the moonlight, her face and figure, covered with soft white wrappings for a journey, looked as he remembered to have seen her the first night they had met in the Boston train. The picture was completed by the travelling bag and rug that lay on the seat before her. Another terrible foreboding seized him; his brain reeled. Was he going mad?

"Joan!" he stammered. *"You?* What is the meaning of this?"

Ezekiel—whom but for his dazed condition he might have seen violently contorting his features in Joan's face, presumably in equal astonishment—broke into a series of discordant chuckles.

"Wa'al, ef that ain't Deacon Salisbury's darter all over. Ha! Here are ye two men folks makin' no end o' fuss to save that Mexican gal with pistols and ambushes and plots and counter-plots, and yer's Joan Salisbury shows ye the way ha'ow to do it. And so, ma'am, you succeeded in fixin' it up with Doña Rosita to

take her place and just sell them robbers
cheap? Wa'al, ma'am, yer sold this yer
party, too—for"—he advanced his face
close to hers—"I never let on a word,
though *I* knew it, and although they nearly
knocked me off my hoss in their fuss and
fury. Ha! ha! They wanted to know
what *I* was doin' here! he-he! Tell 'em,
Joan, tell 'em."

Demorest gazed from one to another
with a troubled face, yet one on which a
faint relief was breaking. "What does he
mean, Joan? Speak," he said, almost im-
ploringly.

Joan, whose color was slightly returning, drew herself up with her old cold
puritan precision. "After the scene you
made this morning, Richard, when you
chose to accuse your wife of unfaithfulness
to her friend, her guest, and even your
reputation, I resolved to go myself with
Doña Rosita to Los Osos and explain the
matter to her father. Some rumor of the
ridiculous farce I have just witnessed
reached us through Ezekiel, and frightened
the poor girl so that she declined—and
properly, too—to face the hoax which you
and some nameless impersonator of a dis-

graced fugitive have gotten up for purposes of your own! I wish you joy of
your work! If the play is over now, I
presume I may be allowed to proceed on
my journey?"

"Not yet," said Demorest, slowly, with
a face over which the chasing doubts had
at last settled in a grayish pallor. "Believe what you like, misunderstand me if
you will, laugh at the danger you perhaps
comprehend better than I do, but upon this
road, *wherever or to whatever it was leading you*—to-night you go no further!"

"Then I suppose I may return home,"
she said, coldly. "Ezekiel will accompany
me back to protect me from—*robbers*.
Come, Ezekiel. Mr. Demorest and his
friends can be safely trusted to take care
of—your horse." And as the grinning
Ezekiel sprang into the carriage beside
her, she pulled up the glass in the fateful and set face of her once trusting husband; the carriage turned and drove off,
leaving him like a statue in the road.

. . . . . . .

The bell of the North Liberty Second
Presbyterian Church had just ceased ringing. But in the last five years it had rung

out the bass viol and harmonium, and rung
in an organ and choir; and the old austere
interior had been subjected at the hands
of the rising generation to an invasion of
youthful warmth and color. Nowhere was
this more apparent than in the choir itself,
where the bright spring sunshine, piercing a newly opened stained-glass window,
picked out the new spring bonnet of Mrs.
Demorest and settled upon it during the
singing of the hymn. Perhaps that was
the reason why a few eyes were curiously
directed in that direction, and that even
the minister himself strayed from the precise path of doctrine to allude with ec-
clesiastical vagueness to certain shining
examples of the Christian virtues that were
"again in our midst." The shrewd face
and white eyelashes of Ezekiel Corwin,
junior partner in the firm of Dilworth &
Dusenberry, of San Francisco, were momentarily raised towards the choir, and
then relapsed into an expression of fa-
tigued self-righteousness.

When the service was over a few worshippers lingered near the choir staircase,
mindful of the spring bonnet. "It looks
quite nat'ral," said Deacon Fairchild, "ter

see Joan Salisbury attendin' the ministration of the Word agin. And I ain't sorry
she didn't bring that second husband of
hers with her. It kinder looks like old
times—afore Edward Blandford was gathered to the Lord."

"That's so," replied his auditor, meekly,
"and they *do* say ez ha'ow Demorest got
more powerful worldly and unregenerate
in that heathen country, and that Joan ez
a professin' Christian had to leave him.
I'v° heerd tell thet he'd got mixed up, out
thar, with some half-breed outlaw, of the
name o' Johnson, ez hez a purty, high-
flyin' Mexican wife. It was fort'nit for
Joan that she found a friend in grace in
Brother Corwin to look arter her share in
the property and bring her back tu hum."

"She's lookin' peart," said Sister Brad-
ley, "though to my mind that bonnet
savors still o' heathen vanities."

"Et's the new idees—crept in with that
organ," groaned Deacon Fairchild; "but—
sho'—thar she comes."

She shone for an instant—a charming
vision—out of the shadow of the choir
stairs, and then glided primly into the
street

The old sexton, still in waiting with his hand on the half closed door, paused and looked after her with a troubled brow. A singular and utterly incomprehensible recollection and resemblance had just crossed his mind.